Anonymous

The Knapsack

A collection of original short stories, sketches, anecdotes and essays

Anonymous

The Knapsack
A collection of original short stories, sketches, anecdotes and essays
ISBN/EAN: 9783744751292

Printed in Europe, USA, Canada, Australia, Japan

Cover: Foto ©Andreas Hilbeck / pixelio.de

More available books at **www.hansebooks.com**

THE KNAPSACK -- A Collection of original short Stories, Sketches, Anecdotes and Essays. Contributed by the members of the Fire Underwriters' Association of the Pacific, and printed by order of the Association.

"The Special and His Grip."—See page 177.

PREFACE.

THE *Knapsack* is as familiar to the insurance people of the Pacific Coast as fruit and flowers; like sunshine in a shady place, it brings light and warmth where it is most appreciated; it has served to cheer the tedium of an exacting business; and has no enemies.

From a small beginning, experimentally, it has become an important feature of the annual meetings of the Fire Underwriters' Association of the Pacific. In the beginning, papers were only prepared by the chairman of standing committees, and the *Knapsack* was introduced as a convenient catch-all for subjects "grave or gay." In time, the members before whom papers were read, became restive if any part of the *Knapsack* was "grave," and at a later date, one serious paper caused an open revolt; this was hint enough to the editor; and thereafter the *Knapsack* was dedicated to mirth.

The record of its first few years is preserved intact herein, because of its historic interest, but the rest of this little volume is devoted to that which it is thought will best interest the members of the Association—quips and quirks, fun and satire, culled from the records.

Let it be known that the Fire Underwriters' Association of the Pacific is like a united family; there is a willing hand and a friendly interest from one to all; the ready laugh and quick applause is more the outburst of affection than of critical appreciation. The subject of this book being largely local, the interest in it very properly centers at home. Those who edit the *Knapsack* perform a labor of love, and where love rules, criticism is unknown.

HISTORICAL.

ON the occasion of the third annual meeting of the Fire Underwriters' Association of the Pacific, presided over by Mr. A. P. Flint, held in San Francisco, February 18th, 1879, the *Knapsack* was conceived; the subject was introduced by Mr. L. L. Bromwell in the form of a motion, which met the approval of the Association, and then and there was created, in the following words: "A repository for the collection of material, and interesting subjects, not properly belonging to any committee, to be called *The California Knapsack.*" The same to be read at the meetings of the Association.

In the printed list of officers for the year 1880, appears the statement that *The California Knapsack* is managed by Col. C. Mason Kinne and Wm. Macdonald.

After the initial number had been read, President C. T. Hopkins said, with enthusiasm, "The *Knapsack* is too good to be allowed to perish."

Col. Kinne continued editor until the year 1885.

Geo. F. Grant had charge in 1886 and 1887.

E. W. Carpenter in 1888; and

A. J. Wetzlar in 1889 and 1890.

Since that date, to the present time, the *Knapsack* has been under the guidance of Mr. Geo. F. Grant, assisted by Mr. Edward Niles.

Fire Underwriters Association of the Pacific
Editorial Rooms, "California Knapsack"
422 California St. San Francisco, Jan. 15th, 1880.

Mr.

Dear Sir

The near approach of the Annual meeting of our Association, should be the reminder of a duty each member owes to the columns of the "Knapsack". As this periodical is intended as a repository for the collection of material and interesting subjects not properly belonging to any committee;— short, crisp, expression of your ideas can be utilized in making the periodical an interesting feature of our annual meeting. To this end I have to request you to favor me with such an article as you can prepare before February the 10th, in the way of anecdotes, recital of personal experiences or views on various insurance points. Don't procrastinate

Very Respectfully Yours

J. Mason Kinne
Editor.

LAST CALL FOR "COPY."—1880.

CALIFORNIA KNAPSACK.

VOL 1.   NO. 1.

C. MASON KINNE,   -   ·   ·   ·   ·   -   Manager.

PROSPECTUS.

THE manager of the *Knapsack* desires to convey to its subscribers the assurance that it starts out on the troubled sea of journalism with a large capital, vast resources, and an array of talent second to none of the first class periodicals of the day.

Its design is set forth in the resolution which called it into being, and if a realization of its purpose is half as successful as the enthusiasm of its conception—a year ago—all will be well.

Being a 12-months child, it ought to come into the world (as it does) full fledged and vigorous.

We are prepared for any weather—favorable or adverse—our blankets are rolled and strapped, and the cold reception sometimes awarded to venturesome news-mongers will not affect us. The *Knapsack* is filled with good things, "from grave to gay, from lively to severe;" and without more of preface will proceed to show what of our promises can be fulfilled.

THERE had been a fire of some extent in Oregon, and a gathering of insurance people and commercial men was the immediate result. Dining together, it was noticed that an unnaturally good appetite and a proverbial scarcity of good things, sometimes caused one of the genial adjusters to go for things quite early and freely. Some allusion being made to the fact that he represented the only company whose policy called for the expenses of the adjuster to be paid by the assured, one of the travelers quickly put the absence of viands and this clause in juxtaposition after this fashion: "Yes, and I see that he is utilizing the 'adjuster's claws' already." After that the rest of us stood a better show at the table.

APROPOS of the coining of new words and changes in the orthography of old ones, we note that some of the fire companies in writing to their people in the old Mormon district of Southern California, spell the town *San Burnardino.*

THE SCALPER'S SOLILOQUY.

[*Tune*—THE OLD SEXTON.]

Nigh to a house that was newly made,
Stood a "Scalper" bold, and thus he said—
The risk is good, and without delay
I'll measure the width of this alley-way;
Ah! it's only nine feet six I see,
For the "tariff" too narrow, alas for me!
And he sighed from his quivering lips so thin,
I must gather it in—I must gather it in.

I must gather it in—for, year after year
I've shaved the "tariff" without favor or fear;
And rated these houses that cluster around,
Without any regard to "exposures" as found;
"Extra" and "special," "gilt-edged" and "scum,"
Find place in my companies one by one;
But come they from strangers or come they from kin,
I gather them in—I gather them in.

Not many are with me, still I'm not alone,
I'm king of the "tariff" and make it my throne;
In dealing out rates I'm both cautious and bold,
And my sceptre of rule is the "cheek" that I hold;
From cottage or mansion men come at my call,
And I fix up a rating to suit great and small;
Let them dicker for "rebate" or come down with the "tin,"
I gather them in—I gather them in.

I gather them in—and my secret I rest
Far down in the depths of my own guilty breast;
And the "Scalper" ceased -for lo, in the street
He spied a "square" agent he cared not to meet.
And I said to myself, when time is told,
A mightier voice than that ' Scalper's" bold
Will sound o'er the last trump's direful din,
I gather him in—I gather him in.

A FIRE INSURANCE AGENT refused to issue a policy to a man who owned a broken-winged hen. He said the company had cautioned him to look out for *defective flews.*

A SHADOW ON THE BUSINESS.

MUCH has been written on the subject of insurance, bearing upon its origin, science, practice and development.

Much has been said in convention and annual meeting. Happy bursts of impromptu, have told the humorous side. I do not remember to have heard discussed what may be termed the *shadow* on the business.

That there is a dramatic, even tragic element, is well known to the gentlemen composing this Association. It is not known to the superior officer. It borders on sentiment, and is not in keeping with comparative statements, classifications or dividends. If the heart of the special is wrung in the pursuit of his duty, it does not appear in his report. Not once, but often, the sad, sad spectacle of hope destroyed, ambition wasted, homes broken, family ties severed, *and worse*, is included in an adjustment. You do not seek these particulars; they come with the *other* particulars.

In the midst of ruin—with some stricken, dazed claimant, you go over and over the same story, picking out the facts which serve to make proof that no condition of the contract has been violated—or the reverse.

The company's check will hardly suffice to provide new clothing for the children. What is that to you? Your stony face is a terror to that widow. You have need of that stony face to hide your real feelings. Do you remember when the neighbors told how valiantly claimant Blank had worked that he might save his property?

Oh yes, you thought, same old story. You hunted up his dwelling. In reply to your question the gentleman said—"I am not Mr. Blank, I am his physician; he is dead—died suddenly of heart disease, from overwork."

That was a good settlement; the directors approved the application of the removal clause—the claimant did not talk back; but the wail of mourning lingers in your memory.

Then the day we took train together bound for that delinquent agent, that tiresome, evasive, delinquent agent, with his merry-happy-go-lucky disposition, his cozy home, his hospitality.

The limit was reached; he had been warned. We did not for a moment doubt that we would prosecute him to the full extent.

We nerved ourselves to meet his genial denial, with firmness. We reached the spot just after they had cut the body down.

There he was! A suicide! His young, handsome face purple in death. No money to be made by talking to *it*.

Did we sympathize with the little broken-hearted woman?

My friend, we got that balance,—which the President said was doing first rate, *under the circumstances*.

Our sympathy and the recollection of the many good traits of his character are left to mock us.

HARRY SMITH'S STORY.

HARRY SMITH, peace be to his ashes, once gave me a leaf from his experience. Seeing in the newspaper an account of loss, one of his own pet mountain risks, he packed up and started. From the stage-driver he gathered particulars.

It was a hard case; the claimant, an honest miner, with his family, was burned out of house and home and was camping in a shanty. No water to work the rocker—credit almost gone. Driver didn't know if the house was insured; nice house, cost a power of money. Didn't know how the fire started. It was six miles to town, too far to give an alarm.

Harry alighted, and was met by the assured. "Do you remember me?" said Harry. "Oh yes, I remember, you're the insurance man. I haven't got anything to insure now, Mister; yonder is my house under them ashes." "Well," said Harry, "It was insured, wasn't it?" "No! No! I meant to have it done over again, but the time went by and it run out. It's no use my grieving over it, stranger, but it brings us down to bedrock."

"Well, my man," said Harry, "I know more about that policy than you do. It has not run out yet, and I am here to pay you the money." "What!" he shrieked. "What! Mister, don't you fool with me. You mean it! Wife! Wife! we're saved, saved!"

"Here, children! run and call your mother; excuse me, sir, I can't stand it; you tell the old woman." And the honest fellow went off and shed tears, which thumb-screws could not have forced from him.

Harry camped with them that night; there were four children playing about the place, with a big St. Bernard dog.

The host noticed Harry's look of admiration directed to the dog, and after a few words with his wife and the children, said: "Mr. Smith, we want to give you something for a keepsake; we haven't anything but the dog; if you will take the dog with our best love, we give him to you freely. I wouldn't give him to another man, Mr. Smith. Money couldn't buy him from us." Harry accepted the present in the spirit of the gift. Next morning, when the stage loomed in sight, a mournful group of children led the dog forward; each one hugged him in turn and whispered a brief farewell. Harry took in the situation and addressed the children, in that cheery voice we remember so well, as follows:

"My little friends, I think that is the *prettiest dog* I ever saw, but I wouldn't take him away *from you*—no not for the world. I give him back to you, my little friends." The shout of joy that went up was dearer to Harry's heart than a thousand dollar salvage. He mounted the seat beside the driver, and was lost to their sight—*forever!*   G.

POKER BILL.

I.

IT was in the days of stage travel over the Mojave desert from Los Angeles, before the Loop road was completed, that a party of travelers stood shivering at two in the morning of a spring day, waiting orders to get aboard the deep-chested, leather-lined Concord coach bound for Caliente, at that time the railroad terminus. Among the number, your contributor, used up by two days and nights anxious work on a particular adjustment.

At the word he glides into the inside front seat, folds about him his ulster and falls immediately into sleep, deep as a well and welcome as May flowers. No amount of squeezing disturbs him. He sways with the motion of the coach and peacefully rebounds with each concussion; the first streak of dawn reveals him in these airy flights. It lights up the inside passengers, showing the form of a burly, glad-hearted, cheery-voiced commercial traveler, known to the trade as "Old Iron;" also a slight, fair-haired, blue-eyed, boyish-looking young fellow, just up from a two-weeks' vacation in Arizona, sun-burned like a pirate, and armed like a footpad. The other passengers were of the usual variety. They are wide-awake, fresh and buoyant, drinking in the cool, delicious morning air. A dense, almost suffocating sweetness is in the breeze—a pure scent of bud and blossom everywhere. Suddenly a gold and yellow sunrise bursts forth, tingling the senses with delight. The very horses feel the exhilaration. The driver, too, is at his best. He pulls the six plunging *broncos* to a standstill, and tells somebody to get down quick, at the same time informing the off-leader confidentially that he will cut the whole heart out of him in a little minute.

The somebody got down quickly and joined the insiders. He was a timid looking tourist, faultlessly dressed for travel, with an eye for points that smacked of the guide-books. Before many minutes he communicated to the commercial traveler a fear that the outside passengers were a desperate lot. "Their whole talk is of stage-robbers, and all of them carry deadly weapons." "Old Iron" saw his chance and seized it. Pointing to the sleeping special, he said in a tragic whisper, "That's Poker Bill himself!" "Who—who is he?" faltered the tourist. "What! never heard of Poker Bill, the Arizona outlaw? used to live in Baltimore; killed his father in '61; ran away and joined the Turks; turned up last year in Arizona. He is the captain of that gang outside. He's a dead shot. I once saw him shoot a man's ear off—man refused to drink with him. He can pick the end of your nose off, as easy; best natured man in the world if you don't rile him; when he's riled it just seems as if hell *was* let loose. You take a fool's advice and *don't you* rile him. I ain't afraid of him my-self; no, sir. I once saved his life. He thinks the world of me; he is going up to the Bay to keep shady for a while—shot a girl down in Prescott—just an accident—a mistake, as you may say; but the folks wouldn't have it; they draw the line on girls in Prescott. It's near break-fast time, and I'm going to wake him up; mind you don't you rile him."

The passengers enjoyed the sport, and blinked and grinned at each other. The tourist grinned, too, but in an uneasy way, like one who is sea-sick.

II.

When "Old Iron" woke me with a vigorous shake, my remonstrance was couched in such forcible yet injudicious language, that the heart of the tourist sank within him, and the hope of meeting a *mild*-mannered cut-throat died in his breast. A few broad hints gave me the cue. We fooled him to the top of his bent. We waded in *gore* for his benefit, re-hearsed scenes of horrible fancy, dragged to light bleeding hearts and quivering fibers; while his face—now pale, now flushed—settled into a blue-white glare disagreeable to look upon. At this stage of the proceed-ings the fair-haired passenger took a hand.

Up to this time, he had simply assented to the *worst* propositions by silent and solemn nods, as if mentally checking off familiar incidents. He now produced a wicked-looking bowie-knife from his boot-leg and pro-ceeded leisurely to pick his teeth. This was too much. With one bound the tourist disappeared through the stage-door; with alarm we saw him roll over and over in the dust. The stage halted; slowly the victim approached—uninjured, a wretched object. With outstretched arms and a trembling voice, he begged the mystified driver to let him ride outside. He rode outside all day, in the heat and dust. He would not leave his perch; breakfast, dinner, supper had no charm for him. At sunset the passengers held council; something had to be done. Supper was nearly over, and there he sat, alone, on the roof of the coach. By request, I reasoned with him—I said: "My dear sir, get down and eat; don't you see it is all a joke?" No reply. "Get down like a good fellow and have supper." Silence. Sternly then I cried, "Look here, confound you, if you don't get off that stage inside a minute, I'll blow a hole in you big enough to throw a pie through." That brought him. Down he came and did eat—ate like one who had fasted long in the wilderness.

We rode through the twilight and reached the sleeping car on time. As I stretched myself in bed with a thrill of pleasure, in anticipating sleep, I heard a troubled voice inquire:

"Conductor, has Poker Bill gone to bed?" "Who?" "Poker Bill, the Arizona outlaw." "Never heard of him." "Why, I saw you take a cigar from him and ask after his brother not five minutes ago." "Oh! him; what did you call him—Arizona outlaw? Outlaw be damned—that's an insurance adjuster."

It was not the Secretary of a local company, doing a national business, that was recently offered a line on Zion's Co-Operative Institution of Salt Lake, at one per cent. After "hemming and hawing" at the physical inadequacy of the rate, he finally succumbed with the remark, "But, after all, it must be a *moral* hazard. I have heard Zion *very favorably spoken of.*" And the policy clerk wrote it up.

SAN FRANCISCO, February 3, 1880.

Col. C. MASON KINNE, EDITOR *California Knapsack,—My dear sir:* The following clipping, from a recent number of the *Scientific American*, we consider of sufficient importance to find permanent lodgment in No. 1, Vol. 1, of our fraternity's *Knapsack* of useful knowledge:

FIRE FROM STEAM PIPES.

To the Editor of the Scientific American: In answer to D. E. Smith, Oneida Community, N. Y., I will say fourteen years' observation has led me to the conclusion that it is utterly impossible to fire wood, or even touch paper or tinder, with steam in pipes up to any pressure of steam at maximum density—*i. e.*, not superheated—that can be carried on any ordinarily constructed boiler.

Why do not the wooden lagging of steam engine cylinders, portable boilers and large steam pipes on steamships, etc., take fire? or the dust that accumulates on steam coils in woodworking machine shops? Simply because the temperature of the steam pipe is not sufficiently high, and that the lowest temperature capable of doing so is between 500° and 700° Fah.

But some will hint at conditions and make use of the words "concentration of heat" and "spontaneous combustion."

Heat of this description cannot be concentrated, and is not capable of making anything hotter than itself, and spontaneous combustion has no place in our consideration, other than, if we are dealing with substances that are likely to fire spontaneously. heat will assist them, whether from steam pipes or any other source.

No one imagines they can light a stick against a boiling kettle (temperature 212°), but many will say, how would it be if I had 100 or 200 pounds of steam; it would be so much hotter then? It will be hotter. The following table shows the increase in temperature for each 100 pounds in pressure (above atmosphere) up to 400 pounds. Let them judge for themselves:

Pressure.	Temp. Fah.	Increase temp.
1 lb.	214°	
100 lb.	338°	124° 1st 100
200 lb.	388°	50° 2d "
300 lb.	422°	34° 3d "
400 lb.	448°	26° 4th "

Respectfully,

Wm. J. Baldwin, Heating Engineer.

Elmira, N. Y., January 1, 1880.

The other day an amiable looking and quite pretty young lady got into a crowded Mission street car and steadied herself by one of the roof straps.

"I beg you will sit still—don't move," she said sweetly to a young man who offered to rise. The gentleman resumed his seat and waited until the car had gone about a mile beyond Woodward's Gardens and everybody but the young lady and himself had gotten out. Then, turning to his fellow passenger, he said:

"Now, then, Miss, what is it?"

"What is what?" said the lady, beginning to look offended.

"Why, you asked me not to get out—now, what can I do for you?"

The young lady explained, with much confusion, that she only meant to decline depriving the gentleman of his seat.

"Why, you don't say so!" exclaimed the gentleman with apparent surprise. "Why, to be sure—I might have known—how stupid of me. A pity, too, as I was on my way to church."

"I'm very sorry," faltered the young lady.

"Well, it can't be helped now," continued the other sadly; and to show her he wasn't in the least mad he handed her out of the car and walked clear home with her.

IT BURNED a few weeks ago, but the records of Santa —————— county failed to show that the assured had any title to the nice little dwelling. So the adjuster quietly "hung up" the claim. On his next visit to the town he was approached by the agent of a rival company, who had evidently been retained by the assured, and who explained that the apparent discrepancy was only the result of a little mistake. "You see," said he, "my friend was instructed to insure the property by its owner (who, by the way, generally insures with me), and by mistake had the policy made in his own name; but the Confederacy Insurance Company, which I represent, would never resist the claim on that account. We always consider the *intention*." "Is *that* so!" said our genial adjuster of doleful name. "Well then, it was doubtless the *intention* of your regular customer to order his property insured with you, and *you* had better *pay the loss*."

AND now, the manager having selected the foregoing from the mass of matter provided, he realizes that life is short and time is precious, so, with the statistics of a Bromwell, the pleasantry of a Carpenter, the poesy of a Bailey, the pleasing diction or earnest pathos of a Grant, the clippings of a Staples and sundries by myself, we will buckle up the *Knapsack* and go "marching on" for another while.

Having so kindly, considerately, and generously held open the ample flap of the *Knapsack*, in order that the charges of rhetoric and humor might be fired in by the anxious and waiting throng of contributors, we propose to thank one and all alike for their assistance in this, the first essay in the journalistic realm.

CALIFORNIA KNAPSACK.

VOL. 1.   NO. 2.

C. MASON KINNE,   -   -   -   -   -   -   Manager.

FIRE UNDERWRITERS' ASSOCIATION OF THE PACIFIC,

Editorial Rooms *California Knapsack*, 422 California Street,

San Francisco, Feb. 1, 1881.

MR.———:

Dear Sir—Again the Editor of the *Knapsack* has to call upon its patrons for copy. The manuscript that you have, no doubt, prepared long ago for this demand is expected to be sent to our Editorial Rooms on or before the 12th instant.

The success attending our first issue should prompt you to give us a sample of your brightest thoughts, tersely expressed, embracing such matters as properly pertain to the very "broad gauge" of an insurance man.

It is hoped and expected that your missives will "fall in promptly."

Very respectfully,

C. MASON KINNE, Editor.

EDITORIAL ROOMS *California Knapsack*,

San Francisco, Feb. 15, 1881.

In entering upon this, the second volume of our valuable and valued journal, we have to congratulate ourselves upon the flattering reception accorded us last year, and to not only congratulate but *thank* our members who have so kindly answered the demand for "copy."

As this periodical is intended as a repository for the collection of material and remarks on interesting subjects not properly belonging to any committee, it was deserving of success, and this issue as well as the last proves that some such *omnium gatherum* was a requisite, and furnishes a vehicle for much that is rich and racy, valuable and entertaining.

From the many contributions to our columns, the manager selects those he proposes to present to you, with the statement that the others are fully as deserving of a place; but life is short and time is precious, and we have no desire to weary you beyond endurance.

BLACKSMITHING IN INSURANCE.

A CASE came under the observation of a special some time ago, while in the general office of a company doing business in California, which tends to show the importance of full particulars in making diagrams of risks.

It seems the local agent of a small country town some years ago sent up an application, stating that as he did not clearly know the rate on the risk, he wished the company to affix the proper rate and send policy. This was done, and policy renewed year after year until the year 1880 rolled around, when the agent paid a visit to San Francisco, and while there called at the office of the company and represented that Jones' risk was very hard to retain, as the rate was so high. The application was looked up and showed two buildings situate within ten feet of each other—one marked "Jones' dwelling," and the other "Black Smith." In making the rate, the general agent had taken as a basis D class *blacksmith* shop, 3.25; exposure, dwelling, .50; stove-pipe and cloth-lining, 1.25—making tariff rate 5 per cent.

The *local* wanted to know if the rate could not be made less, and explained that the building marked "blacksmith" was no *blacksmith shop*, but was a dwelling occupied by a colored man named Smith, whom he had designated *Black Smith* on the diagram. 'Tis needless to say the rate was reduced, all parties were satisfied, and the risk retained on the books of the company.   S.

A "WATER CLAUSE" NEEDED.

Editor Knapsack—*Dear Sir:* The following letter was received by the secretary of one of our mining companies, and is interesting as showing the broad ground that some writers take of the hazards covered under a fire policy. We can no longer rest in fancied security from loss by floods, but must at once establish a rate for this risk and insert a "water clause" in our policies. The orthography of the letter also indicates that the "spelling reform" has taken possession of the claimant:

" —— ——, Secretary:

Dear Sir:—We are still on top, though the storm for the past few days has been most sevear. My house was flooded on night of 30th, and carpiets well nigh ruined, otherwise suffered no loss. Suppose we are entitled to damiges from insurance companies. Are we not? I may be able to use carpiets again. Shall have them washed tomorrough and

see what can be done with them. Those bought in my time cost
$121.77. Then thare is another that used to be on sitting room of which
I have no bill. Some bedding and blankets were soiled, but not enough
to take into account.

Truly yours,   —— ——."

RAILROADING IN THE FAR NORTH.

IN the month of September, some six years ago, the writer stood upon
a rude wharf at the old fur-trading town on the Upper Columbia,
called Wallula. Across an expanse of sand some thirty buildings,
comprising this once prosperous town, were to be seen, perhaps a round
dozen of which were occupied, while the rest were more or less dilapi-
dated and nearly covered up by the drifting sand, which in some instances
reached to the second story or roof.

The immediate object of the scrutiny was to determine which of the
inhabited buildings laid claim to being the haven for travelers. The
afternoon was, moreover, cold and gloomy enough to cause the few
arrivals by the river steamer to seek shelter without delay. The only
available place betrayed no sign, but one of the very few residents disclosed its whereabouts, and it proved to be a combination of general
merchandise store, hotel and apothecary's shop—as a matter of course
presided over by an American. Careful inquiry failed to afford any
information as to whether the train would leave for Walla Walla that day
or the next. The landlord said no "time table" had been prepared, and
frankly admitted that the president of the road and himself were not on
good terms, and carefully neglected to tell any one just when a train
would start. The captain of the steamer was equally unable to give the
information, and finally supper was announced, causing a temporary sus-
pension of the questioning. Later on, we gathered around the "inevitable" stove and listened with great interest to the many stories about the
railroad, furnished by a person who had arrived on the train from Walla
Walla the day before—time, seven hours; distance, thirty miles. Until a
short time before, he said, the rails in use were made of wood, but iron
had been procured and laid; that the rolling stock was of a very poor
character; and, impeded by sand drifting across the track, the result was
that the trip ordinarily consumed more time than would suffice to walk
the whole distance. To these was added a story of a dog belonging to
the president, which, until an accident had occurred by which its life was
lost, used to trot along with the engine and drive cattle off the track.

An early rise was the order for the succeeding day, because it was said that the train might come in and return to Walla Walla at any hour; but it proved to be 11 o'clock before a very diminutive locomotive was espied backing down two small cars toward the wharf. Next, two men came out of a saloon near by with common water pails in each hand and went to the river and began bringing water to the engine. This was poured into the boiler through a hole on top fitted with a lid to screw down. The smile with which the three or four new-comers greeted this operation was only equaled by the non-concern of the old citizens, in whose eyes the proceeding was altogether usual and in order.

In a short time the conductor announced that the train was ready to start; so, taking our seats, it moved away. The features of the trip consisted of three or four stops at stations, including the taking of more water at least twice, and the frequent halting of the train until the train hands should shovel sand from the track. We finally arrived at Walla Walla in four and a half hours, and believed the assurances that the trip had been a quick one for that road. The object of the journey having been attained, arrangements were made to return by "*fast freight*" to Wallula early upon the following day. Before leaving, however, the president inquired for and having found that a San Francisco insurance man was in town, he applied at once for insurance on freight carried by his road and which might possibly be destroyed or damaged by fire from the engines; which, although they had no spark catchers, he said, were perfectly safe, owning up, however, to several fires. Promising a speedy reply from Portland, the return was commenced. The conductor kindly consented to throw a bench across the floor of an ordinary close freight car partly filled with freight, leaving the side-doors open. This proved to be quite desirable, and enabled one to look (until tired) at the waste of sand, relieved here and there by scanty vegetation and fences.

After some time had passed, I became conscious of the presence of an unusual degree of heat, and, casually looking around, was much surprised to see the end of the car on fire and the freight in a fine blaze. How to attract attention was a question, and to add to the dangers of the situation, the train was on a down grade, and for once it was going altogether too fast to admit of a jump. Anxiously looking from the side in hopes that the engineer's attention could be gained, a water station appeared in the distance, and the surmise was rightly made that the train would come to a stop and the writer be released. The stop was made and the fire immediately attacked with water from the tank. After this the train went on and finally reached Wallula late in the afternoon with at least one thankful passenger.

It is hardly necessary to add that the president was never troubled with a reply to his insurance proposition. X-ELL.

THE following clipping may have been read by many of you, but is good enough, as an evidence of the average insurer's idea, to read to you now:

INSURANCE AGAINST NEIGHBORS.

HUMAN nature is the same the world over, as the following incident will help to show. A local insurance agent called on two of his customers whose premises adjoin, for a renewal of their policies. The first one is a grocer. The agent said to him:

"I suppose, Mr. ——, that you will renew your policy, which expires next week? I have called to see about it."

"Well, I suppose I'll have to," said the grocer. "As far as I am concerned, there is no need whatever that I should insure. I am here all day to look after things, and there ain't a bit of danger of fire from my place. But there is no telling what that fellow next door may do, and as long as he is there I've got to keep insured."

The agent called on the customer next door, who is a baker. He could not help reasoning that if the danger in that establishment was so great there was a possibility of having the amount of his policy doubled, at least.

He told the baker why he called, and hinted that there might be a probability of a desire to increase the policy.

"No," said the baker, scratching his head thoughtfully, "I don't believe I'll add any to it. I wouldn't insure at all if I wasn't where I am. You see, I'm up all night baking, and can watch things, so there's no danger here; but there's no telling what that chap next door will be up to. If it wasn't for him I wouldn't insure a cent; but as it is, I've got to do it."—*Ins. World.*

CONSOLATION.

'Twill be a great comfort to many to know,
Insurance adjusters to heaven *must* go;
For if a just man is bound to get there,
Most surely *adjuster* no worse will fare.
Besides, I am told, it chanced one day,
An insurance adjuster to hades did stray,
(The chances are, 'twas the fervent prayer
Of a policyholder sent him there),
And at once aroused the devil's ire
By investigating the cause of fire.
He annoyed him so, old Satan swore
Insurance adjusters should come there no more.

D. M. B.

THE following is from the same pen that gave us the excellent article on "Shadows" last year:

SUNSHINE IN THE BUSINESS.

HOW BLESSINGS brighten as they take their flight; how the scenes and incidents of ten years ago stand out a pleasing contrast to the toilsome present. I remember a special trip from Oregon to California in that happy past. Roseburg was the starting point. Roseburg! dreaming in the lap of a luxurious valley surrounded by brave hills.

At the time of which I write, it was Bohemia. To know *one* of the boys was to be welcomed on every hand. There was Van and Asher and Mac, the Colonel, the Senator and the Judge. The freedom of the city was extended and accepted with more of hospitality and less of ceremony than in—London, for example.

The Senator was sole agent there and monopolized everything from dwelling to brewery. The stage for Redding left in the morning, but there was a *night* before that morning, all owing to a song, a simple camp meeting song. No sooner did its notes strike the Colonel's ear than he was aroused. As a circus band rouses the neglected charger, so roused it him, this song, that Colonel. From away down South in the land of cotton came a host of memories, bright days of his boyhood, long forgotten in the race for wealth. Tears welled to his eyes, while his smooth-shaved lip quivered the pleasure he felt.

We went from one friend to another, gathering a chorus in our wake; the Colonel led the choir, and we sang this song until circumstances made it advisable to pull off the Colonel's boots and put him to bed. We left town at 6 in the morning. To be hurried from bed at candlelight, to scour the town for a mislaid overcoat with a lantern; to bolt a useless meal, is neither impressive or inspiring, but a dozen outstretched hands, a dozen voices saying good-bye, friendly packages that open with a pop and shut with a gurgle, these are the charms of Roseburg. Where else in the world do people get out of bed on a cold day in the dark to say good-bye? The stage agent, known familiarly as "Van" most of the time, is now loading the coach, solemn and unapproachable as a chief engineer at a fire; trunks go on the hind boot, mail sacks and treasure box in front, small traps under the seats, over them the passengers.

I have the seat of honor, beside the driver; the man at the right of the off wheeler buckles in the trace, the man at the head of the leader springs aside, crack goes the whip, six horses plunge madly forward, the brake scrapes a moment, and we are off. In the coach is a man who telegraphed from Portland for an *inside back seat;* he wears a silk hat. He confided to " Van " a desire to quicken the usual schedule time by a day or two; he told the driver at the first watering place of a bet to beat the time of a friend gone down by steamer. Do I need to tell a special agent that a back seat is the worst in the coach? That a silk hat in traveling is an impossibility? No more than I need add that *this* man was a salesman from the *East.* He became a nuisance, he and his hat, and his friend, and his business. At the first piece of "corduroy" we came to, the driver gave us a hint to hold on and then let out his team. Such a shaking up I never experienced. We held on and howled; above the din I could hear the voice of the salesman, first loud, then fainter. When we stopped, which was at a station, he crawled out; his back was bent, the crown of that hat had disappeared, the rim was around his neck; he had not held on; *he* was a wreck. In reply to threats and im- precations the driver said: "So! that's all the thanks I get for trying to help a man. You want to get to 'Frisco, don't you? want to beat your friend? Well, I drove fast on purpose to help you out, and now you growl; want to be an angel, don't you?" The salesman laid over, and his friend reached San Francisco seven days ahead.

After stopping at Jacksonville over one trip I was uneasy about my seat on the incoming coach. "Jerry," the driver, was a character in his way, besides being a perfect encyclopedia of slang phrases. In due time she hove in sight with Jerry at the lines, and alongside him a moon-faced traveler with helmet hat and spread umbrella. There was a quick and expressive interchange of glances between Jerry and me, though not a word was spoken. "Go up to the barn," he said later, "and get on the box seat when the hostler brings her down." I sat there unconcerned while Jerry had a pow-wow with the others; there seemed to be con- siderable excitement, with violent gesticulation, and Jerry rattled a long iron chain which he held in his hand; he got them all inside at last, and and after riding a few minutes in silence, he said: "So you're a maniac, are yer—a raving maniac, escaped from your keeper, did yer? Don't you try no crazy tricks on me, sabe? Cos I'll just chain yer down to the boot, I will; that's about what I'll do. Oh you're a nice lunatic, you are, with a bad eye; chawed up six men already, *you* have. Why don't yer give us a Stockton yell? Let out a Napa file-scraper, will yer?"

And he chuckled and ogled me, and turned red in the face, and rolled himself about, until I expected to see him go over the dash-board head first.

"What in the world are you driving at?" I asked.

"Oh, he never tumbles!" said Jerry. "He don't drop—can't see it yet, eh? Never traveled much, did yer? Ain't no insurance drummer, be yer? only a minister, perhaps—a Sunday-school teacher, likely. Ain't up to the ways of a wicked world. He's a little lammie—has to have his eyelids tucked back to see anything, *he* has. Oh, oh, oh!"

"Jerry," said I, "if you don't stop this infernal nonsense, you won't get a cigar the whole drive."

"Mean to say you didn't hear the racket I gave 'em?" he said, in an altered tone. "Why, Lord love you, thought you took it in as it went along. I told 'em you was escaped from an asylum—mad as a March hare; I wouldn't trust yer inside for fear yer might tear 'em all to pieces. Got it now? See it? Good, ain't it? Now give us a yell—a regular blood-curdler. That's right—keep it up—send it into 'em! Oh, oh, oh!"

All day, at change stations and watering-places, those deluded insiders consulted with Jerry in whispers about my case. Jerry was fertile in resources—too fertile, for he mixed his stories up in such a fashion that it dawned on them at last, and we made peace at Cole's Station, where we took supper and parted with Jerry.

The home drive was made with Charlie McConnell, whose skill at the lines is only equaled by his gallantry and elegant manners to lady passengers. One of the fair sex was beside him; but his love for a good cigar overcame other obstacles, and he made room for me also. After a while the lady observed a little white post by the roadside with a large figure 2 painted on it.

"What is the meaning of that?" she asked.

Charlie shot a glance over to me, and solemnly replied:

"Madam, that is a grave. Two people are buried there. On a dark night the stage upset. Two people—strangers—were killed. The driver escaped as by a miracle. We buried them there, and erected this simple shaft to mark the spot."

"Dear, dear!" she said, "how sad!"

After a while she said:

"Why, there is another head-board with 5 on it."

"Yes, madam—the result of another accident. Here in this lonely spot lies all that is mortal of five persons—all strangers—who met their fate by being thrown over this cliff on a winter day. The driver escaped as by a miracle. We read the funeral service over them and buried them together, erecting this simple shaft to mark the spot."

"This is too horrible! Do accidents often happen?" she asked.

"They do—they do, alas, too frequently," said Charlie.

Some hours later our lady passenger gave a scream, and started from her seat.

"Mr. Driver," she said, "There is a grave-post with 13 painted on it!"

Charlie's tone of solemnity was sublime. "My dear madam, I am so sorry. That was indeed a frightful affair. Coach and horses, passengers and driver, went down this precipice with one grand crash. I was spared as by a miracle—caught on the projecting limb of a tree. Hours after, when I reached the wreck, all were dead but one, and I finished him off with a kingbolt. It was hard to do, but these survivors always sue the company for damages, and I am simply working for my employer's interest. Madam, we read the funeral service over them, and buried them together, erecting this simple shaft to mark the spot."

"Driver," she said, "I do not wish to discredit any statement you may make, or to appear to doubt your word, but I must say this otherwise agonizing narrative seems to me like a fairy story."

"Madam," said Charlie, "you have guessed it. I really must apologize for the kingbolt; otherwise I think it is a shame to spoil a good story."

And so this jolly ride had an end, like all else in life; the stage-load became diluted in the larger accommodation train, and we drifted into the big stream of humanity rushing to "the bay." G.

WHERE WAS THE DEACON?

IT was at Sacramento, last year, during the "session," time midnight, when two of the boys parted thus: Said one, "Good-night, old man—I leave you here. Have to sit up with a sick friend. By the way, do me the favor, as you pass my room on your way to bed, to step in and disarrange it; turn down the clothes and rumple the pillows. My door is never locked, and when the others look in at breakfast time they will see that I am off. Understand?"

"All right," said No. 2.

They met at noon. In reply to vigorous upbraiding, No. 2 said: "I did disarrange your room, put water in the basin, rumpled the towels, tore the bed to pieces—why room 17 looked as if there had been a fight!"

"Seventeen? Good gracious, that's wrong! That's the *Deacon's* room!"

"The dickens it is! Then, *where* was the deacon?"

HAVERSACK PHILOSOPHY—CRUSTY HARD-TACK.

Mr. Editor: Nutritive and brilliant extravaganza in your spicy department is always enjoyable and appreciated, and this fact warrants the relegation of these meagre and crusty rations to the knapsack's accompaniment—as anticipated by the title of our contribution. It need not be inferred that we are starting out on any well-defined long march, and that our haversack is replete with dry "crumbs of comfort"—on the contrary, ours is a *foraging* expedition! We may camp in dangerous fields, and tramp on the corns of friend and foe alike in these chosen philosophical meanderings—brief, because obliged to be, but nevertheless realizing that the practical teachings of the association admit the broadest toleration of individual opinions, and steadily ameliorates all prejudices incident to the denominational or varied interests of fire underwriting. A little healthful, plain talk, therefore, in an Association where there is no distinctive line drawn as separating local, Eastern or foreign, Board or non-Board, experienced or inexperienced, may tend to strengthen and sustain a common brotherhood of underwriters in their efforts to elevate our business, not only by discussing *fresh* topics, but by putting *older* ideas into fresh and practicable shape. Therefore,

1st. It is most obvious that members, one and all, should take a deeper interest in and *participate* in all regular meetings; instead of *shirking*, take rank among the workers; *produce* something, and not, like a sponge, absorb all that comes along, waiting to be squeezed into reciprocity.

2d. Life is too short for men in this great business of ours to attempt the remodeling of characters we find in it. Active-minded *idlers* are even worse, and certainly more dangerous, than the throng of microscopic busy-bodies who magnify trifles, but are incompetent to grasp greater ones. All these characters add a zest, and amount to a necessity, towards perfecting our underwriting drama; otherwise it would drift into a monotonous and enervating comedy—a kind of goody-goody humdrum, without progress or enterprise.

3d. We may sermonize, declaim, exhort, harangue, and lecture, but the members of the Pacific Association must give results—the *motive power*—if the fraternity is to feel the benefits of such Association; quarterly outbursts of courtesy and annual assentation to creed-bound practices amount to naught unless carried into everyday life and honorably adhered to, because appropriate, becoming and comfortable.

4th. It is a lamentable fact that adjusters on the Pacific Coast are becoming gradually extinct, and their places supplied by a class at present without epithetic distinction, unless we introduce them here as "settlers." The over-anxiety of the companies themselves to pay losses, and the thin-skinned make-up of executives, are the responsible causes for the extinction of the former and the epidemic of the latter.

5th. Legislative prodding creates too much noise, fuss and cackling among underwriters. If this exhibition and characteristic virtue of insurance men could be spread out, and some attention given by them to politics from the primaries to election day, their power and influence could be so deployed as to economize all these periodical anxieties and wastes of time, chin-music and bullion.

Lastly, fully equaling a military campaign in discomforts, inconveniences and hardships, is the continuous life of the faithful, plodding special agent and adjuster, and with just about the same consequences; if *successful*, the generals in command secure the credit; if defeated and routed, we must then be prepared to selfishly shoulder the blame without any division whatever. There are several sides to this picture at variance with the above, as every special present verily believes.

We have now finished our tramp. If results shall be fruitful of the good intended, then our reward is ample and sufficient. In the meantime permit us to subscribe ourselves merely a

MALICIOUS SKIRMISHER.

EDITOR *Knapsack,—Dear Sir:* Your valued reminder of the 1st inst. is just received, and I am sorry found me not like the wise virgins—for no manuscript was ready or even thought of, and only to give you "copy" do I presume to take your valuable time. As you want "broad gauge," I give it to you, entitled

"THE BASE LINE."

Some years ago an adjuster for one of our Eastern companies was sent to Humboldt county to settle a loss on a livery-stable building, owned by the well-known stage man, Tom S——. The claimant and adjuster arriving at the scene of the conflagration too late in the evening to do anything, it was agreed to meet at 7 o'clock the following morning for work. Promptly at seven, both parties were on the ground The measure of the building was "taped off"; sizes of sills, posts, plates, joist, rafters and other necessary memoranda made: whereupon the claimant was asked if he knew of a reliable builder in town who was well up in estimating on buildings and contracting for work of that kind. He said that there was a first-class man who thoroughly understood the case, and he soon had him at the place. On propounding the question, the adjuster was convinced by the emphatic and confident answer of the builder that he was the man looked for, and opportunity only was lacking to launch upon the world the result of a well-stored mind. The ground plan was again *taped*, the sizes of timbers and general construction of the stable gone over, and then the builder was ready to go to his office and *figger*.

When asked how soon he would return with his estimate, he said in a couple of hours. It being then nearly 8 o'clock, and as he wanted to do his work undisturbed, this gave the adjuster plenty of time to fill out his proofs (except the amounts) and also to look around town. Having rained for a number of days previous, the country was not in a favorable condition for extensive pedestrian exercise, so ample opportunity was afforded to watch the clock. Ten o'clock soon came, but no builder; then eleven and twelve. Dinner here came to the rescue and was quickly disposed of, and then the wonder was, why does that man delay so much? One o'clock, two, and at three o'clock, with patience well nigh exhausted, the adjuster proceeded to the office to interview the builder.

On arriving in front of a small one-story frame dwelling, situate a little back from the road, the builder was seen in his shirt-sleeves, standing with a table before him. Shortly he began walking back and forth; then he would stop and look at something on the table, and take a pencil he had in his mouth and point at the something on the table; then he would resume his walk, only to stop again and look at the table. How long this had been kept up, is hard to say, but it is fair to presume for nearly all day. Finally the adjuster opened the gate and walked up to the house, knocked and was invited to enter. On going into the room his curiosity was excited to see what was on the table which had interested the occupant so greatly. Imagine the surprise when it turned out to be only a large piece of brown paper spread over the table, a steel square and a *straight line* drawn on the paper. Desirous of knowing how the builder was progressing, the adjuster asked him how he was getting along, and was rewarded with the encouraging reply, "Splendidly; I've got the *base line drawn;*" at the same time pointing to the straight line on the paper in a sort of triumphant way.

Mr. Editor, I will assure you it was extremely difficult to refrain from smiling audibly. Not wishing, however, to wound the feelings of the party, the adjuster proceeded to give the builder the benefit of his figures, and in an hour the estimate was made and written out by the adjuster. When asked for his bill, the *builder and contractor* said it was $10. To this a demurrer was made, the adjuster wanting to know what his regular charge was for a day's work. Was informed that it was $3.50, but he thought his superior knowledge as a builder should entitle him to the full amount. He reluctantly took $5, and no doubt often wishes for opportunities to earn a V so easily.

Yours, etc.,   S.

A LITTLE TALK TO SPECIAL AGENTS.

WHEN one attempts to talk on a subject of common interest touching our business, there are so many heads of subjects springing up that bewilderment follows. There is so much to say, so much that ought to be said in clear, ringing tones, which would find their way to each one, and *wake him up*. It is common for our members to tell the wrongs we know of and do not mend—it is so common that if it were not told we would wonder. Yet here we meet each year, and, having read the lesson, go our way, quickened, but unheeding. Why is this? Do we not take pride in the fact that our business draws its rank and file from the best stock in the land? Is not society, art, literature, strengthened by the workers in our profession? Let me confine myself to one suggestion: The simple fact is here—there is *no good faith* among us. East, West, North and South, the same charge is made—*no good faith*.

I fear me it is true. It springs from cowardice, nothing less—moral cowardice. The will power which carries us through danger and trial in all else falters and is weak in this. My friends, let us mend it; let us talk less and do more; let us make a *start*—let the year 1881 mark this step, viz: Having each in his own mind fixed the way to bring good faith into the business, follow it, stick to it.

You are the managers of the future—before long you will guide and teach others. Teach correct practice; observe it that you may teach. Whatever the condition of things, *keep faith*. Do not agree to a compact until you are ready; if you promise, keep it; when your are ready to break the compact, let it be known; release yourself openly.

Let us think less of our neighbors' business. Each one of us is a neighbor—each one can take heed for himself. In all the town, is there another business worked by men—*gentlemen*—where a mere rumor of bad faith does such harm?

Is it because of the willing ear? Already this Association has done much—so much that the special agent is on terms of cordial friendship with his brother special; so much that strife, and sarcasm, and ill feeling has melted away, and a spirit of unity is found in its place. What is possible in the adjustment of losses is possible in the field and in the office. Let the past go; work faithfully for the present; the future will be here soon enough—too soon for all.

COMMISSIONS.

[Written for the *Knapsack*.]

The morning mists were fading fast,
As through a mountain village passed
A traveling agent, early bird,
Who uttered low the magic word
    "Commissions."

His form was bent, his haggard face
Showed traces of an ancient race,
While ever as he strode along,
He muttered in a well-known tongue,
    "Commissions."

Touch not that mill, the "local" said,
The "lead" is "petered out" and "dead";
The moral risk is something "snide";
But still that anxious voice replied,
    "Commissions."

Oh, stay! the Piute maiden said,
And rest awhile your weary head;
A wink lurked in his dexter eye,
But still he whispered with a sigh,
    "Commissions."

At midnight hour as homeward sped
Two jolly miners to their bed,
Bright flames leaped forth with lurid glare,
Reflecting through the murky air,
    "Commissions."

Morn on the ashes warm and gray,
Disclosed the traveler miles away;
While from the "local" standing near,
A voice came with a hearty cheer,
    "Commissions!"

BUZITE

A MOTTO FOR AN INSURANCE MAN.

My friends, we have met in our own social way,
  Where all may be happy, you know;
But whilst music and wine make us gladsome and gay,
  We'll think of the duties we owe—
We'll drink to the friends who have ever been kind,
  Who will stand by us all when they can,
Advice in my song you will certainly find,
  And a motto for an insurance man.

Chorus—So we'e will sing and banish melancholy;
    Troubles may come, we'll do the best we can
    To drive dull care away, for grieving is a folly,
    Put your shoulder to the wheel
    Is a motto for an insurance man.

In our business pursuits, when troubles **arise,**
  Our principle **is to adjust—**
To act on the square is prudent and wise,
  Each brother in **business to trust:**
The merits of **each we rate at the best,**
  Their *exposure* we gladly hide.
Nor seek for a fault in the East or the West,
  In faith with each brother abide.

Nor can we forget our adjusters and specials,
  Their trips and their troubles are legion;
We have seen not a few hang on to a trestle,
  Or the limb of a tree grimly **freeze** on.
On the road they are known as **the stage-drivers' friend;**
  Oft times they have carried **the stage**
Their grit and their shoulders, if ever they **bend,**
  'Tis sorrow and care to assuage.

We know what hard fare and rough tack they must take
  When traveling a loss to report.
To-day, chills and ague; to-morrow, an ache;
  On duty each hardship they court;
They'll fight to the death for justice and right,
  Nor do they forget the assured;
Their duty they do making sad hearts light,
  When fair play is fairly secured.

We drink to the health of our chieftains all,
  For jolly good fellows are they;
Though fat and at ease they answer each call,
  And their losses with promptness pay;
We'll drink to our aids and our brokers too;
  No small share of the work is theirs
Though some time proposed to cut rates 'tis true,
  But we all have our troubles and cares.

And whilst we are glad and our wine cups are full
  Let us drink to our home offices too;
They are men we esteem, and never will pull
  A man who his duty will do.
They have stood by us all when calamity came
  And strengthened us every one;
And when our slight faults they have honestly blamed,
  'Twas kindly and gently done.

And now, old friends, let us drink to ourselves,
  Our homes and our household gods,
To our wives and our sweethearts, the dear little ones,
  Against the world we give them the odds.
Whilst we gladden their hearts we gladden the world;
  For gladness is catching, you know,
So up with your glasses love's banner unfurled,
  We'll drink to them all ere we go.

W. J. CALLINGHAM.

    And now, comrades, having opened the *Knapsack* for your inspection, and showed you the good things in the Haversack, we will husband what further ammunition we have, and take a pull together at the old canteen when we meet around the festive board to-morrow evening, where neither rebates nor "commissions" will trouble us; and, trusting the "consolation" we'll draw from the occasion will long be remembered, I beg to roll my blankets, buckle my knapsack, and "close up" generally.

C. MASON KINNE, Editor.

CALIFORNIA KNAPSACK.

VOL I.   NO. 3.

C. MASON KINNE, Manager.   GEO. F. GRANT, Associate.

The following circular was dispatched to each member of the Association :

EDITORIAL ROOMS, 422 CALIFORNIA ST., }
San Francisco, Jan. 28, 1882. }

MR. ———

Dear Sir:—Once more the demand for "copy" goes out to our patrons, and as an inducement for the brightest scintillation of wit and sparkle of talent, the associate editor has provided a valuable testimonial, which he offers as a prize for the best article which may grace our columns.

There is also an admonition with our demand this year to the effect that some of the latent talent, which as yet has not unearthed itself, *must come to the front* or there will be a court martial of two or three that we have our managerial eye upon.

Between the above intimation of reward and punishment there is a broad highway of peace and happiness leading down to our editorial sanctum, which you should travel with steps of pride, and it must be a cold day when you cannot provide something in the way of anecdote, personal reminiscence, or views on various insurance points.

All manuscripts to be handed in not later than Feb. 15, 1882.

Fraternally,

C. MASON KINNE, Manager.

TO OUR PATRONS.

Another year has rolled around, adding more gray hairs and wrinkles to the heads and features of all of us, but the bright smiles and warm hearts are as youthful as ever.

As to the specials and adjusters, of course, *we ought not* to grow old. With good salaries, nothing to do but travel about in the palace car, dine at the best hotels and amuse ourselves for an hour or two in some pleasant village talking to our agent, or pleasing our claimant by paying him all he asks, is certainly not very wearing work, from the average manager's stand-point.

But at all events we are here to-day, forgetful of expense account, of stage coach and buckboard, of dust and rain, of hash and hasheries, of dead towns and lying claimants. We are not worrying over ambiguous contracts, non-concurrent policies or excessive profits sweeping a just salvage out of sight, but looking into each other's faces, bearing such an imprint of honest devotion to strict business principles as preclude the thought that you would go for each other's best agent to-morrow, if you got a chance. For one day at least we are brothers in the true sense of fraternal business relations and can let each other see the better and more unselfish side of our natures.

But as the meat of these meetings is expected to be found in the reports of committees and addresses of members, it is only the purpose of the *Knapsack* to give it a flavor, add a certain amount of pleasing aroma to the solids and an enticing bouquet to the fluids.

Speaking of things gastronomically, reminds us that our associate editor will have to see that the *Knapsack* is properly supplied with rations at the contemplated raid on the commissary, as stern duty calls the manager in another direction. We are sorry for this, for even insurance men appreciate the necessity of well-appointed kitchens, and, with the rest of mankind, believe that Owen Meredith is right in saying:

> "We may live without poetry, music and art;
> We may live without conscience, and live without heart;
> We may live without friends; we may live without books;
> But civilized man cannot live without cooks.
> He may live without books—what is knowledge but grieving?
> He may live without hope—what is hope but deceiving?
> He may live without love—what is passion but pining?
> But where is the man that can live without dining?"

C. MASON KINNE, Editor.

ABOUT BRINGING GOOD INTO THE BUSINESS.

If experience teaches anything, it teaches us that a mighty change is taking place in our business. Observe the insurance literature of to-day. It is plain, pithy and *free* to all. Printed instructions now mean just what is said, whereas in those elder days the bewildered student construed ambiguous sentences which intimated more than they expressed and gave wide margin for varied opinion. The agent of to-day is *made*. Instances have ceased of adjusters springing full-fledged into the field and gaining laurels off-hand without the drill of preparation. The leader of the future is grinding at his desk, giving ten good hours of conscientious work for a consideration. There is a change in the hazard created by new machinery, new appliances, experiment and invention. This changes the rate and alters the nature of exposures. The tone of the business is changed; it has gained dignity and importance. In our intercourse, one with the other, there is no longer the "mental reservation"—a promise of to-day has a value on the street. I do not claim this as a moral reform. Said Hamlet to the Queen, "Assume a virtue if you have it not." There is a change. On the bench, and in the jury-box, cases are not lacking where the verdict rendered in accordance with law and evidence is in favor of the defendant. Authorities are multiplying from decisions in various courts which have felt constrained to mete out even-handed justice and defeat the schemes of evil-minded ones whose claim is based on false representation. These changes suggest this lesson: keep abreast of the time in which we live; keep step with the march of progress. It will bring good into the business.

There are endless questions concerning a variety of topics which rise to the lips and get no farther. Ask plenty of questions, but apply to the right source. The freshman is timid and has good fear of being set back by his elders. The sophomore is big with importance and chaff— above criticism, yet ever sensitive. The junior is your true mentor, for he is mellow with study, patient, having sympathy for a plodding brother. The senior—(take heed least you forget that he *is* the senior!) his knowledge is for himself and his livelihood; yet in a community no larger than our own it should be no difficult matter to get below the surface even of one having authority and gain information of a general nature. As I look through the list, I find those who stand best in the good opinion of the profession are not miserly of their thoughts. Thoughts!—it is a great gift, thinking. Few of us get farther in it than to *think* we think; for, to be a legitimate thinker, is to be one picked out of a thousand. All but idiots have minds that reflect, like a more or less perfect mirror, what they see, read or hear; to the few is given the power to invent by mental process, to analyze criticism. Next to thinking, and as an aid to thought, questions come naturally and spontaneously. Questions provoke discussion, and discussion fixes ideas. If you are pertinently in earnest in your business, you will find other earnest men ready to meet you on fair ground.

It is the latest popular custom at meetings of this kind to comment on the faithful, hard-working "Local," to weave for his brow a chaplet,

to portray his virtues even to the border of sentiment. He is deserving
of it all, and more. I have thought of him, and wish to offer a suggestion
for the consideration of this meeting. It is only a suggestion, for it is out
of the common routine and wide open to criticism. My plan is to collect
together at a convenient time and place the local agents of the Coast in
convention, for the purpose of mutual exchange of ideas, and mutual
benefit, all for the advancement of insurance and to bring good into the
business.

GEO. F. GRANT,
Associate Editor.

And now, gentlemen, we'll thrust our hand deeper into the recesses
of our pack, and see what we shall bring forth of the good things stored
away.

CIRCUMSTANCES ALTER CASES.

SCENE, a large clothing store. Proprietor, Mr. Moses, behind
counter. Enter to him a gent with a book under his arm.

Moses (aside)—Ah! here gomes that damned assessor; I'll fix him!
(To gent)—Goot mornin, my frent. How you vos dis fine day?

Gent—Oh, very well, thank you. You have a fine, large store here.
Big stock of goods, too. Now, I wonder what amount of stock you
must keep on hand to fill so large a building?

Moses—My frent, not so much as you dinks. You see dimes is hard
and trade is very pad. I joost sell noting at all, so help me, Gott. But
von must make a goot show, you know, so you see dese goats, dese
pants, dese vests (handling them), all sheep goots; not much money in
dem. All spread out zo as to make goot show, but not much vort.
Times never vas zo pad; I never sells noting. Yesterday von dam Irish-
man gome in and he says to me, Moses, vot you ask for dem goats? I
show him mein goats and pants and vests—one kind, anoder kind, every
kind—but he shtay here one half hour, never say one word while I try all
I knows to sell him a goat or someding. Bymeby he says, "Vell, Moses,
times is bad and goots is low, I vant one goat. Sho you just gome mit
me to der saloon across der shtreet and treat me to von brandy smash,
and I makes you an offer for de goat." And ven I go and dreat him vat
does de dam rascal do? He just wipe his mouth on der sleeve so, and he
valk right away, and never make me no offer at all! And dats der only
customer vot gomes in dese dree days.

Gent—Well, I'd just like to know about how much coin it takes to
stock such a store. Say, how much, Moses? Perhaps I'd like to go into
the business myself.

Moses—Vell, mine frent, I am an honest man, and I tell you the truth, so help me, Gott! Dere is just nine hundred and forty dollars in de shtore!

Gent—Nine hundred and forty dollars! Why, man, what are you talking about? Why, it is only six weeks ago you 'told me you had thirty thousand dollars' worth, and do you forget I am the broker who insured you for twenty thousand?

Moses—Oh, you bees de insurance man! Vell, I vos one d—n fool not to know you again! I taut you vas dat d—d assessor, and you know dose fellows just rob a pusiness man—rob him—rob him all de time. So I fix up de goots for de assessor, you see. But you bees de insurance man! Gome, I show you dat I am an honest man. You knows I been insured mit dose gompanies five year, and I vas burnt out only dree times. You know I am an honest man. Gome! (Takes the gent down stairs.) Dere, you see all dem goots, I takes no advantage of the insurance! Dere, my friend, I gif you my word dere is dirty tousand tollars' vort of goots, and you insure me only dwenty tousand, you know. Mein Gott, vat a fool I vas to take you for dat d—d assessor!

Gent (taking out his book)—All right, Moses; I assess you for thirty thousand dollars.

Moses—Vat you say? You bees the assessor and de insurance man, too? Mein Gott, for what you not tell me you change your peesiness? So help me——You bees one d—d rascal to sheet an honest man like dat? Vot for you play such d—d tricks to rob a poor man. D——n!!

Gent—Good morning, Mr. Moses. Next time be sure of your man before you show your hand. Remember, it's a bad rule that won't work both ways. [Exit.]

WATER PRIVILEGES.

IT is said, once upon a time, that our good friend who now leads a lion about by the mane, waiting for the sexton's bell to ring him to his meal off the agents scooped in from the field, did, in his first trip for and under the tuition of the "general," proceed to Truckee, and soon thereafter forward to the said "general" agent an application for insurance that he had worked into shape, and which included, among other items, certain amounts on a Turbine water-wheel, and also on the dam.

All was satisfactory from the company's stand-point for some two or three years, when the assured began to think that to pay the premium for insurance on a pile of logs with twenty feet of water behind and running over it, was not profitable—to him—and so cut it out of the next renewal.

The dam is there yet, with the silvery sheet of water still flashing back the rays of bright sunlight; all of which goes to show that Domin always did believe that the best of anything was good enough for him; but this not being satisfied with writing on the water-wheel, but must go for the dam also, is a little too *gilt-edged* entirely.

REGISTER EARLY.

INSURANCE men are ever on the alert for circumstantial evidence and it is not strange that their wives, by association, should exhibit a similar tendency. A case in point recently occurred when Winsome William, of San Jose, stopped over night in the city for the purpose of criticising, in company with his friend Carpenter, the fire hazard of a spectacular play. Mr. C., who then did his regular sleeping on the other side of the bay, left his satchel at the hotel where both were to stop, early in the day and registered, but as William never thinks of carrying any baggage for a trip of less than a week's duration, he had no occasion to visit the hotel until his dazzled eyes and excited brain sought rest, after the calcium light had cast its last reflections on the Amazons, and the theatrical fairy had kicked her last kick. It was, therefore, a little difficult for him, or any one else, to tell whether he made his hotel registry "last night or to-morrow morning."

The next night, having descended from the delectable mountains of San Francisco burlesque to the dead level of domestic San Jose, he was expatiating on the glories of the previous evening, when his wife, in as casual a manner as circumstances and a remarkable self-control would permit, asked:

"Where did you stop?"

"Oh, Carpenter and I staid at the Lick House."

"You did? Well, here is a copy of this morning's *Chronicle*, in which I find Mr. Carpenter's name in the list of guests, but I don't find yours."

William doesn't often take a back-set, but he was non-plussed in this instance, and when his name appeared in due form in the next issue, he felt that he lay himself open to the suspicion of having "seen" the newspaper man. He now makes it a rule to register before dark, so that his name may get in the book in time for the next morning's paper. Not having much hair to lose, his practical good sense as an adjuster teaches him that the salvage of that which he has, more than offsets any financial loss resulting from the payment for a night's lodging six hours in advance.   C.

A DREAM.

For a whole year past, since the agents found out
That adjusters and specials were safe without doubt,
Their minds have been greatly perplexed
As to what in the future will be their fate,
If they too can pass through the heavenly gate
When they go from this world to the next.

Now, in order to set troubled minds at rest,
And to aid them in settling their anxious quest,
　I will tell you a little dream
That came to me one night as I slept,
And worried me so that I fairly wept,
　So real did it seem.

Methought I stood by the little door
St. Peter watches so carefully o'er,
　And looking the wicket through,
Found a goodly company in sight
Who seemed to think surely *they* were all right,
　And many of them I knew.

There were Flint and Spencer with Capt. Magill,
Firmly marching straight up the hill,
　And close behind them came
Jacobs and Easton, Haven and Pope,
Faces beaming with pleasure and hope,
　With others that I could name.

Following them in unbroken rank
Came Hamilton, Dickson, Hunt and Frank,
　Andrew Smith and Chas. R. Story,
Carpenter, Bromwell and Landers, too,
All looking as happy as if they knew
　They were on the road to glory.

Brown and Bailey, Syz and Grant,
Naunton and Butler, looking askant
　At the Lion led by Dornin.
Potter, Jones and Farnsworth came in sight
With Laton and Speyer, looking as bright
　As a beautiful May morning.

But Peter said—"Ere I unlock these gates
You must each assure me you have never cut rates;
   Also explain your position
On the troublesome subject which all of you know
Has made such '*bobbery*' there below—
   The matter of commission."

"If while on earth you can truthfully say
That you kept your agreements every day,
   And did not once deviate;
Ne'er around the stump have the devil whipped,
Nor in any way from the right path slipped,
   I will hasten and open the gate."

I saw that they all seemed perfectly dazed,
And mournfully on each other gazed,
   And sadly they turned away,
Save *one*, who could stand the required test;
I could give his name, if I thought it best,
   But prefer that *you* should say.

COMMUNICATION.

PORTLAND, Oregon.

EDITOR *Knapsack*—So many good things will be offered you, that my mite will, I fear, not be entitled to even a place in the outside, with the panikin.

Things *don't hopper much* in Oregon to adjusters. Railroads in which accidents are not allowed to occur run to all the towns where fires occur. *Sleepers* are common. The dangerous streams are all bridged. Where railroads are not built, magnificent steamers ascend the smallest rivers to their very source, or Concord coaches, drawn by elegant horses over macadamized roads, carrying you smoothly along. The highway robbers have all joined the church; the Indians have become *rational* beings, and only go on the war path when Uncle Sam's grub gives out, and though occasionally you meet a "buck-board," the bucking horses have all been broke to ladies' use; and so I cannot, like my California brethern, give you very blood-curdling adventures.

A snow blockade of ten (10) days—having to keep moving for thirty hours to keep from freezing—no grub to pass the time; ascending rivers in a crazy Indian canoe with only Indians for companions—where every sharp bend in the river had its legend of drowned miners—these things, while adding spice to the usual dullness of Oregon life, are of course mere trifles to those who travel in the wilds of California. I therefore spare you details.

I recently met an adjuster who thought I was a Californian, who gave me the following, which I forward as a contribution from a wild untutored Oregonian.

A LEGEND OF THE RHINE(O).

In a beautiful country, where everything is evergreen, because the sun never comes out to dry the pearly rain drop which comes with delightful regularity, is located a beautiful city, grown fat with wealth and prosperity. The city is beautifully situated on a magnificent river, broad and deep. The country is called Oregon, and it is supposed that the dirt with which it was built came from Ireland. One thing is certain, no poisonous snake or reptile is found on its western slope.

The people do not speak Irish, but the oldest inhabitants, the first families, speak a "jargon.' The people are known as "Webfeet." This name was given to them by the first Californian who came, who supposed they were aquatic, because they found their nests so *well feathered.* The people generally took things very easy, making money without effort, but in the days I write of, existed on a well-known class who were an exception to the general rule. They were known as insurance agents. Existed, I say, because at present the race is extinct, *nearly.* They were so active and energetic that they were a source of great annoyance to the old business fraternity, who didn't believe in activity and enterprise. Every one supposed they were getting rich, but people were not aware of the goodness of heart and generosity of these agents, for, while they were supposed to be making large commissions, some of them were secretly returning all their profits to the needy persons buying insurance from them. Such generosity should have brought its own reward. It did. A disease called the "rebate" broke out among them and became epidemic. When the disorder was at its height, a meeting of all the agents was called to devise means to arrest its progress. One peculiarity of the disease was, that everyone thought himself the only one free from it. After many plans were suggested, some one said that there was a fiddler in town who could cure any disease by the magic of his bow. Every fellow wanted to see the other cured, and it was decided to employ him. The fiddler made the rounds of the offices, playing enchanting music; the insurance man could not resist the bewitching strains. Principals and clerks followed the fiddler until every one in the business had

joined the festive procession. The fiddler led them to the river bank and plunged into the water, still playing; all followed—all, save one; he was an adjuster as well as agent. When young a fairy had kindly stood for his godmother, and had given him a charm against water; some people said he wasn't born to be drowned—water didn't agree with him. He didn't believe in the water cure, so took a *ferry*-boat across the stream, expecting to meet his comrades on the other side. Alas! they never came. He mourned their loss, but consoled himself with the reflection that now he had the entire field to himself, and would do a smashing business. Strange to say, this was not the case. People quit insuring, and it was impossible for him to live on the business, and he was obliged to shovel dirt for a living. On being asked what charm the music had for him, he said, "I thought it said, 'Come, I will take you where there is a gilt-edged steam planing mill. Well, where there is no rebate.' The man has just arrived from California, where no such thing is known. Other agents don't know of it, because the lumber is not on the ground yet."
                                                                                    X.

"X" is a little mixed in his metaphors, but the moral is good.

EDITOR *Knapsack: Dear Sir*—To supply your demand for copy, we give the Association the benefit of three letters received by us during the past few days, from our agents at different points on the Coast. They merely show the "stuff" the different agents are made of. Our best wishes to the insurance fraternity is that every company doing business had an agent at every point made out of the same stuff as writer of letter No. 3.
                              Yours truly,   ———, Gen. Agent.

Letter No. 1 is from one of our agents, who having failed to remit for premiums after policies had been in force three or four months, and had failed to take notice of at least two accounts sent him, was gently reminded that *coin* was wanted. It reads, viz:

                                                  ——, February 15, 1882.

MESSRS. —— ——: Yours of the 10th at hand; contents noted. Now, in regard to balance due you of $60, nearly one-half of it is for my own policy, and I felt you could well afford to give me that, or at least wait until I could pay it; but you seem to be in such a hurry about it that I will try and relieve you before long—pay up and quit business. I have done your business for a long time, and as I supposed satisfactory, but I see you are not satisfied, and I think we had better dissolve. I have been urged by other companies to do business for them, who have offered me 20 per cent. for the warehouse insurance, and 25 per cent. for standing grain. They are good reliable Board companies, I have some money due me next month, and if I can collect it, will send you every cent due, and also all the books and papers that I have of yours, and will try my hand in doing business for other companies.

Yours, etc.　　　　　　　　————

Letter No. 2 is from an agent to whom we had returned a dwelling house application for $150, at ¼ per cent., explaining to him it was too small a premium to issue a policy for. It reads, viz:

————, February 18, 1882,

MESSRS. ———— ————: *Gentlemen*—Yours of the 12th inst. at hand, and will say that you have placed us in a very embarrassing position. We accepted the application and approved it, and now you refuse a policy. We are compelled to insure it in one of our other companies.

We are perfectly willing to listen to any suggestions you may wish to make, and while we do not presume to dictate the manner in which *you* should do *your* business, *we* must reserve the right of knowing something of *ours*, and with all due respect, we think we are better able to judge applications and their attending circumstances *here* than you can be in *San Francisco*.

This must not occur again, and if you are to refuse to issue policies when we ask for them, unless some radical error exists in the application, we think it would be best to return our certificate.

Yours truly,　　　　　　　　—— & ——

NOTE.—It has been suggested that we keep the above as a copy, so in case our companies criticise any of our risks, we can answer in same terms as our agent has written.

Letter No. 3 is from an agent, it is a pleasure to correspond with, and from one who has his company's welfare at heart. It is in answer to a *rigid* questioning regarding moral hazard of the assured under one of his risks, and also regarding water supply, and reads, viz:

———— ————, Feb. 19th, 1882.

MESSRS. ———— ————: *Gentlemen*—Your favor of 18th at hand, and we are pleased to see you are wide awake to your business interests, as there is no better guarantee to us and the assured of stability of your agency, and that our clients in —— —— Co., are *insured*.

The fire of December 13, 1881, originated in the building adjoining Mr. A, and there was not the slightest question of moral hazard. His clerk, a most estimable young man, narrowly escaped *cremation.* At that time Mr. A was insured in the —— —— for $2,000, which was fully paid after six days' close account of stock by ——, adjuster. Mr. A has a family here, and has been in business a number of years.

We trust you will accept no risk from us that you are not *perfectly* satisfied with as a business proposition. If it is not a proper risk for our companies, it is not for *us*, and we would prefer to refuse it altogether.

A committee of citizens have recently chosen sites for new cisterns, which are in place, and are to be provided with 5-inch pipes from the mains, and have taps for fastening or coupling hose to the pipe in the absence of engines.

The new cisterns are small, but the supply-pipe is supposed to furnish water to them as fast as the engine will draw it off. We are moving to thoroughly reorganize for the summer campaign. The main pipe of the water company is not as large as it should be, and in case of a large fire, would not furnish water for a large number of hydrants; but we are aiming to beat the common enemy at the threshold, if possible.

"Capt." Dimond, of the Phœnix, and "Col." Kinne, of the L. L. & G., were with us a week, recently, and from them you may obtain information of value.   Yours truly,   —— ——.

CAUSE AND EFFECT.

A fire on the premises of Dr. Port at Chollas Valley, near San Diego, Cal., destroyed a small barn or cow-shed, causing a damage of perhaps one hundred dollars. The fire occurred while the doctor was in town, and for some time its origin was a complete mystery. Determined to find out, if possible, how it occurred, Dr. Port on his return instituted an investigation, and arrived at results which make the affair one of the most singular we have ever heard of. In the morning some brush had been burned some distance from the barn, and when the doctor left home the fire had ceased to burn—the brush being all consumed. Among the pets on the place is a fine young dog, whose chief delight is to chase the numerous colony of rabbits (jacks and cottontails) abounding in the valley. Noticing the dog to be quite lame, Dr. P. proceeded to make a diagnosis of doggie as well as the fire, and found the dog's foot to be quite badly burned between the toes, which led the doctor to follow up his "lead," by which it was doubtless correctly determined that the dog had been in pursuit of a rabbit, whose flight had led him across the burned patch of brush. The fire was apparently all out, but the dog had stepped upon a small smouldering brand which became fastened between the toes. The sensation to the poor dog doubtless made him think he was the pursued instead of pursuer, and "turning tail" he fled for home and jumped the fence into the small yard adjoining the barn. The yard being covered with loose hay, the brand became detached from the dog's foot in jumping the fence and fell among the hay, thus setting fire to the premises.

SOME INSURANCE TALK AT A COUNTRY HOTEL.

WE were sitting before a roaring fire in a dimly lighted hotel office. Office by courtesy only, for it answered the requirements of a bar room, trunk room, reading room, card game and billiards. Not to forget a unique affair in the corner for lavatory uses, including three yards of revolving stuff not unlike sand paper in feeling, while to the other senses it was an ancient and fish-like satire on Turkish towelling.

Outside, rain poured gustily. Inside, dampness penetrated. An incessant drip, drip, drip, fell on the ear with the monotony of a sad heart-beat.

We had the room to ourselves at last, discussing points of adjustment and what not, until "Aretas" straightened himself, and was delivered of the following: "Gentlemen, talk about total depravity, I tell you the country hotel is the root of all evil. The country hotel is original sin, it is the father of cussedness, and the nurse of crime. Attacking the human victim at the seat of intelligence, the stomach, it spreads through the entire system, leaving it a hopeless wreck. We eat, we drink, what? Food, in its primal state fit for gods and goddesses. Fresh from gardens and shambles, rich, juicy, teeming with all health-giving qualities; but in the hands of that arch demon who rules over the frying pan it becomes a substance, a variety of substances, calculated to bring a nightmare that will attend your waking moments. A peaceable man by nature, I have seen times when I could shed blood, could dance on the grave of my dearest foe with maniac glee, all because of the leaden substance taken to support life, and familiar to your ears as 'beef steak, mutton chops, bacon and liver, tea or coffee,' and as for the drink, infusion of penny-royal and thoroughwort, ground beans with chicory. I hold it is a crime, a punishable crime."

"Oh, stop!" said "Gravely." "These extreme and extravagant words destroy the very argument. I admit there is much to complain of, but that portly form, 'Aretas'—that clear eye and fresh complexion—deny the waking nightmares. I concur as to the location of your seat of intelligence, but let me tell of a meal in a country hotel. 'Omega,' over there, remembers it. It was at Lake Tahoe. Too busy to fish, we sent out a man. He returned with a trout which must have weighed ten pounds—a beauty, still alive, swimming in a tank, when we gazed at it. 'Did the landlord know how to cook a trout?' 'He should smile.' 'All right; serve it for breakfast.' What a night of anticipation! How we paused over scorched and soaked books of account to recall the trout breakfast! How at last we toyed with knife and fork, an expectant light in our eyes! It came—ah, how we beamed! It came—ah, how we shivered! Cooked? It *was* cooked, until, in its charred remains, nor man nor surviving member of its family could recognize trout. Dry and greasy and bad, it might have been sturgeon or shark; it was *not* our breakfast. I do not go so far as you, 'Aretas,' in wishing to dance upon that landlord's grave, but if I had heard of his accidental yet shocking death, a holy calm would have filled my breast."

"I do not wish to choke any one off," said "Altamont;" "but what crazy nonsense this all is! Now, I have been on the road as long as any one here, at a time, too, when there were no railroads—when days and nights in a stage coach were as bad as any hotel could be—and I have always found plenty to eat that was good and wholesome. I have adjusted more losses, and probably know more about California, than any one. As for tea and coffee, why, if you don't like it, take milk. I never found any of their lawyers who would not admit that any proposition was correct; and if you can't get milk, water is good enough for the time being, or whiskey for that matter, although I don't need it. I can dictate two letters to different people on different subjects, all on the food and drink I get at country hotels. If that is not proof, what is? If any of you fellows want help in your cases, call on me. I am going to bed."

"Just one minute," said "Berg." "I have a good thing on 'Altamont.' Some years ago I invited him to make a fourth at a little dinner given in honor of two Eastern brothers. We went to the old Louisiana Rotisserie. 'Altamont' didn't want soup, and, after eating a pound of bread, what, in heaven's name, do you suppose he called for? Pudding!— by the eternal—and, dash my buttons, if he didn't order *soup* while we were at dessert—that's the sort of a liver complaint he is."

"Wild" here got the floor. "If I am allowed to get a word in edgewise with this convention, I put it up that the Oregon landlord takes the prize. Let me give you our experience. Time, 6 A. M.; season, winter; air, frosty—raining all the same. Drowned-out old stage dumped me at the door; inside old man asleep by the stove, boots nearly burned off him. 'Hello, pard,' shouted I, 'where's the landlord?' Long stupid stare. 'I be,' said he. 'I want a room—nice room.' No answer. 'I want it now—right off.' Not a burned boot dropped. *'Can I have a room?'* 'Waal, yaas, I presume so.' 'All right; lead the way.' With a blink that would have turned an owl green with envy, he pointed a long finger, saying, 'Take any of them left-hand rooms as is empty on the left-hand side up-stairs.' I was making up sleep at the rate of forty-eight hours a day when I became conscious of a riot outside my door. That landlord had given me the room of a regular boarder—a gambler." "Wild" was here interrupted in his narrative by a voice, saying, "Gentlemen, it is late, and the guests complain that they cannot sleep for your conversation." "I don't doubt it," said "Wild;" "this house is like a drum—you can hear what is said in any part of it. I remember once a young married couple came here"—but another beautiful reminiscence was lost in the general break-up.   G.

DEAR *Knapsack*—Open the inner pocket of your "old pack" and tuck this away for the next tea fight—if you want to.

"CONSEQUENTIAL DAMAGE."

The ideas of the great unwashed majority of the "plebeian herd" regarding the liability of insurance companies are as varied and vague as those of "a hog on a holiday," and happily illustrated in the recent experience of "one of us" in an adjoining county.

Due notice of loss was received at headquarters, and one knight of the Draft-Book hastened to the scene on his errand of mercy. The damage to building and furniture was found to be trifling, but the internal effects of mater familias were rent and disrupted as if by a volcanic eruption, and, though the smoke aud ashes had drifted away, great distress still prevailed.

Right here came in the question of "consequential damage." The loss to building and furniture had been amicably settled, and the adjuster was on the point of taking his departure, when the claimant brought him to the "right about" with a claim for damage through the premature birth of his infant son William. To arrive at the measure of this damage was a puzzler for our adjuster, but, as we all would do, he fell resolutely to work, and first satisfied himself that the damaged article had been properly covered and the thing was legitimate, and William would have been due thirty-one days from the date of the fire. Then arose the problem, what would be the present value of a bill maturing at 31 days—interest, 9 per cent. But here he was startled to bethink himself that he was ignorant of the face of the bill, and a sight of it was refused him. Still, always fertile in resources—like all of us, he took a horn of the dilemma, and knowing the usual bill for such things—he started out with $50 as a basis. Then, turning to his "Tiffany" for a proper table of depreciation, he concluded that "nut and bolt works with gravel roof" would be the correct guide.

This question of depreciation is always vexatious and prolific of more trouble than any other in the line of our calling; but, going quietly away by himself, our adjuster tackled it. Q. E. D.—If nut and bolt works will depreciate 5 per cent. in a year, how much will it depreciate in 31 days, figuring from an *in*verse ratio? After laboring earnestly for some hours to bring the thing to a solution, and having "reached the base line," he was surprised by the claimant suddenly exclaiming, "Look a-here, old man, you just pay the doctor's bill and I'll let you off." "How much is it?" asks the adjuster. "Ten dollars," says the claimant; and ten dollars was the compromise figure.

Yours,   **

HOW I KILLED MY MAN.

ONCE killed a man. He was a perfect specimen of his kind; of him it may be said society met a long-felt want in his demise.

He was short in stature; round, thick-set, swarthy; had broad shoulders and black bead-like eyes; to him a necktie was a useless appendage; summer and winter he appeared in shirt-sleeves; his eyebrows were bushy; his hair stood upright on his bullet head, "like quills upon the fretful porcupine;" his voice was a subdued roar—he spoke in thick gutturals, producing an effect not unlike *solid extract of sound*. I am in doubt as to his nationality; he appeared to combine traits of every known race, and his characteristics were of the four quarters of the globe.

Not having killed a man before, my emotions were varied. This is how it happened: He kept a general merchandise store, and, like a prudent merchant, had policies with two companies, but, unlike a prudent merchant, when the fires occurred from causes to him unknown, he had made such an unequal distribution of coal oil about the premises, that the little room in the rear alone was damaged, while the tell-tale stock in the main store stared sullenly from the shelves, silent witnesses in the case. Before I reached the spot, the district agent of the other company had settled his loss, paid it, taken up his policy and departed, as a precautionary measure, telling the assured that the *other* policy contributed its full face value.

Let me draw a veil—two veils—over the picture of my progress with this good man. How he did swear! Swear—he swore in seventeen languages—swore in all the minor keys, from baritone to double bass—swore to the top of the flag-staff on Mount Davidson and down to the lower level of the bottomless pit. When he had finished this volunteer crop of oaths, he swore judicially in the presence of a notary. Suffering truth, how he did swear!—swore that in this little room 10x12 and 8 feet high was stored every variety of merchandise, sewing machines, agricultural implements, hay, grain, feed, groceries, provisions, hardware, nuts, candy—*everything!* It was the nuts and candy "broke the camel's back." An itemized statement footed up fifteen hundred weight of nuts, and a ton of candy, all in sticks. I stopped him right there.

"Hold on, friend," said I, "whatever happens, I do *not* want you to forget anything. Take plenty of time; talk it over calmly with your partner. True, he is not interested in this policy, but he can make suggestions. Come to town by and by and see your friends and the people from whom you buy goods. Get duplicate bills and statements of accounts; that will help you some. Don't forget the candy man; he can, no doubt think of something not down on your list. Prices may be higher than when you laid in your winter's stock of nuts. You are entitled to every consideration in this matter. Bring the nut merchant round to the office. I would not see a poor man ruined knowingly. Our instructions are to point out to the assured any loss he has suffered which may escape his eye in the excitement of the moment."

Thus I spoke with him; thus I reassured him, while his breast heaved with emotion and his eye burned fierce and fiercer. Suddenly, without warning, he went mad right there; he raved, foamed at the mouth, and bit at the air. It was a merciful Providence intervened and struck him to the floor, a senseless lump of clay. They took him up, carried him out, and that week they buried him. It was the public administrator paid him this tribute; said he, "He was great—for one thing. He was the greatest *liar* in the world."　　　　G.

Conundrum—What is the difference between a livery stable and an omnibus building?

This was asked of the writer by one of the prominent (?) agents of a large Nevada town, after he had received a liberal share of the special's instructions, and when he was endeavoring to inform himself as to the intricacies of rating.

AND now, being of the opinion that we have got right down to the bottom of the thing—of the *Knapsack*, I mean- -the manager and his associate are ready to consider the inspection over and "fall in." Methinks we hear the merry tones emitted with jangling jar from the metal throat of the bugle, sounding the well-known "dinner call," and we sling knapsacks with alacrity and are willing to go marching along for another season.

CALIFORNIA KNAPSACK.

VOL. 1.   NO. 4.

C. MASON KINNE,   -   -   -   -   -   -   Manager

EDITORIAL ROOMS, 422 CALIFORNIA STREET,
SAN FRANCISCO, January 15, 1883.

DEAR SIR:—The *Knapsack* again needs replenishing. We have been dividing our stores among our comrades so lavishly, that the supply of rations is nearly exhausted; and in consequence we propose to make a raid on the talent and wit surrounding our headquarters and see if our intellectual commissariat will not be stocked with good things as of yore.

The soldier can do better fighting when well fed; and the *Knapsack* is at its best when most plethoric.

The great fraternity of specials and adjusters make a goodly company; and now that orders are issued we expect you to *fall in promptly*.

Give us short, concise and pointed sketches of personal experience, ideas and anecdote that the past year has stored up for you, and don't be too long about getting them ready.

The flap of the *Knapsack* is wide open and will so remain till February 10, 1883.   Urgently yours,

C. MASON KINNE, Manager.

EDITORIAL.

In commencing another year of our existence, we have to offer this number just as it is. It ought to have been better: it might have been worse.

Let it be plainly understood by contributors and patrons alike that *our Knapsack* is not one that is piled with the rest when the battle begins, but that it is carried with us onto the skirmish line. Of course it would become burdensome were it loaded down and packed full with the varied impedimenta of the raw recruit; and the old campaigner knows just what to throw out. Luxuries for the commanding officers, but essentials only for veteran soldiers.

The special agent or the adjuster is the man who is detailed for picket duty, or as one of the skirmishers, and while under fire or over it, he sees things as they are. He is not fighting the whole battle; statistics don't count for much just then. The man in his immediate front is his meat for that fight; and whether it is a slippery agent or an unjust claimant, it engrosses all his attention and his best thoughts.

The generals in the back office may direct the plan of the Battle of the Underwriters, and carry it out according to all the rules and regulations of modern insurance warfare, but without his efficient field officer to point out the dangers of the the "ford" and the "pass," his infantry in the way of Tariffs, his field batteries of Statistics, and his cavalry charges of Special Ratings, all are met and demoralized and finally routed by the onslaught of partisan rangers and guerilla warriors, frantically brandishing the spear of rebates and cut rates, excessive commissions and expensive supplies.

Insurance is a peculiar business, fraught with dangers as certain as those of bullet and shell. We meet the onslaught of the fiery foe first of all; we have to bear the brunt of the battle. Every loss, imaginary or real, that can be put upon the shoulders of the insurance company, is carefully rammed home and fired with a short fuse. The adjuster now and then gets in a little good work, but ordinarily returns home feeling that he went, he saw, and was conquered. His knapsack is full of experiences—good, bad and indifferent. He is at once a student and a teacher. Losses educate the people to insure; adjusters inform them of details and necessary preliminaries that hedge about the path of indemnity, that they never thought of before. It is a new schooling for them, and the adjuster is the tutor.

But the field man finds his capacity is of a dual character. To-day the wearied adjuster, to-morrow the worried special. Tutoring a claimant in the paths of rectitude to-day, but a few hours finds him schooling the local agent how not to cut rates and yet talk business to win; trying to convince him that commissions for himself is not all he has to think about, and that the tariff is not the immaculate personification of insurance judgment. That Book 4, as applied to a California town, or village in eastern Oregon or Washington, is to be construed simply as a minimum guide, and not a maximum solution of what to charge for a broken frame range or a B-class building exposed by a long row of frame houses, in which cloth-lining and stove-pipes predominate.

But it is not for the *Knapsack* to moralize. Its duty is to convey such facts and experiences as may be placed within its protecting folds, and not manufacture them; to absorb and not theorize. We have to give you to-day a little of all sorts; from grave to gay, from water supply in San Francisco to whisky straight in the mountains.   There might have been more; there ought to have been much more offered us from out the varied episodes in the work of our specials and adjusters, supplemented by the careful thought and wise experience emanating from those who occupy the *sanctum sanctorum;* who sit at the helm of the various ships sailing with their mingled fair winds and foul, over the troubled sea of insurance.   But what we have is good, and of a character for such a receptacle; while the various committees can deal with the weighty problems of losses and adjustments, forms of policies, statistics, etc., with suggestions thrown in of how to reform evil practices and elevate the profession generally.   THE EDITOR.

THIS, from a paper read by a prominent underwriter before the Association of the South, fits our climate so close that it will bear repeating.

Report says that the paper was repudiated by that Association; and it must have been because truth is unpopular in that neighborhood.

He says of the "candid agent," Arkansas is a good place to draw an example from on this score.   An agent up there offered a company a risk—a ten per center; making a big, fat premium—in an Arkansas frame row, the character of which was so hard that it would simply have scared the average manager to death to see it.   The company wrote back to know what especial feature recommended the risk.   Agent replied that the chief thing that recommended it to him was "the *commission that was in it.*"   Yours,   X.

THE following is a good deal better than no response at all.   We thank "C" for small favors.   Try again.

PORTLAND, Oregon, February 1st, 1883.

C. MASON KINNE, ESQ.

*My Dear Sir:—*Your call for contributions to the *California Knapsack* is received.

The self-assurance and cheek of the special agent is proverbial; but I am yet too young in the business to presume to offer any sketch that would be of interest or entertainment to the members of the "F. U. A."

Oregon is too slow and plodding to furnish any startling experiences; but she can boast of more fires and larger losses to the premiums written, and more unprincipled insurance solicitors and agents, than any other country on the globe.   If ever I have an experience in this country of perpetual mud and slush that will be of interest to the Association, I shall be only too happy to contribute it.   Wishing you a joyous reunion, I remain,   Very truly yours,   C.

Editor *Knapsack:* If you have found, as I have, a lamentable ignorance of the most common rules, perhaps you will add to this list, which is called

HINTS TO AGENTS.

[If printed on a card, why not a good thing to scatter broadcast?]

In event of loss, telegraph the number of policy and probable amount of loss to general agent.

Let the assured put his damaged goods in order, sorting the wet from the dry, and protecting them from further damage.

Do not assume responsibility; use common sense; advise and assist.

Many of your patrons think they have no right to remove or even touch their goods at time of fire. An error. It is their duty to save. The property insured belongs to the party insuring, before, at, and after the fire. Let him proceed as he would if he had no policy.

Save books of account first.

Do not consent to or make an endorsement on policy after a fire.

Office and store fixtures or furniture are not covered under the head of "stock."

Pictures, silver-ware, ornaments, printed books, sheet music, and musical instruments are not covered under the head of "household furniture." Put separate amount on each subject.

Household furniture includes carpets, curtains, bedding, crockery, glass-ware and kitchen utensils.

Awnings are not covered with brick buildings unless specially mentioned.

Give permission for fifteen days' carpenter work free; after which charge as per rule in rate-book.

Accept not to exceed two-thirds cash value on any subject.

Cash value is the value of "to-day," notwithstanding the circumstances.

Refer all special hazards to headquarters without binding the company.

Cancel and return policies when your judgment dictates; for instance:

 Misrepresentation on the part of the assured,

 Danger from incendiarism,

 When property is in the hands of sheriff,

 When building is vacant,

 When business is not profitable.

Render your account current the first of each month.

When rate is increased from any cause during the life of policy, collect additional premium.

Never consent to assignment except on actual sale of property insured.

The words "loss, if any, payable," will protect other interests.

The first payee must release his claim before a second can be recognized.

Enter every change in your register.   X. Y. Z.

[IN this connection we add some of the printed instructions an ex-special, now Secretary, sends his agents. They, as well as the preceding ones, are all good.—ED.]

N. B.—Please be careful and give us the size of building to be insured.

ATTACHMENTS.—When property insured is attached (before a loss), immediately cancel our policies on said risk.

DISTINCTNESS.—If the signature of the assured on application is indistinct, write the name in lead pencil on the margin.

REMITTANCES.—All remittances and letters address to the company, and not to the officers.

TOUCHING LOSSES.

NOTICE.—Upon receipt of information of a fire in your town or district, "At once notify the company by telegraph, giving number of policy; *where issued;* loss, if supposed total, or amount of partial; name of assured, and names of other companies interested.

INVENTORY.—Schedule immediately all property saved.

CUSTODY.—Request assured to take charge and protect property saved until loss is adjusted.

PERISHABLE PROPERTY.—Use all legitimate means to dry and preserve property damaged. Iron and hardware have dried by rolling in bran or shorts to prevent rusting. Cigars, tobacco, dry and fancy goods, clothing, linen-ware and such, expose to air to dry.

SUSPICIOUS CIRCUMSTANCES.—Take the name and address of every person who knows or professes to know anything about the fire, and note all the facts relating thereto.

PROOFS OF LOSS.—Should an assured file proofs and a statement of loss with you before the arrival of the adjuster, "At once notify him that you have no authority to receive and accept the same; but, if he desires, you will hold and deliver them to the adjuster of the company for him, upon the adjuster's arrival; and that the assured must furnish said company such **further** statements and **proofs** as **the** said adjuster may require, the company waiving **none of the** conditions of its policy **or** objections to the receipt of said proofs, or **their correctness."**

INSTRUCTIONS.—Whenever in **doubt on any point** relating to your conduct at time of a loss, telegraph us for information and instructions.

WATCHMAN.—When property saved and in a damaged **condition** amounts **to over $1,000, put** on a responsible watchman until the **adjuster** arrives ; and no outsiders must be allowed on the premises, or to handle said property, excepting those designated by the assured **to assist in** separating the damaged stock **from the** sound, **and to save and protect** his property from further injury, **or to take an account thereof.**

P.

GETTING BOARD RATES.

It is said there is nothing new under the "sun." Here is the last in the way of getting Board rates :

Property insured : a two-story brick building, occupied as a butcher shop on the first floor and dwelling on the second.

Dwelling rate, .50. Butcher shop rate, 1 per cent.

Copy of policy:

$........**on** his two-story metal-roof brick building, occupied as a dwelling, **situate** ....corner **of**........**and**........streets, town o. ...., county of........, California.

Term, 1 year. Rate, 50 cents. Premium **$**........

"Permission granted to **cut and sell cold meats on first floor, day** time and evenings." Yours, X.

[The above is a true fact and speaks for itself.—ED.]

A LESSON IN RATING.

Recently in a small village I was accosted **by a local agent of a prom-**inent Connecticut company, and requested **to settle a dispute, viz.:**

"**What is the rate** on a detached frame **dwelling?"**

"Seventy-five cents," **I said.**

"Well, I mean a dwelling **without fresco,"** he answered.

"Without fresco? Please explain."

Said he, "Under alphabetical table **of hazard, page 12 of rate book,** I **read: Frame** dwellings, **see** frescoed work; D class; 75 cents; now, if you **can't see** any frescoed work, what then?"

Sadly I turned **to the other man, and asked, "What is your idea?"**

"Well, *I* claim that under rule on page 4, *all* frame buildings rate 2½ per cent.," he replied. Explanation follows: "Confound it, my company has insured my own dwelling for the last three years at 2½ per cent. per annum, and never told me I was wrong."

X. Y. Z.

HOW OUR LOSS WAS FINALLY SETTLED.

IF YOU should search the whole world through you would fail to find such another united family as ours. Our love for grandmother is woven in with our daily lives. Left without father or mother at a tender age, she became to us at once guardian, parent, adviser, friend. We are three children—Charlie, just coming of age; Kate, two years younger, and I, "sentimental sixteen." From infancy that blessed grandmother has nursed us through sickness, conquered our stubborn pride by loving means, and instilled into us habits of industry and economy. We lived in the family mansion of the old Harkinson estate, a few miles from town; just a few acres of ground, with a fine chestnut grove leading to the house, a well-kept garden, and two or three out-buildings; but oh! how dear to us. Perhaps you think this a strange story for the *Knapsack*,—wait and see. On the 27th of December, only two nights after Christmas, we were scared out of our sleep and bundled out of the house helter-skelter. "Fire! fire!" was all we heard. Wrapped in odds and ends of blankets, table-covers and overcoats, we watched that dear old home melt away. Huddled together at the dairy-house window we saw the angry flames, and saw the cause of them, too —an earthenware chimney! Heat within and cold air without had cracked it just below the roof; no knowing how long the fire had smouldered.

Even in our terror we noticed the most ridiculous incidents. We saw that what was brought out of the house was mostly of no value; nothing was complete; *something* was gone from everything.

Of course there was insurance. Charlie informed us with pride that he had attended to the matter *himself;* grandmother was beginning to trust matters of business to his care.

Well, next day we knew no more what to do than so many kittens. The local agent of the insurance company was dead, and we had to call in grandmother's lawyer, who notified the company. Next came an elegant-looking young gentleman to adjust the loss. He was so kind and explained everything with such ease, he quite filled us with admiration. We had a builder's estimate and an appraisement, and made out a long list of all that dear old furniture, and the adjuster helped; and when he said, "let me look at the policy, please," Charlie produced it with quite an air, as if to say, "I am the business man here." After a look he said, "I want the last policy." "Last one?" said Charley, "last one—why *that is* the last one." "Oh, no," said he, "this expired in July." "Expired?" said Charlie, turning pale, "expired—*that's all the policy there is.*"

Oh, dear! such another time you never saw. Charlie was as limp as a caterpillar. We brought ammonia and cologne and handed him over to grandmother. Throughout this trying scene the adjuster seemed to do just the right thing at the right time, and said good-bye, leaving us with the impression that we had cruelly deceived him. When the lawyer told us we had no claim, you may be sure we were a solemn quartette. Then it was for the first time we learned how grandmother, in the love of her dear heart, had educated us, clothed us, and reared us at the expense of her own little fortune, which was nearly spent. How the Harkinson estate yielded nothing; and in her extremity she had no one to turn to but God. Then it was we children put our talents to good use. Kate painted water-color sketches, which sold quickly; I formed a music class, and Charlie—well, Charlie seemed suddenly to become a man; not that he changed much in appearance, but his upper lip seemed to become perfectly straight, which gave a determined expression to the whole face. One day he told us he had talked with the president of the insurance company, and was to meet the board of directors. What for? Well he hardly knew; there was some awful mistake about the whole miserable business, and he could not rest until he had tried to unravel it.

The day came—he stated his case to those twelve men as I have told it to you; his whole heart was in the story, and he only faltered when he spoke of the wrong he had done grandmother. The directors were interested. Said one: "Why if the policy had expired, did you send an adjuster?" This to the Secretary, who answered: "The property has been insured with the company for years and renewed annually; the adjuster was sent at once without consulting the books."

"Was there no application for this policy?" asked another.

"No; here is the only application; the original, marked *renewed*, you will see from year to year."

"If the agent who took the risk were alive," said Charlie, "I am sure he could explain the matter." One old gentleman who had quietly watched proceedings asked if the agent had not written a letter ordering the policy renewed.

The Secretary retired a moment and brought in a file of letters; selecting two, he glanced over them, and, with a slightly changed color, asked to see the policy; then, with a dry little cough, he said:

"Gentlemen, the mystery is solved; this policy was ordered renewed for *three years*. By this application you see the *annual* rate; the amount of premium paid on the policy is double the annual rate, or what we call a three-years' rate; clearly a clerical error on the part of the policy-writer."

Well! if it had been a matter of life and death, I don't believe there could have been more joy manifested. Talk about corporations not having souls; those men congratulated Charlie, and shook hands all around with enthusiasm; and the President, laying his broad palm on Charlie's shoulder, said: "Young man, there is a vacancy in my office for just such a boy as you, and who knows but some day you may fill that chair," pointing to his vacant seat.

Out came the nice young adjuster again with proofs of loss, and a check for $5,000; and weren't we happy?

And since that day the young adjuster and I have agreed to a contract of our own, requiring certain proofs—of affection. But that is neither here nor there.   G.

The following has already been honored by appearing in print, but is pointed enough to bear reading again:

GOING FOR HER BALD-HEADED.

A certain officer recently received a report of a policy written, covering, among others, this item: "$150 on her wigs, braids, puffs, rolls, curls, and other hair for her personal use, etc."

The particular old covey, the presiding genius of said office, exhibited an *alarming* ignorance of the subject in writing the agent as follows: "This is an uncommon item; and as we find no blanks for an appropriate survey, you will please speedily answer following interrogations: What color is the hair? and if red, decline. Is assured married or single? If married, is her husband quick-tempered? Does she 'fire up' quickly herself? If single, has she beaux, and do they smoke? Does she use a spark arrester? Is she a church member, and does her pastor smoke? Does *she* smoke? Is she near-sighted or cross-eyed, and are her dressing-mirror lights globed or basketed? Is she a match-maker, and is she subject to 'em? Is she a cremationist? Has she sparkling eyes, and is she an heiress? (Does not seem to be hair-less.) Limit degree of heat of curling irons and toilet chemicals to bay water and champagne, and not more hazardous. Strike out lightning clause if steel hair-pins are used, and make policy cease at death—that is not good on hairs to heirs in any hereafter place. Celluloid pins, back-combs, bang-supporters, and other articles prohibited, and powder limited to twenty-five pounds in metal packages. If any moral hazard or enemies, decline."

QUERY.

Should the cigars the adjuster smokes be charged in the expense account, or to loss by fire?

A MERCED COUNTY DAY-BOOK.

The folling is handed in by one of "ours," and goes to show with what good things the *Knapsack* might be filled, if each of us would take the pains to jot down the amusing part of his experiences:

DEAR *Knapsack:* I hand you some actual notes from the day-book of a Merced county claimant, made while trying to arrive at his loss last summer. He made a diary of daily experiences of this book, and of which the following are a few extracts:

JUNE 2, 1882.

Mrs. Brown—
    10 yds. Calico $1.00
    By 2 pds. Butter .... .50
                                      ————
    Balance ....$ .50

Am going to Merced to a ball with Lena to-morrow night.

JUNE 4, 1882.

William Stevens—
    1 pr. Boots....................................$3.00

These boots came from the "United Workingmen's," at 'Frisco, and give satisfaction all around.

Alex Whitman—
    1 Jumper .... .87½

Speaking of "jumpers," I took Lena to the ball last night, in my new gig. Staid until 3 o'clock this morning. Had ice-cream and cake at Johnnie Smith's. Cost 50c. apiece. Charge expense account for whole thing, $2.60.

Lucky I came home this morning; the sow littered last night—9 pigs, all boars.

JUNE 6TH.

Mary Anderson—

    1 Box Hairpins...................................$ .10
    1 pr. Shoe-Strings .... .05
    1 pr. Drawers 1.15
    1 Dung Fork................................... 3.50
                                                    ———
                                                    $4.80

    By 10 doz. Eggs 2.00
                                                    ———

    Balance $2.80

Thermometer 98°.   Old sow not doing well.

JUNE 8TH.

No sales to-day.

Lena came in this afternoon. Had a good time. Shall marry this girl sure if things go on this way. Gave her a pair of garters.

    Charge expense .... .15

JUNE 10TH.

Mrs. Allison—

    5 yds. sheeting $1.00
    1 pr. Shoes...................................... 2.50
    1 Corset Lace .... .10
                                                    ———
                                                    $3.60

The old sow died last night. It was mournful to hear the poor pigs lament the loss of their mother.

I have the honor, etc.,

ONE OF THE RANK AND FILE.

[The *Knapsack* is pleased to announce that the above-mentioned claimant has since married the girl.]

EMBARRASSING.

To bluff an assessor in a country town regarding a taxable valuation, and be compelled to look the same man in the face a few days after, when he is acting as adjuster for the company in which you are insured.

A "BAR" STORY.

LIMBER Jim Witherspoon was a character. Physically he was weak-kneed, and hence his nickname; but mentally he stood pat on the most astounding and intricate propositions. He prided himself on a latent genius which did not find full scope for its exhibition in the menial occupation of wood-sawing; but he patiently bided the time when "Limber Jim Witherspoon" should be a name that would awaken the envy of the world. His time came. Having artistically arranged the stove wood of the camp so that the usual proportion of sticks would be just long enough to prevent the shutting of the stove-door unless they were driven through the other end of the heating apparatus with a sledge, he betook himself to the mountains, at the head of Grizzly Gulch, intent upon chopping government timber for the benefit of his own private and diminutive exchequer. The air was cold, and braced him up to that extent that he was compelled, in order to keep from freezing, to put more energy into the building of his cabin than he had ever been accused of before. Even the seams of his cheap clothing, entirely unaccustomed to such antics, began to laugh as he plied his lusty strokes; and so Jim worked the harder. With death behind him, Jim *could* work.

That was a luxurious rest that he enjoyed as he spread his blankets before the fire and watched the blaze roar up the chimney during the week after the cabin was finished. He had not yet chopped any wood for market; it was "too damnation cold," as he expressed it; and he "guessed they'd have a chinook pretty soon," so that the weather would be fit for a white man to stir around in. So, between his naps and his meals and his day dreams, he "puttered" around inside the cabin, trying to make it comfortable by the addition of such improvements as would commend themselves to a man of his genteel predilections. One of the most indispensable articles to a person of his tastes was a table; and, as the roaring fire had sufficiently thawed out the frozen floor of the cabin, he straightway dug the holes for the table legs. He wondered, now, if there might not be some gold in the dirt that came out of those holes. It was still awful cold outside, and he guessed it would be easier to stay inside and experiment than to go outside and work. Of course he had a pan with him (no outfit was, in those days, complete without one). Now, Jim was one of the most "patient" men with his hands that was ever seen. There was no nervousness, no hurry, and he seemed to be humming a gentle lullaby to his pan as he sleepily moved it to and fro with a "go-to-sleep-my-baby" motion, that now and then allowed a spoonful of amber-colored water to slop over, but often didn't.

The next day was colder than ever, but Jim was out doors. All his worldly possessions were on his back, and he was headed for town. The "prospect" from the bed-post holes had confirmed the suspicion raised by the table-leg holes that he was a rich man. He had in his pocket a few grains of gold to prove his statement, that he had struck diggings that would "go a bit to the pan." He did not, however, make his discovery known upon his arrival in camp, but essayed his old occupation of wood-sawing. To his dismay he found that during his absence his old customers, unable to get along without the warning influences of the profanity which his long sticks promoted, had been hiring a swarm of Chinamen that had come freezing with the last blizzard into camp. It was not until the dust in his sack required a plentiful admixture of black sand in order to make it hold out "four bits" that Jim became desperate and appealed to his old employers and to his old associates to give their own flesh and blood a chance. The result was that the Chinamen were "run out" of town; and as Jim saw them winding their way along the Grizzly Gulch trail that he had so recently traveled, he concluded that the balance of that day should be set apart by him as a season of rest and thanksgiving. But from that time on it was noted that Jim tried, in a forlorn hope sort of a way, to infuse more energy into his work than ever before; and when, at the close of winter, he engaged to "whack bulls" to Fort Benton, it was surmised that it was something more than the usually lonely plug of tobacco that swelled his off-pocket to its exceptionally well-developed proportions. Fortunately the bulls of Jim's team had been grazing on icicles all winter, so he had no difficulty in keeping up with them, and he arrived at Fort Benton in time to work; or, perhaps, we should say, "wash" his way down the river as dish-cleaner on the steamer *Octavia*. The June rise made the waters of the river thick with mud, so that the sepia representations of cloud-bursts and murkey weather generally, that appeared on Jim's "plaques" were generously attributed to the mud, rather than to his laziness. So he was not thrown overboard, but arrived at Yankton all right. Here he found more good luck awaiting him. A considerable section of land which he had taken up one day, several years before, when it was too hot to work, had become very valuable, and he found himself at once in a position to put into effect the scheme which he had kept secret in his breast ever since the day when he had prospected in the table leg shaft.

It took some time to have his apparatus manufactured; and it was not until one year later that he was on his way up the Missouri River with an iron pipe, a foot in diameter and a half a mile in length, with which, when placed in a "V" shape, he proposed conducting the only available water down one side of Grizzly Gulch and up the other, on to "Witherspoon's Bar."   *   *   *   *   How his spurs jingled as he gave his horse's bit an extra twitch while riding at the head of the bull train bearing his "machinery" through the old camp where the buck-saw and the accompanying horse, without a horse, were his familiars. On the way up the gulch the occurrences of eighteen months before were recalled by the appearance of a straggling band of Chinamen staggering along under their heavy burdens. Were these ever his competitors? Well, even if they were, that time was now passed forever; and Jim eagerly hastened forward to the turn in the gulch which should bring with him in sight of his fortune.

A drizzling rain set in, and the night closed in thick and dark upon him and his train earlier than they had anticipated. Still they pressed on, for Jim was certain of his road, and knew that they would reach their destination in a few rods more. Soon, however, the road became so rough and rocky that they were compelled to halt and await the grey of the morning before proceeding further. The morning came, and for once Jim was up before the sun. He found himself standing on a slippery boulder, rubbing his eyes and gazing upon other slippery boulders and rocks and gravel, wet with the rain of the previous night, that made up a picture of monotonous desolation unrelieved save by the ruins of a single cabin that seemed to have been only recently undermined and toppled over by its last occupants. Little shelves and other conveniences were still attached to the logs which formerly composed its sides, and, as broke the day, so broke upon Jim's intellect the realization that he stood upon what was left of " Witherspoon's Bar."

What became of him nobody knows. His gaunt outlines, with more limber pace than ever, were last seen in bold relief against the morning sun, as he passed over the "divide" to Hell Gate Cañon.

Now, all this has nothing to do with insurance; but when the *Knapsack* told me yesterday that I must have something for its columns, I thought of Limber Jim, who had his "field" all worked out "by hand" by a lot of Chinamen, who utilized the waters from the melting snow, while he was getting ready to do the work on a grand scale by the aid of magnificent machinery; and I wondered whether I could not make the story fit the case of the insurance agent who wants a half column "ad" in the village paper, a big sign, allowance for office rent, power to appoint "subs," a bushel of blotters, and who never gets through wanting *something* before he gets ready to go to work. I will rely upon the intelligence of the reader to trace the smile without a "diagram."

C.

THE following rhythmetical sketch of what will occur to-morrow night has been ground out by our poetic assistant; and, in anticipation, portrays the scene which will follow this feast of reason when the battle of knives and forks begins.

IN MEMORIAM.

ANNUAL BANQUET, FEB. 21ST., 1882.

At "Dingeon's" when the sun was low,
All fiery was the kitchen's glow;
And swift and savory was the flow
  Of *potage* boiling rapidly.

But Dingeon saw another sight,
When the gong struck at seven that night,
Commanding jets of gas to light
  The Pacific Fire fraternity.

Then rang the halls with orders given,
Then waiters rushed by "specials" driven,
And swifter than the bolts of Heaven
  The "boys" were seated merrily.

By host and waiters fast arrayed,
The "adjuster" drew his shining blade,
And, *sans formality*, made raid
  On all in his vicinity.

The banquet deepens! on ye brave!
Fear not dyspepsia or the grave;
Wave Leon, all thy napkins wave,
  And "charge" with strict impunity.

Ah! all must part, though many meet;
But months roll round with flying feet;
And thus again we hope to greet
  Our seventh anniversary.

A CASE OF ARSON.

About midnight, not many months ago, the clanging of the fire alarm bell and the ruddy emblazoning of the fog overhead, called the citizens of Gilroy from their beds.

Breathless and hurriedly they gathered from all points, and while some did service in the way of aiding to remove a $400 stock from the locality describing a $1,500 policy, others resolved themselves into the invariable "standing committee" on the sidewalk. As one small group of the numerous body was conversing about the peculiarity of the matter and of the many suspicious attending circumstances, one of the party said, in a manner showing he was in earnest, "Well, I'm satisfied that's an incendiary fire."

This seemed to be a safe proposition, but somehow did not exactly meet the exigencies of the case in the mind of a rough-looking stranger near by, who excitedly broke out with the exclamation, "Incendiary be d—d; somebody *set it afire!*"

WHAT'S THE USE?

THE *Knapsack* has proportions large enough and capacity ample enough, not to be compelled to turn its microscopic eye in every direction to see things as they are. The real knapsack is essential to the soldier, and the old soldier is a constitutional growler; *ergo,* the *California Knapsack* has *its* growl.

What's the use of our getting together here semi-occasionally, unless some good comes of all this preparation—this grouping of the thoughts and ideas that bother us during the year. What's the use of one writing and reading his paper here unless something results from it?

We'll listen to the emanations of our *Pope* on "Local Agents" to-day, and, at the risk of excommunication, whip the devil around the stump in some way so as to steal our neighbor's best agent to-morrow.

Chalmers will tell us what he thinks about the best way of a-*Dornin* our policies with proper forms; and then some smart Aleck will sneak in a permission in a policy covering a frame dwelling, so that a horse and cow may be kept in the basement.

Despite the advice given us by our Clark on "Losses and Adjustments," you're pretty apt to go right out and adjust your loss to suit yourself and apply the rule that works the best for you in the apportionment when it comes to contributing to paying under a non-concurrent policy, or dividing the expenses of a mutually contested case.

Mitchell tells us what articles should be considered *Staples* when it comes to "Legislation and Taxation"; and then somebody will advise trotting the "sack" up to Sacramento to stay the onslaught of Solons who know more about whiskey straight than valued policies; more about draw-poker than equitable taxation; of ward clubs than re-insurance; representatives who talk and vote, vote early and vote often, returning to their constituents with a calm complacency of a duty well performed, and brag of how they cinched the insurance companies.

Our chairman of the committee on fire department and water supply, he of the sepulchral name but genial features, who believes in live issues and not those requiring the attention of a *Sexton*, gives you new ideas of the subject, and how we bleed ourselves to pay for the services of a fire patrol that the dear public may reap an unrequited benefit; and at the next meeting of the Board the assessment comes in and is paid without a murmur.

We find it a *Cole* day for "Statistics" when he and Bailey get down to real warm work in the matter; and yet you go on writing up "Specials" and bob-tail ranges with a comfort only based in the big premiums they represent.

Our library evinces the *Spencer*ian system of getting volumes in great profusion without cost to the Association, which is heartily to be commended, but only results in our being possessed of a nice case of books, but seldom referred to, and is mainly advantageous in enabling us to say, "we have the finest insurance library on the Coast."

Grant, the President, has told you about "bringing good into the business," and gives all kinds of fatherly advice; and yet you'll pounce on a North British or German-American risk next week and laugh with glee as the genial George stands aghast at your effrontery.

We listen to good advice about excessive commissions ruining the business, and then some fair-faced philanthropist will issue a 10 per ct. city policy through a 20 per ct. Oakland agency, and beat the best of us.

We're jolly good friends, and the best of business enemies; there's many a way to skin a cat past finding out; and so the *Knapsack* concludes as it began,— *What's the use?*

EDITORIAL, 1884.　　C. MASON KINNE.

CIRCULAR.

EDITORIAL ROOMS, 422 CALIFORNIA STREET,
SAN FRANCISCO, January 18, 1884.

DEAR SIR—The *Knapsack* seems to have become a permanent institution and almost a matter of necessity. This result has been brought about by the valor displayed by those who have contributed to its contents—again proving the pen mightier than the sword. You are graciously permitted to know, however, that another engagement is impending, and the *Knapsack* expects every man to do his duty.

Some of you are like the old flint-lock musket; a good deal of promise, but plenty of flash-in-the-pan. We are using the needle gun now, breech-loader and central fire, and while no ammunition will be wasted, we can utilize an almost unlimited quantity. We want quick, sharp and decisive reports.

Very earnestly yours,
C. MASON KINNE, Editor.

EDITORIAL.

Our exordium for the first issue of Volume V is not to be long. We have simply to say that this number is worth reading, and that is enough. The time has gone by when the editor was worried about copy; he now only has to fret about whose effusions he shall consider the least available—all of which is just as it should be, as it is a feature of our broad-gauge organization, one which has representatives of all the varied species of the *genus* insurance. So, within the protecting flap of our *Knapsack*, we find articles of all kinds, useful and ornamental, some emanating from those who believe in that mainstay and bulwark of the profession, the Pacific Coast Board; some from representatives of the compact and energetic California Board; and others from those who belong to the free lances of the business, and float along on the troublous sea of insurance without any board at all. All have ideas and thoughts regarding matters of mutual interest, and what they cannot express in reports of committees and on the floor, find nooks in our commodious and weather-beaten *Knapsack*, where we file away anecdotes, suggestions, and such other supplies as seems proper.

The commanding officer who plans and manages the interminable battle of business and indemnity as a whole, can here meet his own and other field and line officers, and give his notions about how the fight may be bettered in some important detail. The officer of the day—the special—who unexpectedly visits the outposts in mountains and valleys, and gives the well known countersign "business" to those in charge of the picket line, comes home with a personal knapsack stored with information, and here gives to all such of his experiences as he thinks may bring some good into the business. The adjuster, who quietly conveys himself as a scout into the camp of the enemy, who may have been playing havoc with the supplies which have been figuring as assets, returns and reports to his chief, and can now give to us some episode or new idea from which all may gain a point.

The divisions of the great army, all fighting in the same cause, are commanded and officered by those between whom there is a natural and proper rivalry as to who shall win the brightest laurels, but who meet here and give each other good advice, strengthen their line of battle, and harmonize non-concurrent essentials.

Thus we gather them in, and the *Knapsack* fulfills its part in the good work. Here you have the emanations from our brothers, who don't give their names, and who sometimes hit a blow that hurts, but never below the belt. They help us to get our second wind, and sometimes talk so much like themselves that you can put your finger on the writer and make no mistake.

And now let me say that if any one feels aggrieved because his supply of ammunition was not thought to be of the right caliber by the officer in charge, let him report to us after the meeting, and holding ourselves entirely and solely responsible, will then give any and all satisfaction he may demand.   THE EDITOR.

GOOD ADVICE.

"Mr. B., I vould like to speak mit you brivately."

"All right, come into my back office."

"Mr. B., you know my store vas burned?"

"Yes; so I have been informed. What can I do for you?"

"Vell, I vant your adwise on diss point: Sol V. says I burned dat store, and Sam V. says he can brove it. Now, vat you dinks I had better do?"

"Well, if Sol asserts it and Sam proves it, you will be in a h—l of a fix."

"Vell, I dinks so, too. Dot is good adwise, and I acts on it."

THE COUNTRY AGENT'S LAMENT.

BY D. M. B.

'Twas a pleasant day in the month of June,
A beautiful, sunny afternoon,
When, as I had often done before,
I sat on the porch of my country store.
The farmers were all at work afield
Preparing to reap the summer's yield;
My family were all away
Out in the country to spend the day;
So, being alone, with nothing to do,
And no hope of trade for an hour or two,
I sat me down in the open air,
Lit my pipe and tipped back my chair,
The very picture of content,
And so a short half-hour I spent.
But a sudden pause came in my dream,
For a man drove up with a double team,
And, jumping out, he seized my hand,
Saying, "You're Mr. Jones, I understand;
And from what your neighbors say to me,
You're just the man I want to see.
I'm the special of the world-renowned
Owl Fire Insurance Co., known all round
As the strongest company, take it all in all,
That ever was formed on this earthly ball.
Now, I want you to take our agency,
For I know it must be satisfactory;
Fifteen per cent. commission we pay,
And I'll put up a sign this very day."
He didn't give me even time to think,
But rushed me in and took a drink;
Nailed up a sign, ere I could turn round,
Jumped into his wagon and was off with a bound.
Alas for me! 'twas an evil hour
When I put myself in that man's power;
For ever since then I've been overrun
With specials who did just as he had done.
They have covered with signs the front of my store;
I expect soon they'll nail them across the door.
There are American, English, German, and Greek,

Some whose names I can scarcely speak;
From the Cannibal Islands even are some,
  And I know not from where next they'll come.
Each one confidentially says to me
That my commission still more shall be;
What once was large, now seems too small,
And I think they may end by allowing me all.
One says, "We pay losses when the fire is done,"
Another, "We pay when it has just begun."
One will give credit for half the year,
Another says, "Pay when renewal is near."
At New Year comes a clock, a knife,
A "chromo," a breastpin for my wife.
I have scarcely room to eat or sleep,
For my rooms are covered six feet deep
With calendars, blotters, cards and blanks.
And letter paper to write my thanks;
One far-seeing company sent to me
Diaries for 1893.
I live in a state of constant fear
Lest some new Special may appear,
And I've made up my mind if a single one,
From any company under the sun,
E'er sets his foot in my store again,
I'll throw up the whole thing there and then;
I'll shovel the trash right out of the door,
And return to peace and content once more.

RUNNING A LOCAL BOARD IN MONTANA.

Smith, Brown & Co., bankers, represented the Grizzly Bear and the Unicorn insurance companies in a small Montana town, but the town not being rated, the general agents at Helena carried off all the good risks at lower rates than S. B. & Co. were allowed to write at. The special of the American Eagle, seeking food for the noble bird, called on the above firm, and found Smith, the local manager of the firm, grumbling because of losing his town business, and wanting to get out of a business that he could not be protected in, nor compete with others. Mr. Special suggested a local board and rating the town. Mr. Smith answered, "No other agent in town, and no one to make an agent of." Mr. Special suggested that Mr. Smith take the American Eagle, and

Smith, Brown & Co. having the Grizzly Bear and Unicorn, Smith, and Smith, Brown & Co. could form a board. This was agreed to, a board formed, the town rated and rates printed. Mr. Special put the rates on frames pretty well up, particularly on a nice risk in a log building, which was fixed at 7 per cent. This risk was written before the end of a year by Smith, Brown & Co. in the Grizzly Bear at 6 per cent. Mr. Secretary found by the special rating that it should be 7 per cent., and sent back orders to raise to 7 per cent. or cancel at once. Upon receipt of the order, Mr. Smith referred it to the special of the Unicorn, who happened along that day, who pronounced the rate 6 per cent. a good rate, and suggested that the *board* meet and reduce to 6 per cent. Acting on this hint, Smith immediately wrote to secretary "*that the board met and reduced the rate to 6 per cent.*"　　　　　　　　　　　　　　X.

THE FINE OULD UNDERWRITING BOARD.

I'll tell you a fine ould shtory, which I'll aither sing or spake,
Of a fine ould Underwriting Board which for all the Pacific Coast the
　　　insurance rates did make,
Except for some, like H. & M., who always thought they could afford a
　　　little less to take,
And who got lots of business by this same token, much to the dissatis-
　　　faction of others on the strate.
Yet this fine ould Underwriting Board was one of the rale ould shtock.

So the Phœnix bird that has its *Home* with Arthur E. Magill,
Rose from its ashes, crowed, cock-a-doodle-do, and said, I never will
See Oakland dwellings filling up some other rooster's crop
At 50c. when at 45 they'd add plazin' variety to me special hazard diet ;
　　　so from off this board I'll hop—
From this fine ould Underwriting Board—however ould its shtock.

Now, this kind of progress by the bird some thought a fou(w)l pro-
　　　ceedin'—
In fact, the flop gave such a shock, the board commenced a-teeterin'
Until it looked, indeed, as if its balance it would lose
And fall down and break into smithereens, and lave nothin' for a single
　　　chick of us to stand upon but mud wid the corn tramped down into
　　　it so dape we'd all be shtarvin' wid the blues—
Did this fine ould Underwriting Board, all of the good ould shtock.

This might have been our plight—to bad—had not a friend Teutonic,
With Easton and ten companies, jumped on just as the other hopped off
    from it,
And so helped Staples in the middle to keep his seat,
Thereby restorin' the equilibrium, and lavin' us happy as could be con-
    siderin' we see so many chicks gettin' fat below, and so much corn
    rollin' off the board that we don't have half enough to eat—
Off this good ould Underwriting Board, all of the good ould shtock.

So this fine ould Board is not broken up just yit in two,
But if 't had more on it, 'twouldn't be half so likely to warp up or to
    split, but be just as good as new,
And ye'd all get your corn nice and clane, and lots more of it too,
And not be fightin' and pullin' and turnin' a pacable poultry yard,
    figuratively spakin', into a roarin' cock-pit, if you
Would join this Underwriting Board, made of good ould shtock.

EDITORIAL, 1885.   C. MASON KINNE.

CIRCULAR.

EDITORIAL ROOMS, 422 CALIFORNIA STREET,
SAN FRANCISCO, January 30, 1885.

To the Officers and Members of the "1st California Underwriters"—

GENTLEMEN—Those of you that are not on the sick list, are expected to provide supplies for the *Knapsack* without delay. You know what is needed, and it would be useless to suggest to old campaigners like yourselves; but as the undersigned has to provide transportation, it is quietly hinted that we would like to know by the 10th prox. just about how much hard-tack we shall have to haul.

It will depend largely on yourselves as to how the provisions hold out when on the march; and we promise to properly care for all supplies sent us.

EDITORIAL.

At the time of the writing of this article, the turning up of the flap of our *Knapsack* reveals a yawning breadth and a cavernous depth of nothingness. But we have sent out our order for copy, and will say a few words and then lay them carefully away at the bottom of our commodious receptacle, as a nest-egg which shall soon be increased by the outpourings from many a fertile brain and facile pen.

We say this with a certain degree of confidence, as the *Knapsack* has become a feature, if not a power, in our Association. We have solid meats served up to us by the various committees at this our annual feast of reason, but the *Knapsack* furnishes the salad and the dessert that renders the regular courses more palatable, and now and then pops in with a flow of sparkling fluid that makes the still wines of useful and labored addresses all the more palatable. Add to this the aroma and bouquet of spicy anecdotes, and what more can be wished?

Of course, there may be a little of egotism in all this; but as the fledgling of six years ago has shed its pin-feathers and is now fully arrayed in all the panoply of adult plumage, and as we propose to turn over our sanctum, our quill, and all our right, title and interest in the plant and profits of the *Knapsack* at the close of this volume to some fresher and abler man, we may at least be permitted this little expiring cackle.

But really, we have done some good with this frayed, aged and well-creased receptacle. We have increased our capital—brains—by the emanations from others, and have gotten many good ideas evolved by those who never would have dared to start in on a regular essay over their real and true name. We have asked, " *What's the use?* " of doing certain things; and you have replied. We have admonished you, " *Don't forget!* " and some at least have borne in mind the good things suggested. We have given an opportunity for those not regularly appointed on committees to be heard from annually, and we think the result has been, that all along the line some good has been brought into the business.

A SLEEPY AFFAIR.

"The *Knapsack* without its K."
This is intended as a joke on the editor.

A STRONG ARGUMENT—A FACT.

A San Francisco general agency office having received word from one of its local agents at quite a distant point of the total loss of one of its risks, mailed the local a blank form of "Proof of Loss," and instructed him to adjust the matter. The form of the policy covered items as follows, viz.: $350 on frame building; $350 on stock of wines, liquors, and cigars, and $50 on barroom and household furniture.

When the proofs were received at the San Francisco office, it was shown that the loss under each of the items considerably exceeded the insurance on same. But the local explained he was able to make a salvage of $50, as he had found out that a week or so before the fire occurred, the assured had sold a bedstead and the bedding belonging thereto, for the sum of just fifty dollars; and even though the loss on barroom and household furniture amounted to $150, he thought the $50 the assured had received from the sale of his bed was as good as the company's $50, for which it insured his furniture. The assured had but lately received $50 for furniture. What difference did it make to him, whether he received it from one source or another? He had his money; what more did he want? The local so argued to himself; then to the assured, and what is more, *convinced him!*

THE STORY OF THE ENCHANTED LAKE.

AWAY up North, in the wilds of Washington Territory, where the people live and wax fat on the products of the skill and energy displayed by insurance companies in picking up premiums in other parts of the world to distribute among them; situated in a desert of alkali sand, where nothing animate is seen except occasionally a jackass rabbit or a cayuse pony, is located a dark and dismal looking lake. It is a little lake, but its depth is yet unfathomed. Dark volcanic rocks lie in wild confusion upon its precipitous banks, as though at some time giants had hurled them from some mountain height. It is remote from towns and little visited by whites. The Indians avoid it because an evil spirit dwells there. Space will not permit me to relate the terrible legend connected with this lake, but I know the legend is right in one respect—*the devil's in the lake.*

I was adjusting a loss in the little town of C———. The assured and myself could not agree. He wanted $1,100. I was willing to pay $100. He wanted it badly, and stuck out long and valiantly. I told him country life agreed with me, and I would stay a week or two with him. He was a nice man. He said he enjoyed my society, and would try and make it pleasant for me. He proposed going hunting. I borrowed a handsome shot-gun, and the next morning he hitched up his team and we started. Now, I was not a gun sharp. I had not hunted since I was a boy, and then only such game as old sledge, euchre and rounce, and I didn't expect to kill more than one or two ducks. We arrived at the hunting ground on the shore of this desolate lake—"The Devil's Lake." My friend had filled me full of stories about this lake: said that the water was enchanted, etc. But I didn't feel at all alarmed, for I thought it was a mighty poor adjuster that couldn't stave off any spirit that lived on water. I started up one side of the lake, my friend the other side. Ducks were abundant. I killed two the first shot—the first ducks I had ever killed. I was wild with excitement. I didn't wait to get them out of the water; thought I would wait until I came back. I continued to kill ducks and left them in the water.

After I had killed a thousand ducks, I became tired of the slaughter, and concluded to return and pick up my ducks on the way back, but being tired and thirsty, I took a drink of water from the lake, and as it was enchanted water, I thought I would let spirit fight spirit, and so diluted it with a little fine old whisky from my flask. Almost immediately after drinking, a delightful feeling of rest came over me, and I sat down to enjoy it; but suddenly I was alarmed by a most terrific vision. The clear sky became darkened. Long peals of thunder seemed to

shake the earth ; the vivid lightning rent the clouds into a thousand frag-
ments.   The quiet waters of the lake were lashed into a seething foam,
and from its surface arose the thousand ducks I had killed, and as they
arose they changed into demons, and, leading this wonderful throng was
a gigantic form whose hideousness no pen can describe. I will not
attempt to describe him, as you are all more or less familiar with him.
It was the devil. He approached me, and in tones that made every hair
on my head stand on end, said: "Why have you come here to disturb
my rest and kill my people? Who are you? Know you not the fate
which awaits the rash mortal who trespasses here? You will be dragged
into this lake and turned into a little devil!" "I beg your majesty's
pardon," I stammered, "I didn't know your highness was so near. I am
only a poor adjuster—" I did not get any further. His majesty's face
underwent a sudden change, and he looked quite an amiable fiend. "Why
didn't you say so before," he said; "I am always glad to meet one of
your profession. I respect ability, and you are the only fellow that can
stand off my best subjects on earth. I am sorry that I cannot ask you to
spend a few days with me in my country seat, but I hold this part of my
domain under a pretty good contract, and I fear that if one of your
adjusters get hold of it, you will find that I have violated some of the conditions, turn me out and run the business yourself. Don't be *too* hard on
my friends. Good-by," and he suddenly disappeared. The thunder and
lightning ceased, the darkness disappeared. All nature was again at
peace. I looked for my gun—it had disappeared. I walked back over
the road that I had come looking for my ducks. Not a duck, dead or
alive was to be seen. I finally found my friend waiting for me. He had
a wagon load of ducks. He laughed at my story, said that I had been
asleep, that I hadn't shot any ducks, that some tramp had stolen my gun.
When I got back to town, there was a great deal of "treating." I paid
for it. I paid the owner of the gun $45. As there was an adjuster's clause
in my friend's policy, he saw the joke when we settled. The owner of
the gun paid me the $45 back, said he had another one and didn't want to
be mean.

If any adjuster should have to travel in that part of the country, I
would advise him not to rely too much upon my experience, for they have
had so much experience up there of late that they are able to stand off
most any adjuster, and his majesty therefore might have lost his respect
for the profession. I don't imagine that any friend of mine will think
otherwise than I do. I don't think I was asleep. I know I killed 1,000
ducks. I don't think my friend stole my gun and ducks. I think that
lake is haunted. Up to that eventful day, I saw no reason to be glad that

I was an adjuster, but I am satisfied that if I had been anything else, there would have been, on that occasion, the very d—l to pay.

A "STAR COMBINATION" CONUNDRUM.

What prominent hotel risk would properly be "star rated," if the rules of the Pacific Board attached in New York? The Astor-risk.

A YOUNG ADJUSTER'S POINTS.

In one of those towns up yonder, which burn with such regularity that I always pack my grip-sack on the third Monday in June, I met a special who gave me more of joy than I had experienced in thirty-six months, for he said a new thing—a funny thing—and to this day he knows not that it is so, which is the best of all.

It was thuswise: For reasons of importance it was necessary to reduce the builder's estimate to the minimum. Hence each item was scanned, examined and talked about to that extent that the worthy contractor gave signs of rising irritation.

Window-glass was under discussion, when suddenly my special gave a start, his eyes bulged out, he gasped for breath, and in a tragic voice exclaimed:

"*Glazier's points? fifty cents?* FIFTY CENTS??? Why, my dear sir, any glazier would be perfectly willing to give you all the information you require for *nothing!*"

A SPECIMEN WITNESS IN AN ARSON CASE.

An adjuster holding an inquest on the stove-pipes, nails, door-locks and hinges, iron hooks, tin cans, and other fire-proof remains of a cowboy town in New Mexico during the lively times of 1882, learned that a valuable witness—a deputy sheriff, who knew all about the fire and the parties who started it, who was cow-ranching a few miles out—would be in town that evening, and as such a chance to get out of paying a loss was not to be missed, Mr. Adjuster laid for him, and a little after dusk found his man, who was fixed with a big pistol on each hip and a half bottle of whisky in his bosom, his appearance and gait leaving no doubt as to the disposition of the other half of the bottle of whisky.

An adjournment to the plaza, away from eavesdroppers, was necessary, and, after patiently listening to a little of everything except evidence in relation to the fire, and being a little nervous, Mr. Adjuster said:

"Mr. Sheriff, your testimony might be of some use before a vigilance committee, but would not do in court. You know enough of court proceedings to understand this." "Know enough of court proceedings," said the would-be witness; "I guess I do. I was tried for murder three times in this county."

Mr. Adjuster's heart came up in his throat, and inviting the witness to the nearest saloon to take a parting nip, quietly and gently let go of him, paid a total loss and retired in good order.

A MIGHTY NIMROD.

IT IS not often we get an opportunity to repay the pensive proprietor of the *Coast Review* for the many little attentions of a personal nature scattered like "chips" through the columns of his journal. It is with pleasure at the originality of the sensation, also with good natural liberality, that I give away the incident which comes at second hand, but is high.

Listen! In the season for rest and recreation he fled from business cares to the mountains. Loaded to the muzzle with traps, he went off— discharged himself so to speak—his aim, amusement, heaven save the mark!

In due course of time those of us who knew him least, were startled to hear of his deadly use of the rifle. We knew of his "*game*" hand, also his skillful use of the tomahawk, but were surprised to hear that each day he brought to the camp the body of a fine deer, each deer shot through the heart by a single ball. Old hunters sought him out. Lady campers from other springs came to gaze at him. Newspapers made mention of it. The members of his favorite club dined on venison sent with his compliments. In short, with modest pride he consented to be the hero of the hour. Here the story ends to make way for facts.

Last spring an overworked special was told by his doctor to "let up," or die. He preferred to die, but was persuaded to seek the balsam of the redwoods. Here he found a trout stream and an old woodsman. His winsome ways won that woodman's soul; one day in a burst of remorseful grief the woodsman confided to him his one great sin—which like the worm in the bud gnawed ever at his heart, and like a deep toned bell rang ever in his ear, de-ceit-de-ceit-de-ceit. This was the story: Once upon a time dazed by the sight of gold, his scruples overcome by the sweet voice of the tempter, in an evil hour, after vain spasms of resistance, he fell. Each day for five successive days at a secure hour he brought to the wily stranger the dead body of a deer, each deer shot through the heart, and for this act he received the gold which ever since had been to him a curse. Faintly breathing the great journalist's name, the woodsman fell into a deep swoon. Suffice it to say the special agent by the power vested him by his sacred calling, absolved the man and parting bade him go and sin no more. It is now brother Edwards' turn to "chip" or "pass the buck."

RABBIT-STEW—A LA FARNSWORTH.

'Twas way up in the mountains, and the sun was pouring down,
While tree and bush were quivering as the over-heated ground
Reflected back the fervency of Nature's strong caress,
And the youthful green of spring had assumed its summer dress;
When a group of sweltering specials came swinging down the road
Mid clouds of dust and rattling wheels. 'Twas an awful silent load;
Their gems of thought and jokes had risen with the sun,
Been offered to each other with an interspersing pun,
Till everybody tired of the almost ceaseless chatter,
And the wheels were left to roll with never-ending clatter.
Some miles were traversed thus, and we all were getting crusty,
The horses getting wearied, and everything quite dusty,
When a pair of cotton-tails came jumping from the brush,
And darted 'cross the road with kangaroo-like rush.
A shout from all in chorus was followed by request
That Ned should pull his shooter and prove to all the rest
That his early-morning boast of steadiness of aim,
Was not an emanation from his ever active brain.
The team was stopped instanter and out he quickly stepped,
While cotton-tail sat quiet as closer up Ned crept;
Then halted, raised his arm and accurate he drew
A bead on little rabbit. We all wanted rabbit-stew
To add to the lunch in waiting at the famous " Boston Ranch,"
So hardly dared to breathe, or any more than glance.
The silence grew intense, till the pistol loudly popped—
The rabbit gave a kick; his further ear he flopped;
But never moved his body from the bloodless scene of slaughter, (?)
While we fortified ourselves with another drink—of water.
We offered some to Ned, for mounting to his brow
We saw the deadly purpose—it's never or it's now;
But gracefully declining, he pointed Smith and Wesson

At foolish Mr. Rabbit, who should be taught the lesson
That only he who kicks and smartly runs away,
May ever live to kick upon some other day.
Again we held our breath; again did Snyder shout,
As the living target winked and simply turned about,
Till the cottony appendage which giveth it the name,
Gleamed in all its splendor, and like the glowing flame
Of deceptive *ignis fatuus*, led our marksman on once more,
To try another shot and drench the ground with gore.
Again the echoes sounded from the foothills lying shimmering;
Again the sun looked down; hot, and hotter glimmering;
Again the rabbit kicked; again did all look sad,
For cotton-tail had skipped.   The words Ned said were bad
As he reluctantly got in and we started on the team;
For we knew it all had happened; he thought it was a dream.

EDITORIAL 1886.   GEO. F. GRANT.

EDITORIAL.

IN presenting to you the contents of the *Knapsack* at this tenth annual meeting, I am depressed by the solemnity of the wit and humor therein contained, which is but partly relieved by the fun of the pathos interspersed through its pages. How true it is that experience alone can surely teach.

From a cheering notion that the position of editor on a paper like the *Knapsack* was one of pleasant relaxation and profitable enjoyment, I have learned to regard it as a trap for the unwary, where, having become entangled, one can make a free spectacle for the curious gaze, only "breaking out" by means of a cold perspiration, and thus by the sweat of his face earn his freedom.

What's in a name? A *Knapsack* by any other name would be as melancholy; yet have I thought the "Gripsack" a more appropriate title, for from such a traveled article have I taken these choice contributions during the last twelve months, and in every quarter of the Pacific Coast have I struggled with them, pounding them into shape for your delectation, disguising them with what ingenuity I could, that the Commission of Lunacy in its official capacity might pass the matter without finding a true bill. Whatever you may find of a painful nature, kindly consider it the work of the editor, but if by chance you meet a chestnut still in the burr, that, dear reader, is a "contribution."

When you stop to think, (provided you do not evolve ideas while in motion) this Pacific Coast presents a most alluring cover for an underwriter. Insurance is an out of door business, ours is an out of door climate. For seven and thirty years our Coast reputation has lived on air (barring mineral), within that time insurance people have waxed fat and lazy over easily acquired net surplus, also the result of wind. We are superior to our more Southern neighbors, who are popularly supposed to distort facts in the morning and lie in the shade of an afternoon, but all the same we are the most brotherly lot of antagonists extant.

It cannot be denied that the march of civilization, including the influx of insurance talent from the Atlantic, has disturbed our semi-tropical habits, although they have made it *warm enough* for us in all conscience, while as a direct result, low rates and increasing fires have rendered it red hot, with an ever rising thermometer; you will find this more elaborately stated in the annual statistical chart.

But in spite of all opposition, good nature and modesty will characterize insurance people on the Coast for some years. Our modesty is but half understood. It is this quality which prevents the solicitor from being a bore; it also impels the assured to yield lest he wound the sensitive nature of the broker. It is modesty which calls a halt to this editorial.

OH! FELLERS, OH! FELLERS, SOLDIERS! SOLDIERS!!

EDITOR *Knapsack*—I received your order for supplies, and I have tried to think what I could do or say that would result in filling an acceptable corner of your voluminous receptacle.

I have tried, *tried hard*, but it seems to be of no use. I have plenty of fixed ammunition, but I can't seem to make it fit your bore. My calibre is too small for the *Knapsack's* blunderbuss, and I don't want to have it scatter too much.

Again, too, the knapsack, properly speaking, is a useful receptacle for more things than are intended to comfort and make pleasant the life of a campaigner. But, are you, Mr. Editor, aware that it is one of the first things he throws aside when he is tired and worn, and every ounce weighs a pound. Yes, the knapsack, with all its odds and ends, its relics of early comforts and necessities of army life; its remembrances of home, its bible and pack of cards, its pins and pills, its threads and plasters, all have to go before the reliable *haversack* is thought too heavy. Yet, when on a long tramp, and rations are getting short—for you have eaten them— you look about for further useless encumbrances, then what goes? Why, *that* greasy old friend which smells of sow-belly and coffee, with its few crumbs of hard tack and grains of sugar, is quietly chucked into the nearest fence corner, and on you plod with blistered feet and ponderous musket, wishing that night or the enemy might cause the dusty ranks to halt.

But on you go, with bending back and sweating brow, and at every swing the cadence of your personal route-step is relieved by the rhythmical pressure of a faithful companion that is almost a caress in its clinging and lingering contact. It is your old canteen, that has been a solace and a joy forever; rusty, musty, battered and worn, it is faithful unto the last. The very name brings to mind thoughts of days gone by, and causes the pulse of old age to leap with the ardor of youth. Dull prose will not do, and in rhyme alone can the poetry of thought of those who have drank from the same canteen be adequately expressed. I am in no mood to offer excuses for what and how I shall write, but if any apology is necessary, then choose another name for your journal, or else expect the veteran of a quarter of a century ago to say something in the *Knapsack* about

THE OLD CANTEEN.

How dear to my heart are the scenes of the army,
  As fond recollection presents them to view.
The guard-house and sick-call; the cunning grey louses;
  Those dear little insects that each of us knew.
The sutler's old tent and his outrageous prices,
  The little brush house in the rear with its smell;
But dearer than these is the faithful old canteen,
      The battered old canteen we all loved so well.
      The rusty old canteen, the blanket-wrapped canteen,
      The battered old canteen we all loved so well.

That blanket-wrapped canteen was hailed as a treasure,
  For often at night when returned from a scout,
We found it a source of hilarious pleasure,
  As the apple-jack gurgled from its copious spout.
How ardent we seized it with hands that were grimy;
  How quickly the fluid into our open mouths fell
From the faithful old canteen that in fancy is by me,
      The battered old canteen we all loved so well.
      The apple-jack canteen; the musty old canteen,
      The battered old canteen we all loved so well.

Whether filled with pure water from the streams as we crossed them,
  Or conveying fresh milk from the cool spring-house floor;
We think of the thing as of friends when we've lost them,
  And burn with desire for its jingling once more.
So now, far removed from the battle field gory,
  The tear of regret will intrusively swell,
As fancy recalls the camp-fire and story,
      And sighs for the canteen we all loved so well.
      The rusty old canteen; the battered old canteen;
      The faithful old canteen we all loved so well.

But what has all this to do with insurance? Simply this. Draw a moral from "the old canteen." As specials, fill your *Knapsack* with the requisites of such soldiers in the field, so that you can produce lots of reliable capital and comforting assets from its bulky depths. Keep in your haversack the salt and sugar of your vocation; truthful records of premiums and losses to show that your brigade is active and aggressive; can win victories and suffer defeats, always ready for duty on the line of battle with a purpose to stay and fight it out if it takes all summer.

If Texas hurts, quit it. If Idaho frames foolish laws, jump the territory, but don't give up the ship, and remember always, that the oil of the machinery is in your hands, and like the *canteen* of yore, the special must learn how to use the can. An agent kicks; you are the one to pour oil on the troubled waters. Explain all about insurance to him. Rates, commissions, losses, hazards (moral, immoral and physical) and everything else must be squirted and poured out from your fertile cruse, and like the widow's of old, don't let it run dry.

The company is the knapsack, with its essentials to rely upon in case of a rainy day. The insuring public, the haversack which feeds us and provides the supplies for the hungry claimant. But the special and adjuster is the old canteen which moistens the parched tongue and dry lips of the faint-hearted agent or famishing sufferer. With kind words and just acts, he so lubricates the one and washes away the troubles of the other, that happiness reigns at home and abroad.

Keep yourselves filled with the pure waters of integrity, the milk of human kindness, and the stimulating apple-jack of devotion to the principles of your profession generally, and to your own company in particular. Then will the manager, the agent and the assured, each be glad to drink from your depths, imbibe solace from your every act, and all will say, long live   THE OLD CANTEEN.

SCARCELY an hour passes that the mind of man does not assert its superiority over mere conventional rules. Said my friend the broker to his client: "I cannot rebate by as much as a penny; I cannot divide commissions with you—it is against the rules—but, *my friend*, you shall take lunches at my expense for thirty days. Shall I write it up? Thank you."

EDITOR *Knapsack*—Mr. Willikin Sale lost his dwelling by fire. The claim was paid. Was this a sale to the insurance company? Answer: It was a sail, directly he raised the wind.

ASSOCIATE HINE of New York says: No you don't! That's just the sort of mendicant I am myself! I have had the *Monitor* scrap basket strapped to my back for seventeen years, and I am a habitual "picker up of unconsidered trifles," but they all go regularly and inevitably into the insatiate hopper of that bottomless pit!

I am everlastingly pouring in, like Mark Twain's bluejay into the hole in the roof of the deserted cabin, but I shall never get it full any more than did the bluejay aforesaid. I am sorry for you, but you can't get a single cent's worth of fun out of me, nor a reminiscence, nor nothing.

As you appear to be in the same condition as the boy who was digging for the woodchuck, I suppose I shall have to "come down"; but I think you may be perfectly certain of getting the flattest sort of provender from me, because whenever a man undertakes to be funny, or bright, or smart to order, he is pretty sure to serve his dish underdone or overdone, or hurt it in some way in the cooking. Nevertheless, I will in my great compassion remember you, and will endeavor to furnish something for your *Knapsack*, if nothing more than a soiled shirt or a rumpled collar.

Here it is:

A REASONABLE CLAIMANT!

The fire was a small matter. The stove-pipe had run through the ceiling many years, and the double thimble which surrounded it had somehow got crushed so that the heat had gradually charred the woodwork, and one cold day last month an extra boom in the old stove ignited the trap overhead and created a brief household panic. A few dippers of water put out the fire, but the whole Pacific Ocean could not quench the distress, mental and financial, which raged in the bosom of ye gentle claimant.

In due time the gentlemanly adjuster arrived on the scene, and the lady whose property had been the prey of the fire fiend, thus addressed him: "In the first place, I want money to pay those friends who helped me put out the fire, and then I want your company to take immediate steps to have a better arrangement of the pipes and the supply of water near my property if I am to continue to give you my business. And now in regard to repairs: all these rooms have got to be torn out and rebuilt; I am not going to have any smoked walls or blackened timbers about my house. You needn't try to get out of it," continued she, observing the deprecatory air and the argumentative attitude which the adjuster was assuming; and she went on with great volubility and eloquence to enumerate in detail the inevitable carpenterings, and paintings, and plasterings and paperings which would have to be done—and right away, too!

After much long suffering, the crushed adjuster got a chance to remark that it was a case of great importance and intricacy; that he hardly felt equal to its settlement unaided, and suggested an appraisement by competent disinterested parties. She might select some distinguished architect or builder, a friend of hers, who would see that her interests were duly protected, and he would select another competent and honest contractor or carpenter. She bit at the idea, and the wily villain got her signature to an appraisement paper on the spot! Appraisers were duly appointed, and the heartless wretches returned an award of fourteen dollars and twenty-seven cents. The sequel showed its inaccuracy, for the man who finally did the repairs made a clean profit of ten dollars out of the job. Herein do we see the soulless nature of bloated corporations!

TIFFANY'S Instruction Book contains this advice: "Agents should remember that the expense incident to telegraphing is a matter of no little importance, especially when a company is doing an extended agency business." The agent who sent the following telegram "collect," never had the advantage of Tiffany's acquaintance.

The dispatch reads: "Send me rate on wardrobe, scenery, organ, violin, wagon and jewelry of small traveling show, estimated value about one thousand dollars. Answer immediately."

My reply by letter said: "Rate one hundred and fifteen per cent., with ¾ limit and watchman clause in policy," but by the time the mail arrived the show was stranded in an adjoining town, and was subsequently sold at auction for $375!

AFTER four days' hard adjusting work at Red Bluff last summer, a small evening entertainment was tendered by the charming wife of a local agent. Seated on the veranda enjoying after-dinner cigars, the talk turned naturally to losses and adjustments.

Said the Colonel, "My work represents $42,000, and I have drawn checks in payment of that amount." This aroused a judge of local fame and noted peculiarities. "Forty-two thousand dollars!" said he; "why, I never saw any mention of it in the newspapers."

"Of course not," said the Colonel, indignantly, "you don't advertise the fact of doing a plain duty, do you? You don't put it in the paper when you pay your butcher bill, do you?" "No," said the judge, "I never did; but no doubt the butcher would—if I paid him."

A DEFINITION.

A SPECIAL agent in the field gets at the true inwardness of many a racy scheme. He unearths the plans of many a rival office to control agents and business. If he is wise he makes a mental note and files it away in the recesses of his mind for appropriate reference, good naturedly pursuing his journey.

If he is dyspeptic he exposes the sophistry, ridicules the sentimental slobber, unhinges the logic, and "cuts a watermelon." Generally gets himself disliked even where he is not feared, and in compact times drifts to the rear with the other tide wash.

These gentle words are called forth by the recollection of an incident in which some good fellows figured. One was a large-minded, well-to-do local agent, and like all locals with means, he controlled a big business. He was a prosperous, self-made man, and was sometimes requested to adjust losses, which he did with laborious earnestness.

At the time of my story, with an anxious eye and apologetic mein, he laid a gnawing trouble before one of the boys traveling his way. This boy was a genial, fun-loving special as ever scalped a scalper. After some time and a good deal of preliminary consultation, a letter from the office was produced. The letter was the main trouble. It seemed that at a recent adjustment where policies were not concurrent, one adjuster had settled up satisfactorily with a fifty per cent. payment, while the proofs of our friend showed a total loss on the same plant. He had given the manager all the facts of the case, but that fifty per cent. salvage for the other company was as gall and wormwood at headquarters. Hence the letter, which insinuated that since it didn't come naturally, it should have been forced. Hence the disturbed state of the honest local's mind.

"I don't mind their criticism so much," said he, "I done the best I knew how, fair and square, but what worries me is the doggone gibberish I don't understand. I can read American language, but this Dutch lingo gets me ; besides, it seems as if they were saying something mean about Arthur, the other adjuster, you know, and I won't have it. He acted white all the way through." A glance showed the objectionable feature of the letter to be as follows:

"As for Mr. Arthur, from a long and varied experience, our advice for your future guidance is that you take his *ipse dixit cum grano salis.*"

"Now," said he, "you have read the letter. What's it all about ; what does it mean?"

"Mean?" said his genial listener with a beaming smile and a reas-

suring tone; "it means that whatever you hear Arthur say, you bet your
life it's so."

"Right they are, by gosh," said the local.

HIS LAST TRIP.

66 I HAVE taken my last trip; I am going home," said he as the clock
struck the midnight hour. The nurse looked at the doctor with
a significant glance and whispered, "His mind wanders."

Presently he lifted his feverish head from the pillow.

"Any letters from the manager?" he inquired, "there ought to be
letters here."

Then he slept, and in his sleep he was a boy again, babbled of fish-
ing streams far up among the pines and cedars of the mountains, where
the trout played; of school days, and of those who had been his companions in the misty past, while the wild winds of an Arizona desert
rattled the windows of the little inn where he lay.

At one he suddenly awakened.

"All right!" he exclaimed in a strong voice, "I'm ready." He
thought the porter had called him for an early train. The doctor laid a
soothing hand upon his brow, and he slept. In his sleep he murmured:

"Business, my boy, we want business; what have you done? That's
a good risk, who took it? I must get business. I'm off, good-bye."

He dozed off, and the doctor counted his pulse; suddenly the sick
man started up.

"Give me a letter from home. Ellen always writes to me here. She
never disappointed me yet, and the children—they will forget me if my
trips are too long—only one more stop to make, and I will be home—
home—home for Christmas."

He slept again, and again wakened with a start.

"No word from the manager yet?"

He is going fast now; the doctor bent over him, and whispered in a
comforting voice the words of promise:

"In my Father's house are many mansions. If it were not so I would
have told you."

"Yes, yes," said the dying man faintly, "it was a clean loss, and
shall be paid promptly. Ah, a splendid company that—deals fair and
square with its customers and men."

The chill, cold morning dawned, the end was very near. The sick
man was approaching that undiscovered land where all losses are honest

and all claimants are fair; that mysterious land from whose bourne no traveler returns.

"I'm going off the road;" he murmured faintly, "the manager has sent for me. Write to Ellen and the children that I am coming—coming— her picture and address—in my breast pocket—call me for the first stage— it's my last trip, and I'll see Ellen and the children on Christmas.

They laid his head back on the pillow; he had finished his trip—he had gone home for Christmas.

He had been appointed but a short time, and his letters gave evidence of unusual zeal and intelligence. At last he sent in a daily report— an excellent risk. The next day came another—a duplicate of the first; and so day after day he poured in daily reports of the same risk, all in first-class order. In reply to a telegram, he said that the printed instructions on the blank read, "To be forwarded daily, application and survey must accompany each report." "Now," said he, "if I have not followed instructions, what have I done?"

Another good fellow, bent on following instructions, if it broke him all up, after receiving supplies transferred from a former agent, sent in his first account current promptly, embracing not only the premiums for the month, but a copy of all the business shown on his register, and this it seems was his idea of what was required for all future statements, a monthly recapitulation of all outstanding risks, and yet he proved to be an excellent solicitor.

Many of you will recognize a familiar note in the following bit of "human nature:"

"That durned speckled critter with a broken horn," said an exasperated farmer, "makes more trouble than all the cows I've got put together. I'd a gi'n her away if anybuddy'd had 'er, but they wouldn't. I'd a fattened her for beef, but 'twould cost more'n she's wuth."

That night the cow was killed by a railroad train, and the farmer, with tears in his eyes, told the railroad official who came to pay for her, that "if it had been one of his other cows he wouldn't care so much, but to lose that valuable animal, the only thoroughbred he ever had or expected to have, was a misfortune almost beyond money remuneration."

An active special, whose home is on the rail and homestead in "the City of Oaks," having had three days at home without hearing of a fire or a non-remitting agent, began to yearn for the gentle voice of the heathen Chinee as he sings, "Beefee takee, mutton clop, ham and eggee, tea or coffee," and for the dingy room, the cold, clammy sheets, and the delicate perfume of the bedbug poison. He found fault with the dog, kicked the cat, and was showing his nervousness generally, when he was gently chided by his better and more sensible half, thus:

"My dear, take your valise and walk around the block, and you will be in a better humor."

One of the few men outside of the profession whom I have heard speak in glowing terms of adjusters, is a resident of Yolo county, who once had an experience something like the following:

He was a claimant under a policy which covered on hay, grain, harness, and the barn containing the same, a separate amount on each. In making proofs he was free from nervousness and apprehension, answered all questions readily, and gave detailed items. Between the commencement and the signing of proofs of loss, he ordered two bottles of Extra Dry, and was about to insist on a third, when the adjuster claimed his attention by the simple statement that the proofs were a sulphurous lie from beginning to end. Continuing, he said: "You are certainly entitled to the prize for ingenious and lofty lying; your statements put Ananias to blush, while Sapphira trembles for her long-sustained reputation. Compared with you, Beelzebub is a modest exponent of truth! The hay you so carefully described existed only in your imagination, while the wheat is a fiction of the brain; the amount in bulk would fill the barn from foundation to the peak of the roof; as for the harness, there is not even a buckle to be panned out of the ruins; while the barn itself, from what I have been able to learn, was worth $438 at time of fire, instead of $1,200, as insured by the policy. I respect talent when I meet it, and your talent for falsifying is of the highest order. In return for your policy of $2,500, I will give you a check for $438, less my expenses."

During this statement of facts, the Yolo man was apparently an earnest and admiring listener.

"Can I cash your check right away?" he asked.

"Yes," was the reply.

"All right," said he; "hand it over. And now, gentlemen, suppose we have that bottle of arnica."

THE assured was an undertaker, the renewal was being pressed warmly by competing agents; finally, with a funereal twinkle in his left eye, he offered the risk to whoever would "take the premium in trade."

This same chap, complaining of a rival undertaker, accused him of cutting rates, so to speak, and influencing by unprofessional means the patronage of the town. "Why," said he, "the unrepentant disciple of Jimmy McGinn, in order to steal my trade, throws in three hand grenades with every coffin."

AT a recent loss, when the adjusters' clause was in, the assured seemed most anxious to secure the comfort of the boys. This was in the early stages of the proceedings. Before the week closed, however, he had become indifferent, I may say antagonistic. At the close he paid the adjusters' bill of expense, at the same time saying:

"I see you have forgotten nothing which you have used on this trip, including the cigars and wine which I presented to you, and which you have charged to me in your account."

Tableau!

A SAN FRANCISCO special, examining his risks in a Montana town, had a nice hotel to look through, and, as usual, was attacked by the landlord owner with a low rate (and, by the way, what a hotel keeper don't know about the hotel fire hazard and the exorbitant rates charged by insurance companies, is only equaled by what an insurance man don't know about hotel keeping). But this particular hotel man had purchased a first-class, red-painted fire extinguisher, generally considered by the insurance fraternity as more ornamental than useful, expressly to get a reduced rate.

Mr. Special talked the other side, and they parted with the understanding, on the part of the hotel man, that he would get a lower rate or not insure, and on the part of the special that if he got a lower rate it would be in some other company.

About three months later the hotel burned; fire started in the lamp-room under the stairway, and the adjuster found everything burned except the red extinguisher. An inquiry as to how it was saved developed the fact that the night clerk on duty that night was a new man, and when the fire started, seeing this "thing of beauty" behind the bar, took it across the street and put it in a fire-proof building.

Moral.—Fire extinguishing appliances are more useful as rate reducers than as fire extinguishers.

DIAMOND CUT DIAMOND.

"THIS is my story, sir; a trifle, indeed, I assure you. Much more perchance might be said, but I hold him of all men most lightly who swerves from the truth in his tale."

"Adjust loss J. L., on Canyon City Road, — miles from The Dalles— see Dallas agent," read a telegram which I received at Portland, Oregon, on the 3d day of January, 18—.

The prospect for a pleasant trip was anything but promising. The weather was unusually severe, and the route I would have to travel was through an almost uninhabited country. Consoling myself with the reflection that adjusters can't always have soft trips, I started for The Dalles.

Arriving there, I called on the agent of the company having the loss and obtained a copy of the policy and such information as he had in regard to the assured and his loss. The policy read as follows: "$5,000 on his stock and general merchandise, including jewelry, while contained, etc., situate — miles from Dalles, Oregon, two miles west of Canyon City Stage Road."

The information that I received from the agent was that J. L. had formerly been a jeweler in the town of X, Oregon, but had gone out of business some months prior to the fire, and purchased a stock of merchandise for trade in the mountains. Being well known as an industrious, temperate, honest, though eccentric man, the agent had not hesitated in giving him all the insurance he wanted. He presumed that the jewelry mentioned in the policy was a portion of the stock that he had retained from his jewelry stock when he sold out.

The morning was bitter cold when I started, but the sleighing was excellent, and, warmly wrapped in blankets and furs, I enjoyed the ride over the smoothly beaten road. Just before sunset the driver pulled up his team at the bottom of a deep canyon through which flowed a large creek, and remarked, "There comes your man."

Looking up the ravine, I saw a man rapidly approaching, and was soon introduced to Mr. L. He was a powerfully built German of about forty years of age, but notwithstanding his apparently vigorous frame, he had not the appearance of one who lived in the mountains, his face being almost lividly white, and his eyes had a glittering, uncertain, peculiar expression, suggestive of intense nervous excitement.

He greeted me pleasantly, and apologizing in good English for the necessity which would compel me to walk the remainder of the distance, about two miles, we started over a rough trail, deep in almost untrodden snow. He was a pleasant conversationalist, and though the road was heavy, I was surprised at the apparent shortness of the trip, when we arrived at his cabin.

It was a rude log affair, whose interior had, however, a cosy appearance, when, with lamp lighted and a generous fire blazing in the ample fire place, we sat down to a supper of venison steak and bacon. All of his papers were saved, having been kept in his cabin, which was situated on a creek about one hundred feet from the store building which was burned. On examining his books and papers, I ascertained that he had not sold a dollar's worth of goods, and that his entire purchases amounted to less than one thousand dollars. On questioning him, I found that he had sold no goods because he had only had the goods there a short time, and that a deep snow had fallen, cutting off communication with the world generally, and his expected customers in particular.

It had struck me when I first arrived that it was a queer place to start a store, for it was surrounded on all sides for many miles by a mountainous wilderness. Satisfying myself that he had produced all his bills of purchases, I remarked to him:

"You have lost only about $1,000. You never had more than $1,000 worth of goods in your store, and yet you have five thousand dollars insurance on your stock, which to say the least appears strange."

"You have forgotten the jewelry," he said, interrupting me, "the diamonds worth ten thousand dollars," he added.

There were four diamonds, uncut but mounted, he stated, but for a long time I was unable to get him to tell me where he obtained them; but finally, after placing me under the most solemn oath not to reveal his secret, he made a statement which, as nearly as I can remember, was as follows:

I was born in Amsterdam, and learned the trade of diamond cutter and setter. I read much about diamonds, and in a work I came across, found the information that in America were places where persons seeking might find diamond mines. I was ambitious to become rich, and for several years pinched and starved myself to save money to take me to America to prosecute a search for diamonds. I felt sure of finding them, and built many castles in the air, based on their discovery.

A relative opportunely dying, leaving me several thousand dollars, I started for America. Traveling and prospecting for several years, I gave up hope and settled down in the town of X in Oregon and opened a jewelry store. I did not entirely abandon my original idea of searching for diamonds, and spent a portion of each year in the mountains ostensibly prospecting for gold.

One, day, only a few weeks ago, I came to this place, and searching in the creek, to my great joy I found four diamonds. I made no further search, but immediately went home, sold my business, and purchased a stock of goods, principally provisions, telling the merchants I was going to the mountains to prospect for gold, and would take a stock of merchandise to sell to Indians to pay expenses.

Meeting an insurance agent, who had learned of my intention, he asked me to let him write a policy. I told him to give me a five thousand dollar policy on merchandise and jewelry. I had set the stones as rings, roughly, but sufficient as I thought to make them come under the head of "jewelry."

By the time my store building and cabin were completed, the snow had fallen heavily, and I had not searched further for diamonds, but was waiting patiently for a "Chinook" wind to come to clear the snow, so that I might work.

Before the completion of his story, he had become frightfully excited, and the terrible conviction forced itself upon me that I was dealing with a madman. It seemed as if my heart had ceased to beat, and I trembled violently in every fibre of my body. Alone with a madman, who at any time might become a maniac. No chance for help. The thought was appalling.

With a great effort I managed to regain partial composure, and racked my brain for some scheme to escape from him. I finally decided on my course. I conversed pleasantly with him, talked diamonds, talked partnership, to which he seemed favorably inclined, and after awhile he lost his excited manner, and was again the affable, agreeable host.

I told him just before retiring for the night that it was unusual to allow anything on such slender proofs, but that his reputation among the business men of The Dalles was so good that I would allow him a total loss, and make out the necessary papers in the morning.

The cabin had but one room, and the only sleeping accommodation was a rough bunk. My host told me that I could occupy this bed and he would sleep in his large easy chair. I went to bed, but not to sleep. I had made up my mind to escape as soon as he was asleep and take my chances of finding my way to some house before he could overtake me. I was unarmed, and I knew that he had a revolver.

I waited anxiously, counting the minutes, which seemed to my impatience, hours, before I dared make a move. He was apparently asleep, and after cautiously dressing, with shoes in my hand, I made my way stealthily towards the door. I was in the act of lifting the latch, when my ear, painfully acute to every sound, caught the sound of a movement behind me, and looking around, found my host wide awake, sitting in a lounging position with a cocked revolver pointed at me. "That is your little game," he remarked; "you thought to escape without paying me," he added.

He then told me it was useless for me to try to escape him, that he would kill me if I did, and then commanded me to make the necessary papers and draft for five thousand dollars. I was forced to do as he required, but signed the draft "A Boarder, adjuster." The driver had said when he introduced me, "A boarder for you, Mr. L," without mentioning my name, and he evidently thought that was my name, for he had addressed me as "Mr. Boarder" during the entire evening.

I told him he would have to get the endorsement of the draft by The Dalles agent before he could cash it. He had told me that he would go to The Dalles on the stage the next day, and would securely fasten me in the house until his return. On inquiring when he would return, he replied, "in about three days, if I don't forget it." I felt sure he would not return, and my only hope was that the signature to the draft and my non-appearance might result in inquiry.

After taking a receipt from him, I went to bed, but there was no sleep for me. I schemed and plotted until morning to devise some plan to outwit a crazy man.

After breakfast I asked him if I could try my luck in his mines. He consented, but told me that with snow and frozen ground to contend with, I would not be able to find anything. With pick and shovel I worked with all the strength and energy I possessed. He had described minutely the stones he had lost, and I had a desperate hope of cheating him with other similar ones. It was almost a hopeless task, but it was a question of life and death.

After several hours of incessant toil, I discovered four stones which I thought might answer my purpose. Just before noon, I returned to the cabin, and informed Mr. L., in answer to his inquiry, that my search for diamonds had been fruitless. I then asked him if he had searched the ruins for the diamonds, to which he replied that he had not. I then remarked, "if the diamonds are genuine, fire will not injure them, and we ought to be able to find them, and if we find them, he could not of course expect the company to pay for them." He assented to all this, and informed me that the diamonds had been put in a giant powder can, and were on a shelf in the northwest corner of the store.

I told him I would search while he was getting dinner. I found many cans, and selecting one which had been broken by a falling timber, placed the stones I had obtained in it, and then covered it with ashes. I went to the cabin and informed him that I had not found the can. After dinner I proposed that he should go with me and continue the search. He agreed to this, and showed me where the can was at the time of the fire. I had hit the place exactly, and after a pretended search of a few minutes, pulled the can from its concealment and handed it to him.

This was the trying moment, and I felt as if a terrible weight had been suddenly removed, when, taking out the stones, he exclaimed in an excited tone, "they are here—they are all right. It only required this test to prove that the stones are genuine, and I suppose you are convinced that they are real diamonds."

I was only too happy to be convinced, and to agree to pay for the gold in which they were set, which had undoubtedly melted and disappeared. He surrended the original papers I had made, and I made out new ones, with which he was perfectly satisfied. I was not, however, happy, until I was safely on the stage.

When I arrived at The Dalles, I placed him in charge of the sheriff and he is now in the asylum at Salem. When we searched him for the stones, they could not be found. If you doubt my story, go to the insane asylum at Salem and ask for Mr. L. He will tell you that an adjuster, to cheat him out of his insurance money and steal his diamonds, had him locked up in the asylum as a crazy man.

A SAMPLE JUDICIAL DECISION.

A farmer, from loss to be secured,
For many years his *dwelling* insured,
But at last one day when his luck had turned,
His house and all his buildings burned.
The adjuster no chance for salvage could find,
So he filled out his proofs to have them signed,
But the farmer read them and shook his head,
" You will pay for the house, I see," he said,
" But where in the world will I get any pay
For my barn and sheds, my tools and hay?"
The adjuster tried, but all in vain,
To make the matter very plain,
But it only seemed that the more he tried
The less was the farmer satisfied.
At last the farmer a lawyer employed,
Thus made it impossible suit to avoid.
So the case was tried and the judge's decision
Was given as follows with great precision:
" It really seems to this court very funny
That, having for years use of this man's money,

The company now to pay should refuse,
And this court such action will never excuse.
They say that the policy the barn did not mention,
But the plaintiff claims that it was his intention
To insure all he had, and it is very clear
That the word dwelling, as it is used here,
Every barn, every pigsty and shed does include.
This court at least will decide that it should.
This large British policy I hold in my hand
In *size* ought to cover any barn in the land.
It surely holds good in law all the world over,
A building of any kind its contents must cover,
So the court here decides that defendant must pay
For all that the plaintiff lost that day,
For all that he *meant* to insure, but forgot
To mention when he the policy got.
And I really think that the company ought
For even allowing this suit to be brought,
And this matter the mind of the court to trouble,
For contempt of court to be made to pay double.''

ONE OF MANY.

SEND a recollection of a trip. Distance lends enchantment. Time
has repaired the damage.

It was a call to a remote settlement to adjust a loss. First came an
ocean voyage. Then it was I won my sea-legs, for the sickness of the
time was such, I threw up all hope of seeing home again, folded my
wasted hands over my hollow chest, willing, even anxious, to join the
''great majority.'' I have never pretended to own a liver since.

Reaching port, my road lay through a forest of redwood—a ''short
cut'' of sixty miles, by saddle. Now, I am an admirer of horseback
riding—in others, and up to the time of which I speak, had gained some
knowledge of it by means of books and conversation. Sixty miles
seemed a big distance, but could anything be worse than that sea trip? I
tackled it, taking for guide and companion our local agent the faithful
Peter.

The scenery was magnificent, the air bracing. The Anna Maria river
danced and sparkled at our feet; I took notice of this early in the ride. I
was also conscious of sitting my steed remarkably well, contemplating

with much pleasure future exercise of the kind in the park and else-where.

Soon we came to a precipitous place, which Peter was pleased to call a "little sideling." Down we pitched, leading the animals. Remounting, I was pained to find the seat much harder than before. Still, as we picked our way through the woods, chatting gaily, the scent of balsam and the sight of moss and fern distracted attention for awhile. We lunched at a farmhouse, having made good progress. All that was amiable of my disposition, I left at that farmhouse. No freak of imagination, no charm of nature, could henceforth disguise from me how hurt and bruised that miserable saddle had rendered me. The horse became a stumbling, torturing brute. The Anna Maria river sprang up unbearably in all directions, having as many forks as one would need at an annual banquet.

Peter, too, was exasperating, he rode so fast and so uncomplainingly. Why! he would drop the reins and clap his hands to urge the speed, singing at the top of his voice, and in other diabolical ways show his enjoyment of the time. Eventually I learned to know the danger of the four sharp jolts when we came down to a walk, and the painful bumps when we start up. I avoid a trot, find a lope preferable, change position often, now leaning forward, now backward, now sideways, I cling to the horn of the saddle—there are pains where were never pains before; each leg seems to weigh a ton. I think of all the expletives which a varied experience has rendered familiar to my ear; I am saturated with mental profanity; I hate myself; I hate Peter; I hate the world; I am tortured and groan aloud, my sand has run out, I give up and cry for quarter; from that time we walk the horses.

The sun goes down, we move silently on, moonlight casts weird shadows, no sign of human habitation; up and up, down and down, we go; new sensations come, hunger, thirst and cold; we cannot see the trail; we are lost! It is nine o'clock; we reach a clear spot; water reflects the moonlight; it is the refreshing Anna Maria. I tumble to the ground; the faithful Peter builds a fire and mounts guard; I shiver myself to sleep and troubled dreams. At daylight we grope about to find an out-let. There within one hundred yards, with blue smoke curling from the chimney, stands a house, the house of a rancher, an old friend of Peter's. We share his breakfast, and meditate on the irony of fate.

By noon, still walking, we are at our journey's end. The details of the adjustment are conducted standing. My desk is a mantelpiece. When I am told my horse has the "pink-eye," I rejoice aloud; it is the hand of Providence. I take the long way back in a wagon; wagons are good enough for me to this day.

"A GOOD AGENT."

I HAVE been running a merchandise store in this country town for some years with success and comfort; have made a little money, and have an interest in a number of small ranches whose owners have been dealing with me. Not long since the special agent of your company came along and persuaded me, much against my will, to accept an agency of the company. I must say this view of the subject was an attractive one. I having a commission on the premiums, and nothing to do with the losses—that feature captured me. He said he would send a few blanks when he got back; but my God! I had no idea I would get such a consignment; blank applications, blank endorsements, blank monthly statements, blank expiration notices, and blank policies. I haven't tackled the job of filling any out *yet*.

I got a letter from you as general agent, confirming my appointment, and you express a desire to hear from me freely in case anything should come up in the course of the business to puzzle me. Now, the first thing that puzzles me is how to make a rate on the first application I got—the Eureka Hotel. That infernal little red book called the Rate Book, I thought the special had made quite clear, but now I don't believe he understands it himself—I don't. I never had much to do with mathematics except calculating interest, adding up an account and guessing at the weight of hogs. This little innocent book is worse than an algebra.

The first thing I tackled naturally was the rule for determining the rate of premium; my customer (do you call him a customer or a client?) was waiting while I read the rule before making out his bill. I had to tell him to come back in half an hour. Just as he got out the door I saw the *explanation* about star hazards and called him back, saying here was an explanation, and I would tell him in a minute; but when I read the explanation I told him to come back in two hours and a half; that "explanation" stumped me. The rule would be bad enough without all the stars and daggers, but they would puzzle anybody. I turned to "Hotel" on the list, and it there says, see Rules 6 and 18, also see Fresco work. What the devil fresco work has to do with a country hotel, I don't see—we are used to "fly fresco," but nothing else. I looked at Rule 6, which goes on about buildings occupied for a *common* purpose. The "Eureka" is a perfectly respectable house, so don't fit that rule—we've none of that kind of houses in our town anyhow. We go to the city for that kind of thing. Rule 18 fits the "Eureka," for transient guests come there, and there is a bar for regular visitors. A part of the "Eureka" is an old cloth-lined structure, and part is brick, frame and plaster; there is a grocery store at the corner room on the ground floor; that is in the frame part of the building and comes under Rule 7, about the compartments.

There is a wooden awning at this corner, a coal yard next door where there is a steam engine for chopping wood, and a livery stable next to that. When I came to figure upon the brick, iron, cloth-lined grocery with coal oil, awning, coal yard with steam engine, and consider all the daggers, stars, explanations, etc., I thought I would write to you, for I haven't cheek enough yet, being only in the insurance business a few days, to tell him how much he would have to pay; besides, that alphabetical table of hazards, and classification of buildings rather bothers me; when you find it is a "B" class, something in the rule puts it in "C" class, and when you fix it in that, then you find another rule that shoves it in "D" class. I haven't been able to keep it in one class long enough to fix the rate.

There is a woolen mill here, and I tackled the proprietor. His stock is mainly cloth and blankets, but I find a blanket policy is prohibited, so I couldn't do anything with him. How about that? he said he had no trouble before, and I said it was probably due to the compact, and he thought the compact was a fraud. Is it?

I can't get that "exposure" business through my wool. Most of our buildings are on the main street, and the outbuildings are on a corresponding row on the rear of the lot. Do these outbuildings constitute an exposure? They all have separate entrances on the ground floor. I always come back to that explanation pasted between pages 4 and 5. Does not the man who drew that up also draw a big salary? I'd like to fix the basis rate with the stars and daggers to the man who got up that red book. I had no idea insurance business required so much figuring. I thought all we had to do was to accept the premium and dispute the losses, which is easy enough.

Now, if you can give me any lucid explanation of how to definitely figure a rate on a building without 47 exceptions and provisos, I will stick to the agency.

FARNFIELD'S SONG.

Be-hold the pop-u-lar un-der-wri-ter,
   A per-son-age of mar-tial rank and title,
A dig-ni-fied and po-tent ad-jus-ter,
   Whose func-tions are par-tic-u-lar-ly vi-tal.
     'Tis Charlie Kinne—Charlie Kinne;
     To insurance halls we welcome him.

He has strug-gled with non-con-cur-ren-cy,
   And for his rule has fought with might and main ;
Suc-cess now crowns his id-io-syn-cra-sy ;
   We ne'er shall hear of non-con-cur-ren-cy again.
      'Tis Charlie Kinne, etc.

So hail our pop-u-lar sol-dier chair-man,
   He's a man in the pro-fes-sion stands very high ;
Twelve months he's pre-si-ded o'er us no-bly,
   But this night he's del-e-ga-ted to die.
      'Tis Charlie Kinne, etc.

EDITORIAL, 1887.   GEO. F. GRANT.

GENTLEMEN of the Association, and friends of Underwriting, I greet you.

In the budget called the *Knapsack*, for 1887, we find all of the pathetic, humorous, corrective and personal, which active minds have been willing to contribute during hours stolen from business. I use this phrase as a figure of speech.

Stealing is a serious matter; it not only involves a perpetual endeavor to conceal the act, but it lays upon the conscience in unexpected and inconvenient times and places. Why should one steal that which is his own?—a species of kleptomania which shifts an article from one pocket to another, the pocket being on the person of the thief.

The hours of business cannot be stolen. There is a popular impression to the contrary, but it is incorrect. An aimless, heedless clock-watcher can "soldier" through days of time in an office. A no-account special can read novels in a shady corner of a summer hotel. An adjuster can demonstrate the accuracy of calculation on a billiard-cloth. This is not theft—it is fraud. If you think by the rules of *Knapsack* philosophy I have demonstrated these acts to be theft, I will, in accordance with *Knapsack* ethics, yield the point for the sake of harmony.

An earnest, interested worker will put in all his working hours for the benefit of the office for which he toils. If he is not a strong, independent, tactful person, he is out of place with insurance. Being a fit person, he should be encouraged to imbue his work with his individuality. This individuality is strengthened and improved by writing *Knapsack* articles. See?

When I say this business of ours is carried on at too high a pressure, I speak a truth well known to all of you. From a business conducted in such a way that an applicant submitted himself and his risk to close scrutiny at the office during office hours, we have reached a point where solicitors in every grade of station and education, or the lack of both, pursue all classes of people for all classes of risks by day and night.

Your company and mine were the last to wheel into line and follow sorrowfully at the tail of the procession; but we have been poked at and prodded into until at last we have determined to lead the stampede; the whole mental effort of our wonderful and incomprehensible being is strained in an endeavor to "get there." It matters not how long or how short a time this is to continue. It is all wrong.

As I look upon the faces of this calm and dignified body of men before me, I wonder why our business should not be one of elegant deliberation. The feverish day of stock gambling has gone by, we have no Wall street clamor in our midst; we are removed from the world's strife just as far as the western boundary of a continent will permit. We take no note of the orb of day except to watch his lazy decline into old ocean as he winks good night after a long day's methodical work; our climate is one of open doors and windows, our breezes fan odors of palm and spices across sleepy plains, yet here we plunge and rear and kick ourselves into a state of delirium in the vain hope of outdoing our neighbor, in the vain hope of attaining the unattainable.

Underwriters of the Pacific, the *Knapsack* says to you take more time, relax, give up stimulants, drop brain and nerve food, let gentle exercise and moderate action govern mind and body, that we may turn into legitimate channels the business of fire insurance. Then will you have time to prepare your brainy articles for this annual intellectual feast, without fear of the accusation of having stolen it from your business? "May the Lord love you and not call for you too soon."

It is matter for comment that so many of our Pacific Coast insurance people have been fighting soldiers. To one who never faced fire, to whom war is a page of history, the offering of life for a principle seems little short of martyrdom. It is heroism of the loftiest type.

When I see these veteran underwriters marching to the tune of old-time battle songs, or strewing with sweet spring blossoms the graves of fallen comrades, I feel that our business is honored by them, that such material is in accord with our best endeavors to strengthen and purify the profession of ligitimate underwriting.

I thought of this while in Seattle at the time of the labor riot. That same courage which prompted the clerk in 1861, impelled the citizen in 1886, to take up arms to defend the peace of his home and fireside; among them my old friend and former local agent. True, he had never faced fire on the gory field of battle, but he had smelled powder at a target shoot. One cold and stormy night he patrolled a beat laid out for him. At midnight he saluted the officer in charge of munitions and requested a few rounds of cartridges, on the plea of possible failure to kill his man at the first fire.

"More ammunition!" said the officer; "why, you have forty rounds on your person this minute in that box."

"Great Cæsar! are those cartridges? I thought it was my lunch," and the courage which prompted him to face death oozed away at the thought of hunger.

A CHARACTER.

PERHAPS there is nothing more distasteful to a boy or young man than a person who is known as a "character." In the days when the influence of home, the study room, the play ground and the chapel is on the growing youth, such people as have peculiarities, strong-minded notions, or eccentric fads, are regarded with disfavor bordering on hatred.

In after life, with broadened business experience, that experience which seems to teach that the truthful lie, the honest steal, and that virtue has no reward whatever of a tangible nature, men regard the cranks of other men with amusement, not to say interest, and often study them for literary use, as lay figures in novels and magazine sketches.

In my friend Overton is a deep vein of fantastic sobriety; I have taken no end of comfort in watching his intelligent inconsistencies. It was he who studied the effect of various kinds of medicine on himself, and because he was feeling unnaturally disturbed from his last allopathic venture, tried something else homeopathically to set him right.

He was a special agent, and one day came to the committee room with a box of pills which he had found in a drawer of his bureau; no one knew what kind of pill, so he proposed as there was just enough of them to go around, we all take one and watch the effect. He was eating lemons by the dozen just then, but he stopped and tried *eau sucre* on reading the benefits of the drink in a French paper. One day he splashed a suspicion of ammonia in his eye, and went about telling how slowly but surely it was destroying his sight; he negotiated for a dog to lead him by a string when darkness set in.

When the history of the Garden of Eden was under discussion, it was he who said, "show me a sworn statement from the snake and I will adjust the case."

In appearance he was not unlike a clergyman, and in the rapid one-day stands, a special agent makes in towns, secured much business for his company and retained the good will of every one who met him once, for like dead sea fruit, the second taste was away off. He bought a scalper's ticket and paid his fare over again with bland politeness to the conductor who said, "your a h—l of a cattle drover."

Once I met him at a famous hot spring resort; he was really feeling seedy and worn out. The other boys—there were four of us in all, advised him to lay off a week and take a course of baths under the direction of the resident physician. He consented. We went to the office where a printed notice gave terms for bathers, fifty cents in advance per bath; no discount.

He objected, "Suppose I don't like it; suppose I only take half a bath, my money is gone." The clerk put the other view, "Suppose you die in the bath, we haven't got anything." "Oh, Lord! do they die often?" he asked.

He objected to the custom of depositing valuables at the office, but did so finally, preferring to be robbed by the boss rather than in the dressing room.

We took him to the "tepidarium," clothed in a turban and a waist-band, not unlike a Patagonian warrior in appearance, provided the Patagonian had not eaten missionaries for some months; in fact a skele-tonized Patagonian. Here he buttonholed the attendant (that is, if it is proper to say you can buttonhole a person dressed like Adam before the fall).

"Look here! you are the man in charge here. You have been here a long time, may be for years; well, you look like an intelligent man, a very intelligent man; I will venture to say you know as much about the effect of these baths as any doctor; of course you do, in fact more than the doctor, for you haven't got any fool reputation to sustain and no fees to charge; that's it, fees; bleed you to death these doctors, I know them. You just prescribe for me and I'll make it all right. You see at a glance what's the matter with me; liver all gone, nerves used up, no appetite, no strength, see? Now what kind of a bath ought I to take first? Mean to try everyone of them before I get through, but the main thing is to start right, see?"

The attendant saw the solemn winks at the eyes of the party, and dropped to the level of the situation; he prescribed hot air first. He told Overton to step into a dark box of a closet where the thermometer marked 180 degrees, and wait there till he called him. There was a place to sit dimly outlined and no handle to the door. When Overton stepped in, the attendant laid his hand against the door and closed it; Overton had not been in three seconds before he called out:

"Hi! hello! I want to say something! Say! hello! hi there, say! there's something wrong here. Say! open the door! let me out! Help! murder! I can't stand it! Oh, for the Lord's sake open the door!"

Suddenly he jumped against it and sprawled at the feet of his friends, who were convulsed with laughter. After one glance around he grinned and said, "I thought the darned old door was locked." Upon his form hung beads of perspiration and a deep blush of pink marked the brief period of rest he had taken inside.

"Mister," said he to the attendant, "feel of the muscles of my arm, if they are done, I'm cooked all through."

A SHINGLE mill was recently destroyed by fire near Detroit, and the night-watchman was burned to a crisp. The dangers that beset a night-watchman when on duty are not properly recognized by a giddy and heedless world.

"WELL," said he, as he placed one foot carefully on the other, both being raised to a convenient elevation, "an honest man has always been my admiration and delight. You know most of my life has been passed here on the Coast. I have been engaged in various kinds of insurance, but fire insurance is my first love, although adjusting is more my natural forte.

"I am a born adjuster, although I am willing to admit the study of law has made me more proficient than I otherwise would have been. I have seen many queer characters, some of them honest—but not many. I do love an honest man! I had a case once where a claimant was so honest he quite won my heart, and I have entertained a warm friendship for him ever since.

"You know I am a positive man, a very positive man; there are few men more positive. This has made enemies for me, particularly in adjustments. People treat me with indifference at times principally from professional jealously. Being a lawyer, I have that much advantage, which seems to cause a petty feeling in the breasts of my rivals. But this claimant I speak of was a rare one. He had a fire, and claimed loss on some goods left by customers for repair, on the ground that he was responsible, and would have to make the loss good. It was a small affair, and I compromised the case. Well, sir, some time after that, in fact, after I had retired from the fire insurance business—for you will remember, my company withdrew from the Coast and reinsured—some time after that this man came in, and said he: 'I have settled with all my customers, and I find I have $30 over; here it is; I wish to return it to you.' I was so taken back you could have knocked me down with a feather. What did I do? Why, took it, of course. Well, yes; I kept it—you see, the company had retired from the Coast. He was the most honest man I ever met; and in these days an honest man is a novelty—you hear me?"

THE UNDERWRITER OF THE FUTURE.

"SUFFICIENT unto the day is the evil thereof," says the philosopher. "Act well your little part; there all the honor lies," sings the poet. At times a strange desire to pierce the veil of the future comes to me. I would look beyond the working plans of to-day and know something of the possibilities at least of underwriting. Keeping up with the procession, as it is called, seems to be best accomplished by adopting every loose, tenantless vagary of every theorist, no matter how illogical. At the annual meeting of all associations the goal seems to be personal aggrandizement. The papers produced are for the most part a vehicle used to create or sustain a reputation; the writer arrays his facts and figures in a manner calculated to call attention not to the wants or needed reforms in the business, but to himself. Theories are thrown out as carelessly as pitching broadcast a handful of beans, with no more interest in the root they take. He who writes in favor of a scheme to-day may oppose it to-morrow, and receive applause for each effort.

When I apply to my nearest friends for an opinion on the future of our business, they good-naturedly laugh me out of countenance. Those who are recognized as our great minds receive my question with a cold stare and intimate that *now* is the very fruit time and harvest of insurance progress, while others who are working on new and apparently reckless lines are quite happy in the advantage gained, and "think" less seldom than when they were not in the lead.

Compared with the safe rules governing life insurance fire insurance is floundering in a sea of doubt. The cheerful and well fed air with which our leading managers guide their companies to disaster through paths of unquestioned ruin is perplexing. Fortunately the Pacific Coast is still too far from the American center to be entirely stripped bare of its adequate rates, its protecting safeguards. The march of time is doing us a mischief all the same; with it comes changed opinions. Some of our best field men are adopting plans of action which would have been odious in their own eyes a few years back and, worst of all, these plans are not boldly proclaimed as of old, but are know only by the fruit they bear.

Is not reputation dear now as then, or is ours in truth a business to demoralize, to harden the finer sensibilities and make dull the moral perception? In other words, is now the future of ten years ago, and, if so, is it all correct? If agreed, let us say "check," and pass on to the next item.

Thoughts like these have made me somewhat persistent in my endeavor to gain information, so that I am in a manner avoided by my former associates. This disturbs me. One night after dinner I sat thinking of it when a card was handed in, followed by the person whose name it bore.

"Pardon the apparent intrusion," said he; "my excuse shall be a slight service which it is in my power to render you. If you really wish to know something of the underwriter of the future, I can show him without inconvenience to yourself, nor will it take up much of your time. There is but one condition, simply that you will abandon yourself to the thought that a century has passed away since you last took an active part in fire insurance matters."

I assented, and we passed out into the night. To my surprise I experienced no new sensation. The streets were familiar and we paused at the building where my own office is located. Here a determined looking but silent man in uniform kept guard.

"Conduct this person to the center," said my companion. I followed along the familiar hall, saw him open my own office door, heard myself announced and stepped into what at first seemed a spacious auditorium, but which by degrees I observed to be an office of about sixteen feet square, partitioned off with huge plates of glass from other rooms or offices, so that on the right and left in front of the room in which I stood could be plainly seen all objects and tenants of other rooms or compartments on the same floor.

There was not time to fully realize this peculiar and unusual arrangement before I was greeted by the only occupant of the "center," as it was called. In saying the only occupant, I do not take into account a silent man in uniform, for I soon learned to know that such people were stationed everywhere about the place like articles of indispensable furniture. The voice which greeted me was low and sweet, so gentle and winning indeed that I immediately contrasted it with the rude, not to say surly salutations of my own time.

"May I ask whom I have the honor of addressing?" said I. This seemed a trifle absurd, considering the formality of my introduction.

"It is with pleasure," said he, "also with pride that I announce myself Lieutenant Director of the Center of the Pacific Coast Department." (Here he mentioned the name of my own company.)

While he was speaking I notice the peculiarity of his dress, which at first I mistook for a bathing suit. It was of dark silk, knitted, fitting the form closely—a costume, it was explained, in vogue for the use of bank officials, county officers and those in positions of trust or who handled the funds of others. There were no pockets in the clothes. It was a most becoming dress, and my entertainer seem so much at ease that I am sure if he had worn the clumsy apparel of my own time it would have made him appear a guy.

"I knew of your coming," said he "from the general director, he who visited your home and invited you here. The general director is the only one of us who goes outside the building, you know; the rest of us take our meals, our exercise and our sleep inside. We often have a hop on the roof when a few ladies are included, but while we are em-ployed by the company we do not talk to strange men. These silent things in uniforms are called 'Pinkertons.' They are to us such informa-tion as the calendar used to be to insurance offices—albeit they are fewer and less expensive."

"Is that because their days are numbered?" I asked. He only frowned, and continued:

"I am allowed to talk to such people as are introduced by the general director; but I take little pleasure in such talks, since my conver-sational limit is cut out for me in advance, as this Pinkerton in the corner well knows. To really enjoy a conversation, one must be at liberty to tell secrets, lie about his friends, and abuse the other company, as you are no doubt aware."

"We are all employed here for a term of seven years. During that time we surrender ourselves to the company by contract, after which we can re-enlist or be pensioned off, each according to his length of servi-tude." "Much more just than working all your vigorous life for a com-pany, and then be turned out in the streets in old age to make room for a better because a younger man," I could not help saying.

"Yes, no doubt," replied the lieutenant; "still it cannot be denied that the strain on one in my position leaves him little to hope for mentally when his seven years are up. I have five years more to serve, and I feel the strain already. I commenced as a boy under Class I, in this very office, and worked my way around the house to the center."

At this moment our attention was attracted by two dark shadows which fell upon the white top of the table before which the lieutenant sat.

"Two risks being taken," he explained, "if you look into the right hand apartment you will see two people making application. That object into which they are talking is a "voice wave." It catches and records the words, also reproduces them in print, making five impressions. These are held as evidence. This voice wave can be made to repeat aloud the words spoken into it, and is conclusive in a court of law. Of course a man may say he didn't know what he was talking about; lawyers and judges know only too well what a valid excuse that is.

"The shadows on my desk are from the 'reflex' hanging yonder on the farther partition. This same machine also gathers light. Thus as daylight fades away the office is kept at an even state of luminosity. We take every risk that is offered. Nothing is excluded. The rates are found in the directory of rates, such as that hanging beside the Pinkerton yonder. A directory is issued annually, the old one being legal until the new is distributed. The time has gone by for any one to say he knows the correct rate for any particular hazard from experience, or time tables, or classification. That instrument which looks like a piano, situated in the next case on the right, is the most accurate rate maker yet found. You throw in all the statistics and strike the corresponding chords and keys, and you have a rate which is positively correct. We use it in cases where the directory fails to contain a hazard. This one is called a petty organ. The grand organ at Chicago now makes rates for the whole world. You knew that Chicago was the greatest city in America, didn't you?" he asked. I blushingly said I had heard Chicago people say so.

"This system is the outgrowth of the compact series. The grand organ is a more endurable machine than the compact manager."

In the compartment directly in front of us, which was larger than any other, were twelve or fourteen men who seemed to be constantly engaged in receiving and transmitting messages through machines which spoke the words and recorded them in print at the same time. Everything that went on was audible in the "center," but so soft and musical in tone as not to interrupt or interfere with conversation.

"There are no female clerks, you see," said my host. "Women are now engaged as sea captains, railroad conductors, and in such like business. That is the finance department," he continued. "We are receiving advices from our investments all day long. All of our premium receipts are invested in lottery coupons."

At this I started.

"Ah, I see," he said, "you are not informed. Well, to commence: The National Lottery at Washington is drawn every ten days and is the largest investment, conducted by the President and Cabinet officers. This puts capital and labor on the same plane. Then there are State lotteries, county lotteries and town lotteries, all conducted by laws enacted in the Senate and House of Representatives. The prizes are drawn promptly every thirty days. Perhaps you now see why clerks are not allowed to leave the building for seven years. Companies put no more faith in their employes than they did in your time."

I sighed.

"Ah, well," he said, "honesty is the best policy. It is a long way better than an insurance policy."

"We have had a good year," he continued. "Our premium receipts for San Francisco alone are two million dollars in round numbers, our losses a million and a half, and our coupons realized four millions. This is unusual. Last year we were not so fortunate; our out-go was 209 per cent."

"Millions!" I cried. "Premium receipts of millions! How can it be done!"

"Ah, yes, I forgot," he said, "You do not know. There are but fourteen insurance companies now doing business in the United States; the others went to the wall under the old hazardous system. That is why we have no solicitors or brokers. The assured comes to the office and records his voice and receives in return a printed evidence. His insurance is in force until ordered cancelled, and is paid for by the week in advance."

"And the loss claims?" I gasped.

"Oh, yes, about the claims. Well, each claim goes into court and is examined by a jury, or, in case of appeal, by the judge of a higher court. The office deals only with finances. See?"

"Yes," I admitted, uneasily; "I think I do, but I don't quite understand. Have you no adjusters?"

"Adjusters!" he said scornfully. "No; I thank fortune we have no such butchers in these days. I have read of them in books, and I am vexed whenever I think of their abominable practices. Such of them as were half-way honest were wholly incompetent, and such as were competent played the mischief with the companies' money and reputation. No, we have no adjusters. When a claim is presented it comes at first hand through the lawyer of the assured in the manner of a suit for the full amount of policy. We pay the amount into court at once and await the process of law."

"Dear me," I said, "I don't grasp this point."

"Don't mention it," he replied, encouragingly; "I am not surprised. How should you?"

Just then we became aware of what seemed to be a faint round of applause, and upon looking into the left-hand compartment saw a number of elderly men with happy, smiling faces, listening to an address or lecture.

"These," said the lieutenant, "are retired officers, who have served their term of seven years in the chair I now occupy. One of them has been a general director; all are known as extraordinary men. I will not conceal from you (lowering his voice) that in my opinion some of them are crazy on the subject of insurance—but for that matter men have been so in our business, time out of mind. These gentlemen are living on a pension at the expense of the company. Most of them are allowed to come and go at will, always of course, attended by a Pinkerton, so that they may not disclose the inner workings of the coupon investments," this in reply to an inquiring glance.

"These men," said my informer, with as much of enthusiasm as he had yet allowed himself to show, "are engaged in the inductive principle of evolution; the goal of yesterday is the starting point of to-day. They have outlived such questions as local agents, fire department and water supply, tariff rates, legislation and taxation, forms of policies, etc., etc. Saw-tooth diagrams and cube illustrations belong to the far distant past; the common mechanic who dealt with such material is dead and gone to his account years and years ago ; sweet oblivion prevents such from knowing how futile and childish their efforts have been. The paper of to-day, which caused the applause you heard, is on 'the survival of the ligitimate,' and is an able argument in favor of issuing no evidence of insurance other than a loss receipt !"

"But," I said, "This is gambling, this is putting the money of the people on the hazard of a die; millions lost last year, millions won this year—no stability, no guarantee of indemnity. Why, sir, the whole system, inductive or no inductive, was born in the brain of a madman and means everlasting ruin."

"Sir," replied he, severely, "do not forget that you are a privileged guest. You lose sight of the fact that these stern rules of ligitimate business emanate from brains of extraordinary men, bent on making money."

"As if," I cried, "as if history were not made up of the bad actions of extraordinary men, as if all the most noted destroyers and deceivers of our species, all the founders of arbitrary governments and false religions, had not been extraordinary men, as if nine-tenths of the calamities which have befallen the human race had any other origin than the union of high intelligence with low desire."

"One moment, sir," said he, "is not that a quotation?"

"Yes, sir," I replied, "it is from Macauley's Essay on Francis Bacon."

"I thought so. I regret to inform you that your visit is at an end.

One of the cardinal principles of the office is opposition to quotation. We are original in our methods, whatever else we may be."

"Sir," I replied with some warmth, "there is little in what you have said to me that has not been taken from the mouths of others. Remember that those who live in glass houses—"

"Stop!" he fairly howled, "don't do that, don't finish that sentence. That is the worst crime you can commit in this office. Pinkerton!"

I felt that I was disgraced. I saw the uniformed dummy advancing upon me when a voice fell upon my ear, saying:

"Well, dear, if you are ready we will go."

It was the voice of my wife. I had seen the underwriter of the future in as much time as it takes a woman to put on "her things" and make ready for the theatre.

I RAN into a story which caused a merry laugh. Ever on the alert for something to please the readers of the *Knapsack*, I dressed this story up in a painfully alluring manner, and at a distance from home tried the effect of it on a solemn companion. He said he saw it in print in the *Monitor* before the war, or before the Chicago fire, or before some other remote event. It matters little when he saw it; the wretched fact remains that Brother Hine had printed it.

If there is anything touching upon the subject of the heavens above, the earth beneath, or the waters under the earth, which the *Monitor* has not published, aye and "originally" published. I should very much like to know it.

It is particularly painful to always hear that senseless remark, "I told you so." I wish the editor of the *Monitor* would take a vacation; go off and catch cold and be laid up with something painless but confining, while things were going on that others could see and hear and print which would be news to him.

In regard to this story of which I speak, he not only had it in print, but he put in all the fine lines of the picture, had names and dates and locations, described the kind of chromo, gave the company away, broke up the business—in fact forestalled me in every particular. It seems only fair to give a faint outline of the story, for we were not all born a hundred years ago, and it is time the tale was sent the rounds once more. Here it is:

Once on a time a local agent was appointed by letter. At the remote distance where he lived such small matters as bonds or instructions were not thought of; an exceedingly liberal outfit of supplies reached him, and here the business of that agency rested for some weeks, when one day a letter was received, saying : "Insurance business is dead in this place : but I have sold the picture cards you sent at $2 apiece. Inclosed please find remittance less my commission. I don't know if I charged enough ; I can sell a few more at the same price. Please be more particular in your instructions to agents.

THE LOCAL AGENT.

THE local agent is generally supposed to be a man—that is, most of them wear men's clothes, but I have seen lady local agents.

Lady agents do first rate until they get married, then they don't care for anything, such as business.

Local agents have strong convictions. Some of them have a strong conviction that they can't get a risk—and they never try. Others have a conviction that they know more about it than the man at the office, and you can't knock it out of them until you pay twenty per cent.; that seems to be an argument they can't get around. Anybody is willing to follow twenty per cent. instructions.

I know a local agent who made more than the company. He loaned the company money at twelve per cent. per annum, and bought a lot of their stock at ten cents on the dollar. Then he got himself elected president, and pretty soon he pulled the company out, paid his money back to himself, sold his stock for $1.35, and returned to his local agency. After that the company busted. I don't see how he did it.

Local agents are like cats. You stroke them the right way, and they will stay quiet and be sociable, but if you rub the fur against the grain they show claws and howl, and get mad enough to bite the buttons off your clothes.

It's funny how some local agents manage. I know one who fussed around and got a fine office, and the companies paid the rent and helped furnish it, and painted big expensive signs all over the widows, and all such things, and there was a modest little man next door, who never got an extra for anything, and his commission even was never raised although he lived in an excepted city, and he worked right along and sent in ten times as many premiums as the first man, and one day, when he called attention to the difference, his insurance office people told him to mind his own business. "There want any kick coming to him," and talk like that. The harder you work and the more you do, and the better you do it, the less thanks you get. It is just like the woman who poisoned her husband.   No sooner had the jury perjured themselves, than she received thirteen offers of marriage, one of them from a clergyman.

Sometimes I think a good square man has no business with insurance—but that is when I am bilious. Half the agents I meet seem to think the business is a grand swindle. They act as if they were not getting their share of the loot, and if you don't give more they will squeal and give the whole snap away, as the slangy people say. The other half work on the principle that it is the only ligitimate calling in the world, and they abuse the people who don't insure with them, and give them short answers, and take their money as if they were doing them a favor; and when a man has a loss they want the Grand Jury to indite him right away, and start stories about how mysterious the fire is, and tell the adjuster not to pay a cent, and so forth and so forth. Then, in a month or two, they write to the office and ask how you can expect a man to get any business if the company don't pay its losses. I sometimes get real cross with local agents; the only consolation I have is the thought that there are exceptions to the general run of them.

I used to be a local agent myself, and I know how it is. I never had any trouble, because I worked for a home company, and the board of directors could make it all right; but I paid a loss in full once before I adjusted it, because I thought the other locals were getting away with me. I never was an adjuster, anyhow; and I think by the time the man's papers were finally made out, the company people thought they would have saved money if they had sent a regular adjuster. If I had to be a plumber or a local agent, I would be a local agent. The season is longer.

At Alturas last summer bed and board were matters of importance. Beds were secured with difficulty at one end of town, while board of the most primitive service scarcely filled the bill at the other end of town. In the middle was a waste of blackened ruins where the business houses had been. Every one was good natured over the discomfort, and many a cheerful conversation lengenthened out over the simple fare at dinner. Judge White and family, burned out of house and home, shared the " second table " with the adjusters, and his sweet little four year old daughter listened sedately to the oft-discussed points of insurance. One day as we met on the bridge the little one eyed me a moment, then raised her face and said, " Pa, is that the man who set the town on fire?" Quickly he answered, " No, my pet, that is the man who sets the claimant on fire, and he burns him up, too."

CALENDARS.

THE Fireman's Fund sent in what I assume to be a calendar. It is a beautiful picture representing a chaste young thing, dressed in her best clothes, leaning out of a two-story window, and on the chest of a young insurance solicitor. He is imprinting with great accuracy of aim a cold salute upon the point of her chin. He poises himself airily with the slight assistance of one foot upon a rope ladder. He appears to be taking a risk. I commend this new manner of soliciting to the young of our profession.

Of all the calendars received at this office that one which bears the figures of three beautiful girls on its face made the greatest sensation. Fair and elegant types of womanhood were they, gazing into the future with an inquiring eye. But what words are these I see printed directly under their feet?—" Old and tried." Let us hope it is intended in some way to refer to the business of the office.

The German-American sends in a picture of a mother and two infant children gazing steadfastly through an open window in quite a different direction from the general conflagration in full burn across the street. The mother is carefully dressed ; the children in night clothing. A clock on the wall plainly indicates the time to be 5 o'clock. As it is dark out of doors, it is presumably winter. Query, is the heat from the fire sufficient to warm the children, or if this is a tropical scene, as the growing plants at the open window indicate, in what part of the country is it dark at 5 A. M. or P. M.?

Calendars are no good, anyway ; their use as advertisers has gone. I am pleased to think " their days are numbered." I recall one issued by a prominent home company, which, aside from the lurid pigments of its composition, was off color otherwise. It represented an attractive figure clad in an elaborate morning gown presiding over a table containing two bottles of fiz and a hot lunch. In her hand was an invitation to stand in and share the refreshments. The President of the company, a courtly gentleman of the old school, was, in the language of the street Arab, " too fly," hence the whole edition was suppressed.

A " FIRE insurance " and a " hail insurance " man met on a train and compared notes on business. Fire man said business is bad—too many fires, too many losses—and observed that the big hail storms lately must have caused heavy losses under hail policies. Hail man said, no—no losses—had hail storms and *assured* had losses, but the hail policies provide that during a storm or at night time all crops insured thereunder must be taken in and put under cover, and a neglect to do this voided the policy.

MORE CORRESPONDENCE.

YOU may remember me as the individual whose letter on the rate book was handed you by the general agent, and which you paid me the compliment of printing. I can't say that I fully understand that book yet, but I find that I'm not so much worse off than others, after all. Since then I've taken more interest in insurance matters, and have read all I could see on the subject in the papers. I notice that the newspapers seem to know more about insurance than the insurance men themselves, though that seems strange. But what a bad time we've had of late. So many big fires have occurred, and we're having a session of the Legislature to add to the disasters. And now another insurance paper is to be started. When will the luck change?

Speaking of books and papers and legislatures, I find I am not alone in my ignorance of what is in books or ought to be in them. Even Webster's big, unabridged dictionary has no such word as "cinch " in it. Now, we all know what that is, but Webster never belonged to the legislature, I guess, and never was an insurance company, so he didn't put the word in his book. If he had ever lived in California he would have done so. Some of his other definitions are bad also. For instance, he defines Cluniac as one of the reformed Order of Benedictine monks, so called from Cluny in France. Now, Clunie is not in France, more's the pity; he's very much here, and I'm afraid has come to stay. Cluniacension is defined as relating to the reformed discipline prescribed to certain monks. That's not at all the definition our legislative committee would give. The proper " ascension " in that direction would be too high for definition if they had their way. Besides, the reformed discipline prescribed is better adapted to ecclesiastical history than to the present commercial age. It is curious, though, now I think of it, though I couldn't find " cinch " in Webster that I find " clunch " just above cluniac, in the same column, and clunch means to bend the hand or fist. I don't suppose there's any connection, but it's odd.

I hear from the insurance men that the insurance men got away with the Legislature, but I see by the newspapers that the Legislature got away with the insurance men. It usually does, in one way or another— generally in one way. The papers say that one Senator was down on the insurance delegation because they rode up from the depot in hacks, gave lunches, wore kid gloves, canes, clean shirts and plug hats, and drank wine at dinner.　He said he couldn't afford to do this, especially drink wine at dinner.　How dreadful!　Probably he will after adjournment.

I am told that one man—a veteran lob-legislative committee man—was complacently congratulating himself on how he had outwitted the chairman in that investigation before the committee, and while he was doing it another man feelingly confessed that he had been sat on hard when trying to suggest an answer for the first man to one of the questions, and he wanted to know why the first man didn't answer right up sharp when the chairman asked a few pertinent, or rather impertinent, questions about the compact.　Why did he draw neighborhood improvements or other things on the dusty table with his finger and speak so slowly while the chairman was asking the conundrums.　He wanted to speak correctly and conscientiously, he said.　The second man thought it was a bad time and place to wait for a conscience to stretch, and that any insurance man of experience ought to have it well stretched anyhow, so as to be equal to the occasion any time.　He, of course, speaks from experience.

The President of this Association, in his address last year, put in big type his opinion that "agitation is the only means of reform."　That sounds like Dennis Kearney or Coroner O'Donnell, but if it is true, then the insurance companies will presently be reformed, for there seems to be "agitation" enough among them just now.

The President also says that "insurance is the most trustful of any class of business."　Stockholders put up coin and trust directors, directors trust officers, officers trust department managers, managers trust specials (they can't help it, by the way), specials trust agents, agents trust the assured."　That last is the only bad thing about the whole trust business, but this mutual trust talked about is not on faith alone. If we all trusted each other in this golden age manner there wouldn't be any necessity of any compact.　You notice your President didn't say the "companies trust each other."　He knew too much.　I might put the case somewhat like your president did.

Fires make business, business makes agents, agents make specials, specials make managers, managers make companies, companies make cut rates and cut rates make compacts.　Then, compacts stir up public, public stirs up Clunies, Clunies stir up legislatures, legislatures stir us all up.　It isn't, by the way, the fires alone that make all the bad burns in the business.

There is a tendency, I see, to make us all honest by law.　If they applied this principle to all classes of business, this would be all right.

We're no worse than others. Why scarcely a paper is read before this society that does not have something to say about the necessity of our being honest and upright. Perhaps it is on the principle that the " lady doth protest too much " that they don't believe in us. Even your President last year gave us a nut of thought in the expression, " Honesty is the best policy," but he failed to say what company it was in, and until we know that we can't be sure.

MR. JOHN SCOTT WILSON'S SPEECH.

Mr. President :—

THE occasion we celebrate to-night is one filled with special and peculiar interest. It is that we may, with song and story, make a circuit of the festive board, and fill up the chasms of life with mirth and laughter. To feel that buoyancy of spirit which drowns all care and draws each into closer relationship with his brother; for our lives to receive fresh impulse from the hopes which brighten and the friendships which are here formed. Hither we have come to tell the old stories, to sing the old songs, to renew the old traditions, and to add another bright page to the pleasures of the past. How peculiar, then, the delight, how generous the interest enkindled within us as we gather this evening, many hearts beating with one purpose and uplifted in one devotion. No fabled dragon in terrible aspect, as in the elder time, watches at the gates of this garden of Hesperides, lest the foot of the profane should desecrate its fragrant walks, or his presumptuous hand dare pluck the ripening fruit. A mightier than Hercules—the spirit of genial fellowship—has slain the dragon, and thrown open the portals of its sacred recesses; and now the barbarian, as well as the Greek, may enter and eat of those fruits at will. All are welcome, for we meet to the feast of youth, of friendship and of fraternity.

Man is, in the nature of things, a social being; he loves to frequent the society and enjoy the affections of those who are like himself, therefore we can wonder at the entire neglect of the finer feelings of our nature, the social for instance, which mark the character of multitudes of the *genus homo*, in this, our day. Deeply engrossed by their strife after the pelf and lucre of Mammon, they serve him, therefore, with such perfect, such unmingled devotion, that no time is left nor opportunity given for converse with each other, otherwise than in the crowded mart of commerce, the shop and the stall.

From early dawn until the very going down of the sun, and even into the still hours of the night, every thought, word and deed is devoted to the worship of that demigod who rewards his votaries with great stores of gold, and at the same time with bitterness and ashes. Even their sleep is troubled; their dreams are not of the bright realms of sylph and fairy, but of those dark and gloomy caves in the bowels of the earth where hideous and gigantic genii sleeplessly watch over the ingot and the jewel—the heaped-up treasure of their sordid master.

Upon the brows of such sits wrinkled care, while in their hearts is sharp anxiety, brooding over the unattained object of their fierce desire. Their converse is but of cent per cent. of "profit and loss," and of loaded argosies. They tremble from very fear as they hear the fierce winter's wind howling around their homes, and when they meet each other "on change," scarcely have the usual salutations of the day curtly passed between them, ere their troubled thoughts find utterance in solemn talk upon the dreadful storm of yesternight, and their own rich ventures and those of their fellows, for friends they have none, though they may name them such. There is no time to enjoy nature's beauties; no leisure hours to spend with those grand old masters of English literature; none for social duties; no time to pray.

> "How quickly nature falls into revolt
> When gold becomes her object."

Beecher in his "Life Thoughts" says: "Many men are mere warehouses full of merchandise—the head—the heart—are stuffed with goods. * * * There are apartments in their souls which were once tenanted by taste and love, by joy and worship, but they are all deserted now, and their rooms are filled with earthly and material things." But who is this Diety—Mammon, that man so worships? Indeed its power is great; it transforms the beggar into the aristocrat, clothes the bandit with respect, makes the outlaw a citizen, and bequeaths to him the name of Christian. It is a justifier of wrongs and a repulsion to truth, an idol whose worship is almost universal, the possession of which is sought with the utmost zeal to the exclusion of pursuits more worthy. Fame and wealth are indeed great rewards, but they should not be the entire aim and end of man.

Alas! they oftimes come too late. Fame when the laurel wreath crowns a head white with the snow of age; wealth, when disease prevents the gratification of even innocent desires; happiness, when death is at the threshold, when riches are the only fruits of fifty years of toil and labor to the exclusion of higher and happier ends. If you succeed your reward is

> " Praise—when the ear has grown too dull to hear,
> Gold—when the senses it should please are dead;
> Wreaths—when the hair they cover has grown gray,
> Fame—when the heart it should have thrilled is numb.
> And close behind comes death, and ere we know
> That even these unavailing gifts are ours,
> He sends us stripped and naked to the grave."

Forbid that it should be said that there are no brilliant exceptions—those who say to their worldly affairs "thus far and no farther," who cultivate the finer feelings or their nature and glean from the rich fields of literature precious products, and are guided by the light of moral principle; who see in each rounded pebble, little leaf and tiny blade of grass, as well as in the jutting rocks, the majestic tree and meadows carpeted with verdure, the hiding place of God's power. For what were our feelings of consociality so liberally bestowed upon us by the wise author of our existence, if not as pure sources of enjoyment, if not to adorn and beautify life.

Oh! ye who waste the best and brightest hours of that life in carking cares and material pursuits, little know ye how you lose and throw away that time which might be made so fruitful of the truest and most exalted happiness. Eager for gain, looking forward to a period which never comes, ever anticipating and never realizing, before you are aware the evil days come when you have no pleasure in them. First—Go with me to the house of a friend who can sympathize with my taste and feelings. Second—Go with me into your library where are enshrined the souls of the living dead, and let us commune with them for a moment. There you have Milton to sing to you of paradise; Shakespeare to open to you the worlds of imagination and the workings of the human heart; Franklin to enrich you with his practical wisdom, and Bacon to teach you his deductive philosophy. There you meet the gentle loving Spencer, characterized by Hallam, as "the delight of every accomplished gentleman, the model of every poet, the solace of every scholar."

There you meet in true friendship, poet, historian and novelist. How could you better pass your time? You pick up the poets' pages and there you find brilliancy of fancy to captivate, creations of genius to surprise, tenderness of conception to raise us above every day life, all embodied in beautiful and harmonious language. His is the master mind that sweeps among the trembling chords of our hidden and mysterious nature, and wakes the dim melodies we dream we have heard before the present, in some other world—that shadowy memory of some more beautiful existence, which dwells in every soul.

Then you commune with men like Dickens and Thackeray, men full of human love and hope and charity, whose works and lives are but one long poem, wherein all may hope for comfort and sympathy. Here is an honest, and therefore beautiful sentiment towards mankind, in its highest and lowest grades, a broad, universal and catholic faith, that includes in its creed the love of all, even the saddest and most degraded of our human kind. Theirs are the works which bear the stamp of heaven on the broad page, whereon they trace hopeful words to their fallen and deserted brother.

The field of literature is a province wherein have labored the greatest and best of earth's gifted ones; wherein have toiled philosophers and poets; men of science and earnest inquiry; men whose midnight visions have been lit with a strange and mystic light; men whose great and superior intellects have, Columbus like, explored untraversed seas of thought, and brought back wonderful treasures from lands else unknown.

Yet our bond is not that of scholarship or literature. If we still love literature, if we still cherish the sweet sympathy of scholarship, it is that their true purpose may be fulfilled, that like squires and henchmen they may burnish the armor as bright as gold, and tip the spear with diamond lustre, for which we are to do our part in the great good fight for human welfare; they are the means to ends. Ours is an age that demands songs for the army of pilgrims to the arts, the sciences, the mechanical—songs of labor, of sympathy, of hope; songs that hearing, the mighty heart of the great working nations may gather fresh strength and vigor for their daily and weary way onward; songs that shall nerve the sinking heart and give broken gleams of eternal summer. We should, therefore, cultivate literature and a love for books. It gives to us the precious thoughts of our own generation, and the brilliant minds that have gone before us. It enlarges the intellect, improves the understanding, allays and soothes the passions, but above all these it emplants in the heart of man the true principle of universal brotherhood. Where else, save in the rare communion of friends, are hours so short and moments so swift? Where else, save in their tried friendship, do we awake from pleasure into surprise that whole hours are gone which we thought had just begun; blossomed and dropped which we thought had just budded?

As each succeeding year is added to the calendar of the past, let it ever be our pleasure to meet together and keep this feast of genial fellowship, not forgetting that

> "Great souls by instinct to each other turn,
> Demand alliance, and in friendship burn."

WE CALL the head of our office the "old man." He is not so very old, but he is absent-minded to a degree; not so bad as the person who put his umbrella carefully in bed and stood himself behind the door all night, but absent-minded enough to make the boys grind their teeth when he forgets points they carefully tell to him. Now and then we have some fun out of it, as this incident will show. Christmas fell due on Saturday, perhaps you will remember. On Thursday evening the old man beamed all around with his top coat buttoned and umbrella in hand, which he waived airily so as to include the whole force, and with a voice modulated by a recollection of Scrogg and Marley, said, "Young gentlemen, I bid you good evening. It is perhaps needless for me to remark that I do not expect to see you at the office to-morrow." Then he went away to find that to-morrow was not Christmas. He had the office all to himself on Friday.

EDITORIAL, 1888.   E. W. CARPENTER.

CIRCULAR.

Editorial Front Window, 410 California Street,
San Francisco, Jan. 25, 1888.

Dear Sir—presuming that the work pertaining to the preparation of annual statements is over, hoping that the figures thereof were full of satisfaction to all concerned, and that I may now find you in just that good-natured mood which may incline you to devote a little time to the filling of the *Knapsack*, I say, " Send along the copy."

Write it up before the close of the month. Write it with pen or pencil, on brown paper or white paper, or unused agency—bond blanks— *but get it in.*

Every one to whom this circular is sent can remember some humorous incident, or some quaint conceit, or some sage suggestion that may have achieved existence during the year just closed. Put it down and send it in ! *Do not wait,* thinking you will make it the subject of a " labored effort " at a later date, for the *Knapsack* does not aspire to being considered the acme of literary perfection or the condensation of universal knowledge.

While my able predecessors have filled considerable portions of the *Knapsack* with the choice products of their own brains, I feel that neither time nor talent will permit me to follow the precedent thus established, and I shall, therefore, content myself with loosening the buckles on the 20th day of February and spreading out before the expectant eyes of your comrades a repast which shall be generous or meagre, in proportion as you do or do not respond liberally to the foregoing appeal.

EDITORIAL.

A *KNAPSACK* editorial has great advantage over those usually published, from the fact that it does not suffer the common fate of its fellows and remain unread. The editor reads it himself, and pours it into the ear of his patron, as the waiter did the soup into the ear-horn of the deaf person, whether he wants it or not.

The temptation to write an editorial under such circumstances is exceptionally great, and so you must sit and take it. It will, at all events, teach you a practical lesson in resignation, and that is what we all need in our business.

If the "other fellow" alienates the affections of a pet broker, and secures a choice line of business, we all know how we feel inside, and how we make a bee-line for the P. I. U. office to see what can be done about it, and how all our threats of resignation from the Union result in resignation at last.

If a customer is taken away from us by an agent who explains to him that he can never recover anything under the printed conditions of the policy, or that we have failed to insert the electric light permit, or to provide that goods in show windows are covered, we interview the person who has been so "shamefully deceived," and who is "so sorry" that he did not understand the true situation before, but who has accepted the other policy, and it is "too late to change," and then comes resignation again.

If a claimant wants payment for loss on property that we never insured, we say, "Go to glory, if you're headed that way;" but he goes to a lawyer, or possibly two; he talks to his friends and the newspaper men; he writes to his leading San Francisco creditor; we say we won't pay, but we do—and here's resignation again.

If our companies want facts, year by year, more and more, showing all sorts of things about towns on this shore, we kick (in our minds) and mentally roar, then bury them up in statistics galore—just here resignation comes in.

If the compact makes rulings unjust to ourselves, and puts all *our* pleadings upon the high shelves, we wish the Union was "busted"— gone, we'll say, to the elves; yet we swallow the doses, though our stomach rebels—and here's where lots of resignation comes in.

If a man who is buried in business so deep that he has hardly time for his meals or for sleep, runs the *Knapsack* one trip, he's likely to leap right out of the straps, and out of them keep—so here's where *my* resignation comes in.

THAT the frailties of humanity are not singular to the insurance business is below illustrated. At a time when all the railroads were in the pool, I had occasion to borrow an electrotype at one of their offices. Accosting a clerk I said: "The manager yesterday agreed to let me have a 'cut.' Can I get it to-day?" Sweeping the restricted horizon of his office with a cautious eye he eagerly asked, "Where to?"

SMALL CAUSE OF A SMALL FIRE, AND A HEAVY LOSS AND HEAVY ADJUSTMENT.

EARLY last spring a wealthy retired New York merchant, with his family, moved into a handsome dwelling, which had been thrown in with some climate he had purchased, in a fashionable suburb of Los Angeles.

Shortly after the family had become settled they gave a dinner to some friends. During the night, or rather the early morning after the dinner party, the family were awakened by a loud crash, which had evidently occurred on the first floor of the house. The various members opened their bedroom doors in much alarm, but gaining confidence by numbers, and each one assuring the other that they were not " frightened a bit," the head of the family, with one of the older members, mustered up courage to descend the stairs to investigate.

When they opened the door into the dining-room they found considerable smoke in the room, and although no flames, they saw many places on the table cloth, carpet and heavy portieres that were smouldering and smoking. They lit the gas and smothered and stamped out all that was burning. The room looked as if a whirlwind had struck it, and on the dining-table the wreck was complete.

After the table had been cleared a heavily embroidered tablecloth had been spread, and in the middle had been placed the epergne which had graced the table during the dinner. Among all the handsome furnishings of this luxurious home there was no article of which the owner was so proud as this epergne—heavy with solid silver and much cut-glass of the clearest crystal, it was indeed a marvel of the artizan's cunning, and as a work of art its value was not to be estimated at the mere sum of $1,200, which represented its original cost.

This beautiful ornament was shattered. Portions of its clear facets were seen sparkling in the gas light all over the room, on the floor and on the furniture, and of the silver portion of it there was not a piece left in its original shape, nor of a size larger than one's thumb.

The tablecloth, carpet and portieres showed a number of holes burned in them, varying in size from an inch in diameter to as large as would be covered by a soup plate.

What had caused this disaster the astonished and frightened family could not imagine. They decided, however, to leave everything as it was, and have the matter investigated by detectives.

After breakfast the retired merchant reported the fire to his insurance agent. It so happened that the special agent of one of the companies which had a policy on the furniture was at Los Angeles, and in the local agent's office when he called.

The special and local accompanied the gentleman in his carriage to his home, and the three at once proceeded to the dining-room. The special was appalled at the sight, for his quick eye took in at a glance that even though the fire had been so easily smothered, a heavy loss had been entailed by the really complete ruins of the embroidered tablecloth, the Moquet carpet, the Turcoman portieres and three embossed leather chairs, to say nothing of the epergne, whose value he did not then realize.

While he was mentally calculating what his company's proportion would be of a say $3,000 claim, he was startled by a crush and rattle of the glass ware on the sideboard.

The three men looked at each other helplessly for a moment; but the special broke the silence and reassured the others by at once moving towards the sideboard, and saying that whatever the cause of the commotion might be it came from under that piece of furniture, as could be plainly seen by the smoke which was beginning to curl up around it.

The three men had to exert their united strength to move the heavy piece of furniture, but when they had done so a remarkable spectacle met their gaze. Several holes were burning in the carpet, the back of the sideboard and the wall were spattered with blood and gore. The ex-merchant recoiled with a cry of horror, but the special and local began to stamp out the fire. They noticed peculiar fumes while they were doing this, and after they had completed its extinguishment, they began to closely scrutinize the carpet. The special uttered an exclamation of surprise, which was instantly followed by one from the local, and each at the same instant held up something for the other's gaze. What the special held was apparently a rat's tail, and the local held up what was undeniably the complete head of a very large rat. They were satisfied they had found the source of the blood bespattered on the wall, but what it all meant was certainly a puzzle.

The gentleman of the house had drawn near when the insurance men had held up the extreme end of a rat's anatomy, and during the surmises which were being made, he said he doubted if he could ever get his place free from rats; they had been the bane of his existence ever since he had moved into the house, which was completely overrun with them.

An idea seemed to strike the special, for he suddenly interrupted the old gentleman by asking what means he had employed to rid his house of the pests. The ex-merchant replied that they had proved themselves too wary for cats or dogs, and too cunning for traps, and they had lately been placing poison about the premises—in fact, he knew that some had been placed in the very room they were in. He called his butler, who showed a box which had contained the poison, "The Ready Rat Eradicator." The special looked at it, read the directions and the effect it had on the vermin, and among other matter read that it greatly puffed up the animal that ate it, and death was due to its bursting the stomach, but this effect was slow in being accomplished; the pain would lead the rats to look for water, and they would therefore leave the house to find it, and die outside.

The special smelt the inside of the box, but could not detect the peculiar odor of the fumes that had been noticed when they moved the sideboard. He asked if any other poison had been used, and the butler said he knew the coachman had used some around the stable, but whether it was a different kind or not he could not say. The coachman was called, and he said he had procured phosphorus, such as he had seen used for squirrels in grain fields.

A self-satisfied smile came over the special's face—he understood it all; the cause of the last night's crash and the explosion under the sideboard but a half hour before were both clear to him. He explained to his astonished listeners how using the two different kinds of poison had caused the whole trouble—the rats had eaten some of the phosphorus, and had come into the house and into the dining-room, and had there taken some of the "Ready Rat Eradicator;" then one had been attracted to the table by the fruit or bonbons on the epergne, and while on or near it the "Ready Rat Eradicator" had done its deadly work, had blown the rat up, and scattered the phosphorus it had swallowed in every direction, burning whatever it came in contact with. The force of the explosion was severe, as shown by the complete wreck on the dinning-room table, and by the breaking and rattling of the glassware on the sideboard. There was no doubt but that the special's theory was the correct one.

After the matter had been thoroughly discussed, the special said they had better proceed with the adjustment then and there. The old gentleman replied that ought to be short work as everything was in plain sight, and the estimate of damage was simply the value of the same things new, and he could show his bills for everything, as he had bought them less than two months previously.

The special asked him to get his bills, and as the old gentleman left the room he heaved a deep sigh, as the probable cost of the handsome furniture would rise up before him; and turn it over in his mind as he would, he felt the articles were completely ruined, and he could make only a "total" for them, as they were brand new. The old gentleman returned in a minute or two with his bills and also his policies. The special looked them over, put some figures down on the back of an envelope, which he took from his inside breast pocket, added them up and saw his total of $3,570; he paused a moment, and then told the old ex-merchant he regretted, but he must knock off $1,200, the cost of the epergne, as that article was destroyed by explosion which preceded the fire. The old gentleman looked at him for a moment in a pitying kind of a way, as if he felt rather sorry for him for making such an assertion, but the special accommodatingly opened out each policy and pointed out the lines in their printed conditions referring to property damaged by explosions. The ex-merchant read, and saw the special had taken the right ground, and without further delay they agreed upon the billed prices for the furniture, which, less the $1,200, footed up $2,370.

The three then drove back to the local agent's office, where the special filled in the proof of loss blank for his company, and then handed it to the retired merchant to read over so he would know just what he was to swear to before the local agent, who was a notary public.

The old gentleman held the paper some time, apparently reading and re-reading it; at last the special, who was leaning back in an arm-chair smoking a two-bit cigar, asked him if there was anything in the proof which did not appear to be in order.

The old gentleman looked up sharply and said: "Young man, there is much truth in the saying 'never too old to learn;' an hour ago I learned something about fire insurance by your pointing out to me a clause in the policies which made me bear a loss of $1,200, and now you hand me a paper which I must swear to before I can recover for the damage done to my furniture. Now this paper I cannot sign, let alone swear to, for I find in it this clause: 'The said fire did not originate by any act or procurement on my part.' It was certainly my act setting poison for the rats, and had I not done so, or rather had I not caused it to be done, the explosion and subsequent loss by the igniting phosphorus would not have occurred. No, no, young man, I cannot conscientiously sign that paper. I am too old to go back on the truth now; my reputation has always been that 'my word was as good as my bond.' This is another point in fire insurance I have learned within an hour. It may be a good and profitable business for you to follow, but there is nothing in it for me. So I will bid you good day!" and with this he walked out of the office and entered his carriage, leaving both special and local in a dazed condition.

The special recovered himself, and taking his cigar from his mouth, blew out a cloud of smoke, and exclaimed, "Great Scott! that is the heaviest old adjustment I ever participated in."

The local muttered something indistinctly, but the special's sharp ear caught the word, " Rats!"

INFLUENCE OF ASSOCIATION

I ONCE heard a paper read at one of our annual meetings on the subject of the "Influence of Association." At that time it seemed fit and full from the point taken. Not long since I listened to a touching story tenderly told, and in twilight hours and at various unexpected times thereafter this story came and came again, until I realized that it had taken a dwelling-place in my mind, so to be free of it I write it away, putting it in the *Knapsack* like a bit of leaven.

Once there was a man, a laborer. He was not intelligent above his fellows; there was nothing commanding in his appearance; he was only a serious, sober man, who day after day worked patiently, faithfully at his bench, going and coming with scarcely a word to any one, and yet there was something about him which prevented his comrades from rudely guying him.

After many days it was whispered that he had a sick boy at home, and from time to time he found in his hat when the day's work was done, a bit of ribbon, a piece of colored glass, a shining pebble, or some such trifle. Nothing was said; he understood the intent, and accepted it as quietly as it was offered.

At his approach the profane jest or rough horse-play would stop, and in course of time it ceased altogether, and what was formerly a tough gang became civil and decent to each other. What they could not see was the effect of their small gifts.

In an attic room, ever in his little bed, was a small, deformed, invalid child. Before him on the counterpane lay spread the ribbon and the glass, with which he feebly played. There was no other person about the room, and when he heard his father's heavy tread on the creaking stairs a light came into his faded eyes and a wan smile played about his wistful lips. Any new gift was placed in his thin fingers tenderly, as with a woman's touch.

As the cold days of winter approached the father became more and more serious. Deeper lines marked his face; and one day when he carried the form of the little child out of the house and over to the graveyard, there followed him at a respectful distance, every one of his fellow-workmen; they had forfeited half a day's pay that they might help to bury the boy they had never seen, that they might show sympathy for a man who had never spoken of his sorrow.

Mr. President and gentlemen, there seems to be a subtle "influence of association" which is controlled by something besides constitution and by-laws.

SOME years ago, when the adjuster's clause was more in use than now, a fire occurred in Pomeroy. The policy had the adjuster's clause. The adjuster figured up a loss of $150, and his expenses at $155, but told the assured that as he wished to make a liberal adjustment and leave him perfectly satisfied, he would throw off the difference of the extra five dollars, and call it square; and to this day that adjuster seriously insists that it was a liberal adjustment, as he could have figured his expenses much higher, but somehow the assured don't seem to understand it. He knows he had a policy, and knows he had a fire, but does not know where the liberality of the adjuster came in. However, he is still keeping that policy as a souvenir of that adjuster's generosity—as he threw off the five dollars. The Connecticut can tell this story much better than I have done.

ALL SPECIALS and adjusters who have traveled in Oregon in years ago, will remember Berry, the cheerful landlord at Junction City (with the best bedroom off the parlor, with the thick feather bed that smelt like Florida water), who made up in attention and cheerful words to his guests all that was otherwise lacking. Berry always kept his property insured, and was very anxious to have any additions or improvements approved by visiting insurance men. So one time your special was met by Berry at the depot, when the conversation ran as follows:

Berry—I want you to come right over and see how safe I have got my wash-house arranged in the rear of the hotel.

The special went with him and found a large kettle nicely set in brick, with about two feet of brick chimney, with a stovepipe passing from the brick chimney up through a shed roof.

Special—Why, Berry, this is elegant, nice; very safe, indeed! I did not think you had sufficient knowledge of insurance and the fitness of things to make everything so absolutely safe! I see you have made but one mistake.

Berry—What is that?

Special—You have got your chimney on the wrong end of your stovepipe.

Berry—You go to hell—and come in and take a drink.

MODEL AGENT.

WHILE traveling through Colorado some little time since, I happened to hear of a very good thing in the way of country agents. The story runs about like this:

Some few years ago, in a remote country town having a bank and other first-class appendages, with weekly stage communication with the outside world, lived a gentleman of considerable intelligence, well known in the community, and whose financial reputation was considered excellent. He wished to become a full-fledged insurance agent. He thereupon sat down and wrote to one of the secretaries of an Eastern company, stating what his condition was in the town, making reference to the bank as to his financial standing and integrity, and requested the agency of the company, believing that he could do a good and profitable business. After making inquiry the secretary sent forward supplies, together with commission and a batch of policies.

The special agent who had charge of that particular department was not at home at the time, and somehow in the press of business the secretary neglected to make a memorandum to call the attention of the special to the fact that this agent had been appointed, and request that he call upon this agent and make full report of the town and other conditions. So the matter rested about three years, when probably the supply clerk or some other circumstance called the matter up; and the secretary then requested the special when he visited the vicinity to make a call upon this appointed agent and ascertain why he had not transacted some business, inasmuch as the promises which he originally made were "couleur de rose," and he expected to do quite a large and flourishing business.

So in due time the special visited the agent and after being favorably impressed with him sat down to ask why he had not done something in the way of the insurance business. The agent turned upon him with astonishment and said: "Why, not do business? My dear man, I have been doing business for the last three years; have done a fine business. The premiums that I have taken in amount to nearly $4,500. I have nearly exhausted my supply of policies and intended to make an application for a new supply. I cannot understand what you mean by not doing business. Why, just sit down here and I will show you the amount of business I have done." Whereupon Mr. Special and the agent sat down and went carefully over the register; found that he had issued policies in their numerical order, all appearing to be in good shape and covering as if he had been an old underwriter.

"And, by the way," said Mr. Agent, "during this time I have made my regular deposit of the premiums in the bank, and everything is in good form; and in these three years of representing your company I have had a few losses, which, of course, has reduced the amount somewhat. I will call your attention first to the Smith loss; that was caused by defective flue. Of course, in my capacity as agent it was necessary that I should attend to this matter, and I have done so. I have paid the loss, which amounted to $150, and taken receipt therefore. Then there was that Brown loss; that was caused by the explosion of an oil lamp. The damage amounted to—let me see—$75, yes. Then Jones he had a loss of some $300, caused by sparks on the roof. That I paid, so that is all right. Then Jacobs had a loss of $200. I never was able to discover what the cause of that fire was. At all events, the amount of the losses that I have paid foots up $725. Now, take my commissions off of this business (amounting to $675), and there is in the bank to the credit of the company the sum of $3,100. If you wish it, I will give you an order for this amount, check it up, and we will square the thing and start again.''

The special then wanted to know why Mr. Agent had not made his daily reports, and sent copies of endorsements, reports of losses, etc., to the company; whereupon he expressed the greatest astonishment to think that it was necessary to take any such course. He supposed when he was appointed the agent of the company, that he was a little company all by himself; was to issue policies, take the premiums, deposit the same in the bank, and simply retain his commissions from the same; that the balance of the money was to be held in bank subject to the company's order, or to be paid out in the event of loss. The question as to whether losses would exceed that amount had never entered that agent's head. Of course, after due instruction by the special, he left, giving the agent to understand that he would send him out a new supply of policies, and at the same time requested that hereafter all daily reports of policies issued should be forwarded in due course.

SOME three years ago a fire occurred in New Mexico to a general merchandise stock, with damage of several thousand dollars; insurance, $2,000, in a California company. The stock was large and many goods saved. The local agent, who evidently had had much insurance experience admitted a total loss of the $2,000, but said he must have as many goods as he was to pay for, to show the agent of the company when he came up. So he took $2,000 worth of the saved goods, secured them safely, then telegraphed Cobb, Winie & Co., general agents at Denver, to send up an adjuster, not knowing that he himself had made the best adjustment ever reported. For further details and proofs, ask the Commercial.

DAMASCUS BADLAM.

I WAS born bad; my parents gave me a bad name; the boys call me Dam Bad for short, and I like it. What's the good of being good, anyhow? Now I go to school when I don't play hookey, and it makes me tired to see them good boys studying away for dear life, afraid to look up or whisper, or throw a paper wad, the teacher is all the time watching them so sharp, just hoping he may catch one of them so as to make an example of him. You betcher, when I prance in I make things howl, and it would amuse you to see how the teacher has to be wiping his spectacles, or blowing his nose, or regulating the stove, or fixing the window just that minute! He knows I'm bad, but he don't want to see the proof of it, for it would take all his time lickin' me if he treated me as he does the good boys, and he darsn't try that, for he knows I would bust up the school if he did.

I don't mind telling you that the school was started for the express purpose of keeping me quiet. You see, I always did make things pretty lively in our neck of the woods, cutting up and down (principally down), getting in on the apple orchards in a loose and independent style, running a free lance into the biggest watermelons, and "sapping the vitality" of fresh laid eggs in a way that made the other fellows wonder what they had been born for, anyway. So the folks started the school, and they sent a committee of boys that they thought would have some influence with me, because they were the worst boys they could think of except me, and they begged me to join in, and told me how much happier we would all be if I would put my name down on the list of scholars. You'd have laughed if you could have seen the style I put on when that committee showed up. I told 'em that I had a contract for a term of years to rob henroosts for a city poultry dealer; that come what might, my commission merchant must have his regular supply of fruit and melons, and that they knew what that meant, and that under my physician's instructions I would be compelled to suck eggs all my life. Do you know this didn't phase 'em a bit? They just said: "Baddie" (they called me 'Baddie'), we'll twist the rules anyway to suit you, and give you exclusive privileges in the particular directions which you have mentioned, if you will only come in."

Well, it seemed to me as if this last proposition looked like business, as it gave me a sort of dead thing on the melon and orchard and henroost business all to myself, for if one of the goody-goody milksops should ever get up courage to try his hand in my line, he would be barred out. But I didn't let on that I was the least bit willing to join. So they kept coming and coming and coming, and telling me how anxious every one was that "that Dam Badlam should' come into the fold." They agreed to have a teacher that used to be a "free lance" himself, and that would sympathize with me, and would see that the good boys didn't pick up any of the stray apples when I shook the trees ; and they agreed to make a rule that if any boy left the school, the whole thing was busted; so this, you see, made me "cock of the walk," for they all know they must treat me mighty fine to keep me in, for I'm bad, with a big " B."

You ought to come around some day and visit the "Cornpatch School." "Cornpatch" is the common name for it, but when we want to be high-toned we call it the Polytechnic Interior University, and some of the boys have gold pins with P. I. U. on them, but I just think that carving the letters on the watermelons I pick out is good enough for me.

It is as good as a circus to see the good boys try to live up to the rules. They start in and think they are going right, then first thing they know they run slap up against something that means different from what it reads, and then they get licked, and then they start again, and are certain they are right, when the master makes a rule for that "train and trip only," as the railroad tickets say, and *then* they get licked, and finally they get rattled and don't know what to do, and don't do anything, and *then* they get licked, and then when they see me pulling down the corners of my eyes at them, as they lay across the master's knee, it makes 'em feel happy.

I just had great fun the other day with a putty-blower, and hit the teacher with it. It gave him a pain in his eye, but the putty was there to glaze it with, so guess it was all right. (This is a joke.) The Boardman boy hit a fly with a potato-blower, and you ought to see what a whaling he got. He blubbered out that that Dam Bad boy had not been punished for using his putty-blower, but the master said his ruling was that there was no similarity between potatoes and putty, and that the latter had nothing to do with the case. He was lucky he didn't get whaled again, for the teacher could just as easy make another ruling that would have given him one.

I told the teacher one day that if I were one of the other boys I wouldn't stand it. He said that they *had* to stand it, and it was no more than right that they should ; they were born good, and had been familiar with rules and regulations all their lives. "Do you suppose," said he "that an untutored child of nature, an Apache Indian, who whoops up and down the main street of a city, clothed in nothing but his war paint and his scalping knife is to be treated the same as a good young dude that walks totteringly along in a stylish costume, and with an oversized penknife in his vest pocket? Not much. The latter must be 'run in ' for carrying a concealed weapon, while the former must be conciliated, must be furnished with scalps fixed up to order from the nearest hairdresser, must be provided with warm blood from the most convenient slaughter house, and every precaution must be taken that nothing be done to excite his anger in a way which would interfere with his ultimate civilization. "So it is in your case," said the teacher, "and I shall *always* rule that the boys that are good by instinct and education must toe the mark to a hair, but that the greatest leniency must be shown to one as depraved as yourself. In fact, my dear Baddie," he said, "I make it a point to lick the other boys as often as I can, as an evidence to you of good faith, and as a proof to the trustees that I am a strict disciplinarian."

Let me know what day you can come around to the P. I. U. and I will put some of the other boys up to being brave, and making them think they can do the same as I, and then you can see them get licked.

ALL THE old boys of the profession will remember with feelings of "soreness" the stage trip from Walla Walla to Boise over the Blue Mountains, through Burnt River Canyon, with its heat, holes, roots, ruts, rocks, dust, and doubtful grub. Upon one trip the stage load inside consisted of Sheriff M. and wife, E. C. Mc and wife, a Mrs. C., and your "special." We were all hungry, tired, and badly bruised, and there had been no conversation for an hour, when passing some wild flax by the road side one of the gentlemen remarked that the fiber was good to make cloth, another that the seed would make linseed oil, a third that the seed was good to get dirt out of your eyes, the first that the flour from the seed was good to make poultices, when Mrs. C., who so far on the trip had not spoken a word to any one, said with much emphasis, "If we had the poultices now I guess we would all know where to put them?"

SOME years ago a "special," book in hand, was making a diagram of Lewiston, and going into a China store that was insured in the company he represented for $2,500, and seeing a stock of probably $5,000, the following conversation ensued:

Special—John, how much goods you got here; how much cargo?

Kwong Mow—I done know. What for you want know?

Special—Me all same as taxee man.

Kwong Mow—Very lette; not more a tousand dollar.

Special—Velly good; all ritee, John; you burn up, I pay you tousand dollar—all ritee.

Kwong Mow—Mee too muchee sabe—all same insurance man; hab a cigar?

A TIMID, NERVOUS MAN.

I never was a timid man, I'm a pugilist by birth,
I always hated nervousness more than anything on earth;
I've bragged about my fearlessness when I was in my prime,
But of my change I'll tell you now, and tell it all in rhyme.
So if you will attentive be, I'll do the best I can,
To tell you of the sorrows of a timid, nervous man.

I've battled with Old Ocean and fought all thro' the war;
I've been whipped by Johnny Sullivan and never got a scar;
I've gone down in a diving bell and up in a balloon,
I've twinkled with the *other* star, and sailed around the moon;
I never once was rattled, but now I've changed my plan,
For I'm full of woes and sorrows—I'm a timid, nervous man.

I've read about the engineer who threw the lever back
When he saw a headlight on the curve, and but a single track;
The boy upon the burning deck;—all were cowards along o 'me—
Till I got a lively company, and took its agency.
I assumed to be an honest man and keep my shirts so clear
That Stillman couldn't catch me, and then I'd have no fear.

Now what has made this awful change—for I'm not writing stuff—
What is the fearful trouble that makes me such a muff?
It's only that I want to keep my premiums at the top,
My expenses at the minimum—my losses I must stop;
I want to get the business at any rate I can,
But Stillman and the "Union" make me a nervous man.

I've tried to smuggle stables through, as *dwellings* for a beast,
For if it only could be done thus premiums are increased.
The cheerful, rusty stovepipe, and cotton hanging loose,
I try to cover as I may, but it really is no use;
For Stillman and his horrid ways, his fines and reprimand,
Have made me what I am to-day—a timid, nervous man.
    So I'm nervous, I'm timid—a timid, nervous man;
    I've got to leave a business that makes a timid *honest* man.

EDITORIAL, 1889.　　A. J. WETZLAR.

EDITORIAL.

EVERY editor of a newspaper is supposed to present to his readers a fine salutatory, and custom has prescribed such duty even upon the editor of the *California Knapsack*.

No one more so than this editor, perhaps, realizes the pleasure of this part of the work, as full sway can be given there to all the sarcasm or taffy deserved by the various members who either failed to contribute, or did contribute to the success of this publication.

That the position of editor of this paper is an enviable one, the writer has as yet failed to ascertain, and he was led in the sweet simplicity of his life, to accept the position in the belief that by doing so, the many and varied contributions of the different members could be compiled by him, at the sacrifice of but little time, and with credit to himself and the Association.

How vain and transitory are the things of this life!

The editor believed that all he would have to do would be to compile contributions, which he firmly believed would drop in upon him like an avalanche. Let none of you, my readers, for a moment harbor the same thought; it is to say the least, "illusionary."

This editor issued a plain little circular to all the members calling for their contributions to the *Knapsack*.

Since that time he has been almost constantly employed in drumming up delinquents, and now desires it distinctly understood that to those members who did send in their contributions, not this editor, but the Association, should be grateful, as the editor was struck with the peculiar idea that some of the members thought they were doing this editor a personal favor, by contributing their little effusions to the *Knapsack* for publication, and this fact this editor repudiates, as it should be the pleasant duty of every member of the Association to assist and contribute to the success of everything conducted under its auspices.

Of course contributions come in lively. The editor believes there were just four special items, and as a result anything good that appears in these columns should be placed to the credit of the editor, and the bad and chestnut flavored articles, to the members who so kindly contributed their quota to the success of the publication.

There are a few, a very few members, of this Association to whom the editor feels indebted for their cheering help and counsel, and such members will kindly consider themselves thanked in due shape.

To our numerous contemporaries and exchanges we also desire to express our high appreciations of their columns, as among all of them including our *Coast Review*, not a single article worth the clipping was found. As a sequel we are presenting for the edification of the members, a "pot pourri" of effusions which, whilst not as weighty as though they had emanated from a Grant-Carpenter, or a Staple-Spencer, will remind one of the time-worn joke, not Kinne, but how Kinne do it.

We will therefore proceed and see.　　*　　*　　*

FROM NEW JERSEY.

ONE of the jolliest story tellers in the corps of adjusters, in New York City relates the following joke upon himself, which needs to be heard from his own lips to be fully appreciated. He was called to adjust a loss "way down in the Jarsies," and relates his experience something in this wise:

His name was Levy. The goods—general merchandise. Just enough goods totally burned to make a claim on, besides an unlimited claim for per cent. damage for smoke and water. He wanted $6,000 loss and damage. "And I never will take one cent less, so hold me Moses." I went to work in earnest, labored with his books, with only the success of finding that his whole stock could not have been over $5,000. By inventory of remaining stock, got the totally destroyed down to $1,000. After laboring with him two days on the question of smoke and water damage, I concluded to give him $3,000. Upon approaching that amount in my investigation, he declared with hands upraised, "Oh, I am r-r-r-ruined completely; I am busted. I can never uphold any more mine het in pizzness. I shall mine selluf hang." At last, when I told him that it was the best I could do, he said, "Dot ruins me; but how about the monish? Ven shall I that git, eh?" I told him I would draw a draft on New York as soon as he signed the proofs, and swore to them. "You vill at once a draft draw. Ish good dot draft, mine friend?" "Perfectly, sir." "Vill you to the bank go, and get endorsed that draft?" "I will." "To the bank we go, mine frent." So I went to the bank with him, had the papers signed and sworn to, and gave him an endorsed draft on New York. When done, he said, "Come to mine house, mine frent. Ve will take some things mit mine frau." Having sat down to a glass of extra dry, his frau asked, "Have settled you dot insurance oop dare?"   "Oh yes, we have settled for $3,000."   "Oh, mine Gott, mine Gott, ve was r-r-r-r-ruined.   Mine Shakup, wot haf you done?"   "Never you mind mine frau," says Jacob.   Then turning to me he says: "Ve have settled that little matter, eh?"   "Yes." "You pays me three tousand tollars, eh?"   "Yes."   "You von certified draft gifs me, eh?"   "Yes."   "Vell, den, vot ish de matter wid dot?" "Why, nothing, I hope."   "Dot draft vill be paid, eh?"   "Yes; it is as good as paid now."   "Vell, den, I tells you vot ish de matter with dot." "What is it?"   Putting his thumb to his nose, and twirling his fingers, he said, with a laugh: "I dells you, Mr. Adjuster, vot ish de matter: I—beats—you—shust—fifteen—hundred—tollars!"

MORE CALENDARS.

Not a new subject, Mr. Editor, but at the same time an ever-varying one, especially as this year brings us a number of emblematic or allegorical designs worthy of comment.   Space and time limit us to a few.   The Glens Falls offer a suggestion of a "cold day," and since in the hands of the present agents they are not likely to get "left" we conclude that they are on the lookout for a "warming."   The Long Island shows a picture of an old woman threatening an imp with a switch; we trust this does not mean that they intend to "whip the devil around the stump."   The German-American have an elaborate and well-executed mythological design, but it is so long since we prosecuted our studies in that direction, that we are obliged to put our own interpretation on it, as follows: The central figure, the Pythoness, being a soothsayer or fortune-teller, represents the "profit" expected for the year; the Spirit of the Air will furnish the wherewithal for the blowing of the company's "road agents"; the Earth indicates the sum of their desires, the fence being considerately omitted; the Fire Spirit of the Lower Regions, or "Infernal Spirit," represents the bad whiskey found on the road; and the *semi-ichthyle* (consult your dictionaries, gentlemen) Water Spirit may mean that the company is still "in the swim," or more probably stands for the "fishy" losses expected during the year.   But the climax in allegory is reached when we find our friends Mann and Wilson posing as angels, and distributing Continental policies to the world, though the safe indicates that such action is not entirely disinterested.

Time and space forbid reference to others.

❧❧

EDITORIAL 1890.   A. J. WETZLAR.

EDITORIAL.

FELLOW MEMBERS :—

ONCE more the *Knapsack* greets you on this 14th anniversary of our mutual regard, and as the editor tosses it off his shoulders and unbuttons the straps, its weight calls loud attention to the fact that you fellow-members (with a few noteworthy exceptions) have been, as usual, derelict in your contributions, which bears sad testimony to the fact that you are willing to partake of meats and sweetmeats dished out to you regularly, without doing your share of support. This, therefore, incites us to a loud and vigorous "protest and kick." Any particular part of our annual observance should not be made a hardship upon the one who is selected as editor, and who as a consistent member, cannot refuse to act, and likewise, it never was intended to have the *Knapsack* presented as an individual paper or essay, but everybody is expected to contribute something for the amusement, entertainment or instruction of the members, which the editor is expected to collaborate in proper shape and present to this Association.

"Expectancy!" How vain and transitory is the proposition. Were it not for a few consistent, hard-working members of this Association the *Knapsack* would now be buried with the past.

To all such contributors, the Association, through the editor, hereby returns its thanks, and, so as to recompense them for their kind efforts, it will, in this issue, with the kind assistance of Professors Lowden, Gurrey, and George Grant, present to their astonished gaze such beautiful spectacles as never were, shall or will be seen (again) on this side, or on the other side of the Pacific ocean. In this superier effort they have collected together a number of subjects, deservedly much-talked-of, much-heard-of, ever-to-be-remembered, never-to-be-forgotten, and mirth-provoking, simply as a warning to derelict contributors of what they may expect if they do not respond handsomely hereafter. If, when this part of the *Knapsack* is produced, the members will kindly refrain from hilarity, they may save suspenders and vest buttons, and owing to the veil of darkness that will hang over the audience, all jewelry and valuables should, upon entry into the room, be given to the editor. The associate editors and professors are alone responsible for anything that appears in this issue, as the editor is at the present time doing the kicking.

In this issue we present to you essays upon scientific subjects from the pen of celebrated writers, who have for years gone by been well paid for their efforts. Whether at this time it will be necessary to create an assessment to pay them will be left to your discretion and knowledge of their financial condition.

The first essay is as follows:

The Coast Review, January No., 1890, page 28, says:

"Does water burn at great fires?" and quotes from a Chicago paper, experience at last Boston fire, old firemen and other scientists, that "intense heat resolves water into its original elements, and thereby adds fuel to flames."

This theory is correct when applied to the Gulliverean stream of a first-class city fire department (sprayed) thrown from a three-quarter or inch nozzle, of the style of thirty years ago, into the burning mass of a seven-story building 150 x 200 feet filled with merchandise manufactured, unmanufactured and in process of manufacture—but won't apply to the stream thrown by the You Bet department.

The main part of the town of You Bet is where the big pipe leading to the hydraulic mine crosses the Nevada City and Dutch Flat road. The Corners, so-called, were occupied as hotel and saloon, saloon, brick general merchandise store, whiskey included of K. & Co., and another saloon.

When Red Dog burned, a fire department was suggested for You Bet. To suggest was to act.

At the point where the big mining pipe crossed the road at The Corners, there was a pressure of 160 pounds to the square inch; the supply was 3,000 miners' inches.

A connection was made by attaching to the 16-inch pipe a 12-inch canvas hose banded with a three-quarter-inch manilla rope; to this was attached a Little Giant monitor with a 5-inch nozzle mounted on two logging-truck wheels, with a rear lever like a field gun to keep the hose and nozzle from kicking or bucking. The hose was long enough, fifty feet or so, to cover the business part of the town.

Bill Bangs, foreman of the hydraulic mine, was elected chief engineer. Bill knew nothing about fire departments, but knew that a Giant nozzle of that size, under that pressure would cut down a 100-foot cement gravel bank, and pledged himself to knock hell out of any fire within range.

The fire department was ready for business.

During a dull season, at about 12 o'clock one night, forty or fifty pistol shots called out the fire department.   Four or five shots meant a fight; forty or fifty, a fire.

Bill found smoke issuing around the edges of the iron doors of K. & Co.'s store, brought the monitor to bear on the front of the building, and gave orders to turn her loose—and turn her loose they did.   The stream took doors, windows walls, front and rear, books, stock, furniture and fixtures, safe included, out of the building and down into the canyon; cleaned the building, as the boys said, as clean as a shot-gun; left only the side walls.

The loss by fire was small; the loss by smoke not reported; but as usual with a first-class country fire department, the loss by water took the balance.   Boots, shoes, clothing and other merchandise not more hazardous, strewed the canyon for miles.

The special who, a year before, made a favorable report on that fire department and water supply, and recommended a small appropriation towards its support, and had gotten a special rate on and secured K. & Co.'s risk, paid a total loss.   He didn't know until then a fire department could do such clean work; but to the utter disgust of Bill Bangs (the foreman), refused to entertain a motion for a further appropriation.

The You Bet stream would have been just right in the Boston fire; it would not have burned, and if thrown from a fair distance would have been worth forty drizzling streams, whilst the ordinary fire stream would have been good enough for You Bet.   Both were misplaced, and the companies stand the loss—that's all.

"DOWN WENT ——."

THE RECORD OF A YEAR'S PACIFIC COAST UNDERWRITING.

Written by E. W. Carpenter, and interpreted by him at the Annual Dinner of the Underwriters' Association of the Pacific, February 19th, 1890.

In the Spring of '89,
    Underwriters, feeling fine,
Were anticipating profits, very tall;
    All the cinch bills had been killed,
    Each his field had nicely tilled,
And expected a contingent in the Fall.
    So ev'ry fire insurance man
    To grab for prem'ums then began;
Each strove to place his record near the top,
    When Seattle, on the Sound,
    Did every one astound,
And the hopes of all received a sudden drop.

Down went the entries in our register of fires,
　　　　And though we tried to smile, 'twas apparent all the while
That contingent, profit, hopes were burned in Puget's funeral pyres
　　　　Dressed in their best suit of clothes.

　　　　　　Then adjusters rushed pell mell
　　　　　　To that Northwest corner ——, well,
　　　　To Seattle, which for us had made it hot;
　　　　　　Each intent on winning fame,
　　　　　　And a " promptest payment" name,
　　　　By cashing all his losses on the spot.
　　　　　　This was no sooner done,
　　　　　　And the "ads" had just begun
　　　　To announce the feats of those who felt so great,
　　　　　　When Spokane got her hold
　　　　　　Upon another pile of gold
　　　　In a way that made our mournful eyes dilate.

Down came the drafts which so enlarged the gaping hole
　　　　In our assets very small and extremely hard to call,
And we took the "sixty days" allowed where losses high did roll,
　　　　Dressed in our best suit of clothes.

　　　　　　Now we didn't rave and swear,
　　　　　　For none of us would dare
　　　　To do this save against the P. I. U.;
　　　　　　But we all began to kick,
　　　　　　And to strive to find a trick
　　　　Which would swell our assets ere the year was through.
　　　　　　But then Bakersfield "chipped in;"
　　　　　　Ellensburg next gave us sin;
　　　　And we wondered if the fires would ever quit.
　　　　　　Our cash got low and lower—
　　　　　　Then we drew on "home" for more,
　　　　Yet had nothing left except a little grit.

Down came the letters from headquarters far and near,
　　　　　　Asking what we meant—if 'twas really our intent
　　　　To lay out all the companies upon a funeral bier,
　　　　　　Dressed in their best suit of clothes.

Now the underwriter's pale ;
Thought that '90 could not fail
To make amends for fiery '89 ;
When the smash of rules began
By that wicked "other man"
Who could not be coaxed or kicked into the line.
Then all were in despair,
And they madly pulled their hair
As they stood one day beside Lake Merrit dank ;
So they took the cut-rate knife
And, to settle all the strife,
Committed hari-kari on its bank.

Down went the bowels of our business in the lake
And the vital organs, too ; so that's why all of you
Are at the Maison Riche tonight assisting at its wake,
Dressed in your best suit of clothes.

LATELY a number of fire insurance agents and managers appeared
before the insurance committee of the Washington Legislature. Some of
them *for* and some *against* any legislation. Among the latter was the
secretary and manager of a local company not in very good odor with
the insuring public. When this gentleman got an opportunity to make
his speech he addressed the committee thusly:

"Mr. Chairman and Gentlemen—I am opposed to any legislation at
this time. If you knew how impossible it is for me to collect money from
my stockholders to pay our losses, you would understand that it would
be even harder to get them to put up any capital."

CHARACTER SKETCHES.

DEARLY BELOVED:—

THE *Knapsack* has for your entertainment on this fourteenth anniversary of our mutual regard, a series of pictures representing some
of our members in situations, striking but natural. "With charity
for all and malice toward none," we have tried to catch the prominent
characteristics, foibles, weaknesses, what you will, of the various subjects.

The accompanying lines received with each picture are intended to
be funny. Nobody but the author knows the agony of mind attending
this humorous effort. To be really witty, one must be without food,
money or friends; when the stomach howls for recognition, the brain
takes on its most brilliant tone. What then can a well-fed editor hope

for in his attempts to draw pen pictures calculated to win an honest laugh from an audience like this? The cartoons from the brush of a well-known special are excellent.

The photographic work by another well-known special is in his usual finished style.

Hence, my friends, if you find a sentence here and there with more sarcasm than fun, more personality than wit, please believe it to be intended for innocent amusement; at all events, it will " be all in the family, " for our Eastern friends, editors of insurance journals, never publish the proceedings of our wild and woolly Western Association. This may be because we live so far away that what is funny in February, becomes thin and weak in June. Or it may be part of the courtesy of journalism to ignore what has been first published by a rival.

Whatever the cause, do not forget to promote the interests of the Pacific Coast by claiming superiority in everything home born.

The idea of the lantern slides is new with this *Knapsack*, and such of you as feel hurt, because you have not been held up to ridicule, can be soothed with the thought that next year you will probably suffer double abuse.

MR. WETZLAR'S INTERVIEW WITH MR. SHIPPEE.

Everybody knows something about the "harvester" case now on trial at Stockton. Our artist has seized the moment when Mr. Wetzlar is serving a subpœna upon Mr. Shippee. Mr. Wetzlar says:

"Sir, I am well aware that you do not entertain for me that high regard which Stockton men usually have for gentlemen from San Francisco (hold! do not shoot yet)! I am a representative of the United States Circuit Court (ah, you turn pale); in my hand I hold an order for your appearance before the Circuit Court in San Francisco. Although you have no exalted opinion for me, still I know, sir, that you take an *interest* in me. Personally, Mr. Shippee, I bear you no malice; you are a good man, if you do have fits (nay do not foam so menacingly). What our insurance people most earnestly desire to know is how you can manufacture harvesters at a cost of $165, sell them for $137.50, and make a profit of $40.70?"

To this Mr. Shippee replied, in that sweet-toned Sunday voice which he carries with him: "I am just now particularly engaged, but if you will step outside for a moment, I will explain your problem."

In the second picture Mr. Wetzlar is described in the act of stepping outside.

PETER OUTCALT.

Our next production needs no introduction, for who is there among you that will not at a glance recognize our congenial friend and fellow-member "Peter Outcalt," sometimes called "the Unabridged Webster."

Our artist caught him in Seattle, arguing with an obdurate claimant. Peter is too gentlemanly to bulldoze; he is merely explaining that he will need a few figures from the claimant preliminary to making up his proofs —but let him speak for himself: "In the few remarks which I have had the extreme satisfaction of placing in array before your mental vision— weak and futile though perchance they may ultimately prove to be—I can but hope, and do sincerely trust, that 'Altoego' is not too prominently characteristic to overshadow the impressions which I have, '*ipsi facto*,' sought to make; I should be recreant to those who do me the honor to

pay me my paltry stipendiary emolument, did I not grasp those matters of difference so common between the parties of the first and second parts, and finding the point of dissension get, as it were, 'right to its necktie'— I will therefore be compelled to request of you to furnish the company a tabulated, corroborative data, from which it may be possible to extract in an analytical manner and summarize, as it were, your loss"—

The claimant died next day.

CHAS. W. DOHRMANN.

This subject of our illustration was born on the mutual plan, and raised on a policy originating with his father—a tontine—whereby Charley got all that was coming to him. He commenced his career as president of a company, and having extracted all the credit and emoluments from this humble beginning, started out into the general profession as a "local"—the envy of them all. The forked tongues of envious rivals were continuously clipped by this modern Sampson, until today we find him among the leading underwriters of the coast, and the general agent of the baby company of our State.

"The Alta" Insurance Company is but an instrument in Charley's hands, and the affection between the company and agent, as displayed in the picture, proves that "one good turn deserves another," as there is as much evidence of pleasure in the "Alta" as there is in Mr. Dohrmann.

A. R. GUNNISON.

Our artist here presents a subject ripe in years and full of honors—
and yet, Mr. A. R. Gunnison is not too ripe, nor in his honorable career
has he ever been quite full.   His gentle assurance to the claimant is

couched in the choicest legal language, to-wit: "It is clear, this fire was
not accidental ;   the fact that no one was at home, that no fire had been
built in the place for a week, that your wife took her best dress and all
her jewelry when she went to town on a visit—all this goes to show a
motive ; then, again, there was no insurance on the furniture, *prima facie*
evidence of a deep-laid plan to avert suspicion.   I will give you one dollar for your policy, not necessarily as an evidence of an adjustment, but
merely as a precautionary measure."

To this the claimant replied: "You come along with me, it ain't
far, only to the river ; I sized you up the minute I seen you ; says I, durn
a man who wears black gloves—like he was at a funeral."

FAYMONVILLE.

The next on exhibition is ye genial Faymonville—Bernard, for short. By his broad and massive brow ye shall know him as a most earnest co-laborer. Our artist caught him in the field, where he was rushing madly along the road from Tuscon to Quijotoa. It seems Faymonville

had heard at Tuscon that a man was contemplating the erection of a store on that road, and with his usual eye to business, he rushed off to secure the insurance, and the man as agent for his company. At one time, Mr. F. belonged to the cream of the earth, to-wit: was a local agent, notary public, coroner, justice of the peace and undertaker; in fact, gathered honey all the day and raised cattle at night, when there was no moon—this he did for his health.　His ambition, however, led him to this city, and luckily for us, he is now safely housed with the Firemans Fund.　Under high temperature his massive brow troubles him by the hair falling out, but in this great and glorious climate he thinks clearly without reference to his every-day conversation.

MR. SEXTON.

This picture represents William Sexton feeding the lion; one can plainly see there is but one William Sexton and one lion.　This animal stood for quite a season on his exalted pedestal in front of Manager

Dornin's office—one of the signs of the times—but one day he came off the perch and said he was too thin to fool the boys, so Assistant Keeper

Sexton undertook the dangerous task of filling him up ; for this he was particularly adapted, having associated with lions all his life, and being something of an "intellectual monarch," himself. He stuffed the lion so vigorously that digestion was impaired. The chemical action of the stomach resembles that of a geyser spring, and the lion commenced to steam and smoke, and give signs of internal fire. In short, his stock was away off, but by judicious watering he regained his accustomed footing, and is now "on deck" once more.

Sexton's "bete noir" is baggage ; it is confidently asserted that when he goes on a trip he puts a spare collar button in his grip and never neglects to have it regularly sent to his laundry.

A. A. SNYDER.

Mr. A. A. Snyder—or Professor Snidirini, sword-swallower and magician (the professor always works in his pajamas) born, not made,

our hero left Maine, U. S. A., by merchant marine for *la belle* France at a tender age. Here, amid the sunny slopes of that vine-clad land he contracted an accent, together with that graceful repose of manner for which he has since been truly notorious.   After a protracted absence of seven months, he returned to his native shore by the county road and canal route. It was then he studied legerdemain.   With him the sword is mightier than the pen—he can get away with the sword.   This is also true of his manipulation of the assured.   Loved by all, he has had a correspondingly active life.   To be one of a select few when he orders a basket of wine is to breathe indeed.

May the Lord bless him at His earliest convenience.

C. MASON KINNE.

Let all be hushed in quiet silence whilst the band plays "Marching Through Georgia," for now will appear that great warrior in battle and non-concurrent policies.

"Col. C. Mason Kinne," who has been in many frays and always comes out unscathed and on top.   Kinne is nothing if not consistent; an enthusiast and scientist.   As an adjuster he is a terror to the incendiary, and as such is known sometimes as "Old Sneuth."

Our artist has caught him in Los Angeles in the act of making a diagram of an incendiary's tracks.   This diagram is elaborately drawn in black, red, yellow, green and gold chalks, while an admiring crowd of fellow-adjusters watch his every movement through the bars—where they

feel quite at home. You will perceive that Kinne is measuring the tracks with his celebrated rule—9-inch ; and it is needless to add that he successfully tracked and convicted his man ; verdict, twenty-four years in State Prison ; and you will next see his man in his present quarters.

Hello ! It appears our artist has made a mistake, and put "Old Sneuth" behind the bars ! Will the colonel, if he is present, kindly explain how he got out ?—for virtue is its own reward.

EDITORIAL, 1891.   GEO. F. GRANT.

EDITORIAL.

GENTLEMEN OF THE ASSOCIATION :—

I GIVE you greeting for the year 1891. The *Knapsack* may be a trifle empty. It may be even comparatively thin ; if so it is the easier to bear.

Possess yourselves with patience; listen with becoming deference and hide your emotions. It will soon be over. We do not write for the *Knapsack* in hope of glory; for a truth, I don't know why we write for it, but assuming it to be for some good object, why not a sermon in place of an editorial?

A few years ago in Los Angeles, while walking to the Santa Fe depot to take an early morning train, being in doubt, in spite of carefully worded directions, I hailed a colored brother on the walk for further proof of my bearings.

With a smile that lit up a broad expanse of glossy blackness he said, "Keep a steppin', Colonel, keep a steppin' and you will get there." In spite of the original manner of the directions, and the unusual sound of the military title, which was enough in itself to distract everyday thought, I detected at once in this speech, crystallized and glowing, a "gem." "Keep a steppin' and you will get there."

Fix your eye upon the goal and never stop until you reach it. Do not grow weary, or if weary do not give up; where there is a will to achieve there is a way to accomplish.

Fight it out on the line laid out if it takes the whole season. That is the deduction I draw from the words of the smiling Ethiopian, who thought to be simply good natured, nothing more.

From time to time epigrams crisp and clean-cut fall from the lips of great men, who are thereby made so much the greater, and these words live in the world's history, reappearing at intervals in print and speech to point a moral. And so the modest words of my dusky friend fell upon my ear, "Keep a steppin' and you will get there"; a seed fallen by the wayside which, springing up wet with morning dew and warm with noonday sun, putting forth leaves and blossoms until grown big enough to delight the eye and give forth perfume free to all who pass that way; so these words took firm enough possession of my mind and stayed green in my memory until now. Thus I give them to you for what they may be worth. "Keep a steppin' and you will get there." Are you young in the business, a special with your fortune all before you? Then you have many and many a heartache yet to bear.

For that genial gentleman who is at the head of your office, although himself once special agent and comparatively only yesterday hurrying over the road at the direction of others to do the very same kind of business he now sends you about, that same genial gentleman will hold you to a strict accounting and rule you with a rod of iron long after the time when you have proved to him that things have changed and he is the one who is not up with the procession.

"Keep a steppin' and you will get there." The day will come when you feel within yourself a strength born of hard and honest work. That day is your emancipation. "Keep a steppin'," but try to remember when you hold the lines and drive, there are other ways of getting the best out of a willing horse besides plying the lash.

Are you an adjuster burning the lamp at night, with a wet towel around an aching head, digging out the Kinne and the Sexton rule, having a catch-as-catch-can encounter with non-concurrent puzzles and co-insurance pigs in clover?

"Keep a steppin' and you will get there." Ten to one you know more now than the celebrated authors you worship, for my dear plodding, soft-hearted friend, it is not the man who knows everything that receives the plaudits of his fellows, but the man who has the faculty of putting what little he knows in a conspicuous place at the supreme moment when eyes are turned his way.

"Keep a steppin' and you will get there." For there never was a square adjuster in this world who did not attract attention to his office, and some day in poring over the pages of this company's business the directors will put you in a conspicuous place as a marker.

Are you a manager with honors thick upon you, while cares and vexations sap your life and send you tired but sleepless to an exhausting bed? "Keep a steppin'," but take the *Knapsack's* advice: Don't try to do the work you graduated from; have the same faith in your clerks as your employer used to have in you. Take a vacation once in a while; pound your ear with the monotonous roar of the ocean surf, or the whistling breeze of the mountain top. Don't try to do everything in one day. Stop a moment and think. You are now on the shady side of life. Your tastes are few, your habits are fixed, your form is set and you are hardened; you are a type, but you are not and have no right to be a flint. "Keep a steppin'," for there is something for you to think of be-

yond the success of this life. It will do you no harm and relieve those
about you, when you have resigned yourself to the thought that you cannot live to carry out your cherished plans forever. There is somewhere
else to go. "Keep a steppin' and you will get there."

CAMP TEN.

ONE day I received a telegram from San Francisco, requesting me to
meet the assured that night, take Marysville train with him and
proceed to Camp No. 10, and adjust a mill loss. The assured was a
total stranger to me, and I did not discover his identity until just before
we reached Oroville. It was then 2 o'clock in the morning; we decided
on an early start and filled in the time until gray dawn lounging about
the hotel office talking in subdued tones for fear of disturbing sleeping
guests. The assured agreed to all my proposed plans and was in perfect accord with the smallest details. As we seated ourselves for an all-
day drive I thought "How seldom it happens that everything is so
harmonious." And yet there was an unsatisfied feeling within me; after a
short attempt to analyze it I gave it up and turned my attention to the
assured as a study of human nature, a favorite pastime with me.

He was long and thin, over six feet in height, with no unusual expression of face. He had taken the lines when we started, and although
not an expert driver gave evidence of familiarity in handling a team. He
sat in a most uncomfortable position, for his legs were so long they had
to be doubled up in the space between the seat and the dash-board, and
he maintained the same cramped position all day long, working the
brake with his right hand. For a few minutes after we started he chatted
pleasantly enough but soon subsided and eventually answered my remarks in monosylables.

He did not care for the rugged and beautiful scenery along the road;
the warmth of noon, the running brook, the gorgeous sunset, had no
charm for him.

He had consideration for the team in climbing an ascent, but rattled
down hill in a rapid, careless way, which caused me to regard him with
unusual scrutiny two or three times when we struck steep pitches; although he was aware of my eyes being on him a great part of the time,
he made no comment and appeared unconcerned. As we drew near the
"Mountain House," where we were to pass the night, he asked suddenly, in an anxious way, if there was a moon tonight? and seemed relieved when I answered no. Why is it, I thought, as I dropped out of

the buggy at the tavern door, why is it that this very common-place person disturbs my peace of mind. I shall be relieved when I go to bed and shut him out of my thoughts.

The "Mountain House" was neither a dwelling nor a hotel. It was a *place* where travelers to and from Camp No. 10 got a drop to drink and a bite to eat; the price paid should have been the equivalent of a downy bed and an appetizing meal, but the reality, alas, how different! Here was a landlord to whom a pallet of straw was a dreamful couch, and a dried-apple pie a luxury, but he gave his guests welcome with an air of hospitality hearty and genuine. After the usual refreshment at the bar, we went in to supper. Now for the first time I saw the assured without head gear. His hair stood out thick and stiff all over his head, an enviable head of hair to a man of forty-five, but it seemed to neither add nor detract from the appearance of this man, and once more I took myself to task for the persistency with which I stuck to the idea that somehow he was an unusual person. Leaving the table first, by accident I took up his hat. It was so small it perched on my head like a child's hat. In a moment he came out and settled it easily over his shock of hair.

"Well," I thought, "he is peculiar for his small head, if nothing else."

The "Mountain House" had just one guest chamber, in which were two beds. I was tired enough and the thought of an early start for a round trip to Camp No. 10, caused me to turn in soon after supper. Directly in came the assured, walked over to the window and peered out, muttering to himself, "no moon yet." Then he pulled a drawer from the bureau, placed it on top of that article of furniture, so that the candle light was shaded from my side of the room, got out a yellow-covered novel, lit two or three extra candle ends which he took from a small traveling bag and, for all I know, read until morning. Once or twice in the night when I awoke he was still reading. As we took turn about with the basin and towel next morning, he suddenly asked if I had money with me. "Just enough for expenses," I replied. "All right, I have plenty," he said. "See, this is where I hide it," and he pulled a good-sized sack out of his pillow slip.

We spent that day at the scene of the fire, returning to the "Mountain House," where the bureau drawer, the candles and a novel came into use again. Once more we were at Oroville, and if my companion had closed his eyes in sleep, I did not know it.

I spoke of the incidents of the trip to my family and, after a day or two, forgot the subject, when one evening my wife gave an exclamation, looked up from the newspaper she was reading and said, "this must be the man who had a loss at Camp No. 10. Listen:

'Sensational proceedings for a divorce.'   'A husband shoots at his wife because she is too lovely to live.'

'Evidence of insanity.'

'He takes a prominent citizen to Camp No. 10 on the plea of selling a mine.'

'He lashes the team and throws away the lines.'

'Arrayed in his night clothes, he shoots at the moon through the window of the 'Mountain House.'

'Curious testimony introduced.'

'Full particulars in to-morrow's issue.'"

MR. C. W. TAYLOR, a clever newspaper man of Puget Sound, writes the following:

"Fire."

The wild cry rang out on the night air.   Heads were thrust hastily out of upper windows, excited voices uttered quick inquiries, and in the distance was heard the clatter of the engines coming nearer and nearer. From a large building around the corner huge volumes of dense smoke poured forth.   The whole floor was on fire.   The flames had not as yet communicated to any of the floors above.

Nearer and nearer came the engines.   They reached the scene.   The firemen sprang to their task with alacrity.

But an unforeseen contingency presented itself.   There was no water. In vain the faithful men made the requisite connection of hose and water plug.   In vain the engines throbbed with superhuman energy.   Something had happened at the water works.

"Must I stand by and see my house burnt to the ground?" shouted the owner of the building, with tears in his voice.   "Can nothing be done?"

The chief of the fire department shook his head.   He looked helplessly at the crowd that had gathered.

Suddenly a great light shone in his eyes.   With the quickness of a man trained to act in emergencies he darted into the crowd.

There was a sound of rapid scuffling, angry protest and loud threats, and the chief emerged from the crowd with a large bundle in his arms.

Calling imperiously to his men he ordered the front doors of the building to be broken open.

It seemed like the freak of a crazy man, but the order was obeyed. With a yell of triumph the chief sprang into the burning building, followed by his men.   Grimy, choked and blinded by smoke, but victorious, they came out a few minutes afterwards, and the chief gave orders to return. He had smothered the flames with the trousers of an English tourist.

———

It is painful for me to make diagrams for other people's jokes, but the fact is these were traveling trousers.

That is why the flames were *checked.*—ED. KNAPSACK.

EXTRAORDINARY CASE.

YOU ask me to give you the most extraordinary case of adjustment in my experience. I will do so, but it will prove disappointing.

In all my experience during a long period of years this case stands by itself; nothing like it has come under my observation.

In the winter of '85 a loss occurred of which I received notice, and as quickly as circumstances would permit I went to the spot, arriving four or five days after the fire. No sooner had I registered at the hotel than a clean, fresh-shaved, gentlemanly-looking man of middle age introduced himself as John Butler, of the firm of Butler Bros., the assured. With great good nature and perfect composure he awaited my convenience, answering questions quickly and pertinently meanwhile. He agreed to follow all my directions, and was so very willing that I mistrusted him from the first.

He conducted me to a building to which his stock had been removed and introduced his brother James, who, if possible, was more smooth and plausible than John. As I glanced along the shelves and over the counters my eyes took in hastily a well-assorted stock of dry goods neatly arranged, and to all appearances fresh and clean. "What is your claim," I asked. "A trifle over twelve hundred dollars," was the reply. I said nothing, but thought, "You will have a sweet time with this precious pair before you are done." Mechanically I went through the usual words demanding an appraisement, at the same time mentally calculating the expense of bringing my appraiser from home. "Will you look at this inventory," said James. "We have just finished it; John and I hardly knew what to do, but concluded to go ahead as if we had no insurance. We have taken account of stock and placed our assessment of damage in this column here; the woolens, white goods, silks and what not are classed by themselves; suppose you examine a piece here and there and see how it strikes you." Eyeing him sharply I complied; we went from place to place according to my direction. Every measurement came out to a fraction. With most of the pieces I found about a yard cut off; this was the outside wrap which was damaged by heat and smoke. I was puzzled and my wits were hard at work I can tell you. "Suppose we visit the seat of the fire," I said. The fire started in a building next door to my claimants in the second story. On entering, the usual odor greeted my nose; here was a scene of ruin and confusion, boxes and cartons blackened and broken, wet ceiling and sloppy floor. "Did you get everything out," I asked. "Yes," said James, "we did, and a hard time we had. We worked all night long the first night, and I thought John would be on the sick list sure."

With a gleam of sense penetrating my foggy brain I asked for their books of account. "Check, tally, check, tally," everything ship shape and in good order. "See here," I said desperately, "can you make an affidavit that your loss is twelve hundred dollars?" "Well, no," said James, "John has just reminded me that our cost mark is loaded ten per cent. We will have to make allowance for that." I looked at him helplessly—all at once I took in the situation. All at once I saw the whole thing as clear as day.

The men were honest; now I was on the right track, and I followed it up carefully and proved that I was right. We had no appraisers from home that trip; we had no appraisers at all. It is the only case of the kind I ever met.

In an interior New York town, the local agent of a fire insurance company is stone blind, and has been so for years, while some of the officers to whom he reports are not aware of his loss of sight. (Exchange.)

"Here's a state of things." It is an even bet that this man knows more about a hazard and sends in a better description of property than the average agent.

He gets his information of a risk from his young son, and gives it more thought than if his eyes were open.

At the same time, what kind of an outfit is a company having this agent for years and never sending a special to find out how blind he is?

A certain manager, whom we will call Mr. X, not because he is, but because we wish him to be unknown, dropped into his agent's office in a town in the Northwest. The agent said: "Mr. X, I wish you would look at that veneered brick building down there and tell me what line you want on it?" So away posted X, and soon returned with the reply that he had tried the bricks with his knife and really could not see any difference between *veneered bricks* and any other, so would carry as heavy a line on that building as on any in town.

OLD JOE BROWN.

HAVING on a recent trip occasion to use a team, and thinking to secure a premium, I asked the stable man if he was insured. His urbane and deferential manner changed at once. "No," he savagely said, "I'm not insured, and what's more, I never will take out a policy on my barn again." He was a subject for me and the following story is the result:

"Did you see that blackened ruin as you came into town?" said the stable man. "That used to be my barn. When the hotel caught fire it set my barn off. It was a good, substantial building, put up in the solid, old-fashioned way, and I kept it painted and repaired so that it looked every bit as well as this stable we are in now. Well, I had a policy of five thousand dollars on the building and I felt pretty good, for we had a chance at the fire to run out all the stock and most of the wagons.

"In a day or two, along came an adjuster, a nice, pleasant fellow, very kind and sympathetic, and as full of talk as a political speaker. 'Now,' he said, 'what you want to do is to pick out the best carpenter in town. I will get another, and whatever these two men agree is the cash value of the building, you and I will stand by.'

"Nothing could be fairer than that, so I picked out old Joe Brown and the adjuster brought in a mild-spoken stranger, and we signed papers and swore before a notary, until all hands were tied up as tight as a bottle with the cork in.

"The adjuster and I agreed to keep away from the appraisers and let them work out the figures. It took a good deal longer than I expected; so when the adjuster said it was 10 o'clock and about his bed time, I decided to turn in, too, and get the figures in the morning. I had a room at the hotel, and it so happened the mild-spoken stranger had the room adjoining, and he and Joe Brown were working there. After I had gone to bed I heard them talking. There was an old stovepipe hole in the partition and every word was plain and clear. They were as friendly as kittens, and Joe seemed to have things all his own way. So finally they footed it all up, and it came to a little over six thousand dollars—no dispute, all fair and square, and Joe was about to fill up the papers, when the mild-spoken stranger said, 'Now, we have to deduct the depreciation.' 'O, yes,' said Joe. 'I quite forgot the depreciation.' 'Ah,' said the stranger, 'it is easy to see you have had great experience in appraising losses. I noticed all along your adaptability.' 'Well,' said Joe in a pleased voice, 'I have had more or less to do with making up figures on losses, but mostly with men who would steal the coppers off a dead man's eyes. Now, you are as fair a figurer as I ever saw in my life.'

The stranger gave a little cough and he said, 'Well, that is my reputation, and I try to live up to it. By the way, have you your Tiffany with you?' 'How is that?' said Joe. 'You see,' said the stranger, talking right along and paying no attention to what Joe said, 'in this matter of depreciation, Tiffany of New York is recognized as authority by all of us expert builders and contractors.' 'Oh, yes,' said Joe, 'yes indeed, he is so.' 'Tiffany,' continued the stranger, 'has devoted the best part of a well-spent life to the study of depreciation. As you know, he has it down to the fraction of a hair, and when Tiffany says a thing, it is recognized as a fixed rule.'

"'So much so,' said Joe, breaking in, 'that I would just bet my life on Tiffany being right every time.'

"'Let me see,' said the stranger, 'I have mislaid my copy; do you happen to have Tiffany's book with you?'

"'Well, no, not here,' said Joe, 'I always keep a copy at the shop, and one over at the house.'

"Here the stranger had a coughing spell that nearly took his head off. When he got his breath he went over to the adjuster's room after the book. If it had not been for my agreement to keep away I would have told Joe right there to hurry up and give me a chance to go to sleep.

"The stranger soon came back with the book, then he rustled around among the papers, and finally he said, 'Where is that paper that tells how old the building is?'

"'Here it is,' said Joe Brown; 'that building was put up in the fall of 1870; that makes it—let me see, seventy—eighty—ninety—that makes it just twenty years old.' 'Why, so it does,' said the stranger, as innocent as a child. 'Just look here, Brown, and see if the depreciation is as much on a barn as on a dwelling.'

"Joe took the book and shuffled over the leaves for some time, while the stranger was writing, then he said something about his eyes troubling him at night, and gave the book back.

"'Ah,' said the stranger, 'that is the only thing I have against Tiffany. He will print his book with such fine type. He ought to give a magnifying glass with each copy. By the way, is your copy like mine?'

"'Just exactly the same,' said Joe Brown hastily.

"'Let me see,' said the stranger. 'Depreciation—depreciation—ah, here it is on page 389. I will read it: 'Frame, livery, hotel, sale and boarding stables depreciate annually 4 per cent.''

"'Does it say 4 per cent.?' said Brown.

"'Yes. Here, see for yourself; and on page 384 it says: 'It should be remembered that all percentages on buildings are based on the actual life of the building, while any repairs, such as painting, renewing the roof, siding or flooring, should be credited to the building, and the per cent. of depreciation reduced to correspond, for the reason that the building to the extent of the repairs has been renewed.' That is clear enough, don't you think?'

"'Well, yes,' said old Brown, sort of hesitatingly, 'that seems clear.'

"'Well, now,' continued the other, 'in this case the question is, has he kept up the repairs?'

"'Yes,' said Joe, 'he has. The barn was in first-class condition.'

"'That being the case,' went on the stranger, 'we are safe in allowing one per cent. a year, which leaves three per cent. depreciation per annum, or for twenty years sixty per cent. I am disposed to be liberal in this, as I have heretofore been, all the way through. Say we call it fifty per cent. and give the poor man the benefit of the doubt.'

"'That seems very fair, indeed,' said old Joe Brown.

"While they were talking, it seemed to me everything was going my way, but when they stopped talking and went to writing, I commenced figuring up in my mind. I am not very quick at figures, so about the time they went out together, I had found that my five-thousand-dollar policy was worth about three thousand dollars. I jumped up and dressed mighty quick and went hunting for Joe. Pretty soon I met the mild-spoken stranger.

"'Hello,' said he, 'how are you? Your appraiser has just gone home. We have fixed up our papers and have been down to the notary public's office. They are all sworn to and I shall be off by the next train. Why, what's the matter with you?' he said. 'Don't you feel well?'

"'No,' said I, 'I am sick.'

"The next day we went over the whole ground and I signed their papers. I tell you I was afraid if I waited a day or two they would bring me out in debt. After it was over I tackled old Brown. When he got as far along as quoting Tiffany, I just snorted. 'Darn your fool skin, Joe Brown,' said I, 'you never knew there was such a man as Tiffany in the world till that doggoned stranger came here. Don't you know, you old mud-turtle, that Tiffany is a big jeweler and never saw a jack plane in his life?' And all old Joe Brown said was, 'I want to know.'"

"No," said the parson, "we will not have our church building insured. Such an act would, in my humble mind, show a disposition to fly in the face of Providence. We can trust God to look out for His own temple."

"Well," said the timid solicitor, "you may be willing to trust Him on the fire hazard, but I see you are afraid of Him on the lightning question," and he pointed to the nickel-plated rods on the church spire.

AS OTHERS SEE US.

THERE were a number of adjusters located at the "Golden Eagle" at Sacramento one time. It was not so much of a loss, nor were there suspicious circumstances; two men could have completed the adjustment in one day, but the officers in San Francisco could not seem to agree, and each company had a representative of some sort on the ground, ranging from office boy to manager; what between "committee work" and individual opinion the assured was in a highly nervous state.

While the committee meeting was in session I walked out to that part of the town near which the loss occurred, taking the assured with me. He was a Southerner and had put his darkey boy Sam in charge of the place as watchman. Sam had followed the colonel and shared his fortune since away back in slavery days. He was a typical plantation hand and always spoke of himself as a "nigger." After inspecting the ruins and just as we turned to leave, the colonel said, "By the way, Sam, have you seen any of those underwriters about here?" "No, sar; no, sar," said Sam, "haben't seen 'em, sar; spec its too late in the spring for 'em, sar." We smiled, and the colonel said, "Why, you rascal, you don't know an underwriter when you see him?"

"Oh yes, sar, I know 'em." "Well, what is an underwriter," said the colonel with mock severity.

Sam looked scared; he began to lose confidence in his own knowledge. Big beads of perspiration stood on his brow, he rolled his eyes rapidly and breathed hard. "I can't jest call his name," said he, "but he's an animal, sar; he's an animal, an' he lib in the watah, an' he dig, an' he dig, an' he dig, an' he burrow, an' he burrow, an' he burrow, an' bimeby the watah git in whar he been, an' the levee break; oh, yes, sar, I see plenty in Louisiana; he bad thing to hab 'round, sar."

"I begin to think so," said the colonel musingly, as we strolled back to meet the band of the faithful quartered at the "Golden Eagle."

QUERIES.

Q. What is a general agent?

A. A general agent is one who combines theory and practice; the theory is for the home office, the practice for the country agents.

Q.   What is a "local secretary?"

A.   A conundrum which, although no one can guess, is not given up.

Q.   What is a special agent?

A.   One who makes or mars the business of a department, but who shares only in the reverses of the department.

Q.   What is a local agent?

A.   He who sells premiums to the general agent.

Q.   What is a broker?

A.   A broker is the person who eats his *pie and still has it.*

Q.   What is a *Knapsack?*

A.   An annual publication in which appears the dullest thoughts of the "brightest minds in the profession."

Q.   What is salvage?

A.   A term used in marine insurance, sometimes improperly used in fire insurance, in which event it is that part for which a company has paid a total loss but which is subsequently dug out of the ruins and sold by the assured, for the benefit of the assured, without publicity.

Q.   What is the future of fire insurance?

A.   Ask me something else partner. I have been in the business twenty-five years, and I don't know.

WHAT is the moral hazard?

"This," writes a new agent, "is an unusual question to me; I do not understand it. If you mean Mrs. Jane Doe, the assured, she is O. K."

Another, where a Methodist church building was the risk, answered the same question as follows:

"My wife is a member of this church," but he did not say what the moral hazard might be.

1ST OREGON CITIZEN—I thought you told me the adjuster who came down here was one of the right kind.

2d Oregon Citizen—So I understood; what is there wrong with him?

1st Oregon Citizen—He called me a thief and a liar and an incendiary, and every hard word he could lay his tongue to.

2d Oregon Citizen—Why don't you have the law on him?

1st Oregon Citizen—Because he can prove it.

THE following is taken from the page of a ledger, recently used in the adjustment of a drug store loss at a remote village.

The spelling is laughable, but the real humor of the thing is grim enough. He who runs can read the lesson therein contained. Don't monkey with drugs.

```
April 28.   Hals Basom...................................$1 00
    "   30.  Wizerd Oil.................................. 1 00
May   1.    Hales Hot Tar...............................   50
    "   2.   Spung......................................   15
            Asid Phosfat...............................   50
            syrip Figes................................ 1 00
        3.  Citrat Magnica.............................   25
            Coton and Linament.........................   25
            Gargel.....................................   25
        4.  Asavitedy..................................   50
            Scitlitz Powers............................   25
            Tetegrof for doctor........................   25
May   5.    Perscripshun............................... 1 00
            Syring..................................... 1 25
            Perscripshun...............................   50
            Bed pan....................................   75
        6.  Perscripshun............................... 1 50
        7.   do   "                     ................ 1 00
                                                        ______
                                                        11 90
May   8.    DED.
```

TO¡TAKE EFFECT AT ONCE.

There is a stringent regulation of the P. I. U.—
　　And I'd like to see it take effect at once ;
That rebates shall not be made, to the many or the few—
　　And I'd like to see it take effect at once.
It's as grand a prohibition as anyone could frame,
　　And those who fail to heed it are very much to blame,
Who breaks this righteous rule should feel the blush of shame—
　　And I'd like to see it take effect at once.

There's another resolution that really should be passed—
　　And I'd like to see it take effect at once ;
It's fully as important as the one I spoke of last—
　　And I'd like to see it take effect at once.

Let all policies be canceled if not paid in sixty days,
  And withdraw those useful papers from their anxious owners' gaze—
This vote should be unanimous without the usual nays—
  And I'd like to see it take effect at once.

And now to be consistent let me name another plan—
  And I'd like to see it take effect at once;
It's as fair for each one of you as for any other man—
  And I'd like to see it take effect at once.
When your losses are adjusted and ready to be paid,
  Either cash should be forthcoming or a certain limit made;
Uniformity of action on a basis that's well weighed—
  And I'd like to see it take effect at once.

There's a sensible decision that the managers could make—
  And I'd like to see it take effect at once;
This concerns the special agent—it is only for his sake—
  And I'd like to see it take effect at once.
Give that useful creature rest when he comes into the city;
  Don't worry him with work, but have a little pity;
Don't make his trips so long but heed this warning ditty—
  And I'd like to see it take effect at once.

In closing let me now propose a comprehensive toast—
  And I'd like to see it take effect at once;
It's aim is somewhat scattering for it covers the whole coast—
  And I'd like to see it take effect at once.
Here's to one who in this business swings the balance of all power;
  Who wrestles with his customers and with ratings hour by hour;
The local! may sound judgment be his everlasting dower—
  And I'd like to see it take effect at once.

NILES.

EDITORIAL, 1892.   GEO. F. GRANT.

EDITORIAL.

AS a matter of course, the editorial of the *Knapsack* is intended as a moral and philosophical guide, but a guide to the young only. This is so for two reasons, the first being that the simple fact of my having lived for more years than the boy pupil gives the advantage of an experience which he cannot claim; hence, he takes my advice believing it to be wisdom, and has faith that my deductions are sound; secondly, my elders—bless their intellectual bodies—have no use for advice in their business. Now, in this edition of the *Knapsack,* it will be my object to warn my young friends against a common condition of mind, which, unchecked or unrestrained, leads on to a disagreeable habit of thought, and in time may develop the "Fuddydud." A "Fuddydud," as I know him, is a man who shares an opinion with himself but with no other person; still he is quite willing that everybody should know what his opinion· is. As there are no female "Fuddyduds," there is no propagation of the species. He is not confined to any trade, profession or calling, and his presence among underwriters is merely incidental. Although, according to holy writ, "A fool is known by his folly," a young fool often escapes notice; so with the "Fuddydud"; he is not ripe as a rule before the noontide of life. The signs whereby you shall know him vary, and I will cite but one or two for purposes of recognition. At a meeting of importance called to consider some matter of mutual interest, at a critical crisis he will speak to the "question" at some length and get the eye of the chair at least three times; thus he can ring the changes on his individual opinions without stint, and he contrives to lend a humorous turn to affairs by a pun or a joke, which was jolly before it had the grippe. The "Fuddydud" always attempts to wear what is known as "a merry twinkle of the eye," but which is more likely to be, as Hamlet says, "a fitful havior of the visage." He is profound on subjects where personal experiences are allowed, but dumb and silent when quick wit and decisive action are most needed. There are moments, however, when he shines, and that is when he is acting as a peacemaker; but, my young friends, the fact remains, that you can be a peacemaker without being a "Fuddydud."

There are a great many good people who do not know a "Fuddydud" when they meet one, and they misjudge him, classing him in their minds as a self-opinionated ass or an egotistical bore, or some such common place type, which is wrong and really an injustice to the "Fuddydud," who is of a different species and a higher family. One pleasant feature of the case is that oftentimes those who knew him well before he contracted the habit are blind to his "fuddydudism," and see him only as they used to know him in the golden past, when his large heart and broad views gave joy and satisfaction to no end of friends. My object, my dear young friends, is to warn you while there is time, just as I would advise you to be grammatical in your speech, because it is the habit of good society, or because it saves you a burning blush of shame-faced confusion, as is the case when your honest-hearted girl corrects your English. There is one kind of "Fuddydud," however, with whom I have no patience; he is the bold, aggressive bulldozer, who, knowing of his "fuddydud" habit, still jams it down your throat, so to speak, in order to see you wriggle, just as little boys cut angle worms in two. But after all, dear friend, if you are growing into that kind of a man, it matters little what the *Knapsack* thinks or has to say on the subject; a spade is a spade and a brute is a brute the world over. I have been told that the most offensive kind of a "Fuddydud" is one who edits a paper. I have had so little experience in such business that I do not know, but, really, I hope it is not true.

The following letter from a Chicago special will prove spicy reading. He adjusted losses in a camp for several companies, some of whose agents report East and some West:

Dear Sir: Many thanks for your letter of introduction. This is a great place and a great people. The first day of my arrival I was presented to ten citizens, classified as follows: Three generals, four colonels, two captains, one private.

I hardly liked to ask these officers where they won their straps, but I learned incidentally that one of the generals got his title from the fact that he was "general freight agent" of the P. I. & Z. Railroad, and that all of the colonels were from Kentucky. This seems to account for the "C. J. Society," of which I soon became a member by acclamation. The only qualification necessary to join the "Corn Juice Society" is the ability to take seven drinks between lunch and dinner.

The one private mentioned is your agent, who seems to have tactics at his fingers' ends. With his assistance I was enabled to adjust the loss with satisfaction to all concerned.

CIMEX LECTULARIOUS.

THE time has come to give to the *Knapsack* the story of my encounter with the *cimex lectularious*. It is true I had met him in a
more or less familiar way here and there, but until now I had
failed to be impressed by him, and had never felt a sensation of fear in
his presence. The other incidents of the trip (for of course it was a
special trip) were sufficiently varied and startling, but the whole would
have been tame and soon forgotten but for the *cimex lectularious*. It
was just at the end of summer. There was but one train each day to and
from Los Angeles, and by the time-card one could plainly see that from
Modesto to Tulare the arrivals and departures were at unseasonable
hours. A stay of twenty-four hours in each town and broken rest every
night is enough to rasp the nerve and spoil the temper of the best-natured
man in the business. Such was my trip and it was five o'clock one
morning when I reached Visalia, too early for breakfast and too late to
go to bed, which I would have liked well enough, for I had dozed against
a stiff-backed day coach since two o'clock. It is plain to me now that I
had no more sense than to wear myself out voluntarily; and I was yet
too new in the work to secure a good room immediately on arrival.
During the day the usual inspection, adulation and devotion served to
keep things going at a lively pace; but after supper nothing but thoughts
of bedtime and slumber were in my mind. I paid little attention to the
landlord's words of apology, "the last room in the house, grangers' convention in town, do better to-morrow," and all the rest of it. The room
had a bed and a window; that was enough; then again there was a
mosquito netting like a huge tent over my couch,—the better for undisturbed sleep I thought. I did not even growl at the half inch of candle.
What matter? I only wanted it long enough to strip off my day clothes.
Oh, the delight of that half-minute of wakeful bliss just before your eyes
close for the last time and your limbs stretch out in a cool new spot,
restful and free.

How long I slept I can't say,—perhaps two hours,—when of a sudden I was wide, staring awake; no noise, not a sound, save a distant
clock with a giddy, rapid tick, and yet I was alarmed, mentally disturbed.
What was it? I felt "creepy," as the girls say; before I knew it I was
out on the floor with the candle lighted. I looked out of the window;
nothing to be seen but bright moonlight and black shadow. Uncertain,
yet firmly, I inspected the bed. Horrors! What a sight! It was given
over body and bolster to the *cimex lectularious*. He climbed the can-
opy in numbers. He was marshaled in company front on the pillow-
case, and performed military maneuvers on the counterpane. Hundreds,

yes, there were thousands of them, every one of them at home and receiving visitors.   To gather up my clothes and shake them carefully in
the hall was the work of a moment.   Descending, I found a knot of owl-
like grangers talking mule.   If there is an unprofitable subject outside
a race-track it is horse talk.   With some irritation I took a seat under
the porch with my back against a post and my feet in a chair.   I slept
like a top until all at once my feet dropped with a dull thud ; and the
voice of the clerk, he who had pulled away the chair, said something
about "time to lock up."   For a few moments the resounding air was
alive with my burning words, until the clerk, who was not more than
half full, realized that it was a sober man who talked so earnestly.   With
something of an apology he yielded the chair and locked me out of the
hotel.   As the sound of his receding footsteps died away I was once
more asleep.   The exact hour of my next awaking is unknown, but in a
bewildered and helpless way I was conscious of much light without the
power to distinguish objects.   While engaged in a futile endeavor to
drive something from in front of my eyes I heard a deep voice growling
out a demand to know what I did there.   In time I beheld a person with
a bull's-eye lantern.   He proved to be the night-watch ; in fact the entire
police force stood before me.   He was uniformed in an Iverness cloak,
slouch hat and carpet slippers, and was armed with a crooked-necked
cane.   I rose and requested the department to be seated while I related
my story.   When I told the experience with the *cimex lectularious* he
was convulsed with laughter, and made such an outrageous noise that I
was obliged to arrest him ; but soon he departed on his own recogni-
zance in order that he might finish his beat.   From time to time he returned, and each time woke me up to inquire how I was getting on now.
On these occasions he swept my feet off the chair quite easily and seated
himself for a chat.

I was dreamily comparing him in my sleepy mind with the hero in
the play called "Nick of the Woods."   This hero held the stage during
most of the performance, and moved about with a step which was often
referred to as "soft as a panther's tread."   While I was groping for information which would explain why the Jibernanessy should carry a dark
lantern I became once more conscious.   This time my friend had chosen
to seat himself without removing my feet, and while I struggled to recover them I talked some plain American language to more fully illus-
trate what I thought.   Imagine my surprise when a cheerful but strange
voice replied in pretty much the same strain as the form of my own address.   This voice gave evidence of indulgence in strong liquor ; and I
was not much surprised when an invitation to go and take a drink followed.   In order to gain time I engaged the last arrival in conversation,

and soon learned more of his past, present and anticipated future than often falls to the lot of a mere chance acquaintance. After parrying the invitation to drink several times, my companion, after fumbling in his clothes, brought out a bright, shining six-shooter, which he held in a wavering, uncertain grasp, at the same time saying in a decided tone, "My young friend, you come along with me and drink." "Why, certainly," I answered, springing to my feet, "which way?" "This way," he answered, pointing his weapon over the face of the country. Grabbing him on the off side of his pistol arm I helped him over to the groggery, which fortunataly was closed.

He was quite indignant that the bar-keeper should dare to lock up the place, and commenced to get ugly. Acting on a thought I suggested that he should go to the bar-keeper's house while I remained to keep guard over the saloon. After considering this proposal with solemn gravity he decided not only to perform his part, but to awaken the sleeper by a shot from his pistol. No sooner was he out of sight than I was back in my chair, again asleep. When next I awoke it was from a shake given by the night-watchman. "Did you hear that shot?" said he. "Come along, there is murder going on." As he sped away, his cloak flapping in the breeze he made, he looked not unlike one of Dore's birds of ill-omen. I never saw him again, for at this moment the long whistle announced the approach of the train.   Gray dawn had come; the hotel clerk reappeared, and mechanically carried my chairs indoors; the 'bus rattled up to the depot and rattled back again with nothing but a mail sack for its pains; the night had passed; a day had dawned.

When the livery stable man came down to the barn I was waiting with my grip. He drove me over to Tulare, and talked all the time. I could not even get a nod. At that time the crowning glory of Tulare was the Railroad Hotel, owned and run by the Southern Pacific people; it was clean and wholesome. If I remember aright I went to bed at 10:30 in the forenoon, and never gave a sign of life until breakfast time the next day. Twenty years of travel has never given me such a shock as that encounter with the *cimex lectularious*.

A NEW agent always wants to write policies; of course I mean an agent new to the insurance business. One of this kind sent in his maiden effort with a pat-on-the-back sort of a letter with it. His "daily" read as follows:

"One thousand dollars on household and kitchen furniture, bedding and such other articles as are contained in a family." In reply I asked him if this was intended to cover breakfast or lunch.

TEXAS is full of small general agents, many of whom do their special work by mail. I know of one of said general agents who made a certain appointment by letter. Not hearing from the new agent in six months he proceeded to take the train to look up his supplies. Arriving in the town he made inquiries for Mr. So-and-So, and found that the gentleman had sold out four months before, and had gone away. After some difficulty he found the purchaser of the business, and made inquiries for his supplies.

"Don't know anything about any supplies. I bought Mr. Blank's real estate business, and he threw in some old insurance blanks, which I burned up."

"But surely you didn't burn them all up. How about the policy blanks and my register,—a book, a good big book, about that long?"

"Oh, let me see. I think there was some kind of a book marked 'register' on the outside. I took *that* over to the hotel and sold it for one dollar."

Repairing to the hotel our general agent found his "book" being used as a hotel register, with six pages of arrivals already "in force."

THE cupidity of the average loan company is admirably distanced in the case of a Utah farmer, who recites that the agent agreed to give him $1,000 insurance for fifty-three dollars. But when he received the policy he found, much to his disgust, that it indemnified him to the extent of $1,500. He writes, "This wasn't your agent's agreement, and if you don't fix it right I won't keep your policy. If that's the way you do your business I don't want anything more to do with you." And who questions the moral hazard of Utah? It might be well to add in explanation that the premium paid was for $1,500 insurance, and that the company, with characteristic exactness, rectified the error.

C. P. FARNFIELD.

Far away on the desert, where Arizona's shimmering sands are tinted by the sunset to a lurid hue; where Yuma's burning plains stretch far beyond the horizon; where the sullen Colorado rolls,—there died our friend, alone. No mother's words of comfort, no sweetheart's soothing touch, were there; but in solitude and in silence he passed over the Dark River to the Unknown Land. The dismal hum of the wires was his only requiem, while the winds of the desert moaned and moaned, as if for our departed friend.

Farewell, Farnfield! May the light of your generous nature illumine your path to the Great Beyond.

CLINCH THINGS!

There 's a motto a manager once gave to me,
A man full of brains you can readily see.
Experience and knowledge in him are combined,
A man of broad views and talent of mind,
Successful in business, ranking high in this State.
He said to me once, "Put this thing on your slate;
Should you wish fame to acquire, success to attain,
    Clinch things.

"If in business transaction a point should arise
Which might be constructed ambiguous-wise,
And you may be enabled to fully define
The point at once clearly, and bring it in line,
Yield not to the impulse and matters delay,
But define your point then, for that is the way
    To clinch things.

"Should an agent default, and you're sent to the scene,
And he meets you with face all smiling serene,
Let him know you are there for justice and right,
And keep him in hand by day and by night,
Till success you've obtained and your money 's secure;
'Tis the only true way the evil to cure;
    Clinch things.

"Should a loss have occurred, and you're sent to adjust,
Don 't look on all claimants with eyes of distrust,
But keep them wide open; with your ears do the same;
Then if things are crooked you'll drop on the game;
Perpetuate testimony, examine the facts,
And success should attend every one of your acts;
    Clinch things.

"Put not off till to-morrow what you should do to-day,
Is an excellent motto and well in its way;
For things once deferred may ere long disappear,
Which makes it more urgent, and the motto is clear;
Delays are oft dangerous, let promptness prevail,
And never admit there 's such word as fail;
    Clinch things."

OH, WHAT A DIFFERENCE IN THE MORNING!

Parody on a selection from the comic opera of Sinbad, Sung-bad, by
E. W. Carpenter, at the banquet of the Fire Underwriters' Association of
the Pacific, at the California Hotel, San Francisco, Cal.

FEB. 17TH "AT NIGHT" AND 18TH "IN THE MORNING" 1892.

The day being done, what queer changes appear
    At night, at night!
We seem to inhabit a different sphere
    At night, at night!
The manager sweetly takes guests to a show,
To a party with "wifey" will placidly go,
Or mayhap to church, humbly bowing quite low,
    At night, at night!
  But oh, what a difference in the morning!
  Vexations overwhelm him at the dawning.
  They come by mail and wire,
  His temper is on fire,
  He's not a "B-class" angel in the morning.

In "Bluelands" a rogue "cooks" his books to a turn,
    At night, at night!
Is caught setting fire to the store he would burn,
    At night, at night!
The judge to the jury makes guilt very clear,
And then locks them up until dawn shall appear;
Adjusters feel certain of verdict severe,
    At night, at night!
  But oh, what a difference in the morning!
  Then comes acquittal with the dawning.
  "Corporations without soul
  Will always hunt some hole
  To crawl through," say the jury in the morning!

The homeward bound special strikes Lathrop so drear,
    At night, at night!
Returning to 'Frisco, his last stop is here,
    At night, at night!
His wife and his babies to-morrow he'll see,
And stay long at home on some sort of a plea,

He's dreaming he feels the cool breeze of the sea,
>> At night, at night!
But oh, what a difference in the morning!
He's paralyzed by lightning at the dawning.
The head office briefly wire:
"Another general fire.
Start promptly for Miles City in the morning!"

Now Armstrong "*selected*" a company rare,
>> At night, at night!
Who "*inspected*" Delmonico's choice bill of fare,
>> At night, at night!
"He'd '*protected*' himself by insurance discreet."
Such news to the guests was a morsel most sweet,
To be rid of the "trio" seemed to ev'ry one meet (meat),
>> At night, at night!
But oh, what a difference in the morning!
That "trio" woke up crowing at the dawning.
With their systems purged of all,
Save their charters and their "gall,"
They resumed the same old "lay" again next morning!

Each year at this dinner we're jolliest friends,
>> At night, at night!
We resolve to be good, for the past make amends,
>> At night, at night!
We praise beyond measure the business we're in,
Pledging honor and friendship 'mid wineglasses' din,
Extolling our calling so guiltless of sin,
>> At night, at night!
But oh, what a difference in the morning!
Love and faith seem blinded by the dawning.
With tricks resembling lies,
And crimes of greater size,
We charge each "other fellow" in the morning.

CALLING on a good friend at the office where he holds a responsible yet modest position, I found his name posted on his desk with the letters "G. A." added. "Why, Charlie," said I, "are you a general agent?" In answer he led me to the front, where an electric indicator with a dozen buttons gave the names of various clerks. Said he, "the buttons gave out, so when I am wanted they sound a general alarm, 'G. A.,' see?"

THE BOGIE MAN.

Come all ye little managers and listen unto me,
A creature somewhat strange has come a sailing o'er the sea ;
One like him you have seldom seen since first your lives began ;
No wonder when you gaze on him you call him " Bogie Man."

> Hush, hush, hush !
> Here comes the Bogie Man ;
> You'd best lie low,
> You stand no show
> Before the Bogie Man.

He has the power to crush you all and make you quake with fear ;
He has the calm and steady stare that makes you feel so queer ;
He has taken in Macdonald, James and Carpenter as well,
And has some others on the slate the British ranks to swell.

> Hush, hush, hush !
> Here comes the Bogie Man ;
> You'll have no show,
> You'd better go,
> He'll bounce you if he can.

He has some blooded backers who give the business tone,
And when he plays at any game the counters are his own ;
He represents more sterling wealth than any others can ;
No wonder that you all bow down before the Bogie Man.

> Hush, hush, hush !
> Here comes the Bogie Man ;
> Your cake's all dough,
> You're doomed to woe,
> He'll catch you if he can.

The locals tremble when he speaks, and wither 'neath his frown,
While the clerks all start side whiskers to help the British Crown ;
And no one has sufficient nerve to even mutter " Damn !
You cannot crush my spirit with a foreign Bogie Man."

> Hush, hush, hush !
> Here comes the Bogie Man ;
> You'd better run,
> He'll spoil your fun,
> And cinch you if he can.

At the time of The Dalles fire last September our office was on the *qui vive* for definite information regarding the boundary of the burned district. The newspapers (as sometimes happens) gave the names of all the sufferers, with a full account of "lurid flames" and "forked tongues," but was silent on the subject of boundary lines. The local agent, with wisdom acquired from books, rushed to the telegraph office and was delivered of a message something like this, "Town burned down; send adjuster at once." Hours went by, but no one knew the limit of the fire; so we decided to wire the local agent as follows: "Please give numbers of blocks burned." With something of pride we answered the questions of our neighbors by saying we had sent for full information, and would soon be able to impart definite particulars. The reply message came; we could hardly wait to tear it open; it read as follows: "Blocks to the number of *eighteen* burned."

TEN LITTLE SPECIALS.

Ten little specials, all in a line,
One cut a rate and then there were nine.

Nine little specials hunting a rebate,
One of 'em found it and then there were eight.

Eight little specials, hardly fit for Heaven,
One got full and then there were seven.

Seven little specials up to all the tricks,
One became expensive and then there six.

Six little specials, all of them alive,
One "sassed" the manager and then there were five.

Five little specials hoping to get more,
One broke the compact and then there were four.

Four little specials from office work quite free,
One asked for a raise and then there were three.

Three little specials, and all rather new,
One played poker and then there were two.

Two little specials eager for fun,
One paid a total loss and then there was one.

One little special whose work was well done,
He became manager and then there was none.

AN ACTIVE agent in the San Joaquin valley having had a number of policies returned to his company by an agent of a competing company in a German colony, visited the locality to learn the cause. The cause was a German agent. The active agent called on his customers and found them in possession of the policies of an aggressive, well-managed company, whose policies are adorned with the head of a celebrated but very ugly "chieftain." This gave a cue to the active agent to work on, and taking a recent importation from Europe aside said to him, pointing to the picture, "That is the photograph of the president of that company. How would you like to have him settle your loss?" The reply was, "Mein Gott, I no vants to settle mit dat kind of a mans," and immediately gave up that policy and took the active agent's policy. Others did likewise, and in a short time a truce was had and an agreement made between the agents to respect each other's contracts.

IT WAS a sight to see the *Monitor* man eat crow pie. After sitting on the fence and holding up the pie labeled, "best pigeon pie," and after being sassy to the little boys who had no pie at all, suddenly he realized he had to eat it; he never changed a muscle, but gulped it down. This was when Lowden got back at him for his criticism of the paper on "Manufacturers' Profits," read by the President at our last annual meeting.

The ruling passion is strong in death; and the *Monitor* man raised his hat to Lowden, and said, "We have always advocated your theory; in fact, the senior editor of this paper converted George Washington's grandfather to the same thing."

THE SPECIAL'S WAIL.

An active special who had been engaged in various lines of work before joining the Grip Brigade says that when a young man he wanted to be a fireman on a railroad locomotive, as he had observed that when the train came in or went out the fireman did nothing but "ring the bell." He got the position, but his experience was that he had to get down out of sight in front of the furnace and shovel coal between stations. He tired of this position, and became a local agent. Here again he noticed that the special agent seemed to do nothing but "ring the bell" when in town, and his ambition was only satisfied when he secured a place as special; but here again he found that in the work of a successful special there is more coal-shoveling than bell-ringing.

A SUPERANNUATED old adjuster, who smiles when he is called the "old man," says, "When I am assigned a room at a hotel I look at the register to see if my room was occupied by a lady guest the night before."

"Then if it was, you of course take it," chimes in a young special.

"On the contrary, no."

"Why not?"

"Because I don't like to be taken for the man who is always 'a day after the fair,'" says Graybeard, with a twinkle in his left optic.

(Memorandum by the editor.) "Not a sound was heard, nor a funeral note, as his corse to the ramparts we hurried."

TELL me, ye winged winds, that daily
    Round me roar,
Is there a spot where adjusters are no more?
Some pleasant, fire-proof place,
    From oxygen quite free;
Where flames are never known
    And smoke they never see?

The wild winds dwindled to a whisper low
And sighed their answer as they murmured,—"Yes!
But 'tis over the river,
    In the mansions of the blest,
Where the Wetzlars cease from troubling,
    And the Treanors are at rest."

DOWN in a certain southern field a peculiar class of risks familiar to you all are known as "female boarding-houses," and take twice the rate of ordinary dwellings. I was walking about town examining our business with the agent, when we passed a comfortable two-story dwelling. Upon making inquiry why said dwelling was not covered by a policy in my company, the agent replied:

"The fact is that dwelling belongs to my widowed sister, and as she had more room than she wanted she took our two schoolmarms to board. You see the rate book says that female boarding-houses shall take double the dwelling rate; and my sister just couldn't stand it."

ANOTHER good fellow with the world all before him, after studying his book of instructions, wrote the following query: "Do I deduct my commission from the rate prescribed in the rate book, or do I charge it extra to the party insuring?" And yet almost all the officers of companies commenced life as a local agent.

SOME one has invented a smoke preventive. Will some one invent "smoke-damage" preventive, and apply it to sundry stocks of drygoods, etc.?

THE SPECIAL AND HIS GRIP.

Through the seasons, in all weather,
  In the valley's scorching heat,
In the mountains, cold storms braving,
  In the driving snow and sleet;
Where the streams in spring are booming,
  Where in fall Jack Frost may nip,
Even on the ocean raging,
  Goes the special and his grip.

Perhaps 'tis thought a risk is stolen,
  Perhaps a balance is overdue,
Or, in the push for business,
  One must seek some pastures new.
Now a loss must needs be settled,
  All which need a hurried trip,
But to these and many others
  Goes the special and his grip.

In the cars and on the stage-coach,
  Though train may wreck and horse go lame,
When others halt and cry *peccavi*,
  The special gets there just the same.
Through stormy day and stormy night,
  Midst pelting rain when all things drip.
Without his sleep, still pushing onward,
  Goes the special and his grip.

Wherever there's a human dwelling,
  No matter how remote 'twould seem,
The special in his travels makes it,
  On wheels or runners, or by steam.
'Long trails on horseback and on foot
  When death would meet him should he slip,
Where other dangers lurk about him,
  Goes the special and his grip.

Where'er he goes his friends they greet him,
  And when he leaves he's bade God speed;
When he gets home he's welcomed warmly;
  Then here's his health, long life indeed.
And as he travels all routes known,
  With cheer and smile upon his lip,
Perhaps upon the road to glory
  May go the special—and his grip.

ASHTON.

EDITORIAL, 1893.   GEO. F. GRANT.

EDITORIAL.

IS there a limit to man's desire? If so, how are we to know where it is found. The old farmer who said, "My wants are few; all I ask is the land adjoining my farm," unconsciously spoke the sentiment of ambitious mankind. Insurance men do not differ from other wide-awake, active business men; all they want is to lead in their profession, and they are actuated by two principal motives; the first, to win the enconiums of their directory; the second, to share in the profits of the corporation, and this is what makes all the trouble with the Pacific Insurance Union and kindred associations.

At the start, with every toe on the line, the compact manager has an easy time; the question of rates is quite enough for his serious consideration, the discipline which becomes necessary because of the infraction of rules is easily applied because the infringement is from misunderstanding only, but with the first published statement of figures, showing the net results of various offices, doubt and distrust disturb the minds of some members; these figures show that premiums are not equally distributed.

Ambition to lead has met with a rude shock, and in place of reflecting that leaders are necessarily few, suspicion is nursed that all is not right; failure to meet expectations is traced to seeming abuse of rules. If ability were all on a line, or if energy was the same in each case; if brains were equally distributed or opportunities evenly balanced, this of course would not be so, and this is what makes all the trouble with the members. A thinking man devises a plan whereby some rule is changed in a slight degree by some innocent looking wording accompanied by an explanatory diagram, simple and clear, but it is found after a time that the thinking man referred to has an advantage over his fellows because of some difference in the management of his particular office, and this is what makes trouble for companies. These troubles grow and magnify, because it is not "good form" to repeal a rule and go back to the old condition of things; instead, amendments are piled on amendments, ingenuity of a superior order is brought into play whereby the latest rules can be made to serve the individual, irrespective of the effect on the association as a body; committees composed of good members wrestle with the problems that arise, and the tangled web is loosened in some places and tied into knots at others; finally, the end of the skein is lost in the snarl, and as time goes on is forgotten altogether.

In spite of all this the compact manager, if he has tact and discretion, succeeds fairly well in maintaining order; moral suasion is as much a part of his diplomacy as the rules of his office, but with moral suasion he is confronted with an entirely new order of culprit—the crank—and now he must beg where once he threatened. Who shall say that the observing member, thinking to obtain from the manager what the rules deny, suddenly resolves to be a crank himself and so confusion becomes worse confounded and hints of dissolution are in the air. Members put their business houses in order for the break; the press gives the daily news and colors the insurance situation with enough spice to make it good reading; some people believe all they see in print, and so comes a nightmare of suspense.

Now what is to be done? Let us reflect. In the beginning men came together and formed this Compact Association for self protection. With fear in their hearts and with pale faces they told each other we have carried our warfare so far that ruin seems inevitable; without mutual concessions and mutual obligations we think we are lost. The concessions were made and the obligations taken; the association has hung together, say for ten years. Members of the Fire Underwriters' Association of the Pacific, what are you going to do about it? This is your affair; the compact question is your business; your influence, if properly directed, can bring order out of chaos. It is your duty to recommend going back to the starting point with each toe once more on the line.

WHEN I was a young special I was afraid as death of the "old man." Nothing I did was just right, and it was long years after I had left his office before I knew how kindly he used to speak of me when I could not hear him. Now that *I* am an "old man," I know that some youngsters must get information injected under the skin or they don't get it; but the particular story I started to give the *Knapsack* runs like this: My "old man" sent me to San Diego to adjust a loss, kindly saying as a parting shot that he expected me to make a mess of it. When I reached the ground I found the claimant stricken with apoplexy. Here was a complication, and I was at my wits' end. Reluctantly I went to the telegraph office and sent this message:

"Claimant dead. What is to be done next?"

Back came the answer,

"Bury him."

A KICK.

THE following letter was written by a Montana agent with whom I have a delightful personal acquaintance. He commenced his career in the Southern States, and after being taken prisoner by the Union side absolutely refused to take the oath of allegiance. Instead, he came West and for years personally conducted the taking of furs and hides from the wild animals of Montana, incidentally, making "good Indians," as occasion required. By nature he has the affectionate disposition of a woman. His generosity is unbounded, but he will fight at the drop of the hat if he thinks an offense is intended. How he came to engage in the insurance business I now forget, but as one who follows instructions he cannot be improved on from the office standpoint:

"SURVEYOR P. I. U.

"*Esteemed Sir:*—Yours of the 9th instant at hand. In response thereto, with reference to your suggestion that a correction should be made in the rating of 'D. R.' ——, would say that you are evidently bilious and need the advice of a physician.

"As you have suggested no particular course for me to pursue in making the correction desired, I would feel obliged if you would wire me just what is the matter with the one adopted by me.

"I feel assured that any one, not entirely blind, or a damned fool, can perceive by a close examination of accompanying diagram that the rate determined by your office *has been maintained*, and the maximum charge established. If this has been done (and it cannot be disputed), then, merely for information's sake, I would like to ask just how it concerns you, or your honorable office, if the charge is in excess of that set forth in Rate Book No. '4'?

"It occurs to me that I have simply done my part of the business correct, and that (in addition to a slight waste of postage stamps) you have made an infernal ass of yourself."

"Now please oblige me glancing over the rate under which No. —— was written:"

Basis (boarding and lodging, 15-20
     rooms) . . . . $2 25   Is that enough?
Cloth lining and stovepipe . . . 1 75   Is there anything the matter
                       with that?

Ex. (mixed) 35-40 feet   35   Is that correct?
Ex. (mixed) 40-60 feet   40   Probably that will suit you?
Ex. Chinese wash 200 feet   25   Too little, of course?
Ex. lumber yard, 80 feet   50   This fixes it.

       Total $5 50

"Now look over this matter calmly and thoughtfully, and candidly ask yourself if you do not need a little rest? How would it do to take a trip to the Arkansas Hot Springs and boil yourself out? You assuredly need relaxation of some character, but monkeying with a Montana insurance agent will neither prolong your life nor add anything to your present enjoyment of it.

"As for the ' D. R.' I return it to you with the hope that you will extend it the careful consideration I am led to believe it deserves. You are at liberty to use it, and I have no objection to your retaining it as a souvenir of of this office, if such is your desire. In any event, I am done with it.

"Referring again to your desire that a correction should be made in the rate of the risk noted, I hardly see how I can charge any more than I have done. Even if this could be done, a spirit of fair dealing to the assured prevents any interference on my part with the one presently established.

"In conclusion, I beg to observe that I believe you are getting tangled up into something that you have no concern in. Your office is a great stickler for rate, and when its desire in this particular is gratified, it should let matters over which it has no possible concern, severely alone.

"If the charge is greater than that established by your office, it concerns you not, but it does the company writing. Please remember this while being boiled out.

"I propose to always charge enough. Maybe sometimes I will not; in such event you can fall in, for it is a part of your duty to do so, and I shall not feel offended, for if I did (judging from the high-handed manner in which you have been running things), you would not give a damn.

"In conclusion, I insist upon it that you look more carefully after yourself. With your irascible temper and delicate constitution, it is a question if you will be able to survive your term of Surveyor of the Pacific Insurance Union.

"With sentiments of the highest consideration, dear sir, permit me to subscribe myself your most obedient servant."

THE fire started at the end of the block farthest from the hydrant, the hose was short, the agent reported that the firemen waited until the fire burned within reach of the hose, and then put it out—good work on the part of the fire department—but as our risk had gone up in smoke we were in no humor to advocate Book 3 for that town, merely because the fire was put out when it reached the fire department.

ASSIGNMENT OF POLICY.

The beauty of five year term business on the note installment plan is beautifully illustrated by the following letter, which, without personality I have been allowed to publish in the *Knapsack*. The incident of an assignment during the life of the policy adds to the spice of the item:

"September 30th, 1892.

"I should like to have this insurance policy canceled, as it would benefit me very little if I was burned out. In looking over the policy this evening I noticed for the first time that I have $500 on grain, and as a matter of fact there has never been a bushel of grain raised on this ranch. I had always understood that this was placed on a stallion, but even if it was it would not be of any use, as I sold the stallion two years ago.

"There is also $100 on a buggy; at present I have no buggy, as it was smashed in a runaway last spring.

"There is also $200 on furniture, while, as a matter of fact, there never was $200 worth of furniture in this house.

"Of course all of these things were given in by the former owner of this place, but I do not see exactly why I should suffer for it."

I HAVE been in the business a good many years; more than I sometimes like to contemplate. I have been under the impression all the time that I knew how to rate a simple frame range, but a newly-fledged agent opened my eyes the other day to a mistake that I have long labored under.

It was a picturesque frame range, embellished with many signs and tottering awnings, held up by posts hacked and hewed by the festive granger, in a small Rate Book No. 4 town in this State. The rate in dispute was on the end building, and I was called in to settle the matter. My decision was, basis, restaurant, $3.25, 8 exposures at 75c. Total, $9.25. "Oh, no," said the brand new agent, with a withering smile of superiority creeping o'er his fair young face, "you are wrong, entirely wrong. You don't have to charge for the eight exposures at all. The proper way to rate the building is, basis, $3.25, 4 exposures at 75c., $3.00. Total, $6.25. If you fellows from the city would only take the trouble to read your Rate Book, instead of thinking you know it all, you would find on page 31 that you are only to charge for exposures on every *other* building in the range, not on each one; so you take the basis rate, skip the first exposure, charge for No. 2, skip No. 3, charge—why—wazzer matter?" Well, its kind of you; its rather early, but still—

I THOUGHT I was going mad last week because I laughed at a joke printed in the *Post Magazine*, and it was only when I found the joke was copied from an American paper that I lost "that tired feeling," the same feeling the newspapers tell about in the medical column of the advertising page, which tired feeling is said to be a sure forerunner of death in twelve different forms, provided, you do not buy (and pay for) the antidote described in the "ad."

I subscribe and sometimes pay for various insurance papers. Others are thrust upon me by due cost of postoffice box and some are backsheesh, pure and simple; thus, the spice and essence, the very zest of the underwriter's newspaper brain is mine to command. I regret to notice a tendency to frivolity in these papers; they have a reserved space for a "funny column," and the most serious subjects are treated with gags, tags, and jags to suit the mood of the editor writer, who would be funny if he could, and some of his readers think he is, because they lack the power to know. So this editor plays the cuttle fish business with his writings, until between sense and the other thing his meaning is as opaque as good bottle glass. Now, the papers of the Old World are different, because they are dead in earnest, as the expression goes; they are serious in what they say. For two years I have studied the difference until I have learned to know perfectly what they say, but still I do not yet know what they mean; hence, when I come upon a bit of tinsel shining amid the heap of *Post Magazine*, for the moment I am alarmed, as aforesaid.

AN ENTERPRISING fire chief in an inland city, when steam fire engines were first being introduced, log-rolled a resolution through the council to send a committee of one of their members to the Bay (San Francisco) to investigate and report on the new fire *masheen*. He came, he saw, and he reported, "That he did not see any need of heating water to put out a fire," in his opinion cold water was just as good, and his city did not get a steamer until after the next election.

"YES," said the old special, "bursting up the Pacific Insurance Union is all very fine to talk about, but seriously it would be too much like the Chinaman's description of the toboggan slide that he had seen in Canada.

"Said he, 'Swishe-e-e' (with a downward sweep of his hand) 'walkee back three miles.'

"It would take us three years to get back."

SPECIAL AGENT IN 1870.

IT may seem strange to you to talk of days when there was no special agent, but in 1870 on the Coast the title of traveling men was "adjuster," and, if he was willing to demean himself by soliciting insurance, he was "no adjuster," in the opinion of his comrades.

For this reason, as I was sent out to solicit business pure and simple, and as a high-sounding title was absolutely necessary, I was called a special agent. My duty was to assist the local agent to secure business, get his good-will, find out the nature of his complaints against the office, if he had any, and visit him as often as I could make the circuit.

In rough-and-ready times, among rough-and-ready people, before the railroad was graded, there was no difficulty at all in carrying out instructions and making a good record ; it seems like a golden dream to look back upon ; but there was one agent who came quite near knocking me out in the very first round, so to speak. He was from the West— that is, the west he came from was a wilderness where log-houses were a luxury, blue jeans too swell for anything, and the frying pan about the only cooking utensil in use.

He got religion, chills and fever, and learned to chew tobacco at an early age, and all of these habits stayed right with him until he grew up, consequently he carried his liver in his eye, so to speak, and, as he was a money getter of the Quaker school, he found a passage of Scripture with authority for every sharp transaction, which enabled him to sleep peacefully after saying his "Now I lay me," while the poor creature who had the small end of the trade walked the floor all night. When I first saw him I thought he was an old man, because his hair and beard were grizzly gray. This hair was long, shaggy and thick, while his beard was of the patriarch cut, and the level-headed fellow knew full well the value of this appearance, just the same as the patent-medicine man who advertises cuts of benevolent-looking old fakirs to make his drugs go off. When I first saw him he was at the end of a long room which had once been a general merchandise store, and there was still a remnant of a stock stuck about on a few shelves. In a corner, between a red-hot stove on one side and a small iron safe on the other, he sat, his chair tilted back against the wall, while his long, thin legs twined about each other so that his feet hung loose and pointed in unnatural directions, as if disjointed at the ankle. Around his form and within a radius of four feet was evidence of a life-long practice with tobacco juice ; he seemed to think the whole world his cuspidor.

As I advanced towards him, his eyes followed me, but in no other way did he acknowledge my presence. In answer to my questions he replied yes and no, until I mentally compared him to an unwilling witness in a criminal case.

"Come, come," I said to myself, "this won't do; we must wake the old man up." So I talked all the topics of the times, amusements, politics, religion, the Indian question, slavery, woman's rights. I was getting awfully dry and was on the point of asking him to join me, when it occurred to me to first discuss the woman's crusade against saloons. Presto, change—there I had him—his feet became untangled, he sat erect in his chair, his eyes blazed, his manner was dignified, his voice pleasant to the ear, and his flow of talk simply surprising. I kept my mouth shut, listened carefully, and helped myself from the water jug; I was not edified, but I was rested. By and by I got the object of my visit well into him. He did not believe in special agents; did not want either my advice or assistance and asked me to leave town at once.

Here was a state of things; almost the first agent I had met trying to prove that I was a mistake.

As fate would have it, at that moment, entered, far away at the front door, another old skin-flint, a rival tomato-can banker, so to speak. With derision in his tone, my agent said, "Here comes old Grimes; I have tried to insure his dwelling for a long time. Perhaps you can secure the risk." "All right," I answered, "introduce me."

I do not know how it came about, but that man Grimes not only signed his application there and then, but he pulled out his old leather purse and paid the premium on the spot. My agent was struck with astonishment (no doubt of that). He looked from the receding form of old Grimes to me, and his mouth was open wide from astonishment at Mr. Grimes' submission. Finally, he said, with an awkward attempt at a smile, "do you like soda water?" "Yes," I replied; so we went to the drug store and drank the doubtful compound at that unseasonable time of year. A bond was thus established between us which only strengthened as time went by.

When Henry Martin was married he had just been appointed local agent for an insurance company, and his sweet little wife took as much interest in that local agency as Henry himself. She used to go down to the office and write up the register in a neat little English hand that made your head ache to read it, and many a risk came in on account of her bright eyes and rosy cheeks. One day she said, "Why, Henry, I do believe you have been drinking. I can tell it on your breath." "Of course I have," said Henry, "had to do it; have to sample everything I insure, you know; rule of the company; must try the goods to see if they are insurable." And so it went on. Henry was not much of a drinker, but first and last he managed to sample a number of risks. When he insured the drug store his wife asked innocently, "if he had to test the medicines." "Certainly," said Henry, "every one of them, but not all at once," he hastened to add. One night he came late to dinner, and the chops were done to death, and the little wife just a trifle vexed, but her brow soon became free from wrinkles when she heard that Henry had been to inspect a risk.

"But what risk is it," she asked. "The female seminary," he replied. Her face was very much troubled, indeed, and she said severely, "Henry Martin, does that horrid rule apply to this risk?"

ABOU BILL SEXTON.

Abou Bill Sexton (free from all rebates)
Awoke one night, from a deep dream of rates,
And saw within the moonlight in his room,
One of imperial stature and full bloom,
Writing in a register of gold.
A Denver trip had made Bill Sexton bold,
And to the presence in the room he said,
"What writest thou?" The vision raised its head,
And coldly answered, "As a test,
I write the names of those whom agents like the best."
"And is mine one?" said William. "Nay, not so,"
Replied the vision. William spoke more low,
And murmured, "Then write me, I insist,
As having no prohibited list."
The spirit wrote and vanished. The next night
It came again with a great wakening light,
And showed the names of those by agents blessed,
And, lo! Bill Sexton's name led all the rest!

The P. I. U. returned a daily report for correction, agent having failed to charge for stovepipe.

Agent replied: "Risk burned; stovepipe *removed;* my rating correct."

FIELD NOTES.

THE colonel once had an experience which he could narrate more fully and with more of interesting detail than I can hope to do.

But his modesty has thus far prevented the *Knapsack* from securing the story.

Some years ago he planted agencies in Arizona, and in one town, as there was no published map, he commenced bright and early in the day, while the coolness was still in the air, to make a diagram of the business blocks. We all know the curiosity of village folks at such a time, they are consumed with a desire to know what the strange man is doing with tape line, note book and calculations. Generally, children are sent to interview the man and find out his business. In this instance, the colonel, who is a natural artist, made a few sketches of the youngsters, which he showed to them and at which they grinned approval. It was well along in the afternoon that the final field notes were taken, and with a sigh of satisfaction the colonel shut his book and walked into a place of refreshment for a lemonade. After his pleasant drink he was about to leave the place, when a group of men dressed in the picturesque Arizona fashion, that is, half miner, half cowboy, stood in his way. One of them, more impetuous than the rest, said abruptly: "What are you doing here, anyway?" but the least demonstrative touched the colonel on the arm, and whispering, "a word with you, sir," he lead him aside, and speaking quietly but with great earnestness asked: "What is your business in this town?" At this the colonel, who had somewhat recovered from the first rude encounter, flushed and replied with a tinge of sarcasm in his tone: "Will you be kind enough to inform me what that can matter to you." "Certainly," was the answer, "but as time is short and my friends are impatient, it might be as well for you to keep a civil tongue in your head." There was suppressed force in the man's tone, and the colonel looked at him fixedly as he asked: "What do you want to know?"

"Who sent you here?"

"The Liverpool and London and Globe Insurance Company."

"What for?"

"To appoint an agent."

"What have you written in that book?"

"I have made a diagram of this town."

"What for?"

"So that the local agent can make rates understandingly."

"Are you deceiving me?"

"Not at all, here is my card."

At this the questioner waved his hand, and **said**: "It is all right, boys." The boys took their hands off their pistols, and went out. **The** colonel heard them talking reassuringly outside, and for the first time noticed a crowd about **the door** of the saloon ; turning to his questioner he asked **for an explanation.** "Well," said the **man**, "it is this **way**: Some years ago, **where** this townsite stands, **was a mining claim—placer** diggings—but they **didn't** pan **out big, and most people have forgotten it.** Right lately there has been **a story that the fellow who used to work** the claim **was** going to jump **on the improvements of the town, claiming** them as his property. So when **the boys saw a city chap going around** taking notes, they put it **up that he was here appraising the value of the** property ; they called a **meeting. Some was for shooting the son-of-a-** gun where he stood ; some **was for** hanging **him after dark, and some was** for trying him **in open** meeting. **We are a peaceful, law-abiding crowd, and we have never had a** hanging **here** yet, **so it was** decided **that the** sheriff—that's me—and **his** deputies—them **that** just **left us—should** interview the stranger, just **to** give him **a chance for** his life, **for mistakes** *is* sometimes **made,** you know."

The **colonel** wiped his brow. "Yes, I know," he said. "Well, so-long," said the sheriff, "no harm done, **but** I say, Mr. Kinne, **you** take **a** fool's advice and while you stay in Arizona don't you be too quick with your back talk. I know a lot of California people ; **got a** sister living at San Jose. I like them and they are the right **sort,** but they can't talk too quick for **an Arizona peace party when** it is after informa-tion.

"I know this town pretty **well.** The boys **will all get on a 'tear'** to-night to even up on the **way you** fooled them, **so if you take the stage** when it comes along it will **put a stop** to **any funny business so far as** *you* are concerned."

The colonel decided **to take the stage.**

DREADFUL **EFFECT OF THE CREDIT RULE.**

GENTLEMEN:—I received your note. I am very sorry I cannot send you the money, because I have not got it, and cannot raise it. I am an old man, and living **alone. I am** troubled with the rheumatics in my legs, I can hardly walk, and your agent, **Mr.** ———— has decieved me, he told me if I could not pay it the insurance would run out and that would be all about it, and I cannot pay it if I would ever so much. My little place don't bring me no more than $50 or $60 per year. I send this note with my neighbor, Mr.————————, he can tell you the same.   I send the insurance papers to you with him, and told him to pay you some for your trouble of making out these papers, I hope you will have a little mercy on an unfortunate old man.

Yours with sorrow and regret.

"IN OTHER RESPECTS."

In that clever combine styled the P. I. U.,
Whose members are in a continual stew,
They have been perspiring for quite a long spell,
But, in other respects they are doing quite well.

High salaried agents have been all the go,
While excess commissions have had a fair show;
And specials have worked, local business to swell,
But, in other respects, they are doing quite well.

Amendments have been ground out by the score,
And its thought there may be a few dozen more;
They are aimed at the agent, his spirit to quell,
But, in other respects, they are doing quite well.

Collections, that once were remote from our gaze,
Or else out of sight, are now thirty days;
There is trouble in Lodi and far Kalispel,
But, in other respects, they are doing quite well.

Some worked up farm business by aid of a note,
With interest old enough, almost, to vote;
While those who got left said, "it is a sell";
But, in other respects, they are doing quite well.

Macdonald and Dutton pulled hard for biz,
And what each didn't get he thought should be his;
When 'Frisco burns they will murmur, "O, h—l!"
But, in other respects, may be doing quite well.

A. Turner, for exercise, leaped from the ring,
Magill's double-decker joined in the mad fling;
They slid back with a thud that is painful to tell,
But, in other respects, they are doing quite well.

Hugh Craig and George Dornin each wrote a letter;
They misquoted Scripture and seemed to feel better;
They shot at a target and sounded the bell,
But, in other respects, they are doing quite well.

Alas, for the pride of brave "Yankee Doodle!"
Foreign companies carried off half of the boodle!
They took in six millions with a bold British yell,
But, in other respects, they are doing quite well.

Of topical songs you've perhaps had enough;
Though easy to write, their allusions are tough;
But when Carpenter sings them none will rebel,
And, in other respects, they are doing quite well.

THE OLD ADJUSTER'S DREAM.

He had kissed the dear little tots good-night,
  After their evening prayers were said;
They had whispered softly, "God bless you, pop,"
  And were off to their trundle beds.

By the soft mellow light from the coals in the grate
  In his own little "Home, sweet home,"
The adjuster leaned back in his large easy chair,
  By his fireside all alone.

Scenes from the past he pictured
  In the shadows around him dark and deep,
And the old gray head fell down on his breast—
  The adjuster was fast asleep.

He dreamed he was young and was just starting out,
  And things were a coming his way,
He was gathering risks from all parts of the world;
  He was writing a thousand a day.

He ordered his blanks by the car-load;
  They put on a hundred more clerks,
Who put in their nights and their Sundays,
  But they couldn't keep up with his work.

He insured all the gold in the mountains,
   All the fruit that would grow on the trees;
He insured all the snow on the top of Mt. Hood,
   And the fishes that swim in the seas.

All the fire-work factories and gun-powder mills,
   And the places they store dynamite,
Were all gathered in, and he marked them "first-class,"
   And said "Business was way out of sight."

He brought in a risk from some underground place,
   From a Mr. D. Evil by name,
And he made it for ten million dollars,
   Just to show he was thoroughbred game.

The ink on the policy hardly had dried
   When D. Evil, he put in a claim,
And tried to collect his ten million
   From this agent of such renowned fame.

He acknowledged the loss, recommended the payment
   To the adjuster, who stood near the door,
Who grabbed this invincible "son of a gun,"
   And with him he swept up the floor.

Mr. D. Evil he threw from the window,
   And as to the bottom he fell,
The adjuster he roared, "I'll be d—— if I'll pay
   One cent of insurance on h——."

Then he cussed in his sleep and tore at his hair,
   And his voice it was higher and higher,
And he woke up to find it was only a myth—
   He'd been dreaming alone by the fire.

Song composed by MR. W. J. CALLINGHAM, to be sung by him at the Annual Dinner.
AIR—"The Bowery."

I.

Again we're here for our annual "meet,"
With H. M. Grant in the president's seat;
His State passed valued policy law,
And gives us another tough bone to chaw.
We've contended with more than our share,

Now Oregon clutches at our back hair;
We 'll have to raise the current rates there,
And they 'll never pass laws any more.

Oregonians!   Oregonians!
They should know better our efforts to fetter;
They surely will box us with their laws, obnoxious,
Oregonians!   Oregonians!
They 'll never pass laws any more.

II.

Then Turner's notice for thirty days
Gave a promise the mischief to raise;
He held out, and justly, too;
The Credit System never would do.
The Compact felt they 'd struck a snag,
The manager wanted to get on a jag;
But his noble head he gravely would wag,
And he refused to go out any more.

The Compact!   The Compact!
It looked as tho' it would surely go;
The Compact!   The Compact!
He refused to go out any more.

III.

Then the manager packed his grip,
Hied him away on an Eastern trip
To that city of excellent beer—
I think they call it Milwaukee here.
He was successful with President James,
Came back and called him affectionate names,
Jumped into harness, pulled hard with the hames;
He'll not have to go back any more.

Milwaukee!   Milwaukee!
They drink good beer and it makes you feel queer,
In Milwaukee!   Milwaukee!
He 'll not have to go back any more.

IV.

Craig stepped in with his warlike shout,
Troubled and worried us all about;
This reform was much too rich,
And every measure he'd try to ditch;
After tossing in bed one night,
At last he saw that the thing was right;
Got into line and he quit his fight,
And he never will fight any more.

The Maori!　The Maori!
He's got New Zealand, we wish him weal;
The Maori!　The Maori!
And like "Slade," he'll not fight any more.

V.

The executive committee is doing good work;
They are pushers and never shirk.
Look! the accounts!　How they all come in!
Agents are rustling and sending the "tin."
The "U. A. P." is the proper stuff;
Stand with the committee and make it rough
For all who offend, till they cry enough,
And never offend any more.

The Local!　The Local!
He's made up his mind that we're the right kind;
The Local!　The Local!
He'll never offend any more.

VI.

And now, before I finish my song,
Let me beg of you always be strong;
Keep your course in your manly way,
No one will ever your rights gainsay;
And I'm sure in another year,
If we're alive and again meet here,
There'll be no one to pull by the ear,
For they'll never drop out any more.

Hurrah, then!　Hurrah, then!
The year's begun fine, with them all in line,
So hurrah, then!　Hurrah, then!
They'll never drop out any more.

AN ARIZONA ADJUSTMENT.

(As related by Monte George.)

AT THE time of the big fire at Tombstone, I was dealing faro for Bill Johnson in the Palace saloon. He moved most of his things and didn't lose much.

"I've got a thousand insurance," said Bill. "I didn't lose more'n five hundred, but they tell me you always get what you insure for. Its like a lottery; you buy a policy, and, if your burned out, you draw a prize. They say it's a dead square game, and I played her up to the limit to win. Vickers, the agent who sold me the policy, sent to San Francisco for a special adjuster to fix the thing up, so as to be sure and have everything all right."

Three days after the fire the adjuster arrived. His name was William Henry Harrison Benton. He was a nice looking, smooth-spoken man, not very large. He looked some like Jay Gould. I saw Gould at Hailey two years ago, and he talked and acted a good deal like Benton. Well, Benton stayed around for a week or so, and finally told Bill he was ready to settle, and we three went into one of the poker rooms in Bill's new saloon to talk it over.

"Now, Mr. Johnson," said Benton, "I've figured up the value of your furniture and fixtures that were burned, and I find they amount to $359.63."

"But I thought I'd get the whole thousand," said Bill.

"Oh, no!" said the adjuster, "because you saved the balance of the stuff. We only pay you for what's burned."

"Guess you're right," said Bill.

"Then there's the depreciation to come off."

"What's that?" asked Bill.

"The wear and tear; the difference between old and new. You had the furniture four months, and I'll figure the depreciation down low, say forty per cent.; that's only ten per cent. a month."

"Isn't that a good deal?" said Bill. "If I'd had it a year, I'd been worse off than nothing."

Benton smiled and replied, "No, that's very reasonable. There's an adjuster named Beard, at Denver, whom we call 'Old Depreciation,' who'd have made it sixty per cent., at least."

"Don't send for Beard," said Bill. "Let her go at forty."

"So, taking off the depreciation, that's $143.75; leaves your actual loss just $215.88."

Bill looked over the figures, drew a long breath, and said, "That's correct. Will you pay the money here, or send it from San Francisco?"

"By the way," asked the adjuster, "what rate did you pay?"

"A hundred and twenty dollars for the thousand," answered Bill, "and it seemed to me rather steep."

"That was reasonable," said Benton, "very reasonable. Now, there's another little proposition."

"Spring 'er," said Bill. (I'll say right here that Johnson was one of the coolest and gamest men I ever met; nothing could startle him.)

"Did you ever read the adjuster's clause?" continued Benton, pointing to some fine blue print on the policy.

"No. What's that?" asked Bill.

"That provides that you shall pay the expenses of the adjustment, because Tombstone is so far from San Francisco."

"That seems reasonable," said Bill.

"Yes, that's only right," said Benton, "and it makes it easier for the companies. I've made up my bill of expenses, and here it is:

```
Fare from San Francisco to Tombstone and back  . . $115 88
Hotel and other expenses, ten days  . . . . . . . . .   50 00
Ten days' time, at $20 a day . . . . . . . . . . . . .  200 00
                                                       ________

                     Total . . . . . . . . . . $365 88
        Less amount of loss . . . . . . . . . . . .  215 88
                                                       ________

Balance due the company from you, just . . . . . . . $150 00 even."
```

Bill thought for a minute, then pulled out seven twenties and two fives, handed them to Benton, and said, "That seems to be according to the contract, and here's your money. I played to win out, and ought to have coppered her; but, look here Benton, I don't want to say anything to hurt your feelings, but I'm not going to insure any more if that d—d adjuster's clause is in. The percentage against me is too heavy."

Benton laughed, and we all took a drink at Bill's expense.

Since then Bill and I have talked that case over a hundred times, I suppose, but we always came to the same conclusion that it was a fair, square game, but an unlucky deal.

Bill tried to hire Benton to stay in Tombstone and run his new saloon for him, but couldn't get him to give up insurance. He said it was a surer thing.   EDWARD NILES.

THE MODEST-MANNERED MAIDEN.

As sung by E. W. CARPENTER at the
Banquet of the Fire Underwriters' Association of the Pacific,
San Francisco, February 21, 1893.

In a manager's office daily sat, with keen, receptive ear,
A typical, clickical, short-hand girl, to every secret near;
Yet she kept this knowledge all to herself, was mum as a maid can be,
Though occasionally heard, with manner severe, to remark complacently,

    Should you seek an explanation,
    Or insurance information,
       I'm a frozen font of wisdom that responds to nary call;
    Yet with underwriting knowledge
    I could discount any college;
       I'm a modest-mannered maiden, but I know it all.

I could tell what agents at Christmas-time get checks for souvenirs,
What brokers have their private plans that DuVal never hears;
I know the girl who draws her pay without a stroke of work,
But whose papa's biz just ten times is her "wages" as a clerk.

    Each of all these high-toned dodges
    In this little cranium lodges;
       I can walk all round the P. I. U. and never trip or fall.
    To the letter keep each ruling,
    While its spirit I'm befooling;
       I'm a modest-mannered maiden, but I know it all.

I see the letter that is sent from "home," indignant with regrets
That the other man pays rebates on 'bout every risk he gets;
Yet, hold your business, come what may (the writer'll always add),
Which is English sly for cheat and lie: the income must be had.

    Our instructions may degrade you,
    But the compensation paid you
       Ought to keep your manhood notions microscopically small;
    So preserve the Union running,
    And we'll jointly gain by cunning;
       I'm a modest-mannered maiden, but I know it all.

I could name the agent whose misfit draft don't pay the balance due
Per monthly statement, so nicely drawn to fool the P. I. U.;
I have seen the cunning special's charge for extra railway fare,
Wherewith he'd buy, at figures high, a local here and there.

> Yet, we flaunt our morals proudly,
> In the Union preach most loudly,
>   And non-concurring brethren we, names, distinctive call;
> Always vote for measures winning,
> Then evade them by our sinning;
>   I'm a modest-mannered maiden, but I know it all.

And I know the genial manager who just drops in, to say
He thought he'd call to see if we were all alive to-day;
Then deftly turns the tide of speech towards what he wants to know,
And we've sometimes lied to dam that tide and stop its babbling flow.

> We would not descend to rudeness,
> So, with underwriting shrewdness
>   We just keep polite and popular by fiblets letting fall;
> We're so choice of others' feelings
> That deceit marks all our dealings;
>   I'm a modest-mannered maiden, but I know it all.

So many were the truths this maiden told, all causing deep distrust,
That to get her off the office force the manager thought he must;
So he married the maid; but within a year the Union went to smash;
And in those sad days it was hard to raise, for *lingerie*, the cash.

> So the mother, once the maiden,
> With much care and trouble laden,
>   Now bemoans the day when honesty gave place to guilt and
>   gall;
> Now her husband's income's nothing,
> She supports him doing washing;
>   She's a wisdom-wrinkled woman, and she knows it all.

Should insurance situations call for further explanations,
She's a broke-up fount of wisdom that responds to every call,
And with floods of frigid knowledge she could deluge any college;
She's a wisdom-wrinkled woman, and she tells it all.

> Moral:—Nothing but the maiden.

EDITORIAL, 1894.   GEO. F. GRANT.

EDITORIAL.

TWENTY-FIVE years ago a man working in an insurance office was taught to believe that the first requisite for making money in his business was an adequate rate. The subject of rates was the theme for private lectures and public papers. So imbued did he become with this idea of rates, that the first printed speech containing a doubt of this theory gave him a shock of disapproval, and the author was regarded in the light of an apostate. It is useless now to speculate on the motive of the author. He may have been a crank out of a job, or one ambitious for notoriety as an advanced thinker.

The seed he dropped took root and bore fruit. Year after year the doubt was nursed, until at last it lost a doubt's identity. Since then, every ingenious theory imaginable has been presented in an endeavor to prove why the net profit should *not* depend upon the rate at which policies are written.

When the Compact office was born, it came for the purpose of controlling the morals of the business. The Compact manager was the keeper of the insurance conscience, and like a faithful monitor stood watch over the just and unjust, holding all to a strict account and showing favoritism to none.

In an unguarded moment the manager, listening to the logical siren, reduced a rate on apparently technical grounds, but before he could, metaphorically speaking, say Jack Robinson, he had reduced the rate on the whole class to which this risk belonged; and this was done, too, under pressure of the "Governing Board" and to the great satisfaction of every competing solicitor and the calm delight of the policyholder.

Then some one advanced the idea that if rates were only reduced *all around* it would prevent the disruption of the Compact, because it would leave the rate-cutter nothing in particular to cut from. For look you, it seems to be better to roll up a large volume of business, and thus demonstrate superiority over one's adversary, than to stand guard over the rate.

Whatever element of chance there may happen to be in the business thus becomes the foremost idol of the hour.

Fortunately for the Pacific Coast we have been too old fashioned to tread rapidly in the footsteps of our Eastern brothers, but we are tending that way. Year after year the wail of "no profit," is heard from over beyond the Rocky mountains. Year after year the conflagration hazard increases.

I leave to others the analysis of the fire waste, but to you members of the Association I recommend the subject of adequate rates on the Pacific Coast.

One constant menace to the rate is the "patent appliance." Sometimes it comes in the guise of an improved fire alarm; again as an extinguisher; but whatever form it takes it is accompanied by no end of printed proof of superiority, and a talking agent before whom logic and reason are expected to fade away, and reduction of rates to then and there obtain. If this were all it would be better; but hardly have we become accustomed to the reduced rate, when an able talker, with more pamphlets, nails us down, demanding a further reduction because of an improvement in the patent.

The older one grows and the more experience one gets in the world's affairs, the more he learns to know that persistent effort will accomplish almost anything.

If a local agent sets his mind on the reduction of a certain rate he will get it. It may take time, but he will get it. And as one good turn deserves another, other agents will get reductions on similar risks, and get them the more easily because of the precedent established.

There never was a better time than now to agitate the subject of adequate rates. We have just left behind us a hard year. All have not suffered alike—the rule is proven by the exception. Before us we face we know not what. But, associates and friends, if experience is worth the lives worn out to gain it, why not accept the advantage which costs us nothing!

Let us return, as nearly as possible, to the theory which controlled men in the insurance business twenty-five years ago. Let us return to adequate rates.

A LADY, writing from Tacoma to a general manager here, complains that she was insured in the Tacoma Insurance Company of Tacoma, Washington; says that she went into this because she thought it was controlled by good men, and she got a little lower rate, but winds up her letter by stating that hereafter she will not insure in *sound* companies.

AFTER THE FIRE.

A bright young special climbed on the veteran's knee,
Begged for a story: "Do tell to me,
Why are you sighing, why do you groan,
Have you no hope left, why that deep moan?"
"I once was cheerful, years, years ago,
What, boy, has changed me, you will soon know;
List to the story, and do not tire,
I lost my faith in man,
After the fire."

   After the blaze is over,
   After the smoke is away,
   After the ashes are sifted,
   After we 've all had to pay,
   Many a heart is aching,
   As the message goes by wire,
   Many contingents are scattered,
   After the fire.

"Once, in Montana, traveling up and down,
I stopped at Butte—a rather rapid town;
An expert was with me—some call him 'Bill';
He and I together soon had our fill.
There was a dry goods stock;
There was a liar;
There was a smoke damage,
After the fire."

   After the flames are over,
   After the hose has burst,
   After the claim has swollen,
   After we all have cursed,
   Then the figures are twisted,
   Till we are in the mire—
   Seventy thousand they wanted!
   After the fire.

"Since then I 've lost my faith,
Do you wonder why?
The loss was not five thousand,
So said Bill and I;

Every rusty piece of goods
That couldn't find a buyer,
Was put in as a total loss,
After the fire."

After the fire is over,
After the proofs are made,
After appraisement is ended,
After the damage is laid;
O, how companies suffer,
And how adjusters tire,
Of paying unholy loss claims,
After the fire.

THE NEW AGENT AT HANGING ROCK.

THERE was a vein of originality about our new agent at Hanging Rock, Colorado, that led us to hope that he would pan out the pure metal, with only a trace, here and there, of lead and copper, but the final assays were disappointing.

When he agreed to act for us, he said: "I don't know much about insurance, but I'm a hustler and willing to learn." That sounded encouraging, and I began to read to him our prohibited list, beginning with "auction stock" and ending with "zinc factories," calling special attention to the combustibility of "hay barns," "Chinese laundries" and "powder magazines"; ringing the alarm on "cigars and tobacco"; calling in the patrol on "lithographic stones," and sounding the police whistle on "wall paper and paint stock."

He interrupted me with the remark: "I can't remember all of those. All I want is to know the risks you *can* take, for after I write a policy, I never will cancel."

I gave him the desired information; cautioned him about limits, moral hazard and prompt remittances, and took the morning stage for Gunnison.

His first letter, received some two weeks later, said:

"I'm working up a big business on a new plan. You will be surprised when you learn how simple and easy it is. I'm careful about getting an A 1 moral hazard and no excess lines. Yesterday, Bill Brown wrote up a policy of $2,500 on the furniture and fixtures and everything in the house, situate in the 'Miners' Home,' a first-rate, third-class, wooden hotel, with stovepipe flues, ten miles from here, at the crossing of

Rattlesnake Gulch and Mesquit Creek. The whole outfit isn't worth six hundred, but Bill is a dead shot, and said if the policy didn't stick, he'd cancel me at short range with a Winchester, and wipe out the agency; so I reinsured $2,475 with the other agent, keeping $25 for us, covering on the cook stove, with patent water back. If she burns, as I think she will, we'll have a salvage, sure."

During the next six months, he sent in nineteen curiously worded reports, with the numbers badly mixed.

We supplied him with fifty policies, numbered from ten thousand five hundred and one to ten thousand five hundred and fifty. None of the numbers of his reports were consecutive. In answer to queries, he merely said: "That's my new system a workin'." Finally, I made a special trip from Denver to Hanging Rock, and asked an explanation.

"This system is simple and effective," said he. "I thought it out myself, and it's a daisy. Of course, I don't know anything about policy writing, and the man who wants to insure knows what he wants better than I can tell him; so I signed all of the policies and distributed them around town, among the business men, and asked them, whenever they got ready to insure, to fill out the policies themselves and let *me* know. Then I let *you* know, and that's the reason the numbers don't run regular. If number forty-nine writes up his policy before number nineteen, I send the report right in. In time, the numbers will check up all right, but it may take a year before they all fit in. How do you like the system; isn't it neat? It suits our people exactly."

I stayed a week; got in all of our policies, except Bill Brown's, and took up the agency.

It was a needed lesson, and I profited by it.

> Little Jack Horner sat in the corner
>   Thinking if profits were stringent;
> He called in his forces to foot up his losses.
>   Good-bye to Jack Horner's contingent.

The Colorado specials, as well as accountants, who have a vivid recollection of J—— B——'s hieroglyphics, will be pleased to learn why his agency was popular and why he controlled so much good business. The reason, as given by one of his clients, was, that under one of J—— B——'s policies one could recover for any property burned anywhere, as no adjuster could prove by the written portion of the policy what property was, or what property was not, intended to be covered.

A COLORADO ADJUSTMENT.

UP to the time of the fire, I thought Isidor was square. He was a Jew, and his ancestors lived in Poland, but his credit was high at the banks. He paid good wages, and made the usual hundred per cent. on cheap goods, and from twenty-five to fifty per cent. on the highest grades. He kept all of the Hebrew holidays, but stood in with Christians, and was considered a superior specimen of his race. When it came to a question of street car fare or postage stamps, he was as close as some Eastern men; but I did think he had too much business sense to match his wits against a Yankee. Still, you never can tell.

The firm name was Wilzinski & Rosenstein. Its members were Isidor Wilzinski and Moritz Rosenstein, the latter having a quarter interest and little to say in the management. I kept the books and occasionally acted as salesman. Their main store was at Pueblo, occupying the basement and first and second floors of the Kirtland Block, on Santa Fe avenue, where they carried a stock of clothing, averaging from $20,000 to $30,000. They were sole agents for the Stetson hats; E. & W. collars and cuffs; Douglas three-dollar shoes, and Jaeger underwear; were rated "B 2" by Bradstreet, and were supposed to be doing a profitable trade. They also had branch stores at Canon City and Cripple Creek.

Pueblo had never been so dull. The Bessemer rolling mills had been shut down several months; the Mesa Hotel had just burned; the Grand Hotel had been closed for a year, and "the Pittsburg of Colorado" looked like San Diego after the boom. Our business had fallen off one-half; collections were almost impossible; creditors were pressing, and ruin seemed near at hand.

The firm had been carrying $19,000 on stock. The policies all expired on October 1st. On September 15th we completed an inventory, showing a stock value of $20,583.37. Isidor kept the inventory, and made no record of it on the books. Our policies had the usual broad permit: "Other concurrent insurance herewith permitted." On renewal, the insurance was increased to $29,000.

About 10 o'clock on Sunday evening, October 15th, the alarm sounded, and a dense volume of smoke was seen pouring from the basement of our store. The Pueblo fire department is a good one; the firemen made a lightning hitch and run; threw two streams in the basement, and had the fire put out within seven minutes after the alarm.

Monday morning the firm notified the local agents that they had sustained a heavy loss, and asked for an immediate adjustment. The companies were advised of the claim, and on the Wednesday following four adjusters arrived from **Denver**. They examined the stock ; looked wise, **said** little, smoked good cigars, and told several stories that **were** entirely new to me, but did nothing definite toward a settlement.   On the afternoon of the second day after their arrival **Isidor** grew uneasy.

"How soon will you get this fixed?" he asked.   "We want to clean up and open the store. Our **expenses** are going on, and we are losing fifty dollars a day, easy."

The adjusters laughed, and lighted fresh cigars, and resumed their anecdotes. Isidor was getting mad. Just then there was a light rap on the front door, which had been tightly closed. Isidor opened it, and in stepped a quiet-looking man, who said, with a pleasant smile :

"Is this Mr. Wilzinski?"

"What's left of him," growled Isidor.   "Who are you?"

"My name is Bird," said the new comer, handing him a card reading as follows :

<pre>
. . . .
.   .
.   A. BIRD,   .
.   Adjuster of Fire Losses,   .
.   1561 Curtis Street,   .
.   Denver.   .
.   .
. . . .
</pre>

"I represent thirteen thousand of your insurance. Is there any damage?"

"Is there any damage?" repeated Isidor ; "there's fourteen thousand five hundred.   At any rate, that's what we first claimed, but the stock's looking worse and worse, and I wouldn't be surprised if we lost twenty thousand."

"May I trouble you to show me your policies?" asked the adjuster.

"Certainly, Mr. Bird," said Isidor, "no trouble at all."

After closely examining the policies, the adjuster inquired :

"Where did the fire start?"

"In the basement," said Isidor,—adding quickly, "that is, we think so."

"Let me see the basement, please," asked Bird.

"Why, there's nothing there," said Isidor, changing color a little. "We didn't keep any stock there ; there's nothing but old boxes and rubbish."

"I'm not particular about going down, myself," answered Bird, in a very smooth, pleasant way—"in fact, it isn't really necessary, but you know the rules of the companies, Mr. Wilzinski ; they expect us to go all through a building. There's no sense in it, but I'll just look down for a minute and let it go at that."

They went down. Bird looked carelessly around and remarked: "There's quite a strong smell of coal oil."

"We filled our lamps down here," said Isidor.

After returning up stairs and looking carefully through the stock, Bird consulted with the other adjusters for a few minutes, during which recess Isidor and his partner had a quiet conversation in the office, of which I caught the words: "Raise him to twenty thousand, Isidor; he'll stand it."

Bird then came forward and said: "The other adjusters have authorized me to act for them. Is that agreeable to you?"

"Yes," said Isidor, "perfectly. I'd rather have it that way. When I first saw you, I said to myself, 'there's a fair, square man, who knows his business.'"

"All right," said Bird, "it won't take five minutes to settle it. Do I understand you to say that you claim a loss under the policies, and, if so, in what amount?"

Isidor rubbed his hands, and said, "Mr. Bird, we've lost twenty thousand, if we've lost a dollar; but I don't want to be hard on the companies. I'll say sixteen thousand, and we'll never take a cent less."

Bird laughed. He had such a genial, pleasant way with him that, by this time, Isidor, Moritz, the other adjusters and myself had clustered around as if we were drawn to him something like iron filings to a magnet.

"Where is the loss?" he asked.

"Where?" shrieked Isidor, "Everywhere!"

"Were any of the goods burned, Isidor?" asked Bird, in a rich, mellow tone, and added: "You'll excuse my familiar way of talking; I'm from Connecticut, you know."

"That's right," was the reply, "call me Isidor. None of the goods were burned; but look at the smoke! the stock is ruined."

"By the way," asked Bird, "do you use gas for lighting the store?"

"Nothing but gas," said Isidor.

Bird smiled, and what a pleasant smile he had.

"Are the goods blackened or discolored?" asked the adjuster.

"Not yet," said Isidor; "it's the odor—the smell of smoke all through everything. We can't sell the goods for ten cents on the dollar."

"What's the value of your stock?" asked Bird.

"About forty thousand. We carry a big stock of the finest kind of goods," replied Isidor.

"Then the damage you claim is a smoke damage?" asked the adjuster.

"Yes!" said Isidor, "it's a smoke damage; they all say that's the worst kind of damage to clothing."

"A damage from the odor; from the smell of smoke only?" asked Bird.

"Yes, that's it; the goods are saturated with it."

"Did you open the store and let the smoke out, after the fire?" said the adjuster.

"No," said Isidor.

"Did you put the goods in the best possible condition, as required by the policies?"

"We were afraid to touch them," said Isidor.

"Is there anything in the policies requiring us to pay anything because there has been the smell of smoke in the store?" asked Bird.

"Isn't there?" said Isidor.

"No," answered Bird, "there is not; there is no liability whatever."

"And don't we get anything?" said Isidor, turning pale and trembling.

"Nothing from us," said the adjuster, mildly and soothingly, "not one dollar."

"We'll sue the companies!" shouted Isidor.

"Listen to me," said Bird; "you don't understand your own case. This is the way it is: You claim a $40,000 stock; you have about $20,000. You are entitled to about $15,000 insurance on your present stock; you have $29,000. The fire was started in two places in the basement, Sunday night, and coal oil was freely used. Your lights are gas; you don't use coal oil lamps. Now, I'll say nothing more on those points. Next comes the question of smoke damage. You claim a damage from the smell of smoke only. A little smoke benefits clothing, and will kill the larvæ of moths, every time. Open your doors, and in three hours the odor will disappear. Now is the opportunity of your life. Advertise a fire sale; throw open the store, and in the next two weeks you will sell two-thirds of your stock at a big profit. I'll tell you how to to it. Get signs painted on cloth"—

"They're all ready," interrupted Isidor, with a sheepish smile, as he went in the office and brought out several bolts of sheeting and unrolled them, on which were painted, in large red letters:

. . . .
"GREAT FIRE SALE!
THE INSURANCE COMPANIES HAVE SETTLED!!"
IT IS THEIR LOSS, NOT OURS!!
THE ENTIRE STOCK FOR SALE
AT TWENTY CENTS ON THE DOLLAR!!!
. . . .

"That's the idea," said Bird. "Your fortune's made. Now, how about our expenses?"

"What!" said Isidor.

"You claimed a loss when there was none, and we could hold you for our expenses, but let it go, Isidor, let it go. Come out and set up the cigars for the crowd, and we'll call it square."

And Isidor did.

The "great fire sale" began next day, and in three weeks the bulk of the stock was sold at a large profit. The firm paid their debts, banked the surplus, and to-day are doing the largest clothing business in Pueblo.

Moritz asked Isidor why he did not hold out for the amount of his claim, and why he backed down so quickly. Isidor answered: "Moritz, that adjuster was born in Connecticut; he was on to the coal oil, and the policies don't say anything about the smell of smoke!"

"Isidor," said Moritz, "you vos yoost right."

AN UNPRECEDENTED SALVAGE.

A special agent, while in Utah recently, had occasion to adjust a loss on a barn and the contents, including some horses, the latter being insured for $100 per head, some three years previous. Owing to the considerable fall in the value of live stock, the adjuster made an offer to the assured of $40 per head. After some little controversy, the figures were accepted and the adjustment closed. The next day, returning to Salt Lake, the special in question observed a notice in the daily paper to the effect that an auction sale of horses would take place on the following day. To acquaint himself with the relative market value of these animals, he decided to attend the sale. He did so, and was surprised and even chagrined to observe that out of eighty animals, one of them brought $10, and the remaining number from $1.75 to $2 apiece. He did not sleep well that night, realizing how inefficiently he had served his company in the adjustment of the day previous. However, relying upon the adage of "everything comes to him who waits," he took note of this fact. Within a week a similar loss took place and he was wired to adjust. Upon examining the daily report he found that the policy covered $1,500 on the barn and contents, $600 of which was placed on six head of horses, with a loss limit of $100. Here was his chance. It was an excellent opportunity to make a record for himself, and he forthwith went to the auctioneer who had sold the animals, obtaining from him a certified copy of the sale and the prices obtained, and, so as to fortify himself doubly, obtained the additional signature of the local agents, that this was true, and that same could be replaced for that figure. His face beamed with smiles as he soliloquized, "While it is possible that the entire six horses are burned, it is more than probable that one or two of them have been saved. My salvage will be unexampled in the history of adjustment." He got on the train, arrived at his destination, engaged a team and drove to the scene of the fire. The barn and contents were a total loss; the horses were saved.

SUCH A NICE MAN, TOO.

From a social point of view we look
　　Upon our fellows, kindly,
And to their business vagaries,
　　Close friendship's optics, blindly;
A "manager" we may detest,
　　Whose ways are dark and dreary,
Yet for the "man" have friendly thoughts,
　　He's socially so cheery.

CHORUS (*Slow march time*):
　　Such a nice man, too, such a real nice man,
　　　　So affable and full of information,
　　　　　　All who know him must admit,
　　　　　　He's a man of brains and wit,
　　　　And a gentleman of spotless reputation.

He says he won't, and yet he will,
　　Give rebate should he like to,
Excess commissions also pay,
　　Through tricks *ad infinito*.
When losses come he stands aloof,
　　Lets others work and worry,
But, figures made, to favor gain,
　　Pays claimants in a hurry.

"There's naught in this great world," he boasts,
    "Shall stop me from succeeding,
I'll make just ev'ry scoop I can,
    Repressing conscience-pleading;
Thus while the honest dolts plod on,
    I'll soon become real wealthy,
Then quick retire from the 'Cosmos Fire,'
    With a gold reserve quite healthy."

And so the choicest gilt-edged risks
    Come crowding to his door,
His prem'ums mounting higher up,
    His morals tumbling lower,
His loss ratio quite modest is,
    His adjustments are made gratis,
He taps his massive brow and says,
    "What brain as this one great is?"

But the "Eternal Fire" (*perpetual plan*)
    Does business somewhat later,
It's "always low as the lowest" bait
    Will "scoop" in our rebater.
Then sizzling there, his sulphured thoughts,
    Revert to cooler creatures,
To the snow-made image of boyhood days,
    With frosty, frigid feature.

That image clothed in coat of sleet,
    Till ice it all seemed to be,
Like all creation he'd like to change,
    With that creation, may be;
But he's struck a special hazard hot,
    Sans sprinklers automatic,
A "fire"-man's lot he'd gladly change
    For an ice man, more phlegmatic.

Chorus:
    Yes, an ice man, true, just a *real* nice man,
        A triumphant work of childish refrigeration,
            Though with sightless, snow-ball eye,
            And a mouth that couldn't lie,
        Yet better far than sin's incineration.

CARPENTER.

ON HER SURROUNDINGS.

W. B. FRENCH, the veteran adjuster and flour mill expert of Chicago, tells the following :

The loss occurred at Joliet, under a 'Continental' policy. The assured was a woman, and the policy read :

"$1,000 on her two-story frame residence; and $200 on her surroundings."

I settled on the building, and then asked :

"Madam, what are your surroundings?"

"What did you say, sir?"

"Your surroundings, madam, what are they?"

"What do you mean, sir? They are quite as good as yours, I think."

"No offense, madam ; please read your policy."

She did so, and then said :

"Excuse me; I didn't notice the wording. Well, sir, what are my surroundings?" she asked with a smile.

I replied : "Ordinarily, I would define a woman's surroundings as her wearing apparel."

"What I thought I was insuring," she answered, "was against loss on the trees and shrubbery surrounding my residence."

"All right," I said, and allowed her fifty dollars' damage on the shrubbery and trees.

It was the only case of the kind I ever had, but I think I made a common sense adjustment.

THE adjuster sent the old man to the notary public to swear to his claim, and the following conversation took place between the adjuster and the daughter:

"You say you have just returned from abroad. How I should like to have been there ; and where did you visit, may I ask?"

"Our travels were confined principally to Ireland," she responded, rather naively.

"Did you see the Blarney Stone?" he queried.

"Oh, yes," was her quick response.

Whereupon he commenced a most eloquent dissertation upon that most famous object, and said that in view of his being unable to kiss that stone himself he wished to do so by proxy. She drew back with astonishment, but with a twinkling eye that betokened intelligence, replied :

"Sir, I did not kiss it; I simply sat on it."

"THE WOMAN'S EXCHANGE."

A TRUE STORY.

IN December last I was in Denver, the prettiest city of its size in the United States, and one having a much better climate than San Francisco. During my stay there Henry J. Lufkin, our agent at Wagon Wheel Gap, Colo., came to town to spend some of his commissions, and, incidentally, called on me.

Mr. Lufkin is one of those genial, whole-souled gentlemen indigenous to Colorado; is popularly called "Hank," and is very fond of a practical joke.

After lunch one day, Lufkin and I were taking a stroll through town and chanced to pass the Cumberland building on Stout street, on the first floor of which is the "Woman's Exchange," so called, consisting of a restaurant and a supply of fancy articles, embroidered penwipers, tidies, lamp mats, canned fruits, cocoanut cake, custard pies and other feminine products, all on sale for the benefit of their makers.

"Hank" gazed on the numerous signs on the outside of the building, setting forth in large letters the name of the association, "Woman's Exchange," and finally burst into laughter and said: "When I get home I'm going to spring a joke on a verdant friend of mine that I believe will prove a good one. If you get a letter from one James B. Ferguson referring to the 'Woman's Exchange' you will understand what prompted it."

A week later I received the following:

"WAGON WHEEL GAP, Colo., December 13, 1893.

"*Honored Sir:* Billy has just got back from Denver and tells me there's a 'Woman's Exchange' in your town, where one can exchange his wife for another woman, and I want to know if I can trade my wife, and how much it costs to do it.

"I have a wife, 31 years old, a blonde, good looker, good worker, and can play 'After the Ball' on the piano; but the altitude is too high for her, and besides, this town is too slow for one of her gait. She wants to fly high, and if I can swap her off for some good girl about 18 years old I would like to do it, and my wife would like the scheme herself.

"If you can send a brunette that would like to come here and take her place I'll pay her expenses and introduce her to the best society and make her life one of refined pleasure.

"Send me her photograph, and if it suits me I will go down and arrange for her legal transfer.

"Please answer by return mail.

"Respectfully,

"James B. Ferguson.

"P. S.—Maybe Bill is lying to me, and if so, let me know, and I will fix him so he will lie under the daisies before spring."

I was afraid to reply, and to this day don't know whether Mr. Ferguson succeeded in making the desired trade.

WHEN THE "SPECIALS" COME HOME.

The old year is past and its duties are done;
And now in my corner I sit in the sun,
And dream of the days when out on the road
I thought that I carried a wearying load—
When I wrestled with agents to get in our coin,
And ate as I could, whether chucksteak or loin.
Still, my burdens seem hard, though no longer I roam;
But I 'll lay them all down
When
The
Specials
Come
Home.

They are coming from near; they are coming from far,
And are sure to ride in on the best palace car.
There's a smile on each lip and a flash in each eye,
As if none among them could ever say die.
They tone up the office with cheer and with hope,
And talk in as certain a way as the Pope.
Their knowledge is gleaned from no musty old tome,
And we all learn more
When
The
Specials
Come
Home,

And I hope, when a few more years have rolled by,
And I 've solved the grim problem that all must try—
When the fever of living has burned out at last,
And my memory is but a dim dream of the past—
That perhaps in eternity's bright sunrise—
In the crystal dephths of Paradise—
I shall see reflected in Heaven's clear dome
The shades of the specials
     As
       They
         Come
           Home.

P. S.—I 'm a little uncertain about the general agents.

"I WANT to be an expert,
 And with the experts stand,
With my forehead full of figures,
 And a ledger in my hand;
And when I 've totaled up a loss
 With much of mental strain,
Someone will coolly rub it out
 And get it wrong again."

EDITORIAL, 1895.   GEO. F. GRANT.

EDITORIAL.

YOU might as well ask me to fly as to request something funny for the *Knapsack* this year, if that something requires time. I need hardly dwell on the reason why.

This is a serious period, this fall of '94 and spring of '95. After many years of mutual understanding we were all at once happily engaged in the most formal manner in general and specific misunderstanding; whispers became commands, and rumors grew strong as words of holy writ. I say *happily* engaged, for to judge by the cheery tone and smiling faces, special agents found the prospect of a fight more than pleasing, and if they did not reflect the manager and his opinion it is too bad. The Fire Underwriters' Association of the Pacific was on trial, and if it had failed saltpetre would not have saved the business, but the seeds sown twenty years ago come October were deeply rooted, and the boys at Virginia City in 1875 are now grave and reserved men; the spirit of harmony and good will, of mutual advantage by associated effort asserted itself in the hour of need and by the very boys who learned to know and trust each other during that cold thirty days of adjustment so long ago, they were able to meet and formulate a new plan, to bury the hatchet and smoke the pipe of peace. It was a great feat well performed, and I congratulate you, each one, on the result. I am not the keeper of my neighbor's conscience, nor is it for me to cast stones at any man; but by the power vested in me as editor of the *Knapsack* I say unto you, if you are by word or deed, by indirection or mental reservation, retarding the progress of a successful and profitable insurance business on this coast, you do that which, enriching nobody, makes you a marked and shining target for boys now growing up in this Association to fire at; it is like tearing down with no intention of replacing or putting the gloss of right on that which is in reality wrong; it is sowing seed which in another twenty years may bring ruin.

Perhaps the first business advice to have weight in the mind of the youth was expressed in the familiar line: "Go to the ant, thou sluggard; consider her ways and be wise." Having been liberally endowed by nature with those traits and attributes, which tend to enlist sympathy with the sluggard, I accepted the admonition as personal, and turned my attention to the ant. The first specimen was found in the sugar barrel and she was particularly repulsive, being black and ugly, and divided in the middle by a hair line, having a pudgy ball on either side; I slew her. Reposing at a later date under an oaken tree in a green meadow, watching milk-white clouds float over a light blue sky, I again found the ant, and she was numerous. When found she was within my trousers' leg; I considered her seriously and changed not only my position but the trousers. This was instinct. Thus far I had not that wisdom for which I yearned. It was many years later, in the town of Merced, before the full force of the proverb was demonstrated. In the capacity of special agent, I visited the San Joaquin district and came upon the ant at Merced. She was of the small red variety, agile and strong. In great numbers she was engaged in removing a pile of sand from one side of the walk to the other, and during my stay at Merced, with unremitting zeal she struggled over the path with a load and trotted back empty-handed for more. Meantime, with varied step and gait, the villagers passed to and fro, representing all ages, sexes and conditions of man, and the point which arrested my attention and caused me to consider the ant was that of destruction. It was the fate of some to die beneath the tread of the passing people, but the survivers kept at their business with no apparent cessation or delay, and the advice seemed plain enough: "Go to the ant, thou sluggard; consider her ways," and be wise enough to go to work. Enter the vineyard in the morning and toil until night; bear the burden and heat of the day with fortitude; be thankful that the brain and muscle, which a kind Providence has given you, can be put to good and everlasting use; consider the ant and her ways; keep right on in your work; take little or no time for your meals; never waste the precious moment by talk with your neighbors, for is not the working ant a neuter, without sex, no family ties, no mating season; consider her ways and be wise; let your motto be *business* first, last and all the time. The male ant has wings and takes a "nuptial flight," accompanied by the female ant, also on wings, and after this short and happy example to the unemployed the male ant dies and the female ant founds a new colony of ants, a large percentage being neuters, or workers. If the male sluggard considers the ant at the nuptial flight season it is quite likely he will think it wise to join forces with a congenial female sluggard. But at Merced I considered another matter—it was the average of chance in the destruction of the ant stepped upon by the passing throng. It was not only possible but probable that many of these ants worked all day on the path and escaped scot-free; some were maimed, but still worked on, and the lesson I took was this: No matter what threatens, attend to your own affairs; let the dread and doubt and fear, the apprehension and the borrowed trouble die in one grave. Give fair attention and honest measure to your employer, but also attend to the wants of body and mind, that health and temperance may follow you to a happy home. You will feel the iron heel which stamps you out of existence all in due time, and perhaps it would be fair to twist the advice to read: Go to the ant, thou sluggard; consider her ways and be otherwise.

BY AND BY.

The weary clerk looked up from his book,
   As the "special" passed him by,
And he gave the traveling man a look,
   And muttered, with a sigh:
"How sleek and saucy he appears,
   How cheerful in his glance;
Of creditors he has no fears,
   Who lead me such a dance.
He thinks that he is fixed for life;
   Just wait and see me try,
I'll get his place without much strife;
   It will be mine, by and by.

     It will be mine, by and by,
       By and by;
     It will be mine, by and by.
     In just about two years,
     He will have cause for fears,
      It will be mine, by and by."

The manager sat in his easy chair,
   And pressed a little bell;
The "special" tumbled through the air,
   And, hastening, nearly fell.
The manager said: "Now, take the train,
   And travel for a year,
Whether in sunshine or in rain,
   And let good work appear."
The "special" started on his way,
   With a satchel in each hand,

And as he traveled, day by day,
  In obedience to command,
He thought : " He seems to have a cinch,
  His job is very fine;
But wait until he gets the ' pinch,'
  And then it will be mine.

It will be mine, by and by,
        By and by;
It will be mine, by and by.
I 'll be quiet for awhile,
But, pretty soon, I 'll smile,
    It will be mine, by and by."

The Death Angel paused in his flight o'er the town,
  With a gloomy air and severe,
And, as he marked his victims down,
  He said, with a ghastly sneer:
"It 's really funny to hear them talk,
  And scheme for each other's place,
While I am ready the plans to balk
  Of all the human race.
An insect has more sense than they,
  As it flutters in the sun,
For *it* enjoys each warming ray,
  And *their* worry is never done.

They will be mine, by and by,
        By and by;
They will be mine, by and by;
I will shut off their breath,"
Said the Angel of Death,
    "They will be mine, by and by."

I MET a local agent who represented our worthy President in an
Oregon town. Said he: "I am surprised to find that my manager, far
from being the strict churchman I had supposed, is no better than he
should be ; why, he is actually profane in correspondence, and that I hold
to be inexcusable." I stopped him and demanded proof. The letter
ran something like this : "We feel that it is high time to hear from your
agency. We find on looking over the expiration book that we have not
had a D—— R from you in three months. This worldly agent had
construed the D to mean dash and the R risk.

A young and bashful special was called upon to adjust a loss on "female wearing apparel" belonging to a plump and pleasing young widow, as fair as a June apple, and whose well-turned foot reminded you of Trilby's. After taking down a list of opera cloaks, silk and satin dresses, dresses cut square, on the bias and gored up the back, dresses high from the ground and low from the ceiling, he came at last to that which even the most hardened of our special agents return in their proof as "underwear"; but this poor, timid, bashful special (a *rara avis* to be sure) was aware of the necessity of having a complete list of everything, and so "corsets" and "chemises" were put down, and his voice weakened, for the lady looked daggers, as he said: "Now, madam, I am nearly through; how many pairs of silk stockings did you say were damaged?" "Seven pairs, and they cost me $10.50 per pair, and I can't wear them again." The price seemed an exaggeration to the special, although he remembered the McKinley tariff had just gone into effect; so he said: "They come high, don't they?" "No," said the lady, fiercely; "not any higher than usual. I always wear mine long." This flabbergasted the young special, and he decided to finish the adjustment at once, so said, "Please let me see your stockings." "Sir," said the lady, "do you dare." This settled the special, but not the loss. Next day our plump and pleasing widow called at the office and told the manager that she had been insulted; that no unmarried man had the right to ask her such questions, smiling sweetly on the manager the while. He took the adjustment into his own hands, paying more, I have been told, than if a valued policy law were in force.

From various sources the following has been sent in, but as no two stories are quite alike I take the liberty of an original version:

One day a telegraph boy brought a dispatch from a remote region, reading:

"Large losses here cause general congratulations; your office has twelve thousand total." Well, I thought, that is candid, to say the least. I know times are hard and business dull; I also have a feeling of uneasiness about incendiarism, and from the tone of the agent's letters heretofore I somehow felt lack of confidence, but this bare-faced exultation over the prospect of a cash sale to insurance companies is carrying bad practices quite too far. It transpired in due time that an error had been made in transmitting the message, which was intended to read, "Large losses here cause general conflagration," etc.

A BRIGHT young agent who hails from the Garden City thought the compact ought not to charge for a cement chimney which was not in actual use. His erudite and "strictly in line" manager told him the charge must be made; that as long as the chimney remained, even if it were not in use, a charge should be made, and that the only way to obtain a reduction would be to remove the chimney. Nothing daunted, this bold but smooth-faced youth, whose smile reminds you of your best girl, would not have it, so he wrote out the following endorsement: "Warranted by the assured that the cement chimney will only be used during the life of the policy for *ventilation purposes*." The aforesaid manager, who loves a joke, sent the endorsement to the compact—*and it passed*.

> If I should die to-night
> And you should come to my cold corpse and say,
> Weary and heartsick o'er my lifeless clay ;
> If I should die to-night
> And you should come in deepest grief and woe,
> And say, "Here's that ten dollars that I owe,"
> I might arise in my large white cravat
> And say, "What's that?"
>
> If I should die to-night
> And you should come to my cold corpse and kneel,
> Clasping my bier to show the grief you feel ;
> I say if I should die to-night,
> And you should come to me there and then,
> Just even hint 'bout paying me that ten,
> I might arise the while,
> But I'd drop dead again.

IT WAS a small town, and he was young, but earnest, when appointed local agent. He soon mastered the rate book and insured his brother's stock. The brother strongly objected to the high rate and produced last year's policy. It was no use, rules are rules and the minimum rate book contained these words :

> Rate on building 1.60
> Rate on contents 1.80

The total of these figures is 3.40, and the brother had to pay that rate, or fight—and he paid.

A NEVADA ADJUSTMENT.

SOME say special work is hard and that experience is necessary for success in that line. I made my first trip last week, wrote up some new business, adjusted a loss and found it easy. I suppose there is a difference in men, but I'm a student. I've read the rate books from One to Four, and all of the Pacific Insurance Union circulars, including those that didn't go. I know "Lowden's" Adjustment of Book Losses by heart, and have studied the Kinne Rule over and over, but O! I hope I will never have to adjust a loss where the policies don't read alike. If there's anything in Tiffany, Griswold or Hine I'm not posted on, it must be in later editions than mine. I've even read the Otey Manual clear through, including the dedication and diagrams. So, when the manager called me up from the supply department and started me on a special trip, I was sure I'd succeed because I had the theory down fine and all I had to do was to apply it. I didn't travel far, but I may go out again next summer and stay longer.

First I went to Elko, arriving there January 3d. Agent Jones gave me $2,000 on the "Diamond Hotel." On the fifth the hotel burned. That was too bad, for it set a splendid table. I don't know why they did not get me to adjust that loss.

Then I went to Be-owa-we and took the stage for Weeping Water station, 30 miles west. There I appointed J. Wesley Ferguson agent. He is also postmaster, justice of the peace, notary public, stage agent, express agent, and has a cattle range of 3,700 acres near the station. I insured his dwelling house and showed him how to make the rate under Book 4.

"First," I said, "the basis is seventy-five cents."

"As low as that?" asked the new agent.

"Yes; but that's on each hundred dollars, you know."

"All right," said Ferguson.

"Then for deficiencies we add seventy-five cents."

"What's that for?"

"Isn't there an old silk hat stuck through a broken window up stairs?"

"Yes."

"Well, you can see by the book that we have to charge seventy-five cents for a stovepipe through the side, window or roof."

"Correct," said Ferguson.

"Now for the exposure charges."

"The dwelling stands alone," said the agent; "there's no other building nearer than two miles east, where I have a wooden house occupied by the men at the round-up station, and west three miles I have a cattle barn."

"Hold on," said I, pleasantly; "we must go by the book. For frame dwelling house situate two miles east of said dwelling, on said ranch, fifty cents, and for frame private barn situate on said ranch three miles west, fifty cents."

"Are they exposures when they are so far away?" asked the agent.

"Well," I answered, "to be fair and square with you, I don't think them very dangerous, even in a strong wind, but we have to charge for them just the same, for the rule says: 'Charge for every other building in the range.'"

"That's all right," said Ferguson. "I see you know your business."

"Any objections to my adding the 'adjuster's clause'?" I asked.

"No," he replied, "everything goes. You're pretty good on addition, old man; add anything you want."

So I wrote $2,000 on his dwelling for five years, annual rate two and a half, term rate seven and a half, premium $150, and then went to Reno, where I made my first adjustment. The policy covered $500 on a frame dwelling house, $300 on household furniture and $200 on one violin.

The assured was a professional musician, well known in Reno, a distinguished violinist, and appeared to be a man of superior education. Everything checked up all right until I came to the violin.

"Professor," I said, "that must have been a fine fiddle of yours to have had $200 insurance on it. Where did you buy it?"

"It was left to me by my father," he replied, and the tears came to his eyes. "It had been in our family for many years."

When he said this I knew I had him, but I never changed countenance, and continued; "What did you value it at?"

"It was priceless. I refused $4,000 for it. It was insured for a trifling sum, for I never expected a fire."

"What make was it?"

"A genuine Stradivarius, and was inscribed 'Antonius Stradivarius Faciebat, Cremona, 1771'."

"Who was Faciebat?" I asked. "One of the firm?"

He looked at me wearily and answered, "Faciebat is Latin for 'he made it.' The violin was made by the great Stradivarius at Cremona, Italy, in 1771."

"In 1771 and this is 1895. Then it was a hundred and twenty-four years old, and we supposed we were insuring a new, first-class violin. Of course you don't make any claim on that item, professor?"

"Why not?"

"Look here," said I; "See what Tiffany says;" and I pulled the book on him. " Musical instruments depreciate annually 5 per cent. You can figure the depreciation yourself, professor. A hundred and twenty-four years at five per cent. a year leaves no value, and Griswold says: 'Where there 's no value there 's no liability'.''

" But "— said the professor,

"Tiffany," said I—

" D—n your Tiffany and Griswold, too," said the professor; "was there ever such an idiot? ''

" Do you mean me ? '' said I.

"Never mind, sir," he replied, "I 'll write to the company."

"Very well," I answered, and left him. But I never understood why the company finally paid him a total loss.

E. NILES.

THE SUPPRESSED VERSION.

(Not allowed to be sung in San Francisco.)

There was once a simple agent came to 'Frisco on a trip,
When the Compact rates were split right up the back;
His cheek was still unhardened, he 'd a smile upon his lip,
Though the Compact rates were split right up the back.
When he landed at the ferry he took a little stroll,
And he met a nervous manager who had lost his self-control;
Said he : " The news is awful. Why, bless your verdant soul,
The Compact Rates are split right up the back. "

But, oh dear, he doesn't look the same;
　When he left Milpitas he was shy,
But alas, and alack, he 's gone back
With a naughty little twinkle in his eye.

He walked up town with a twist upon his face,
For the Compact rates were split right up the back;
It was hard to hold his morals in their customary place,
For the Compact rates were split right up the back.
Of course he knew his manners, he'd been taught to be polite,
So when asked, "Hem, cut rates?" he said, "Hem, all right.
I 'm a stranger in the city, but at home I 'll try to fight,
While the Compact rates are split right up the back."

He took his arm in confidence, he liked his pleasant ways,
While the Compact rates were split right up the back;
And as he passed the offices he stared in great amaze,
For the Compact rates were split right up the back.
He asked on what the cut would go, the answer was "good biz,"
Then he took him into Collins' and treated him to fizz;
Said he, "I think it's nicer than a glass of milk, it is,
Though the Compact rates were split right up the back."

They drank until the artless man so very weary grew,
While the Compact rates were split right up the back;
That a six per centum rate was dwindled down to two,
For the Compact rates were split right up the back.
Then silently he left the town and took the evening train
And wrote up hay barns at a rate that gave the office pain,
Said he, "They'll never catch me with their Compact again,
For the Compact rates are split right up the back."

But, oh dear, he doesn't act the same;
When he left Milpitas he was shy,
But alas, and alack, he went back
With a naughty little twinkle in his eye.

E. NILES.

A WELL-KNOWN broker in a city not far distant, and whom we will call Long, for short, called upon a certain manager, who is known for his suavity of manner, and offered a line of insurance upon a "glucose factory," which risk was on the "prohibited list" of the aforesaid manager. The manager declined the risk, but the broker persisted, and said: "You know there is no 'moral hazard' in connection with this risk"—naming the gentleman connected with it. The manager said: "We are aware of that and our objection goes to the 'physical hazard.'" The broker replied: "I fear you are mistaken; have you ever inspected the property?" "No," said the manager, "but such risks are physically poor." "You are mistaken in this," said the broker, "for I have made a personal inspection of it, and you ought to see the great, big, strong men working there; their arms were bare and their muscles stood out like whip-cords, and their broad chests and powerful limbs were superb. I never saw men better made physically. I am certain you would change your opinion about the 'physical hazard' if you could see these men." The manager smiled, but had strength enough left to decline the risk.

A DETECTIVE STORY.

I HOPE I am not over confident of my own power of discernment, and no one has ever accused me of undue egotism, but I feel sure if I were not a special agent I would be a detective. I pride myself on my knowledge of human nature and my ability to see the motives of men at a glance. This was in a measure demonstrated at the large fire at Traver, and I have given the subject of one particular loss a good deal of thought since then, and I think I have gained knowledge of great value both to a special and a detective. The facts are these: One night, or rather morning, for it was about 2 o'clock A. M., after a long sitting with a claimant I went into the cool air for the purpose of refreshing myself preparatory to sleep. I was drowsily smoking, when all at once I saw a dark shadow moving along the street in a noiseless and apparently stealthy way. With equal caution I followed. It proved to be a man, and he went with great care and precision to the rear of a building situated on the outer edge of the burned district, let himself into the back door by means of a key, fastened the door, lighted a candle and with deliberate action put a pile of rags in the middle of the floor, poured kerosene over them from a convenient can, and applied a match. I saw the flames burst forth, and waiting to see no more I ran at once to the home of the town marshal; awakening that official I quickly told the story, then hastened to the bedside of a few trusty adjusters, arousing them also to action. With much discretion we surrounded the store where the fire had been started. Through the shutters we could still see the form of the incendiary feeding the flames. The marshal had no difficulty in recognizing the man as Alex Wollenslagger, of the firm of Dagger & Wollenslagger, and it was well known they were claimants by the recent loss. After a council of war, so to speak, the marshal beat a loud tattoo on the front door, at the same time calling upon the incendiary by name to come out, and be d——d to him. This had the desired effect, and Wollenslagger came forth. He was the coolest villian I thought I had ever seen. He had the obsequious air of a counter-jumper, and the accent which is a dead give-away. He invited us inside with much apparent hospitality, and his eye never blinked nor did his color once change. This, thought I, is the most hardened scoundrel ever caught red-handed. Finally, the marshal recovered from his temporary stupor and made his arrest, naming all the damaging evidence in our possession and the eye witnesses to the crime. "That is all right," said Wollenslagger; "I settles my loss with the Royal Insurance Company yesterday, and I gets ready for a schmoke damage and a cash sale to-morrow." The adjuster of the Royal was still in town and confirmed

Wollenslagger's story. The smoke was an after thought to influence trade.

I DIDN'T THINK HE'D DO IT; BUT HE DID.

As sung by E. W. CARPENTER.

[A very much resigned ex-company manager.]

The world is full of people who are always on the bluff,
　　And you meet them—ev'ry where.
In our underwriting business we 've found many that are tough,
　　Hardly ever—on the square.
I had an old-time customer whose rate was boosted higher;
　　He "kicked" and said insurance was "no good."
I jokingly suggested he could square accounts by fire;
　　To tell the truth I didn't think he would.

CHORUS:

　　I didn't think he 'd do it, but he did, did, did;
　　He said he always knew it, and he did.
　　He beat me "by a scratch,"
　　With his auburn-headed match;
　　I didn't think he 'd do it, but he did.

Though proof was really lacking, I accused him of the crime,
　　Said I 'd land him—in the jail,
And I quoted court decisions from the early English time,
　　In a way that—made him quail,
But finally suggested that I might not prosecute,
　　So full of human kindness was my mood,
If for one dollar full receipt he 'd promptly execute;
　　To tell the truth, I didn't think he would.

CHORUS:

　　I didn't think he 'd do it, but he did, did, did;
　　He wanted to get through it, and he did.
　　He took his dollar bright
　　Then briskly skipped from sight,
　　I didn't think he 'd do it, but he did.

I trembling, took the policies, was paralyzed with joy,
    But recovered—very quick,
When claimant's many creditors quite promptly did employ
    An attorney—smart and slick,
Who "intimidation" hinted at, and prison bars "to boot,"
    Claimed total loss in manner very rude.
I told him I'd receipts in full—he'd better bring his suit;
    To tell the truth, I didn't think he would.

CHORUS:

    I didn't think he'd do it, but he did, did, did;
    He told me that I'd rue it, and I did.
    On the judge he "had the call,"
    Made me pay claim, costs and all,
    I didn't think he'd do it, but he did.

Now episodes like this one detract sadly from the bliss
    Underwriters—all desire.
But when thereto, through faithless fraud, large loads of acts remiss,
    Are by themselves piled higher,
I was so much disgusted that I couldn't help but tell
    (In vernacular so plainly understood),
My offices I "guessed" I'd quit—the "biz" could go to ——*
                   (*Spoken*) *Well*,
    Of course, you know, I didn't think it would.

CHORUS:

    From present point of view, it seems it did, did, did;
    For *something* happened to it, yes there did,
    But where going to or gone
    Is too deep a thought for song.
    I didn't think 'twould do it, but it did.

---

*Considering the present unsettled condition of insurance affairs on this Coast (to which, as a whole, and not to the "biz" of any particular office, reference is here made) the writer would not hazard a suggestion as to the locality, and the reader can (of rhyme regardless) supply the omission in accordance with his idea of the situation as seen from his individual point of view.

ONE of our managers has a family of beautiful children. They were discussing a gentleman friend at table, when the little daughter asked, "What is a bachelor?" "Ugh," said the little boy, "anybody knows that. A bachelor is a man whose wife does not wear a wedding ring."

"WAIT, MR. POSTMAN!"

The postman was late, and was running along,
To gather the letters in time,
When he heard a gruff voice like a bull-frog's song,
Or a mellow-toned cow-bell's chime.

CHORUS :—

" Wait, Mr. Postman, don't hurry so fast,
   Wait, Mr. Postman, I've caught you at last;
   This letter must go in the mail before two,
   So our Oakland agent will know what to do,
   Wait, Mr. Postman, please bend down your head,
   Wait, Mr. Postman, the compact's not dead;
   Wait, Mr. Postman, for heaven's sake wait,
   Or he'll give us more risks at a deep-cut rate."

THE NAUGHTY MAN.

By R. W. OSBORN, as sung by A. M. BROWN.

(With apologies to "The Bogie Man.")

Come, listen to my song to-night, you underwriters all,
I'll tell you 'bout the naughty man, who's bound to have his fall—
He joins the P. I. U., he does, the rules and laws he'll scan,
But he'll not keep to anything, this very naughty man.

CHORUS:

Fie! Fie! Fie! Oh, what a naughty man,
To join the P. I. U. and promise everything he can;
Just look there, and quickly his face scan,
And tell me if you'd think him such an awful naughty man.

He goes into the street forthwith, a broker for to catch,
And offers twenty-five, but finds the other quite his match;
He offers thirty, thirty-five, the limit of his plan—
Another takes the broker from this very naughty man.

[CHORUS:]

The next step is the country, there an agent for to get,
He 'll not stop short of twenty-five or thirty, you can bet;
To drop or shelve the other one is usually his plan,
You can't find out so very much about this naughty man.

[CHORUS:]

Then comes disruption, threatened so, to all along the line.
The organization fails to cash a solitary fine;
So daily do the members meet to formulate a plan,
To check the work and damage of this very naughty man.

[CHORUS:]

Then one his resignation sends, in hopes to bear good fruit,
When, within a week or two, so many follow suit;
The war gets warm, and each man sweats, some needing much a fan,
And on account the crooked ways of this very naughty man.

[CHORUS:]

The new board forms and to the sea each underwriter went,
To discuss the ways and means, the naughty things we must prevent;
When they returned quite full of joy at a perfected plan,
They bid good-bye to tricks and works of this very naughty man.

[CHORUS:]

LATER. [POSSIBLY A LITTLE PREMATURE.]

The war is fully over and we are all into line,
New hope springs up, bad faith no more, for all is looking fine;
Each man has to his senses come, and every face you scan
So clearly shows from this time on there is no naughty man.

CHORUS:

Ha! ha! ha! each is a goody man,
To join hands with the rest of us to do the good he can;
Ha! ha! ha! just try each face to scan,
And it will be impossible to find a naughty man.

EDITORIAL, 1896.   GEO. F. GRANT.

EDITORIAL.

IT HAS been a subject of comment at home and abroad that the insurance people of the Pacific Coast have deliberately thrown away a large and desirable business. It reminds us of the man who killed the goose who laid the golden eggs.

In the man's case it was curiosity to see where the golden eggs came from; in the case of the insurance people it was different.

The insurance publications of New York and Chicago are particularly satirical and facetious in their comments on the situation, and yet it is not new or strange, *except* to the Pacific Coast. In certain districts in the East there is a mild eruption, with more or less feverish action all the time.

The Pacific Coast has been for many years unusually prosperous, and all classes thrived; money came to all, whether in or out of the insurance business. When I say of the Coast, "It has been" prosperous, that very nearly tells the tale, for a "has been" seldom attains a second time, so far as fame and fortune is concerned, a position where he can be said to be in it, or of it, strictly speaking.

From 1875 to 1890 money was easy to get, everybody seemed to have enough and to spare ; "the wave of prosperity" seemed to be ever at the flood. In insurance business we thought our success an evidence of superior judgment on the part of officers, and we talked freely and learnedly of the "science" of our trade; we ranked ourselves with bankers and financial agents, and plumed ourselves not a little on the keen insight into human nature we possessed which made us particularly fitted for our dignified and scientific calling. In 1891 the wave of prosperity was going out, but we heeded it not. In 1892 we felt something, but did not know what had hit us ; at least I have thus far failed to find the man who claims he then knew what has since been shown to all. While the knowledge of the advent of hard times was slowly filtering into our dull minds, we were irritable, accusing each other, trying to fasten the blame for loss of business on the Compact, on the unprincipled agent, and on the lack of Faith, Hope and Charity in our associates, and on all of them, irrespective of previous reputation.

The Compact was such a perfect machine that it took the place of skilled labor, and when we killed the Compact we were obliged to exercise our alleged brains (Heaven save the mark!)—and after that the cunning instinct which dwells more or less with every man was aroused and put into action. Look at the annual figures for 1895 and read the story; that is the result of our best efforts to prove our eminent and unusual fitness to manage the affairs of an insurance office during hard times. What I was about to say is this: When "good times" return we will have peace—I mean by good times, general prosperity. When money is plenty and easy to get, the insurance business will once more be ranked as a science, but you can take my word you will never see the business as it has been on the Pacific Coast.

It is perhaps needless for me to say my remarks are particularly addressed to the young men of the Association, to whom the "insurance war" will soon be but a part of history.

THE only incident I remember, said the quiet member, which will be at all appropriate for the *Knapsack*, occurred many years ago at Santa Cruz. The town was small and the stage road over the mountain was inaccessible in the winter months. There was no telegraph line, and sometimes the people waited as long as sixty days for a San Francisco paper. The sea also was rough, and steamers could not land. About this time the town folks started a hose company, but as a matter of fact it was more of a salvage corps than a hose company, owing to the limited supply of water. Our office had a policy in the contents of a boarding and lodging house, and a loss was reported. The assured was a quick-witted but uneducated son of the Emerald Ise, and he claimed "everything in sight," as the expression goes.

It was beyond doubt an incendiary fire, and started in the corner of the sitting room down stairs. A quick alarm was given, and the fire boys not content with putting out the fire, moved all the furniture on the second story across the street to an empty building. This they did so carefully that no damage was done, and only the bed clothing looked disturbed; the sheets, blankets and covers were tumbled together, but otherwise uninjured. I went over the ground with the assured, exercising great patience. We talked of the origin of the fire, the condition of the contract, the duty of the assured and the liability of the company; and finally, out of patience, I said, "But you have no claim here; nothing is destroyed." "How about the bed clothes?" he said. "Why, man, it is only necessary to wash them." "Wash them, is it," he replied; "wash them? Don't you know it damages sheets like hell to wash them."

EIGHT WORD POEM.

> Cut rate,
>   Long trust;
> Big line,
>   Soon bust.

SONOMA agents claim that in their county a good article of grape butter is made by churning the wine.

> SPECIAL, spare that rate!
>   O, cut it not in half,
> Nor anything abate,
>   Lest customers may laugh,
> And say, with a broad grin,
>   "Aha, we told you so;
> They're fighting now like sin,
>   And *we* will have a show."
>
> Special, spare that rate!
>   And split it not in twain.
> For years it sheltered me,
>   And may do so again;
> Swing not your ready axe,
>   Draw not your snickersnee;
> Special, spare that rate!
>   If you would happy be.
>
> Special, hold that rate!
>   And at a fair price sell,
> For if you wildly cut,
>   The rates will go to—well!
> They're sure to go below
>   A figure just and right;
> Special, spare that rate!
>   Nor send it "out of sight."

"SOUT' O' MARKET."

AT DE time of de big fire, sout' o' Market, last June, I had me room at Mrs. Muldoon's, on Freelon street, near Fourt.' De old gal had tree hundred insurance; two hundred on her furniture and one hundred on her pianny. De nex' morning after de fire she gives me de policy and says:

"Mickey" (me name's Michael, but dey calls me Mickey fer short), "Ye goes down to de office and ye brings me de tree hundred, fer I *needs* it," she says.

"Well, *all right*," I says, and I goes to de office.

I goes in—it was a dandy office, wid de prettiest gal I ever see in one corner tumping hell's delight out of a pocket pianny—I tought it was—but dere's a pal o' mine on Jessie street dat knows; he told me afterwards it was a type *rider;* and a four-eyed dude steps up to de counter, and he says right off, hot from de bat:

"Well, young feller, wot *you* want?"

Say, I ain't no fool, if I never had no edoocation 'cept dat night school at de Lincoln, and I sees right off he was no good.

"Where's de main guy?" I says.

"*Who?*" he says.

"De foreman; de man wot writes de policies. Dere was a fire at Muldoon's. Say, de poor woman wants tree hundred," and I trew down de paper. "Does she *get* it? She's a poor, hard-workin' woman. She says her beads reg'lar an' she *needs* de dough."

De dude stepped into a room wid glass around it and den comes out and says: "Dis way, sir, if ye please;" jest like dat; smoot' as dose butter cakes at Dennett's.

I goes in an' dere was anodder dude wid his Sunday cloze on, but a pleasant feller, and he says: "Wot's yer name, sir?"

"Michael Free."

He says: "Mr. Free, are ye *square?*"

"On de roof," I says; but say, ye could have knocked me down wid a fedder.

"Ye roomed at Muldoon's?"

"Dat's wot I did."

"Look here, Mr. Free," he says, "you know what Mrs. Muldoon lost? We gives her every cart-wheel she loses—dat's all. Did she lose three hundred?"

"Nit," I says.

"Did de pianny burn?"

"Naw," I says.

"Mr. Free," he says, "you goes and settles dat loss and I pays you. Look out for depreecyashun."

"Is dat de dude wid de blinkers?"

He laughed.

"Mr. Free," he says, "what did dat suit o' han'-me-downs cost you?"

"Nine plunkers at Roos's," I says.

"Wot are dey wort now?" he asked.

"Maybe tree dollars," I said.

"Dat's *depreecyashun*," he says. Say, I caught on in a minit.

Well, I goes and settles wid de old woman. I tells her nottin' goes on de pianny cos it didn't burn. She kicked a little, but not much. Den I figgered de furniture. Say, I know every second-hand joint on Mission street where she got it. De lot cost her a hundred and sixty-six. Den I says:

"Dere's eighty-tree dollars off for depreecyashun"—

"Fat de divil's dat, Mickey?" said she.

"Dat's de wear and tear," I says.

"Holy Saint Bridget, how much does I get?" says she.

"Eighty-tree dollars, net," says I.

"Is it *net* or *nit*, Mickey?" says she.

O, she was a funny old gal; she'd joke on her deat' bed.

"Hurry, quick, Mickey," says she; run, ye divil, to de office and get me de eighty-tree dollars before ye spring any more Frinch words on me."

Dey coughed up de dough all right, den de foreman says:

"Mickey, yere a *fine* adjooster; how much does we owe you?"

"Well," I says, "I makes two cases a day when I works at de foundry. I works on dis half a day; dat's one iron dollar."

Say, he gave me a big twenty, and now I cleans de office and maybe I goes on de road next year in Alameda county. De old gal bought four hundred dollars wort' of new furniture on de installment plan, and I says:

"Say, does we give you tree hundred insurance?"

"*Naw*," says she, "I insures for what I *gits*. You tell 'em to make de paper for *eighty-tree dollars, divil a cent more*."

And so de old gal gets a policy for eighty-tree.

Say, if dere's any more fires sout' o' Market, let me figger on de props. Leave word at de Caffy Royal. I gits a steam beer dere ev'ry noon.

E. NILES.

A CRIPPLE CREEK ADJUSTMENT.

IT WAS, perhaps, the most remarkable adjustment on record. I have had a tolerable experience in that line, but never heard of a similar case. It seems almost incredible, and might not be believed if it were not for the fact that such well-known insurance men as Charlie Wilson, Fred Buck and D. C. Packard of Denver, W. S. McIntyre of Colorado Springs, and John H. Kirtland of Pueblo, know the facts in the case and will bear witness to the truth of this plain, unvarnished statement. Verily, truth is more wonderful than romance! To think that Cripple Creek, with its golden flow of increasing millions, took its start from the burning of an adobe dwelling house, on which there was an insurance of but five hundred dollars! It sounds like one of those glittering tales from the Arabian Nights, and recalls the marvelous adventures that occurred in the days of the good Haroun Al Raschid.

There are many San Francisco insurance men who knew James W. Ferguson when he was special agent and adjuster for the old "Concordia" (that wasn't it's name, but those who know the writer will remember the company well), and who know him now as one of the multi-millionaires of Colorado. Cripple Creek and he both boomed after that adobe dwelling burned. Pshaw! when I think of the many millions that little fire developed I have no patience with my humdrum life, and its petty economies.

"Jim" Ferguson, as we called him, now divides his time between Chicago and Denver. He is a large holder of choice inside property at Denver, and in Chicago is best known by the magnificent Ferguson block on Adams street, a seventeen story office building of marble and steel. It was there that I met him last December when he told me the simple story of his great good luck. He said:

"Five years ago I was at Denver as special agent for the 'Concordia' of San Francisco. While there the company wired me to proceed to Fremont and adjust a supposed total loss of $500 on an adobe dwelling house owned by one Jose de La Guerra. The risk had been written by McIntyre and Hayden, our agents at Colorado Springs, from which Fremont was distant eighteen miles as the crow flies, or about twenty-eight miles by road. To be brief, I made the adjustment, found the assured a gentleman, the loss straight, and everything satisfactory.

"While waiting for my team to be brought up to take me back to the Springs, I carelessly looked through the debris of the burned adobe, and on kicking one of the crumbling slabs with my foot was surprised to see it filled with glittering particles. 'Pyrites of iron,' was my first thought; my next was 'gold!' I decided to take no chances, and before starting secured the assured's stipulation to the effect that he relinquished all claim to the debris. I filled a salt sack with a sample of the adobe and went straight to Denver. The assayer at the Grant Smelter was an old friend and gave me a quick assay which showed that the dirt went $93,000 to the ton in gold. I hastened back, sacked the entire lot and shipped it to Denver. The net returns were something over $43,000, some of the dirt being very rich and some poor, but the average was good.

"I sent the proceeds to the company, which immediately declared a five dollar dividend and the stock jumped from $87 to $105. The secretary acknowledged receipt of my report of the salvage and its accompanying draft, and referred to my action as being somewhat irregular, but on the whole, acceptable. This I thought cold, so I resigned. Then I hunted up De La Guerra, and bought for $500 a two-thirds interest in ten acres which he owned at Fremont, on a part of which the adobe bricks had been made, started in placer mining there, and in six weeks we cleaned up $93,666, of which my share was exactly $62,444. This rich ground, as everybody knows who has been at Cripple Creek, as Fremont is now called, was immediately back of where the Palace Hotel on Main street now stands.

"Then the town began to boom. I put down six shafts and struck it rich in five of them. One of them proved barren, the 'Independence,' and I sold it to Stratton, a poor devil of a carpenter who came over from Colorado Springs, for $250, and told him to pay me if he ever struck it. Two months after, he 'struck it' all right, and to-day is the richest mine-owner at Cripple. He takes out half a million a month from the 'Independence,' and has a standing offer of ten millions for it. Maybe he isn't a good friend of mine! Well, that's all there is to it. Lucky, wasn't I? Let's have a small bottle or two."

E. NILES.

A GOOD friend who loves to indulge in metaphor was speaking of local agents. Said he: "You go to work and build a man up from the ground, and along comes a big fish and swallows him, and you lose the premium it has taken years to nurse to life."

Question in Application: "Have you personally inspected the risk *inside* and out?"

Agents' Answer: "From the outside only."

N. B.—The subject of insurance was a stack of hay.

THE companies' fears for the future are like those of the honest German who was overheard talking to his dog:

"Mein dog, dere is a great difference from me und you. You play all day, but I haf to vork all de vile. You youst have fun. Vell, de time vill gome already ven you haf to die, and den dot is de end of you. But it is different mid me. I have to go to hell yet already."

FOUND IN A PALACE CAR.

One calm, consoling thought
  Comes to me o'er and o'er,
When riding on the rail
  Is something of a bore;
When stages are upset,
  And steamboats make me ill,
This thought relieves my pain:
  The office pays the bill.

When letters criticise,
  And make me rather tired;
When they become so wise,
  Somebody should be fired;
When agents fail to pay,
  And give the "hard times fill,"
I keep my even way;
  The office pays the bill.

That tranquilizing thought
  Steals o 'er me night and day;
I have no board to square,
  I have no rent to pay;
No creditors can come
  My peace of mind to kill;
Expenses are charged up:
  The office pays the bill.

AT THE midsummer jinks last season one of the tents caught fire, and the occupant lost a few articles of clothing. General Barnes, the well known legal wit, stated that the insurance adjuster had compromised the loss. He convinced the claimant that the trousers burned were per. fectly good *below the knee*.

A RESPECTED agent at Healdsburg writes: "We have received one of those 'angel's visits, few and far between,' from your *specialist.*"

Query (from the inside). How many special agents are either "angels" or "specialists"; and if they were either one or the other what would be the effect on the insurance business to-day?

OUR supply clerk is a Swede. He attended a revival meeting recently. The clergyman asked him: "Peterson, are you willing to work for the Lord?"

"Ae don't know," he answered. "Ae got a good yob now. Ae tank ae keep dat."

EDITORIAL, 1897.   GEO. F. GRANT.

EDITORIAL.

THE aim and object of the *Knapsack* is to promote harmony and good will within the Association, and board or no board, compact or no compact, it proposes to carry out its object, even if is necessary to kill a member or two. There is good in everything, even in a kicker, and there is sweetness and purity in everything (when treated chemically), and if it becomes necessary for the *Knapsack* to cremate a fire underwriter of the Pacific, please understand that it is not for the fun of "burning him up," but for the purpose of purifying him.

It is claimed by some that the *Knapsack* is not run for profit—fallacious sentiment. It has profited many a contributor, and this year brings Charlie Hill prominently to the front in the Association with his admirable paper on "The Necessity of Revising the City Tariff." He wrote the same article in a condensed form for last year's *Knapsack*, and it was strangled at the printer's office by some crank and never saw ink. That was a good thing (for Mr. Hill), and whoever did it gave the members the pleasure of the more elaborate paper which deserved and received so much favor yesterday.

THE following was posted on a little church at Palestine, a colony near Fresno:

NOTICE.

There will be preaching in this church, Providence permitting, on Sunday next, and there will also be preaching here, whether or no, on the Sunday following, upon the subject: "He that believeth and is baptized shall be saved, and he that believeth not shall be damned" at precisely half past ten in the morning.

GIVE THE AGENT A CHANCE.

Our agent writes: I shall have a little over six hundred living risks on the books and several hundred that have died in the late war. With the aid of a tariff and a few compact rules I think I can raise the dead.

RULES OF THE GAME.

INSURANCE is a game. It can be played by two or more persons, and the rules differ according to location.

The first player is called the assured.

The prize is called a risk.

The stake is called the premium.

The second player is called the insurer.

The betwixt is called a solicitor.

The between is called an adjuster.

The teetotum is called journalism, and the same can be introduced into the game at discretion.

The assured is the dealer and pays out chips, each player receiving chips according to the rules; but when the assured runs out of chips a new deal can be demanded. If any assured refuses to pay out chips, when in the game, he becomes "red slip," and another takes his place; the red slip cannot again enter without first paying a forfeit; the game terminates when the last assured declares himself out of chips.

The risk is an important factor in the game, but in certain localities it is considered of less value than in others. A cautious player endeavors to secure each risk singly, but if one is playing for high stakes the object is to possess quickly as many risks as possible; a cautious player, if skillful, can often obtain a better result in the long run by single risks with less danger to his chips; if a player be both careless and unskillful, there is danger that he may be absorbed by a winner, and thus lose his place in the game. The risks should be in plain sight of the players at all times.

Each player can select one or more betwixts, according to rules agreed upon before the game commences. Each player stands behind his own betwixt and pushes him forward into the game. When a betwixt secures a risk it is placed to the credit of the player who backs him, and the assured shall pay over the equivalent in chips.

The risk is said to be good when the "between" can find no flaw in it, but if a player accept a risk as good, which subsequently proves imperfect, then he shall pay chips to the assured. If it is a fair game no player will know in advance the imperfect risk, but he shall have the privilege of inspecting it before he decides to take it in. A skillful player learns to know an imperfect risk on sight. If two players lay hold of the same risk they shall be allowed to pull for it, and he who has the greater pull secures it.

There can be many other rules, but it is a very pretty game as it stands.

I ENCLOSE you a contribution for the *Knapsack*, written by a personal friend, who says the name "Palache" haunted him for five years, but that now he had eased his mind, just as "Twain" did when he wrote "The pink trip slip for a three cent fare," etc.:

AN INSURANCE IDYL.

I tell you a tale of the days of old,
A tale that has never yet been told,
    How Whitney Palache
    Killed an Apache.

Kicking-Horse-with-the-mane-of-blue
Had a Wampum belt and a wigwam too;
    So Whitney Palache
    Approached the Apache.

"Pale-faced stranger, let me inquire
What happens in case of a prairie fire?"
    Said the Apache
    To Whitney Palache.

"Pieces of silver we give to you
For your Wampum belt and your wigwam too;"
    So Whitney Palache
    Insured the Apache.

Now it came to pass in a year and a day
That Whitney Palache was going that way;
    So Whitney Palache
    Addressed the Apache.

"Kicking-Horse, this day am I come
To pick up the annual pre-mi-um!"
    Then the Apache
    Looked at Palache.

"Better run off for fear of your life,
This is my sharpest scalping knife!"
    Growled the Apache
    At Whitney Palache.

"An Injun man is best when dead."
This was all that Palache said.
    Then Whitney Palache
    Smote the Apache.

FROM CHICAGO.

THERE is an occasional "happenstance" in this sun-scorched and blizzard-frozen section worthy even of being noted in the *Knapsack*. We sustained a loss last week at a little town in Arkansas. It now develops that the dwelling consumed was the property of a negro. It appears that he is a cook and secured a position in a neighboring town last fall, and while there conceived the wisdom of having his house burn up, upon which he had sufficient insurance to pay his mortgage and interest and leave him $90. He therefore wrote his wife a letter as per enclosed copy. The letter was unclaimed at the post-office, and as he had used an envelope of his employer with a return card in the corner, the letter was "Returned to writer." This darkey having meantime left his position, the letter was opened by his former employer, and upon its contents being discovered was placed in the hands of a prominent attorney in the town where the darkey lived, and thus reached us.

This unworthy follower of our Lord returned to his home and carried out his own instructions, and is now threatening suit to enforce recovery under his policy. The enclosed is an exact copy of the original letter, save the names:

Osceola, Ark., 9–27, '96.

Miss Rachel Snowball,

    Oskaloosa, Ark.:—

My dear wife i received your kind letters today and i was glad to knoe of your Being well but i am not well i Roat you 3 letters and you say you have not goot but 1 letter from me i don't see why you didn't get my Letters. Love i want you to burn up this Letter. i think you had Better let the house get Burnt and then we will get some money out of it i think that is the Best thing to do But you get the things all out we can get $90 and we can Build a house for that money i think is the Best thing to do it Rite now and you let me knoe you Be sure and Burn it up now Love you Burn the house up Love and we will save the place But if you dont we will louse it you be sure and do this Love i want to see you Rite bad i dont knoe what to do give my love to all Love i am sick Rite now But i am at work yet i dont no what with myself. Good Bye i will close.

Yours in christ

Geo. Snowball.

POOR JO. E. O'SHADY.

BY R. W. OSBORN.

If sung to the tune of "Sweet Rosie O'Grady" it will go.

Not far away from where I do insurance as a trade,
  There works another 'surance man at cutting rates I'm 'fraid;
He has a knife that is so sharp 'twill cut him to the bone;
  Just wait until you hear him from his private office groan.

CHORUS.

Poor Jo. E. O'Shady, with his knife so sharp,
  Sings his song of "cut rate" unaided by the harp;
Grief will come to him who fails to clearly see
  That Jo. E. O'Shady is naughty, naughty as Shady can be.

—Repeat.

This same man he does not care how deep he'll cut the rate;
  His company stands back of him what 'ere may be his fate;
So you can see that on the street a mighty man is he,
  To name the figure to which all the underwriters flee.

Chorus and repeat.

O'Shady does not stop to think that companies have souls;
  He seems to feel the "situation" he alone controls;
But he will find that "there 'r others" that do likewise have the nerve
  To fight and cut the rates of all, and thus their companies serve. (?)

Chorus.

The next year came and rates went down still lower in the scale;
  The cutter felt his nerve give way, his face began to pale;
Letters came to show dissatisfaction reigned at home;
  That Cæsar was not loved the less, but more they loved their Rome.

Chorus.

Like Cæsar poor O'Shady lost his head whlle in debate,
  Maintaining his position with the president sedate;
Alas! the Board Directors found the profits were not there,
  And passed a resolution making vacant 'Shady's chair.

Chorus.

AGENT at Milpitas telegraphs: "Small loss on lumber. Needs measuring. Piles non-concurrent. Send Kinne rule."

HE WAS a good fellow, a traveling special. He solicited the hotel risk of the landlord where he put up for the night. Landlord replied, ''I am already insured.''

''What rate do you pay?''

''Ten per cent.''

''Ten per cent.! Why, man, you are being robbed. I am a special agent, with power to appoint agents, write policies and collect premiums for the best company in the country, the Centaur Company, sir, and I tell you ten per cent. is highway robbery. Let me see your policies.'' (Landlord brings policies and exhibits them, the Centaur policy appearing on the list.) ''What 's that,'' said the special, ''the Centaur? That's my company, rate ten per cent. Well, well, I must examine this building; there must be something about it I don't understand.'' He examines the building, and then says to the landlord:

''I am a special agent with full power to act, and I tell you, land-lord, there is more wood in this building than in any building of its size I ever saw. The rate is all right, sir; ten per cent. is a fair rate, a very fair rate—considering the wood.''

ROCK-A-BY Compact on the tree-top,
With adequate rules, you are built like a clock;
  When the rules break the Compact will fall,
And down will come profit, rates, friendship and all.

Hey diddle, diddle, come guess me this riddle,
Ye managers who hope to stay in.
When rates are so low—loss ratios so high,
Where does the home office come in?

Sing a song of low rates, managers full of grit,
  Seven and sixty companies, net profit—Nit!
When the annuals are opened home office 'll begin to sing,
''Isn't this a pretty mess''—''Let 's stop this sort of thing.''

Presidents in the counting room looking for the gain,
Stockholders sat and glowered, swearing might and main;
Manager, far away, was planning how to spread,
When down came a telegram and took off his head.

ONE question on the application of a saloon risk was answered thus: ''There is no steam in the building except what is in the *beer*.''

A PIETY HILL ADJUSTMENT.

THE policy covered $1,600 in favor of Mary J. Riley, "on her two-story frame dwelling house situate on the north side of Porphyry avenue, between Quartz street and Bullion ravine, Piety Hill, Nevada county, California." The building burned last summer and an appraisement was entered into by Adjuster Anderson for the company and James Trevathan for the assured.

Anderson is a well-fed, warm-faced man of cheerful address, bold, shrewd and courteous.

Trevathan is a Cornish carpenter who sequesters himself, and makes lump estimates by some long, mysterious process of wrestling with the lower mathematics. He is inclined to be stubborn, but is open to reason. Being of slow thought and speech, he is susceptible to the quick action of a brighter mind.

The efforts of the appraisers to "come together" were somewhat one-sided, as will be seen by the following:

"Trevathan," said Anderson, "why didn't you meet me here this morning, so we could save time by making our figures together? I have nineteen adjustments on hand; appointments with five men and three women, and we haven't done a blamed thing. Say, old man, what's the matter?"

"I always figure alone," replied Trevathan, stolidly.

"Well," continued Anderson, "I see you make your total $1,650. Do you know, I thought the building was over-insured. I'll take your figures on the lumber, but there's one thing I must say before we go on with this. I want to do just what is right and give Mrs. Riley every dollar she lost. I have a conscience in these things, and you know, Trevathan, we've sworn to be just to the best of our knowledge and belief, and I tell you frankly, that if I find your figures are too low on any item, *I'll raise 'em*. I make no secret of this. I shall do it, and the company will have to stand it. Ain't I right, eh?"

There was an air of frank good fellowship about this statement that had its effect, and the carpenter at once assented to the justice of the proposed line of action.

"And what's the damage for nails?" airily continued Anderson.

"Eighteen dollars."

"You can't build that house with eighteen dollars' worth of nails. It wouldn't hold together. We musn't *rob* the poor woman. I'm going to raise that to *twenty-five dollars*. Isn't that right?"

Trevathan thought it was.

"Now, that's the way to do business," said Anderson. "I believe in being fair and liberal. In fact, I never adjust in any other way. Maybe we won't need the third man. What next?"

"Carpenter work, three hundred dollars."

"What!"

"I make labor three hundred," said Trevathan.

"But *why* do you? My estimate is a hundred and fifty."

No answer.

"*How* do you make it, Trevathan?"

"I wouldn't do it for less," was the reply.

"Well, let's hold that for the third man; but before we pass to the next item I want to tell you a good one on an acquaintance of mine at Anaconda. He was going to get married, and one of his friends started a subscription to get him a wedding present. Among those he solicited was an employe at the smelter, who gave five dollars, and asked what the gift would be. 'We thought of getting him something useful as well as ornamental,' was the reply, 'and have about decided to give him a silver-plated chandelier.' 'Don't you do it,' said the fellow earnestly, 'there isn't a man in town can play on it.' Now, how many doors and windows have you?"

"Six doors and eighteen windows. Eight dollars a door and six-fifty a window."

"Um-m—that's steep. I can get the doors in San Francisco for five and the windows for four, but, of course, labor's high here. It always is in mining towns. How much did you allow for the work on the doors and windows?"

"Two-fifty a door and two dollars a window."

"You're high, but we won't fight over it. I'll accept those figures. Now, let's go back to the carpenter work. Does your item of three hundred dollars include all of the labor?"

"Yes."

"How about the work on the doors and windows?"

"Why, er-r-r, no, it doesn't include that."

"My dear boy, don't you see you've charged twice for labor? Now, while I know the work on the house ought to be done for a hundred and fifty, I'll yield a point there and be liberal with you. I'll say two hundred. Is that right?"

"Well, yes," said Trevathan.

"Say, did you ever hear this?" said Anderson. "Referring to a suspicious fire, an honest citizen of hazy ideas was asked: 'What shall we do with the fire-bug if we catch him?' 'Why,' he replied, 'the *least* he can do is to marry the girl!' That's a good one, isn't it? Now, how much for painting?''

"Hundred and fifty.''

"Too much. Here's an estimate of ninety-three dollars from Avery, Vandyke & D'Auber, the best painters in town. What do you say?''

"They *can't* do it for that.''

"But they *will.*''

"Then let it go at their figures,'' said Trevathan.

"I see,'' said Anderson, "that you've left out an important item, and I'm going to put it in, for right's right. I may lose my job, but I don't care. That's the gutter on the roof—say ten dollars. Am I right, eh?''

"That's so; I forgot that,'' said Trevathan.

"Next comes the porch; what's your figure on that?''

"Eighty dollars.''

"By the gods, old man, I *can't* stand it; I can't *stand* it!'' said Anderson, rising from his chair and pacing the floor. "My estimate is forty. How do you make it eighty?''

"I wouldn't build it for less than that.''

"But *how* do you figure it?''

There was no reply.

Anderson looked reproachfully at the carpenter and said in a deep, mellow voice: "I will concede at the start, Mr. Trevathan, for I know you are a builder of large experience, that we must allow something for the porch, but we must not overlook the fact that most of it is standing, and while I do not claim that it is as good as it was before the fire, still it has a certain value as a *porch*, and just what this is, we are now to determine. At a later period we will consider its value as a part of the *daybree*. Now, come off the porch, old man; shall we say forty?''

"No.''

"I won't go so far as to insist that the porch shall be left standing and the house built against it, although that could be done. Well, say forty-five.''

"No,'' said the Cornishman.

"I won't stand more than fifty,'' said Anderson, "if we pass it to the third man; but I tell you candidly, Trevathan, I don't believe in making any more expense for the assured than is absolutely necessary. She has lost enough as it is. Shall we make it fifty?''

"Well, call it fifty,'' said the carpenter.

"Now, how much for the chimneys?''

"There's fifty feet,'' said Trevathan, "at a dollar a foot; that's fifty dollars.''

"Too high, my boy, too high. It used to be a dollar a foot, but its six bits now. But let it go. How old was the building?"

"Nine years."

"What's the depreciation?" asked Anderson. (And here it may be remarked that everything depends on the style in which it is done. It is said that a certain great actor could repeat the word "Mesopotamia" with such exquisite modulation that his hearers would be moved to laughter or melted to tears. The elder Booth's rendition of the Lord's Prayer was most pathetic ; and Anderson has the same gift of expression. His measured pronunciation of that simple word "depreciation," and his eloquent exposition of its true meaning, have often brought deep sadness to many sensitive claimants.)

"Depreciation," said Trevathan, "*was* there any?"

"Certainly," replied Anderson, "the difference between old and new, you know."

"Oh," said the carpenter, "I don't think there's much ; not more than five per cent., anyway."

"You 're 'way off on that ; you mean twenty-five, don't you?"

"No, five," repeated Trevathan, firmly.

"Mr. Trevathan," said Anderson, with dignity and decision, "I *never* will consent to anything less than fifteen, and when I make it as low as that I'm taking desperate chances of losing my position. The appraisement may go in at five, signed by you and the third man, but it *never* will have my signature on any basis less than fifteen per cent. Never! so help me God, never! There's no man more conscientious than I am, and you must remember that we have taken a solemn oath to do our duty in this case, and if my experience is worth anything (and I believe I know my business), fifteen per cent. is less than the damage to the house by the action of the elements, its occupancy by a family, and its consequent partial disintegration as a frame structure. Ain't I right?"

"Well, call it fifteen," said Trevathan.

"And now," said Anderson, "we have but one item left, and on that I'm *sure* we will think alike. What have you allowed for *daybree ?*"

"For *what ?*"

"For *daybree.*"

"Mr. Anderson," said Trevathan, cautiously, "what's your opinion?" (Anderson, by the way, speaks French like a native, and gives the true Parisian twist to all words borrowed from that language.)

"My estimate of the value of the *daybree* in this case is two hundred dollars."

Trevathan was puzzled. He evidently didn't know what was meant by that strange word, but would not confess his ignorance. After a long pause, he shook his head gravely and said: "I'll leave that to the third man."

"Before we do that," said Anderson, "let me give you my views. The *daybree*, comprising the framework of the dwelling left standing, the porch and the chimneys, amounts to fully two hundred dollars."

"Why," said Trevathan, pulling himself together, "the chimneys are no good; the bricks are damaged by the fire."

"If they could be hurt by fire," said Anderson, "why do they use fire when they burn a kiln of bricks? Those chimneys are better than before the fire. The bricks are glazed and the mortar is hardened. If I owned that property, I would build my house against the chimneys; they *never* ought to come down."

"I'll say twenty-five dollars," said Trevathan.

"No, sir, that wouldn't be fair to the company. I'm willing to give and take, and I ask you, Mr. Trevathan, to do me the personal favor, when this appraisement is closed, to tell Mrs. Riley as a matter of justice to me, that I acted fairly and without prejudice, and I believe you can honestly say that. Now, I'm going to name a figure on the daybree that will surprise you. I will say, in order to close the matter, and this is my lowest figure,—seventy-five dollars—there!"

"Well, call it seventy-five," said Trevathan, with an air of fatigue.

"And now, Trevathan, I will make the footing. The total is $1,121.93, and I consider that a good, fair, liberal adjustment, for the building was over-insured and prices are lower now. Put your name right there, and we will all take a drink; but before doing that, I will take this occasion to say that I have made hundreds of adjustments on buildings all over the coast, from Victoria to San Diego, and have figured with the best architects, builders and carpenters, and, without flattery, I can sincerely say, Trevathan, I never met your equal!"

As we passed out, Trevathan remarked: "Mr. Anderson, you said you might lose your position, but let me tell you one thing—*you never will.*"

Anderson laughed and replied, "The trouble with me is that I'm too tender-hearted. I sympathize with the assured and it wears on me. When I went into this business a few years ago, my locks were as black as a raven's wing, and now look at them." He raised his hat and showed a fluffy head of hair as fine as silk and as white as snow.

EDWARD NILES.

THE claim was on a two-story brick building; this building adjoined a one-story building, and the latter was totally consumed. When the two-story building was put up, the bricks could not be dressed on the outside until the wall reached a height above the one-story building. Claim was made for an entire wall, and to this day the owner (an estimable lady) believes that the heat from the fire *melted the mortar* which ran out rom between the bricks of her building. One adjuster, two builders and fhree friends of the family failed to convince her to the contrary.

REVERIES.

BY MAX BERTHEAU.

Melody: "The Sidewalks of New York."

Merrily together sits a jolly crowd,
Chatting, drinking, smoking; even praising loud,
How in spite of hard times and that merry war,
They are getting premiums—but don't ask how big they are.
Eastern, home and foreign companies,
They all are cutting down the rates as well as salaries.
Five-cent lunches are now for the boys a treat,
While the managers find a place for fifteen cents to eat.

All of us are weary, though some won't admit
That its surely 'bout the time when fighting should be quit.
Some we hear still boasting of last year's result,
Showing in their statement what amount of biz they held,
And with all that say they always showed
The best intentions for a Union—but there is a road
Leading from this world, far away from here,
Paved with good intentions. Let us hope they won't go there.
(*With Apologies.*)

California's record in the days of old
Showed the yearly premiums to be seven millions gold;
But the last year's statement up to the thirty-first,
It showed not quite four millions—for the P. I. U had burst.
Cut rates don't bring premiums, don't you see,
It is the same thing with the babes, they don't grow on a tree.
Some such new ideas, Oh! let them be blessed!
As in either case the "Good old way is still the best!"

"A DREAM."

My Dear Knapsack:

I DREAMED I was standing near the corner of California and Sansome streets talking with George Grant, when I saw the "Giant of my child. hood," 20 feet high, 10 feet across the shoulders and one eye in the center of his forehead, marching along Montgomery, Pine, Sansome and California streets swinging his 10-foot club, and knocking insurance men right and left; he spared none, from the office boy to the President; all were meat that came under his club; he swept the streets, the air was full of hair, the sidewalks were ankle-deep with brains.

As he passed us I saw following him a "mob," "a howling mob," crying out "Give it to them!" "Don't spare them!" "That is a good one"—as a blow from his club sent a leading manager's hair into the air, and his brains over a half acre or so of sidewalk. "Go it, one eye!" "Bully for Cyclops!" "Bust a compact again, will you?" and as this mob passed us (this was a dream, you know) I said, "George, this is dreadful." He said, "Yes." I said "Do you see that mob stuboying that fellow on?" He said "Yes."

I saw, in the front ranks of that mob, numerous agents whose principal growl, when I was on the road, was the tyranny of the P. I. U. They could tell how they could hold their business if there was no compact, how J. Jones Knowitall, whose barn was as good as a dwelling, would insure said barn, if he could get a fair rate; and a lot of such rot —you have all heard it.

I saw in the next rank the "special" who never took the off side, and was always ready to side in with the growling agent, and found it easier to allow five per cent. or so in postage to get a good business in a big agency, than to build up a fifteen per cent. straight.

I saw the manager whose jealous rivals credited his success in getting the best business in an agency to his loyalty to rates and independence of P. I. U. rules.

I saw a strange crowd bringing up the rear. They were armed with what appeared to be spears, with which they would jab at the hair in the air, and the brains on the sidewalk. Upon closer view, these spears were pens, marked *Coast Review*, *Pacific Underwriter*, *Adjuster*, *Sun*, *Monitor*, *Standard*, and others; a cloud of them too numerous to mention.

I pointed the insurance men out to George, and asked him why these old "manifest bad faithers" were so prominent and so noisy in that gang, and he said that it was because they were crooked; crooked people can't live in a fair fight, and are the first *to squeal.*

"Well," I said, "how about those insurance quill drivers, East and West; why are they so vicious, ours was not the first broken compact?" He said, "No, it was not; but you know that when good people fall from grace what a howl society makes about it, while a common, everyday sinner can go right along in his evil ways without creating a ripple. We on the Coast had the best and the only unanimous compact organization that I ever heard of; other places have boards and unions, but invariably have a big non-board, or non-union element, while we had no non-boarders. We kept up this compact for a dozen years or more and made money, and because it broke down, was worn out, maybe, we are howled at worse than if we were pirates, and while we are bad enough, we do not deserve the kicks we get from people who live in glass houses, and who should, instead of making matters worse, lend a helping hand to reinstate the compact."

I said "Yes; but, George! how do you account for the work going right along! insurance men moving around on the streets! all, from managers to office boys, at their regular work, and still their blood and brains are ankle-deep on the sidewalks?"

"Oh," he said, "that is all right, Bill—the business is running without brains nowadays."

I then woke up.

SLANG.

"Are you with me?" as the match said to the kerosene oil can.

"Holy smoke!" as the zephyr said when the church was burning.

"You are not in it," as the policy said to the acetylene gas permit.

"Drop on yourself," as the solicitor said to the detached rate.

"Go off and die," as the annual statement said to the closing year.

TO THE PURE, ALL THINGS ARE PURE.

When asked if the stores were not used for a common purpose, he was quite indignant. "No, indeed," he replied, "the tenant is a most estimable man and keeps the best crockery and dry goods for miles around; he has caused arches to be cut between the rooms, and personally superintends his business."

AFTER the last earthquake a building was renewed at the high rate of six per cent. because it had a "shake roof."

KILLING NO MURDER.

IN THREE ROUNDS AND A WIND-UP.

Round 1.

THE heart of Waldorf Quigley swelled beneath his vest as he rode away from the broad acres of Jabez L. Hayward, situate ten miles due north of the bustling town of La Grande, in the Grand Ronde Valley, Oregon.

And Quigley deserved success.

At the early age of sixteen he decided to play a lone hand, and he played it boldly. He worked his way through the Gervais, Oregon, University, graduated with honor, and immediately went with the Farmers' Mutual of Medford as special agent. With that company he did so well that he was offered a similar position with the Eagle of Hartford, and at the time our story opens he had just secured a promise of a desirable five years' ranch risk of the aforesaid Hayward (premium $525.75), the policy to be written and delivered within two weeks.

And Quigley was happy.

One word about our hero. He had industry, confidence, ability, a clear mind in a sound body and had Heaven's best gift—good nature. In addition, he had fine magnetism and readily made friends with all kinds of people, with no discrimination against sex.

Round 2.

(Ten Days Later.)

"Good morning, Mr. Hayward," said Pat Hexton, in a loud, ringing voice, as he alighted in front of Hayward's barn; "there is my card, sir. I am special agent for the Eagle Insurance Company of Hoboken, and have called to insure you. What are my chances?"

"First class," replied Hayward; "your man Quigley was here, and I promised to give my insurance to the Eagle—but why didn't Quigley come again as he promised?"

"Poor Quigley," said Hexton (as he caught on like a flash) drawing his handkerchief and pressing it to his eyes; "poor fellow."

"W-why, what 's the matter?" asked Hayward. "Is he sick?"

"Worse than that; he's dead."

"You don't say so. That's too bad. Kind o' sudden, wa'n't it?"

"Very; the dear boy worked too hard; nervous prostration and heart failure. What a funeral we gave him! I found a memorandum about your insurance among his papers. The widow gets the commission on your premium, every cent of it. Shall I write it up?"

"Certainly; I'll give you two hundred down and a note for the balance. It's a doggoned shame that Quigley had to die. I liked that young fellow."

Hexton drew a blank policy, filled it up, attached a non-cancellation clause, accepted the money and a note, and drove away.

Round 3.

(Four Days Afterward.)

"Are you there, Mr. Hayward?" shouted Quigley at the barn door. Down from the hay loft came the honest farmer and started back in horror as he met the smiling gaze of the confident young special. .

" W-who is it—not Quigley?"

" Yes, sir; here I am, right on time; and here's the policy."

" Why, ain't you dead? Your man Hexton said you was."

" Do I look like a dead man?" asked the astounded Quigley.

"N-no," said Hayward; "but I'm doggoned if I understand it." Then he explained and showed his policy in the Eagle of Hoboken.

" My company is the Eagle of *Hartford*," said Quigley.

" Sure enough," said Hayward; " what'll we do? "

There was nothing could be done, and with a sad heart Waldorf Quigley departed.

Kind hearer, or gentle reader, as the case may be, this story has one merit—it is true.

THE WIND-UP.

In this, as in a scrapping match, with a fair referee, the better man finally wins.

Pat Hexton, the quick-witted and unscrupulous, now sells sewing machines, cash registers and Dickenderfer type-writers, and his life is filled with care.

Waldorf Quigley is the coast manager for the Dublin, Glasgow & Sheffield Assurance Corporation, and draws his salary every month.

There is a good moral in this true tale. If any one needs it he is at liberty to take it.

ONE of our men complained about the office horse. Said he, "The beast will not go and he won't stand still; you can't drive him straight, and he won't turn a corner."

" Has he ever attempted to roll?" I asked.

" Not yet; but if I tell him not to, he will do it on the spot."

"Cancel and re-issue," I replied.

I ONCE received a report on a small town; with one exception a most flattering report. There was one steam fire engine of modern make; one hose wagon; one thousand feet of hose; a paid chief; twenty-five volunteer members of the company, and steam always maintained in the boiler. But there were no iron mains, no hydrants, no cisterns, *and no water*, except for domestic use. Investigation followed. It transpired that the merchants of the town, in order to earn a reduction in rates, had subscribed and purchased the material of the fire department, and although water had not yet been introduced, the department was the principal feature of the Fourth of July parade. Rates reduced? Oh yes, the rates had been reduced.

AN INTELLIGENT insurance agent disputed a bill for mason work, taking the law of the case from his rate-book.

The mechanic had first put in a stovepipe, but later replaced it with a chimney.

The rule reads, "When a charge has been made for a stovepipe, the charge for an artificial, stone, cement or earthenware chimney need not be added." At last report the bill had not been collected.

I ASKED my scholarly friend what he thought of the grammatical construction of the many circulars issued from a certain Compact office.

"Well," he replied, "at present the author could only be convicted of assault and battery, but last year he could easily have been found guilty of murder."

OUR new special wires from Los Angeles: "Loss on stock of books and stationery. Send immediately a copy of Lowden's 'Adjustment of *Book* Losses'."

METAPHOR: (Assorted.)

"If we are not careful," said the eloquent speaker, "we will find ourselves in a quagmire where we will drift to destruction."

EDITORIAL, 1898.   GEO. F. GRANT.

IF you are that kind of a man, you can make it a safe rule in business never to be satisfied with a *small* amount of worry. Do your worrying on a large scale; by wholesale—as it were. A man who only worries a little is doing practically no worrying at all, and the satisfaction of a long, sleepless night is denied him. Neither does he know the sensation of a moist palm, or a cold mouth, void of saliva. To be a good first-class worrier requires long practice and constant effort. No trifle is too small for attention, and if you can learn to worry on two separate subjects at once, particularly if there are subdivisions in the subjects, you have climbed pretty near to the top of the ladder, and there is room at the top for the ambitious climber. It does not always follow that a person with a large capacity for worry knows what to worry about. Such a person is to be commiserated, and the few hints here given may perhaps save such a one from the evil effect of contentment and help to bring his mind to bear on the subject until the state of acute unrest, so dear to the heart of a true worry student, is really his own.

If your superior officer speaks approvingly of your work, worry! He may have a hidden meaning which you cannot fathom; a long, wakeful night is excellent discipline at such a time. If you receive an official communication couched in excellent English and reading like a book, worry! It may be a bad sign and there may be something "between the lines"; you had better give two days to this case. If by the 21st of the month no fires have been reported, worry! It is an evil omen and may portend great disaster; as each day goes by worry more and more. When a good fat loss occurs, beware! Be on your guard! The excitement of the adjustment will take your attention for awhile, and you may not remember to worry. When traveling on business, if the train meets with an accident—after you have left it—worry over what might have been! Not that you might have lost your life; *that* is *nothing*; but because of the annoyance which might have happened the office.

Is it some time since you have had the services of a physician; let that fact furnish food for your ambition. It means something! Possibly something dreadful! Worry!!

Do not, however, be so foolish as to worry at the request of another. Some jocular people are always to be found who will put up a hypothetical case in the expectation that you will swallow the bait. Beware of them; they are expert at their alleged fun and with the true instinct of an angler never weary of casting their bait. Such people have no worries of their own; some trick of fortune has made them rich in wealth and power. Do not associate with them. Misery loves miserable company. Never forget that, and some day when your work is done, after your eyes and ears are closed forever, men will sing your praises and deliver laudatory speeches in recounting your virtues, but you are past worrying then, and it cannot hurt you. Worry while you can, my hearers, and leave the rest to fate.

HOW HAPPJ!

A special of "Web-Foot" named Fabj
Is wise as a veteran rabbj;
  'Neath a watery sky,
  In garments quite dry,
At each well-sprinkled risk doth Grabj.
  Grab-He—Sabj?

He called on his friend, the manager, the other day—just a friendly call to be sociable—and he said, "You must have a lot of calls from careless people who take up your time and never do the business any good." "Yes, I do," said the manager; "it is an awful bore, but my chief clerk has a good remedy; he sizes a man up and when he thinks he ought to go he tells me I am wanted at the telephone." Just then the chief clerk came in and said, "You are wanted at the telephone, sir."

"Please order kindlings and coal to-day sure," said Mrs. President; "don't forget it, love." "Certainly, my precious, I will order it at once." He did not reach home until quite late and he had forgotten the wood and coal. Business at the office and a lodge meeting had driven the order quite out of his mind. Next morning Mrs. President was repentant of the hasty words she had spoken the night before. "Really, dear," said she, "I could not know that you would have taken it so to heart and be restless and uneasy in your sleep. You turned and tossed and talked about it all night." "What did I say?" "You said, 'Give me twenty dollars worth of chips!' over and over again."

A LOST SHEEP.

WE were gathered at Helena one cold winter night; the snow and wind outside only gave an additional sense of comfort to those within the bright, warm, social room of the hotel.

"Do you remember Hosey Moward?" said the speaker. "He traveled as a solicitor for the 'Eneole' company, and was for years a prominent factor out our way. His specialty was farm business and he dressed and acted like a granger; the hand of the elements was laid heavily over his outer garments, and the map of the West India Islands, in coffee and tobacco, was done on his shirt front. Of course you remember him; that is, all of you but little Rembrant, over there; he is too fresh at the business to remember anything." At this Rembrant sniffed. "Well, I saw Hosey only last week and if it was not for his everlasting pluck and unnatural energy you would have said he wouldn't fetch the price of old junk. He was worse dressed than ever, but he had silver in his pocket, and he was good natured as a friendly squirrel, 'Hello!' I cried. 'What on earth brings you here at this time of year— farm business?'"

"Oh, no! No more insurance for me, I am done with it for good and all,' he said. 'What with the drop in commissions and the wretched collection rule there is no show for an honest solicitor any more. No, sir, no insurance for me! I have a better thing. I own a patent, sir, a patent on an article of my own invention. I own the right to manufacture in the whole United States, and I shall sell territorial rights, and you hear me, I am good as a millionaire already.'"

"Of course I congratulated him. 'But tell me,' I said, 'what is this valuable invention?'"

"'Well,' he said, 'it is the most taking thing on earth; just adapted to suburban and remote residences; in short, it is a movable combination dining table and bath tub.'"

"I was so shocked that I could only stare at him vacantly.

"'Yes, sir,' he went on glibly, 'portable dining table and bath tub all in one; inexpensive, easily adjusted, never gets out of order, and a child can work it. You eat your dinner, remove the dishes, take away the cloth, pull aside one leg and out comes the tub; you jump in, take your bath, go to bed and sleep like an angel; in the morning you set the table for breakfast, and there you are.'"

"'But, wait a minute,' I gasped; 'dear me, how about the water in the tub?'"

"'Serves a double purpose,' said Hosey. 'When you get ready you run it up to the back door and water the garden.'"

"'But, land sakes, man,' I said, 'do people eat and bathe in such near proximity?'"

"'Do they? Watch 'em!' he said.

"I simply looked at Hosey in silence.   Finally, he broke the stillness.

"'Tell you what I will do, old man, just for old association sake.   I will sell you the right for all of Utah.   The insurance business has gone to the bottomless pit.   Now, I will let you in on the ground floor of my combination.   There's *a fortune in it*, sure.'"

"Well, boys, I nearly fell dead, and I never made him a reply."

The little party seated around the fire at the hotel in Helena looked at each other.   Little Rembrant broke the silence.   "What a fool he must be to think he can sell bath tubs in winter," he said.

There was noise enough after that remark.

MOTHER AND CHILD.

What is that, mother?
　　　The agent, my child—
The morn has but just looked out and smiled,
When he starts from his humble place of rest,
And prospects for risks, bad, better and best;
Hard is his toil and slender his pay,
While he tries to follow the compact way.
　　　　Ever, my child, like him pay your debts,
　　　　For now he *remits* the money he gets.

What is that, mother?
　　　The special, my son—
A man who is full of spirit and fun.
His air is bold, his action brisk,
Keen is his scent for any old risk;
And whether young or getting old,
He can do more than he is told.
　　　　Ever, my son, be thou his size,
　　　　Faithful, earnest, patient and wise.
　　　　(Toothpick shoes and sporty ties.)

What is that, mother?
　　　The manager, boy—
Proudly careering his course of joy;
Firm in his native vigor relying,

> Breasting the non-boards, cut rates defying;
> He swerves not a hair, with a course so clear
> That agents look on him with wonder and fear.
> Boy, may the manager's flight be thine,
> Onward and upward, true to the line.
> (Across to Canada, over the line.)

WHITHER ARE WE DRIFTING?

CHARLES DICKENS tells of a dinner party, at which the baby of the family, a child in arms, was handed around for inspection. "See him smile," said the fond mother. "The angels are whispering to him." The wooden-faced butler behind her chair felt an uncontrollable desire to say "wind," and throw up his job. The good or bad in anything is often determined from the point of view. The following copy of a daily report is the cause of these reflections. The wording of the report reads:

"Prof. F. P. Hazal.

$500. On his gas balloon, known as the 'Pride of the Sky,' while in actual service in the counties of Marion and Polk, State of Oregon ; and

$250. On basket and trapeze suspended from said balloon.

"Permission granted to make pyrotechnic displays, without prejudice to this insurance.

"Loss, if any, payable to the Portland Gas Company, as their interest may appear as holders of the first mortgage, and balance, if any, to the Portland Awning and Tent Company.

"This slip attached to and made a part of Policy No. 2,854,561 of the Fire Insurance Company, issued to Prof. F. P. Hazal, December 30th, 1897. Three months, $750; rate 6 per cent."

When I first saw the report I did not like the risk. It was a new subject to me, and I am old-fashioned and like to tread the beaten path. I had no occasion to cancel by wire, as I knew by the morning paper it was raining in Oregon. If I wrote a letter, I might say it was a risk which would not pass the board office, but here my eye rested on the stamp of the secretary of the executive committee, and I read these words: "Board of Underwriters of the Pacific, *relief granted* Jan. 3d, 1898." Here was a chance that the risk had some possible merit, for the secretary of the board never grants relief if he can avoid it. I looked the report over carefully. "While in actual service," it said. Actual service? Actual service? thought I. What in the world is actual service? If it were a dumb brute in the spring time I would know well enough. Actual service must mean during the time it serves Prof. Hazal to ascend and come down. I have a great mind to ask Tom Van Ness for an opinion. Still, I dislike to admit my lack of confidence in my own knowledge of words. "Actual service in the counties of Marion and Polk!" Suppose there is a high wind and the balloon drifts over the county line? How is anyone to know a county line half a mile from the ground? If this balloon is destroyed by fire, Prof. Hazal will never be able to prove *anything*. If his body falls outside the county of Marion or Polk, there is no claim; and as Prof. Hazal values his life quite as much as the company values money, why, there is absolutely no *moral* hazard, and the physical hazard is restricted to a few days in the month, and the rate is 6 per cent. I think possibly I may accept this risk as gilt-edged at this rate of meditation, for really the more I think of it the better it seems. "Permission granted to make pyrotechnic displays." Suppose a rocket strikes the balloon, it means a total loss; or a Roman candle, or a pin-wheel, or a double-headed Dutchman, why there is not rate enough to be named for such a fool risk. But stay! Reflect a moment! The pyrotechnic display is more on the dead wall posters than a reality. I have seen the balloon ascensions at the park, and the fireworks are by day and only make smoke; and then, again, what is Prof. Hazal about during the display? He has no more desire to blow up the balloon than the company. I think better of the pyrotechnic display after this.

"Loss, if any, payable to the Portland Gas Company, as their interest may appear as holders of the *first mortgage*." That settles the matter and I regret having wasted so much time on the blamed thing. I will cancel by wire after all. The Portland Gas Company? Why, of course! the balloon is filled with gas, and in event of a fire on the very first ascension, the gas company is sure of their pay; after that there will be no trouble. These æronauts get a large sum of money each time they go up in a balloon, and the gas company's bill cannot be so very much. I see it quite clearly. Prof. Hazal, like all of his class, is improvident; he spends his money freely, is a sort of a king with the rustic folks, and is no doubt a stranger to Oregon, and the gas company and the tent company want their money secured; but why is the tent company content with a second mortgage? That is not quite right; in fact, it is a suspicious circumstance. The answer to that is that the awning and tent company built the balloon; in fact, it is their enterprise, but it is not intended the public shall know it. They do not care to let it go out that they are behind this man Hazal, so they have worded the "loss, if any," clause in this way. Not a bad plan; in short, quite clever. The more I think of it the less objection I can find to the risk, and yet I don't just like it. I have turned down two risks from that agency lately and I am getting the small end of the business from there. Three other companies are in the agency and two of them have special agents that just stuff the local agent with things to eat and drink. The silver mug I sent to his baby is six months old, and would have been forgotten if I had not put the name of the good old company on it in large letters. Yes, I must carry the risk, but I will re-insure half of it. I don't just like to take it around myself; it will perhaps attract attention and create suspicion. I will send the usual re-insurance clerk. The clerk returned so quickly I was sure the risk was rejected. No. "Took it at once and will write all of them he can get," said the clerk, and here I made a mistake. My own cautious nature impelled me to telegraph the agent to collect before the first ascension. The weather might clear, the man might go up, the balloon burn, and nobody from whom to collect the premium—that seemed plausible enough and worth the price of the message. That was my mistake. The whole thing was a fraud originated by the local; assisted by the special, aided and abetted by the assistant general agent, and they had landed the "old man," but my friend of the re-insuring company went down with me—and that is some consolation.

IF, WHEN you work, you do not shirk,
And never stop to quibble nor quirk;
If it's understood you will be good,
And try to saw your share of wood;
If your heart is light, and you do right,
And aim to keep your record bright,
When you die, you may fly high
To a detached mansion in the sky.

"FATHER," said the happy boy, putting down his illustrated edition of the Arabian Nights with a sigh of intense satisfaction, "Father! what was the most extraordinary thing that ever happened to you in all your life?"

"Son," replied the father, "the most extraordinary thing that ever happened to me was the last fire that destroyed my store."

"And why was the last fire so extraordinary, father?"

"Because it was unexpected, my son."

PURE FICTION.

SOME of you remember Philip Bird, I dare say. He was "counter-man" in the days when steamboat and covered wagons ruled transportation, long before the iron track was laid. He was a serious boy, at school, with large, solemn eyes ever looking earnestly at you. He believed everyone to be honest, and he trusted his associates beyond belief; not that he was lacking in a sense of humor, for he was the first to understand a witticism, but his faith in the integrity of his fellows was almost pathetic. He learned his lessons quickly and recited them faithfully, but he dreamed about them with his eyes wide open and built mental castles of the material furnished to him by his teacher, but beautified by his own inspiration, and he was often punished because he was "idle and listless." That was the way the teacher put it. No one but his mother knew his timid and reserved disposition, and she was disappointed that he was not a big, burly chap to fight a way in the world and early bring something to eke out the scanty larder and modest family wardrobe. Like many a fond mother she sought to mould his mind on her own plan, and barely concealed the disappointment of failure. He suffered while he tried to do his whole duty, as poets and lovers of nature must when all in their lives is out of drawing. With nothing but filial affection to harmonize that which he could not understand, he did what he was told to do. From school to an office as "boy," with a small salary—a proud boy glad to help mother—but a wondering boy trying to understand business; he made few mistakes; did not "watch the clock"; never asked for and never received a holiday; did all he was told to do and more, and yet the president was impatient of the boy who had no "get up" about him. In time, tho man at the desk two removes above him was taken sick, and it was found that Philip had a knowledge of the work and was able to carry it on. The temporary assignment to this desk became permanent, and the clerk over whom he had jumped became a silent foe. The president thought it strange that the "little snake," as he called Philip, had glided so smoothly ahead. "Mark my words," said he, "there is something wrong. I don't like that fellow."

Months ran to years; salaries are raised at intervals; the boy grows to be a man; death claims parents; and loving hearts are drawn to each in marriage. Philip was cashier and counter-man now, serious, earnest, attentive, obliging, and still distrusted by the president. " I don't know what it is, but that fellow makes me nervous. I don't like him; and yet I can't put my finger on a thing that is not all right. Peace of mind is worth something, and I will fire him the first chance I get. He is crawling too near to the head office, anyway."

Then Philip was fired. One day of passionate despair, one day of calm resignation, one week of shame-faced timidity, and then the cooling, grateful, hopeful counsel of a clear-headed wife had its effect. The president was popular, a rustler, a square man. If he discharged anyone, there was cause for it. The street gave Philip a frosty shoulder.

He dropped out of sight. Ten years passed; twenty years. And then the celebrated inventor, Philip Bird, returned to town, a self-contained, scholarly millionaire.

"I brought that boy up," said the venerable president. "I gave him his start in life, and yet he has not even called on me."

IN LAW, technicalities seem to be as valuable as facts:

Over yonder down South, a man thought of taking out a policy on his dwelling. He talked a good deal about it with the agent, made a diagram, and asked for the rate, and was always on the verge of ordering a policy. Finally, his house burned. After a time he decided that the agent should have issued a policy anyway, and he brought suit to recover from the company. The judge gave a verdict for the company on the ground that a proof of loss had not been filed within sixty days of the date of the fire.

MANAGER—Did you offer this woman a rebate?

Solicitor—I did not, and I never told a lie in all my life.

Manager—Good enough. I am getting a little absent-minded myself.

IT IS hard for some specials to remember faces, and it is a point with most specials never to admit that they do not remember an agent. At Stockton, the other day, one of our boys was approached by a smiling stranger, who said, "You don't remember me now, do you?" "Oh, yes, I do," said the special, "remember you perfectly well, but I forget just where you live." "Madera," said the stranger. "Why, of course," said the special; and how are things at Madera?" but all the time he was thrashing about in his mind for the name of the Madera agent. It came to him after the affable stranger had disappeared—also the special's watch and chain.

THROW UP YOUR HANDS.

"Proud man drest in a little brief authority most ignorant of what he's most assured. His glassy essence like an angry ape, plays such fantastic tricks before high heaven as make the angels weep."

ONCE there was a "Ding-dong" who lived in a sweet village near the banks of a running river, and he grew up with the people all around him. As a little, teeny, weeny Ding-dong he was cute and the pride of the valley. Men patted his head and women curled his hair; birds regarded him curiously and dogs used to run with him.

In time he was older and smarter, and knew it, and dinged it and donged it into the ears of his neighbors until he had no neighbors, and houses were to let in the vicinity of his father's home.

Then he studied, and the effect of study was a shock to the legal profession, and he dinged the lawyers and donged the court until he put their eye out. After that, he took a ding at politics and donged his way from primary meetings to nominating conventions, and always he gained his point but lost his cause.

Then he went forth to ding public officers and prominent citizens, and although he killed them dead as Julius Cæsar on paper they were still alive in the hearts of their countrymen.

After this he run amuck and people fled from him, but one day the Governor, a brave man, put the shackles of office upon him and tied him down to his post, so that thereafter and until his term was up he could ding at but one class of people, and the birds sang once more with joy and the dogs barked bravely once again, and lawyers smiled and politicians beamed, and the public said, "For heaven's sake keep him at his post forever," but the poor insurance people threw up their hands just as men do when friendly brigands stop a stage coach—and this never occurred in Kansas and has nothing to do with McNall.

ARE all "board members" wooden men?
No! But some are of pretty good timbre.

ONE of the boys is very proud of his personal appearance and his toilet is always carefully arranged. One time we had traveled all night by stage to adjust a loss. Arriving at day-break, we decided to freshen up and defer sleeping in bed until night. I waited patiently while our friend groomed himself. Suddenly he gave a snort and rushed for the water basin. By some means, known only to a country hotel, a bottle of pepper sauce was on his bureau which he had mistaken for hair dressing.

A SERMON IN LINES.

I.

As we gather at our meeting,
  With old friends on every side,
With our tales of joy and business,
  Songs of mirth, and songs of pride.

II.

Think of those, do not forget them,
  As we tell our stories o'er;
Those who once were here beside us,
  Comrades, who have gone before.

III.

Who shall know or who shall tell us,
  If beyond the Great Divide,
Where the curtains fall asunder,
  And the doors are parted wide,

IV.

Shall we meet them, shall we greet them,
  In that far and distant land;
Shall we see their faces brighten,
  Shall we grasp each friendly hand?

V.

Do they stand with arms outreaching,
  Welcome bearing for us all?
Are they there, expectant, waiting,
  Shall we hear their voices call?

VI.

Shall we join the best and bravest,
  And once more review the past,
All our strife and toil and labor,
  To the winds forever cast?

VII.

Weary hands may drop their burden;
  Weary hearts may rest at ease;
Tired brains forget their labor;
  Care and toil from troubling cease.

VIII.

Look around, see! here among us,
   Shadowy forms are standing near,
With the smile of God about them,
   With the peace that knows no fear.

IX.

They are with us in the spirit;
   Hail them! as the friends of yore;
Dear the thoughts, and sweet the memory,
   Brothers who have gone before!

X.

Oh! companions, stand together!
   Soon, too soon, our day is o'er,
And we leave to join our comrades,
   Comrades who have gone before.

DU VAL.

Why do they always speak of your chief clerk as a man of great push?

Because that is the sign on the door he uses so much, I think.

One of the rules of the office reads: "Vacancy permits can be granted only by the head office." For this reason an agent in a 7 x 9 village wrote to the head office as follows: "Please to excuse me for thirty days, as I want to go to the coast and refresh with the salt air."

HOT TIME IN 'FRISCO.

By R. W. Osborn.

All ye underwriters at this board, list while I sing this song,
It will tell you of the many things to happen here ere long;
Just three years ago we had a fight and rates were cut in four,
(All sorts of bad and senseless things are done in times of war.)
Look out then for your expiration book, don't accuse the other as a
    crook,
Because he gets a risk that you did fail to hook—'twill make a hot
    time in 'Frisco this year,
      By jingo.

CHORUS.

Bow your head in shame for what we 've done,
Thank your stars the war has had its run ;
But if perchance one thinks he 'd like to have more fun,
There 'll be a hot time in 'Frisco this year.

Now Jack Frost got in his deadly work in southern part of State,
Ran right through the orange groves so like the irony of fate,
And the rain it failed to fall in places where the grain is king,
North wind dried up the barley crop and every other thing.
Look out then for the business that 's in force, good risks burn and
       become a total loss.
And if you don't inspect as a matter then of course there 'll be a hot
       time in 'Frisco this year,
             By jingo.
                         Chorus.

Then there 's Clunie, with his dictum and his rulings so unjust,
Saying one day we must not do this, the next day that we must ;
For illegal taxes he is bent, our bonds he nullifies,
Claims our rates are high, the board is bad, these does he criticise.
Look out then or behind the bars we 'll be, serving time at the will
       of Czar Clunie,
And if we don't disband this board now instantly, there 'll be a hot
       time in 'Frisco this year,
             By jingo.
                         Chorus.

Now how charming we would look with prison stripes upon our backs,
Breaking stone in Folsom's yard, or turning jute right into sacks ;
Oh ! how crushing this would be for high-born spirits such as these—
All this will only come about when moons are made of cheese.
Say then, say, to this same commissioner, we 'll do right, yes, most
       respectful sir,
But don't demand our life as executioner.—There 'll be a hot time
       in 'Frisco this year,
             By jingo.

LAST CHORUS.

Raise your heads for we have done no wrong,
Shout our rights and keep the shout up long,
And when you tire, just merge your shout into the song:
There 'll be a GOOD time in 'Frisco this year.

THE CHICKEN DISPUTE.

"I only deal by rules of art, such as are lawful."

THE Farmers' Mutual Insurance Company of Malaria Corners, Oregon, issued its policy No. 41,144, at its Gold Hill agency in favor of Alfred Falfa, for $100, as follows:

"$100 on hens and roosters, plucked or unplucked, in coop, field, hen-house or crate, while situate on or about his ranch of forty acres, more or less, lying in a southerly direction, three miles from Gold Hill, Jackson county, Oregon.

"In event of loss, this company shall not be liable on mixed breeds in a proportion exceeding one dollar for three hens, or roosters, as the case may be, and for 'Plymouth Rocks,' not exceeding one dollar for two fowls of that breed.

"If this policy is cancelled by the assured, it is hereby understood and agreed that in addition to the usual short rates, the assured shall pay for the necessary expense of doing the business."

The hen-house burned from cause unknown, but presumably from spontaneous combustion caused by an excess of phosphorus in some over-heated eggs, and a settlement of the loss was made by A. W. Foote, special adjuster of the Farmers' Mutual, as follows:

"It appears, Mr. Falfa," said the adjuster, "that you lost by this fire 120 hens and roosters of various unnamed kinds, and 120 'Plymouth Rocks'?"

"Yes," said the assured.

"Do you or do you not consider it significant that the exact number lost in each case was a hundred and twenty?"

"O! Why, no; it just happened to come that way."

"Well, we will call it a coincidence and agree on that number. Our contract is to pay you at the rate of one dollar for each three of the mixed chickens, and one dollar for each two of the Plymouth Rocks."

"That is what the policy says," remarked the assured.

"Now, one dollar for three and one dollar for two are equal to two dollars for five, *are they not?*"

The claimant made a mental calculation, and after a long pause, replied in the affirmative.

"Then," continued the adjuster, "at the rate of two dollars for five chickens, a hundred chickens would be forty dollars, wouldn't they?"

"Let me see. Five's in two dollars forty times; that's forty cents apiece; one hundred at forty cents makes forty dollars. Yes, that's right."

"Then two hundred would be eighty dollars, and forty would be sixteen, making a total of ninety-six dollars."

"Well, I suppose that's correct," said the assured; "but when I figured it at home I made it a hundred dollars, and so did the children, and the schoolmaster who boards with us. We must have made a mistake, for 240 chickens at forty cents apiece amount to just ninety-six dollars."

So he signed a proof. Foote gave him a note for the ninety-six dollars, took a receipt, gathered in the policy and returned to the home office at Malaria Corners.

When the claimant returned to the ranch, the whole family, including the schoolmaster, who was regarded in the neighborhood as a mathematical prodigy, sat up till midnight figuring, and by the dim light of an antiquated lamp, calculated in all kinds of ways, but finally agreed that the loss was an even hundred.

The neighbors joked Falfa so much about the matter that he got mad and brought suit against the company for four dollars and costs, alleging fraud.

The decision of the court was as follows:

Al. Falfa

vs.

Farmers' Mutual Insurance Company, } ss.   Mossback, J.

Of Malaria Corners, Oregon.

The defendant company issued to plaintiff its policy No. 41,144, at its agency at Gold Hill, Oregon, in the sum of $100, covering on "hens and roosters, plucked or unplucked, in coop, field, hen-house or crate, situate on or about assured's ranch," etc. In event of loss, the company was not to be liable on mixed breeds in a proportion exceeding one dollar for three hens, or roosters, as the case might be, and for Plymouth Rocks, not exceeding one dollar for two fowls of that strain.

A fire occurred, totally destroying 120 fowls of mixed breed and 120 Plymouth Rocks. The company's adjuster settled the claim for $96. Plaintiff now brings suit for $4 and costs, claiming fraud on the part of the defendant.

The case appears to be resolved into one main question with two collateral points:

First. Did the loss of said fowls by the assured constitute a legal claim against said insurance company for the full amount of $100?

Q. E. D.—that is to say, quite easily demonstrated, to-wit,
namely: $120 - : - 3 = 40 \times \$1 = \$\ 40$
$120 - : - 2 = 60 \times \$1 = \$\ 60$
$\$40 - | - \$60 = \$100$, total loss.

The two collateral points are these, viz.:

(A) The defendant gave the plaintiff its note for $96, pay-
able one year after date, without interest, which is
clearly to be regarded as *collateral* evidence.

(B) In consideration of said note the plaintiff gave a receipt
in full and surrendered said policy.

Defendant claims that $96 is a correct estimate of the loss, based on
the following calculation, which, if figures cannot lie, appears to be
correct: $1 for 3 and $1 for 2 = $2 for 5. Two-fifths of 240 = $96.

Plaintiff does not question the accuracy of this computation.

It is clear that there is a difference of $4, but where it comes in is not
so apparent. Still, it must be remembered that courts are not schools of
the higher mathematics. The legislators of our State have decided that
the amount named in a policy shall, in the event of the total destruction
of a building, be the measure of loss, regardless of the value of the
burned structure, and I see no good reason why this principle should not
apply with equal justice to other kinds of property. The courts have
always given the benefit of any doubt to the assured and justly, for it is a
fundamental truth underlying all law, that corporations are soulless. Or,
as the late Sir Edward Coke tersely said: "Corporations cannot commit treason, nor be outlawed, nor excommunicated, for *they have no
souls.*"

On the other hand, I cannot overlook the fact that the defendant
company in this case is made up of some of our best farmers, whose
rights must be protected. After carefully weighing the evidence, the
decision of the court is that the charge of fraud is not established.
Judgment is given against the defendant in the sum of four dollars, while
the costs, which we assess nominally in a like sum, will be paid by the
plaintiff.

Mr. Foote, the adjuster, rankled under this decision, and asked for
expert opinions in the following letter:

MALARIA CORNERS, Oregon, February 5, 1898.

To the Editor of the Knapsack—SIR: I enclose decision of Justice
Mossback, in a case in which my company is interested, and as I understand your paper has a large circulation, though I never see it more than

once a year, I will ask you to use your valuable influence towards getting opinions on this case from some of the best adjusters (who can figure), and much oblige,

Yours respectfully,

A. WEBB FOOTE,

Inspector of Agencies,
Chief Clerk and Special Adjuster for the
Farmers' Mutual Insurance Company
of Malaria Corners, Oregon.

As we were unable to get written opinions from the leading adjusters and expert accountants requested by Mr. Foote, in time for this issue, we take the liberty of giving what we believe *would be* their views in this matter, based on their instructions in similar cases. From prudential motives we omit names, and simply number the various opinions, which follow :

(*Opinion No. 1.*)

The settlement in accordance with the mode of procedure arbitrarily established by the adjuster in question, which treatment was apparently sanctioned and confirmed by the insurance company interested, ostentatiously develops a latent ambiguity and a maximum of turpitude which cannot be too strongly deprecated. Without attributing absolute criminal motives to the aforesaid adjuster and his supporting company, it will be distinctly obvious to the meanest comprehension that intervention in this case, in behalf of the assured, whose entire good faith cannot be successfully impugned, is imperatively demanded in the interests of that justice which is an ineradicable and inherent right of both of the contracting parties, regardless of preconceptions or prejudgment.

As a mathematical proposition, even if it were based on purely supposititious claims, the solution presents no insuperable contradictions. Primarily, the exact words of the policy must be faithfully and studiously considered, in all their verbal felicities, or infelicities, nor must they be diverted into channels not contemplated originally. The chickens in question, without considering their augmented sound value, or their augmented present value, were insured on an average valuation, not of forty cents, but of forty-one and two-thirds cents apiece. To prove this beyond the faintest penumbra of a doubt, add 33⅓ cents, the proportion of one lot, to 50 cents, the proportion of the other lot, and divide this sum by two. The quotient is the insurance on each chicken, which equals 41⅔ cents. Multiplying 240 by 41⅔ cents, we have as a resultant sum, $100, which is the correct and undoubted answer.

The $96 settlement is plausible, but is tainted with illegitimate calculation and is based on premises radically and diametrically antagonistic to homogeneous and synthetic reasoning.

(Opinion No. 2.)

Both are right. The difference is one of proportion. To solve this quickly, construct a diagram shaped like an ordinary gridiron or pipe organ, through which draw a line broken at various points by irregular angles and resembling a flash of lightning taking the usual zigzag course. Let the top jag of the flash represent the three for one proportion; the middle fork, the two to one ratio, and the tail of the thunderbolt, the five to two proposition. Now, is it not evident that by arranging a series of years on the left of the diagram, extending from its top to its base and averaging the size and weight of the fowls annually, we are prepared, by taking these in connection with the ratios, to arrive at a fair basis for computation? I have built so many of these plans that I am satisfied they give to anyone with good eyesight that instantaneous knowledge which mere words cannot convey. I do not, however, insist on a slavish allegiance to diagrams, for there are other methods. To simplify this further, let me suggest the following: Place 120 chickens of the mixed breeds in a box (redwood preferred, but any old box will do), and deposit 120 Plymouth Rocks in another box. Remove the chickens from the first box in bunches of three, and every time three are taken out, drop a dollar in a sack. Repeat this with the other lot, putting one dollar in the sack for every two chickens.

When the boxes are empty, *there will be $100 in the sack!*

To prove that $96 is also correct, mix the two lots of chickens in one box thoroughly, and remove them in bunches of five, depositing two

dollars in the sack for every cluster of chickens taken out of the box. When the fowls are all out, *there will be just $96 in the sack!*

I might elaborate this statement, and will do so on another occasion, giving full diagrams, but for the present, prefer to allow the young, thinking adjuster a chance to grasp the principle, and then work it out for himself.

If books of account were kept, the loss would adjust itself, and even if the books were burned, my system of cross-examination would so confuse the assured that a solution could doubtless be arrived at within three or four days.

(Opinion No. 3.)

Steps to be taken. (These may be used to advantage *before* the fire if the chickens are roosting high.)

First. Average the fowls into as many groups as the conditions of the policy demand.

Second. Ascertain the loss of each group separately.

Third. *Do not mix the chickens.*

Fourth. Divide 120 by 3; the quotient will be the loss on the mixed group.

Fifth. Divide 120 by 2; this gives the loss on the Plymouth Rocks.

Sixth. Add the two quotients. The sum is $100, which is and must be correct.

Note. It is essential that the chickens be counted separately. *Do not mix the chickens*, and the groups will be so fortified, and the proportions so clear, that the problem is at once narrowed down to an ordinary mathematical one.

(Opinion No. 4.)

This is a simple but interesting problem, and can best be solved algebraically.

Let x = mixed fowls ; and y = Plymouth Rocks.   Then x -|- y = 240. As 3 to $1, 120 are to $40, and as 2 to $1, 120 are to $60.   Form the equation and raise to the 'nth power.   The answer is $100.

Again, by compound proportion :

5 : 2 : : 240 : x

Multiply the means and divide by the extremes.   Answer is $96. This leaves a difference of $4, which may be handed to the assured and charged to traveling expenses.

(Opinion No. 5.)

Adjusters are not born, but made ; and there's a difference in their makes. The problem in question may seem hard to some, but gets easier for me the longer I work on it. The simplest way of doing it is by ledger accounts. Any number of accounts may be used. Personally, I prefer not less than seven, but at this time will give but two, as follows :

Insurance Company, Dr. $100

To Assured, Cr $100

To 120 chickens at 33⅓c $40

To 120 chickens at 50c 60

This comes out just even.

Next we have—Loss account, Dr. $96

To Bills Payable, Cr. $96

This also explains itself.

I rather think the difference of $4 may arise from an ingenious change in the wording of the policy made by the adjuster.

My method of settlement is based on plain cayuse sense, and can easily be done with chalk on a barn door.

(*Opinion No. 6.*)

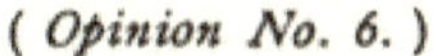

The $4 is there, but you don't see it.

In this case a vital point escaped the adjuster, and that is *depreciation*. Some of the chickens probably had the roup or the pip and the values were too high. Good, merchantable hens have often sold in Oregon for $1.50 to $3 a dozen.

A fair settlement would have been like this:

240 chickens at say 20c apiece $48
Less depreciation for sickness, poor condition,
    etc., 33⅓c 16

Net Loss $32

As the assured accepted the adjustment, the basis of $96 should stand. Ain't I right, eh? An adjustment in favor of the company should *never* be reopened.

Of course, any one can see where the difference of $4 comes in.

(*Opinion No. 7.*)

Was the premium paid before the fire? If not, the policy should have been canceled and all of this trouble would have been saved.

I frankly confess that in this case, so far as I am concerned, there is but one member of the trinity of underwriting involved, and that is agnosticism.

(*Opinion No. 8.* Solution from Chicago.)

You will remember that Gladstone, in one of his lighter humors,
asked: "What are we all doing at the same time?" To which the
Prince of Wales aptly replied: "Counting our chickens before they are
hatched!" May we not apply this to the matter in question?

The old rhyme truly says:

> " This is not so bad a world
> As some would tell ;
> Heaven may be no better,
> And, likewise, hell."

I stood one evening in the maze at Del Monte for an hour, waiting
for some one to show me the way out, and as I gazed at the full moon,
and heard, softened by the distance, the voices of the guests at the hotel,
some of them, perhaps, in the same condition as the moon, I thought:
" How transient are earth's rivalries!" Oh, why should we worry over

trifles? Let us keep our hearts warm and our hands full, for, as the Persian poet so beautifully said:

> "Some wager on a pair,
>   And some on threes will bet;
> A full hand's good enough for me,
>   But rather hard to get."

What we need is more leisure. The lark has always time for a song, and man should always have time for a lark.

But it must not be all play.

Dr. Samuel Johnson once asked an able-bodied individual why he did not work. He answered, "Oh, doctor, I am an insurance manager!" There is a lesson in this for some of us!

In conclusion I would say: "Don't split feathers, nor adjust with a microscope."

EDWARD NILES.

THE EDITOR, THE PROBLEM, AND THE CHICKENS.

OUR PRESIDENT HAS BEEN GOING AROUND PICKING UP POINTS.

THE LOVING CUP.

UPON the conclusion of the reading of the *Knapsack*, the President turned to Mr. Grant and said:

Mr. Grant, before you leave the desk at which you have so acceptably presided during the reading of the *Knapsack*, I have a little office to perform, acting for the members of the Association, your friends. It has been your pleasure and your custom to serve us as editor of the *Knapsack* these many years. The *Knapsack* is a paper that is known the world over. We all appreciate it, and we all come here to listen to it. The writing of such a paper carries with it not merely the performance of the editorial work, and the further duty of reading it to the Association, but it also carries with it a duty that is not always fulfilled by those who have it in charge. Your work is most acceptably done. Your rendition and delineation of the different passages and characters is inimitable. You attain to a position that few of us could hope to gain. If the proceedings lag, the sparkles of wit in the interpretation by your good self in the *Knapsack*, always make us feel that, though the meeting may have been dry, the *Knapsack* always gives it a relish.

Therefore, on behalf of your friends, Mr. Grant, I wish to present to you to-day a "loving cup," a token of that regard which we all feel for you, and which is better expressed in the engraving than I could possibly phrase.

Mr. Grant—Mr. President and Gentlemen: I have sometimes simulated emotion; now I feel it. Indeed, I find it very difficult to speak to you at all. I am completely taken by surprise.

We hear that said often, but in this case it is absolutely true. Whoever had this beautiful memento in hand, has kept the fact from me. I have not even heard a whisper of it. I am sure I do not know just what to say, for I am not in the habit of being presented with such beautiful and valuable gifts. But if the words of others, which I have always enjoyed reading to you, and if anything I have been able to write has

Presented to the Editor of the *Knapsack*, with the love of his many friends.

pleased you, or has given the pleasure I have hoped and anticipated, then am I truly glad. For many years we have met in this assembly room on the occasion of our annual gathering, and I am glad to think that the hearts of those who are here are as young to-day as they were years ago when the Association was formed, the result, as we all know, of the fire at Virginia City. And I do believe this, that the managers who annually meet with the boys will keep more thoroughly in touch with the progress and the changes ever going on in our business, and will be younger in spirit and better able to withstand the attacks of time. And I hope, gentlemen, that I may live long to meet you, and each of you, here. I thank you very much.

AND thus ends the first volume of "The Knapsack." Its sarcasm is without sting; its wit is harmless; its pathos melts only the softest heart.   As a whole, it is intended to bring for the moment a sensation of pleasure to a "body of men" buckled into harness, tugging with might and main.

If, in the reading of it, the spontaneous laugh can for but one instant speak the complacent mood, then is the mission of the "Knapsack" fulfilled, and it has "danced in the sunbeams" to some purpose.

Contents:

CONTENTS: